"Manny!" the redhead shrieked. "He's here! The bastard's here!"

Reese almost wished she would try and stop him, but she stayed clear of him, jumping up and down in frustration and yelling for Manny. Reese reached his car, yanked open the door and jumped inside. Out of the corner of his eye, he saw Bronson and Manny break from the woods across the road, with Blondie stumbling blindly after them, his hands clutching his face.

Reese hit the ignition switch as he pulled the door closed, and mercifully the engine sprang to life. He threw the gear lever into reverse and popped the clutch. Wheels spinning, the car shot backward up onto the road. He jammed on the brake and shifted gears just as Manny and Bronson reached the car. Reese floored the accelerator and shot past them before they could open the doors.

Reese was still fighting mad, and had no qualms about scarring the side of his old Chevy. He swerved right and sideswiped the Harleys as he went by, and the sight of the motorcycles in his rearview mirror, sliding down the shoulder, brought a smile of satisfaction to his lips.

REVELATION

L. CHRISTIAN BALLING

A TOM DOHERTY ASSOCIATES BOOK
NEW YORK

This is a work of fiction. All the characters and events portrayed in this book are either products of the author's imagination or are used fictitiously.

REVELATION

A Forge Book
Published by Tom Doherty Associates, LLC
175 Fifth Avenue
New York, NY 10010

www.tor.com

Forge® is a registered trademark of Tom Doherty Associates, LLC.

ISBN 0-765-35206-0
EAN 978-0765-35206-4
Library of Congress Catalog Card Number: 97-34390

First edition: April 1998
First mass market edition: July 1999

Printed in the United States of America

0 9 8 7 6 5 4 3 2 1

For Livia

Let him who has ears hear the words of prophecy in the First Book:

A thousand upon a thousand years shall pass before the coming of the Son of Man. Then shall the Nations fall, and all that was shall be swept away. The sea shall give up its dead, and there shall be a new heaven and a new earth. Those who know His name shall drink of the River of Life, but the abominable and unbelieving shall be cast into the Lake of Fire, which is the Second Death. Then shall the Kingdom of God be established on earth for a thousand years of Glory.

—SAMARIA SCROLL 1, COLUMN 1.4.7

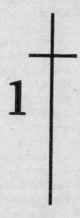

1

John Reese sat astride his black BMW motorcycle in the midst of Baxter Academy's pitch-dark playing fields. Overhead the stars shone brightly, but there was no moon and the light from the nearest school buildings did not reach the fields. Reese stretched to relieve the stiffness in his back and glanced at the luminous dial of his watch. It was 2 A.M.

Spring had come late to New Hampshire, and this was the first warm night of the season. Baxter's students were always restless after the long winter term, and this was a perfect night for an illicit outdoor drinking party. After more than twenty years as a teacher at the elite prep school, Reese knew what to expect. Yet he hoped he was wrong, for he disliked this part of his job.

The rules had to be enforced at a coed boarding school or the kids would blow the lid off the place, but Reese had never intended to become the enforcer. It had just happened that way, and Baxter's successive headmasters had come to depend on him. Over the years, his late-night ambushes had become the stuff of legend.

Legend had it that Reese had once been a Green Beret,

and that was true. Legend also had it that no student had ever escaped him. That wasn't true, but it helped keep the lid on.

Reese shifted restlessly and looked at his watch again. *Christ, I'm too old for this.* The air had cooled, and a patina of dew was collecting on his black leather jacket and dampening his jeans. If there actually were kids out this late, he thought, the damp and dropping temperature should have broken up their party by now. He allowed his hopes to rise. Maybe the kids would surprise him for once. Reese always hoped.

Then, as if on cue, he heard a distant giggle far to his right and his hope died. He sighed resignedly and peered into the darkness in the direction of the bushes at the far end of the playing fields. Seconds later he heard several more giggles, leaving little doubt that the kids had been drinking.

They had partied in the bushes, and now they were returning across the playing fields to their dorms. Reese grimaced and eased the motorcycle off its stand. He would have to bust them, and his only hope now was that no seniors were in the group. This close to graduation, Baxter's rules for seniors became draconian. Any senior he caught tonight would be expelled.

Reese had extraordinary night vision, and it wasn't long before he could make out the indistinct shadows of the group moving toward the dormitories. He slipped on his black helmet and waited for them to cross in front of him. Clad in black, one with his black motorcycle, Reese knew they'd never spot him. The shadowy figures kept coming, and when they were directly in front of him, forty yards away, he switched on the ignition and hit the starter button.

The motorcycle's headlight beam leapt across the field, transfixing four boys and three girls. For a split second they stared into the light like jacked deer, and Reese's heart sank. They were *all* seniors, and one of them was the last kid Reese would have expected to risk his diploma on a lark. Grady, the geek—the star of Reese's calculus class.

"Scatter!" yelled another boy, breaking the spell, and the kids started running.

Reese revved his engine and let out the clutch, but even as the motorcycle shot forward, he knew he was going to let them get away. Reese knew he couldn't bring himself to bust Grady, so he would have to let them all go. Grady was a scholarship kid, and the loss of the Baxter diploma would be a severe blow to him, yet Grady's parents were what Reese saw in his mind's eye as he bore down on his quarry.

He had met them on Parents Weekend, and they'd made an indelible impression. They were a shy, blue-collar couple, painfully ill at ease among the other parents, who'd flooded the campus with BMWs, Mercedes, and Jags. Hopelessly out of their depth, they had clung to their pride in their talented son like a life raft. Reese might have taken the Baxter diploma from Grady, but he couldn't take it from Grady's parents.

The yell for the kids to scatter had been good advice, but no one heeded it. They all ran in the same direction, making a beeline for the safety of the dorms. As Reese closed on them, they finally did scatter, but Grady was an awkward kid and undoubtedly under the influence. He stumbled and fell headlong to the ground.

Reese veered left, pretending that he hadn't seen the boy fall, and pursued the fastest of the runners, slipping the clutch and revving the engine so that it sounded as if he were closing faster than he was. Just before he caught up with them, he veered off again, as if confused by the scattering tactic, and made a show of pursuing the others.

None of the fugitives seemed to realize that they'd been recognized, and they ran from Reese as if their lives depended on it. Aided by Reese's artful maneuvering, they all reached the cover of the bordering woods before he caught up with them. As he braked and turned away, giving up the chase, he hoped they wouldn't realize that he'd deliberately let them escape. Behind him, he saw Grady running toward the woods. The boy stumbled once again, but he managed to stay on his feet and finally disappeared.

Reese returned in a sour mood to the old Cape in which he lived six blocks from the campus. He had never played favorites, and he disliked teachers who did, yet tonight he'd done just that. He knew why he'd done it, but in his own mind, his reasons were no excuse.

He trudged up the steps to the rear door, entered, and flipped on the overhead light in the kitchen. Two days' worth of dishes stood in the sink, and the floor needed mopping. Tomorrow, he told himself. Tomorrow he'd catch up on the chores.

He went to the refrigerator and took out a bottle of Bass ale. He was thirsty and the beer tasted just right, but for some reason he found himself thinking of what Kathy would have said if she'd caught him drinking in the small hours of the morning. He leaned against the refrigerator, listening to the silence in the house.

Two years had passed since cancer had cut short his wife's life. With time, Reese had come to terms with her death, but tonight the silence in the house weighed on him and he felt the stab of loneliness. Once or twice he had met a woman with whom he might have started a new life, but things hadn't worked out.

Despite the late hour, Reese still felt restless, and he walked through to the living room at the front of the house, turned on a light, and settled onto the couch with his beer. Working out his next chess move, he thought, would make him sleep soon enough. The board was set up on the coffee table, recording the moves of a game he was playing by mail with a friend who'd taken a year's leave of absence from Baxter. Reese's position in the game was precarious, and his next move wasn't going to be easy.

Abruptly the phone rang on the end table, startling him. This late, a phone call was unlikely to bring good news, and as he answered, he hoped it was a wrong number. To his surprise, he heard the voice of his daughter, Allison, on the other end of the line.

"Hi, Dad," she said cheerfully, and Reese smiled with relief and pleasure. He could tell from her tone that nothing was wrong, and hearing from her always cheered him up.

"Hi, Alie. What's up? It's almost two-thirty. Why aren't you in bed?"

"I'm working late. Where've you been? I've called every half hour since midnight."

"I was out on my bike."

"Uh-oh. The midnight man strikes again. Did you catch anyone?"

"No."

Allison laughed gleefully. "Good!" she said with satisfaction, and Reese smiled. He was sure that she'd taken a few chances herself when she'd been a Baxter student, and she still rooted against him.

"So, what's up?" he asked.

"Dad, don't tell me you've forgotten."

"Forgotten what?"

"Happy birthday! I wanted to be the first to congratulate you."

"Thanks." Reese laughed. "I must have lost track of the date. Getting old, I guess."

"Come *on,* Dad. You're only forty-eight. That's not old."

But no longer young, he thought, his eyes straying to the family photographs on the end table. One was a shot of him just after he'd returned from Vietnam—a tall, rangy young man with dark hair, a broken nose, and thick, dark eyebrows. Perhaps it was the look in his eyes, or the roughness of his skin, that made him look older than his years, but there was no great contrast with the photo beside it, a picture of him with Kathy more than two decades later. It had been taken the year before she'd died, and they were both smiling.

The years had creased the corners of his eyes and left furrows around his nose and mouth, but he was still slim and his slightly receding hair hadn't grayed. Yet Reese felt the physical effects of age that the photos didn't show. When he got out of bed in the morning, his ankles ached for his first few steps, and although the strength of youth had not entirely fled, he had no endurance.

But these were minor things—in the same category as the reading glasses he now needed—and Reese rarely noticed them. Yet, tonight, perhaps because of the errant attack of melancholy, he felt age creeping up on him.

"How come you're working so late, Alie? You know that

you always come down with something when you don't get enough sleep.''

"That was true when I was a kid, Dad," Allison responded with a good-natured sigh. "You can stop worrying about me. I'm twenty-three, remember?"

"That doesn't mean you can go without sleep." Reese wondered if he would ever stop worrying.

"What do you want for your birthday? I didn't send a present because I can come up this weekend for a visit."

"Great! When are you coming?"

"I'll be there Friday evening. So, what would you like for your birthday?"

"How about a bottle of Chivas?"

"Be serious," Allison chided. "That's no kind of birthday present. I—Oops. Hang on a sec. I'll be right back."

Reese heard a thump as Allison put down the receiver, and several seconds passed before she came back on the line. As Reese waited, he reminded himself to ask her about the incidental aspects of her life, as Kathy had so often urged him to do. By nature, Reese was a listener, not a talker, and to some extent Allison had inherited the trait. He was afraid that unless he made the effort to draw her out, all but the bare essentials of his daughter's life would slip right by him.

"Sorry, Dad," Allison said, coming back on the line. "I heard the elevator and wanted to close the door."

"Aren't you in your apartment?"

"I'm still in the lab—actually in the computer cluster down the hall. The experiment Singer started me out on has worked out well, and he wants me to write up the results. Can you believe it? Only six months into my thesis research, and already I have something publishable."

"I believe it, kiddo," Reese said happily.

Reese had settled for a master's degree in math and computer science, but Allison had more ambition. Professor Singer, her thesis adviser, was one of the top DNA researchers in the country, and at the rate she was going, she would have her Harvard Ph.D. before she was twenty-five.

"I hope you know how proud I am of you."

"Thanks, Dad."

"Why did you close the door? Aren't you supposed to be there this late?"

"No, that's all right. We can work all night if we want. But I heard the elevator, and I think the security guard just came up. Usually there's a bunch of us here, but tonight I'm the only one and I don't want him to know I'm here. He's a nice enough guy, but he talks and talks and talks."

Reese frowned. "Why are you there alone?"

"The demonstrations. They have everyone spooked, I guess, and for the past three nights I've been the only one working late. It's really dumb, because the demonstrators don't hang around at night."

"What demonstrators?".

"Just the Bible Belt crowd, Dad. Haven't you heard about them up there? It's been in the news. Some antiabortion coalition has been out in front of our building all week, picketing Professor Singer. He's fit to be tied."

"Why? What does molecular genetics have to do with abortion?"

"Nothing. That's the nutty part. They're protesting a speech Singer gave last month in favor of expanded fetal-tissue research. The speech had nothing to do with his own work, but he's a pretty famous guy and the speech got publicity. Apparently that was enough to bring demonstrators out of the woodwork."

"If no one else is working late," Reese said worriedly, "maybe you shouldn't either."

"No problem, Dad. Really. And with no one around, I get a lot done. Actually, I shouldn't have said I'm the only one. Kenji was here until about half an hour ago."

"Who?"

"Kenji Hamada. I told you about him, didn't I? He's a postdoc working with Singer on some sort of hot project. Something to do with the DNA they've been analyzing from an archaeological sample—some scrap of mummified flesh. Neither Kenji nor Singer is talking about it, but it's clear they're excited. It's got everyone around here buzzing with curiosity, and—"

Allison broke off, and for a second or two there was silence on her end of the line.

"Alie?"

"Dad, did you hear that?"

Reese heard a note of alarm in her voice and tensed. "Hear what?"

"God! Hang on, Dad. I'll be right back," Allison said excitedly, and Reese heard the thump of the dropped receiver.

"Alie!" he yelled into the phone. *"Alie!"*

Reese waited tensely for Allison to return to the phone. He didn't know what had drawn her away, but her reaction worried him. Straining to hear, he caught the faint sound of a splintering crash, followed by a shout from Allison. "Hey!" he heard her yell. Her voice sounded as if it came from the corridor outside her office.

Again he heard a distant splintering crash, followed by another and another. "Alie!" he shouted into the phone.

Then Reese heard a distant, high-pitched cry from his daughter, and he felt as if an icy hand had seized his heart. There was no mistaking the sudden fear in her voice. Reese listened no longer. He stabbed the receiver hook button and punched in the number for Massachusetts information.

"Come on!" he cried desperately as he waited for a response. "Goddamnit, come *on!*"

"What city, please?" asked the operator.

"Cambridge!" Reese said urgently. "Harvard University Security!"

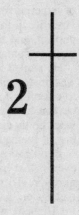

2

Kenji Hamada was tired and sleepy, but he was still in a buoyant mood as he climbed the back stairs to the fourth floor of the Biology Building. He was in the midst of an experiment of a lifetime and consumed with excitement. For Kenji, there weren't enough hours in the day. Yet he would have to get more sleep, he reflected. He was beginning to make mistakes.

He had been almost home before he remembered that he'd left a DNA sample in the PCR cycler. A small mistake, it merely required him to go back, but if he didn't get more sleep, the mistakes might become more serious. He couldn't afford mistakes—not with this experiment.

Kenji could hardly believe his luck. At twenty-eight, with a fresh Ph.D., he found himself on the threshold of a major scientific success. The ramifications of the gene he had accidentally discovered were incalculable. When Professor Singer had given him the routine task of analyzing the DNA from a sample of ancient, mummified flesh, neither of them could have guessed where it would lead. It had been pure luck—glorious luck.

Professor Singer had already mentioned the magic words *Nobel Prize,* and he insisted that Kenji complete a long series of experiments to verify his initial results. He had also advised Kenji to say nothing to anyone before he was ready to publish, and that made Kenji's excitement all the more difficult to contain.

He smiled as he anticipated his father's reaction when he was finally able to tell him. As much as Kenji looked forward to scientific laurels, his father's opinion was even more important to him. All his life he had yearned to measure up to what he thought were his father's expectations, and now, at last, it seemed possible.

Kenji had never wished to follow in his father's footsteps, even if that had been possible, but that didn't lessen his admiration. To the Japanese police, Yoshiro Hamada was but a gangster, but to Kenji, his father was larger-than-life. Yoshiro Hamada was an *oyabun no oyabun*—godfather of godfathers—in the underworld of the *yakuza.*

For three decades he had been the undisputed leader of the Naguchi-gumi, Japan's largest crime syndicate, which he ruled like a feudal lord. His influence extended throughout Japan, and major figures in all walks of life were beholden to him. Yet the stigma of the criminal remained, and Yoshiro Hamada had taken pains to insulate his son.

Kenji had grown up entirely outside his father's world, and only through his mother had he learned his father's history. Yoshiro Hamada had been born in the gutter, and he'd literally fought his way out with a sword. While still a teenager, he had joined the ranks of the local *yakuza.* Through suicidal daring, raw fighting ability, and cunning intellect, he had risen rapidly. Brains, as much as brawn, had made Yoshiro Hamada the undisputed leader of the powerful Naguchi-gumi.

Insulated from the *yakuza* world though Kenji was, the force of his father's personality made it inevitable that Kenji absorb Yoshiro Hamada's precepts of honor, loyalty, and courage. He was as awed by his father's strength as he was ashamed of what he considered his own weakness. As a boy, Kenji had been physically frail, bookish, and introverted.

He'd been an easy target for bullies, for he was easily frightened and had no stomach for a fight.

If his father knew, he'd never said anything, and Kenji's nagging sense of inadequacy sprang from within. Yoshiro Hamada had always taken pride in his son's achievements in school, and he'd never expressed the slightest disappointment in him, but that had never been enough for Kenji. When Kenji thought of the distinction that would soon be his, he thought entirely in terms of the reflected honor it would bring to his father.

As Kenji reached the stairwell's third-floor landing, a series of heavy thumps startled him. They came from somewhere on the floor above—inexplicable and jarringly loud in the silent building. Alarmed, he hurried up the last of the stairs to the fourth-floor landing. He reached the door to the corridor and was about to open it when a splintering crash halted him. Gooseflesh rose on his neck and arms as instinct warned him that something was terribly wrong, and he froze.

He heard a woman shout in the corridor, and he realized that it must be Allison. Through the door he heard more crashing and thumping from the direction of their lab, and his skin crawled with an undefined but vivid sense of danger. He desperately wanted to open the door and burst into the corridor to confront the danger Allison faced, but he felt frozen to the spot. He stood there with his hand on the door handle, his heart pounding, willing himself to act, but unable to move.

Then he heard Allison cry out in fright, followed by a sudden silence, and he grimaced with almost physical pain at his cowardice. He took a deep, gasping breath to steady himself and opened the door a crack. He knew something had happened to her, and he'd done nothing. *Nothing!*

"You fool!" barked a male voice, and Kenji was sure it came from their lab. "What have you done to her?"

"Shut up and get that flashlight out of my eyes," snapped a younger man's voice. "Have you got it?"

"Yes!" hissed the older man. "It was right where I expected it to be. I had it already! You didn't have to hit her!"

"Don't be stupid, Michaels," the younger man shot back.

"She'd have come after us, yelling bloody murder. Come on, let's get out of here."

Footsteps pounded up the corridor and Kenji hastily let the door slip shut. "Not the elevator," he heard the older man shout. "The stairs are faster!"

Seized by panic, Kenji started to retreat, but then he realized that they'd catch him on the stairs. Just in time he moved to the side of the door and pressed his back against the wall. He held his breath as the door swung open, hiding him from view, and the two men rushed past, pulling off the ski masks they were wearing as they pounded down the stairs. Wide-eyed with fear, Kenji prayed they wouldn't look back.

The young man in the lead was short and chubby. Kenji was sure he hadn't seen him before, but there was something familiar about the tall man behind him. He was almost entirely bald, and his head was thrust forward on hunched, narrow shoulders. Where had he seen him? Kenji wondered fleetingly, but he couldn't make the connection.

He didn't move a muscle until he heard the bang of a door far below and the ensuing silence assured him that the intruders were gone. Even as visceral relief surged through him, a rush of self-loathing overwhelmed him. *What had they done to Allison?*

Kenji opened the door and stepped into the corridor. At the far end of the hall, the door to their darkened lab was ajar. The silence was deathly. "Allison!" Kenji called, running toward the lab. "Allison!"

As Kenji rushed across the threshold, his shoes crunched on shattered glass, and he stopped and fumbled hastily for the light switch. He flipped it on and took an involuntary step backward. Despite the violence of the sounds he'd heard, he was unprepared for the devastation he saw. The laboratory looked as if a tornado had struck.

The lab benches had been swept clear of all but the heaviest equipment. Computer terminals, chemical apparatus, and electronic equipment lay upended on the floor amid shattered glassware and pools of liquid. The air was heavy with the smell of alcohol and acetone. There was no sign of Allison, and Kenji was about to call out again when he saw what had happened to his desk in the far corner.

His personal computer had been dashed to the floor, and his store of backup data discs had been attacked as well. "No!" he gasped aloud. He'd been meaning to transfer his data to the university's mainframe system, but he hadn't found the time. Now he'd have to repeat all his—

Out of the corner of his eye Kenji saw that one of the wall cabinets was open, and his head whipped around. The door to the cabinet in which the archaeological sample had been stored was open, and even from across the room Kenji could see that the container was gone. With a strangling sensation in his throat, Kenji stumbled through the wreckage toward the cabinet, desperately hoping to find the container on the floor nearby.

As he came around the corner of a lab bench in his path, he tripped over Allison's inert form lying on the floor. Kenji saw the crimson pool slowly widening from beneath her head and retched.

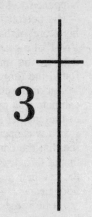

3

Reese was scared. The frightening return call from Harvard Security had sent him racing through the night to Boston's Mass General, and his heart was in his throat as he followed the young surgeon who had come to meet him at the reception desk. The doctor had told him that Allison had fallen and struck her head on something with a hard edge and that they'd had to operate at once. He'd given Reese some technical details that Reese had barely noted. The single word *coma* had blotted out all other thoughts.

As they walked along the hospital corridor, Reese heard the rap of his motorcycle boots on the shiny waxed floor, he smelled the hospital odors, and his eyes took in meaningless details—the scuff marks on the edge of a swinging door, the worn-down edges of the doctor's shoe heels, a mole on the back of the doctor's neck. Reese's senses were alive, but the impressions he registered were unfiltered, slipping at random past the single, terrible thought astride his consciousness: coma.

The doctor opened the door to Allison's room, and Reese took a deep breath in an effort to steady himself. It didn't help.

Allison's face was unmarked, but deathly pale, and her auburn hair was swathed in bandages. The tubes and electronic monitoring cables attached to her bore mute testimony to her precarious condition. As Reese approached her bed, her head turned and her lips moved languidly, as if she were about to awake.

"I'm here, Alie," Reese said, eagerly taking her hand and pressing her limp fingers. "It's Dad. I'm here."

"She can't hear you, Mr. Reese," said the doctor, who was standing behind him. "I'm afraid the movements you see have no significance."

Reese swallowed and steeled himself for the question that he hadn't yet dared to ask. "You said she's in a coma, Doctor, but you didn't tell me if she'll come out of it."

"I wish I could give you a definite answer, but I can't."

Reese turned and looked at the doctor. The young man had given Reese his name, but Reese couldn't recall it. "You must have some idea," he pressed. "You operated, didn't you?"

"Actually, I assisted Dr. McClintock in the operation. We were lucky that he was available, Mr. Reese. He's one of the best. As I told you, we managed to stabilize your daughter and minimize subsidiary damage, but . . . well, I'm afraid she hasn't responded as we'd hoped. The brain scans are not encouraging."

Reese blinked as he felt tears start in his eyes. "Is she brain-dead?" he heard himself ask in a hoarse voice.

"No," the doctor replied, but with obvious reservation in his tone. "There is evidence of higher brain activity, but the scans are outside the normal range. It's too early to say for certain, but I must warn you that there is a possibility of persistent coma."

Reese felt his shoulders sag, and as he looked back at Allison, his eyes blurred. "You mean she may never come out of it?"

"I'm afraid that's a possibility."

Reese took a deep, shuddering breath, but he could no longer hold back his tears. They spilled from his eyes and streamed hotly down his cheeks. "I want another opinion."

"Of course," the doctor said solicitously. "We'll be discussing your daughter's case in staff conference today, and I can assure you that we will consult with other neurological experts in the Boston area."

But to no avail was the doctor's unspoken opinion. Reese could hear it in his voice.

The doctor cleared his throat. "I think it would be wrong for you to give up hope entirely, Mr. Reese. The old cliché is often true. While there's life, there's hope."

Reese turned and looked at him through a blur of tears. "Hope for a miracle?" he responded with a terrible sense of déjà vu. He had hoped along with Kathy as she'd battled in vain against her cancer, and his capacity for hope had died with her.

"I wouldn't put it quite that way . . ."

"But the odds *are* against recovery," Reese said, refusing to grasp at straws.

The doctor nodded and dropped his eyes.

Reese wondered why he wasn't in shock, and he wished he were. He wished he were numb and couldn't feel the terrible ache inside him. First Kathy, and now Allison. If he'd believed in God, he would have raged at Him.

"I'll leave you alone now," the doctor said softly. "I'll be available if you'd like to talk to me some more. Just ask at the nurses' station. In case you didn't catch it, my name is Bob Kaplan."

Reese nodded dumbly, and as the door closed, his control dissolved entirely and he began to sob.

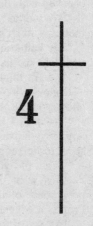

4

A fist rapped on the door to the office in which Kenji had been waiting, and he rose nervously as the door opened. A Harvard Security guard had put him in the office to await questioning by the police, and Kenji braced himself as a burly, middle-aged man with iron gray hair entered. Kenji was going to have to lie, and he knew he was a bad liar.

"Dr. Hamada, I'm Detective Donovan. Cambridge PD."

"Yes," Kenji responded, and he could hear the nervousness in his voice. The detective had a steely gaze that Kenji found difficult to meet.

"You look a little rocky," said Donovan. "Why don't you sit down."

"Yes—thank you."

What else did the detective see besides a nervous, skinny Japanese with an overly delicate face? Kenji wondered. Could those hard eyes see the coward inside? His mother lauded his features as fine-boned, but the bullies had called him effeminate. Maybe they were right; maybe he had no right to call himself a man.

"How is Allison?"

"Not good," Donovan replied grimly, "but I haven't checked with the hospital. Was she a friend of yours?"

"We worked in the same lab, and I liked her," Kenji said, feeling a fresh stab of guilt.

"Do you know of anyone who might have wanted to hurt her? Did she have boyfriend trouble?"

"I don't think so, but I don't know."

Donovan looked at him for a moment in silence. "What about you, Dr. Hamada? How well did you like her?"

"I—well, I liked her—as a colleague," Kenji said, flustered by the detective's cool stare, "but not the way you seem to be suggesting. I don't understand. I thought . . ."

"What did you think?"

"Just what the Security people said—that it must have been some of those demonstrators who've been protesting Professor Singer's speech."

"An act of vandalism?"

"Yes. What else could it be? Why would anyone else want to break into our lab and wreck it?"

"Did you see any strangers when you returned to the lab—in the building, or just outside?"

"No," Kenji lied. He had no choice. He couldn't reveal his cowardice.

Had it not been for his father, he could have accepted the humiliation, but he had to spare his father the shame. The *yakuza* claim to be the spiritual descendants of the samurai was ridiculed by outsiders, but Kenji knew that his father lived by the samurai code. Yoshiro Hamada certainly knew that his son was no fighter, but this—to stand by, paralyzed by fear, while a girl was attacked . . .

"Think," the detective urged him. "Are you sure you saw no one?"

"Yes. I'm sure."

"But you arrived only minutes after the girl was attacked."

Kenji blinked in astonishment. "How do you know that?"

"She was on the phone to her father when the perps started wrecking your laboratory. He heard enough to call

Security, and that was shortly before your call came in. Are you quite sure you saw no one?''

"Yes. No one.''

"And you think this was the work of protesters running amok?''

"I don't know,'' Kenji responded hastily. "It's just what the Security people were saying.''

"Then tell me this, Dr. Hamada. Why in hell would vandals steal some scrap of mummified flesh?''

"I don't *know*,'' Kenji said, unable to control his voice. He felt exhausted, overwhelmed. The sample was gone and most of his records were destroyed. Was that punishment for his cowardice, or simply his karma?

"You told Security that nothing else was taken. Is that right?''

"Yes,'' Kenji replied, rubbing his burning eyes, "but I can't be sure—everything was thrown about.''

"Yes, but only one cabinet was even opened—the one that contained the archaeological sample. There has to be a reason.''

"It makes no sense to me. It was an archaeological sample of no value whatsoever.''

"But they tell me you were quite upset about it, Dr. Hamada,'' Donovan responded coolly.

"Because it was valuable to *me*. A professor at Georgetown University sent it to Professor Singer for a DNA analysis, and Professor Singer asked me to take on the job in my spare time. But to our surprise, I found a startling genetic anomaly, and . . .''

Kenji blinked tiredly and sagged in his chair as despair swept over him. The sample was gone. His records were ruined.

"So, it *was* valuable.''

"No—I mean it was only valuable from a scientific point of view.''

"Any practical applications?''

"No,'' Kenji said automatically, and even as he said it, he wondered why he bothered to be secretive. There was no longer any reason to be cagey. There would be no publication. "Besides, no one outside our lab even knew the sample was here."

In spite of Kenji's exhaustion, or perhaps because of it, his last words released a memory that burst into his consciousness. He knew where he'd seen the bald man before.

Two weeks ago, a scientist had dropped by in search of recruits for a new DNA laboratory he directed, and Kenji had given him a courtesy tour of their lab. Someone had mentioned the archaeological sample, and the visitor had asked to see it. Suddenly the voices Kenji had heard from the lab came back in a rush:

"Have you got it?"

"Yes! It was right where I expected it to be. I had it already! You didn't have to hit her!"

"Don't be stupid, Michaels."

Michaels—the name of the scientist who'd toured their lab.

The detective was staring at Kenji. "Did you think of something, Doctor?"

"No, I—it was nothing." Kenji realized he was blinking rapidly and made a show of rubbing his eyes. "I'm very tired. The shock of it all . . ."

Donovan stared at him for a few seconds longer, then he nodded. "Okay, I have enough for now. Go home and get some sleep. You look like you need it. I'm heading for the hospital. Want a lift home?"

"Thanks," Kenji said, forcing a smile, "but I think the walk might do me some good."

If anyone had seen Kenji trudging homeward that night, they would have thought he was an old man. He walked slowly with his eyes on the ground, bowed by the weight of his guilt and despair. He had left Allison to her fate, and now he had abetted her attackers. If only he'd remembered Michaels earlier!

He could so easily have claimed to have seen him outside the building, just as the detective had suggested. But he had been too exhausted to think—too intent on hiding his shame—and now it was too late. If he told the story now,

Donovan would know he was lying and it would all come out.

Kenji writhed in the torment of his failure. Not only had he shielded Allison's attackers, but he'd denied himself and his family the distinction that had been within his grasp. For the sample wasn't lost; it had deliberately been stolen. Kenji had no idea how Michaels had discovered the secret, but he must have somehow. There was no other explanation.

Kenji's mind was befogged with physical and emotional exhaustion, and he never knew how the idea came to him. But as he neared his apartment for the second time that night, a wild thought stopped him in his tracks. He *didn't* have to tell the police, he realized. There was another way.

Something happened to him in that moment that he didn't even try to understand. For the first time in his life, he rebelled against the weakness that had dogged him since childhood. He knew what he had to do, and the fear that clawed at him at the prospect only hardened his conviction. He was Yoshiro Hamada's son, and for once, he swore to himself, he would act accordingly.

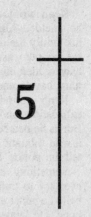

5

Reese didn't know how long he'd been in the room with Allison when the doctor returned. "Mr. Reese," the doctor said, "there's a detective from the Cambridge Police Department waiting outside in the corridor. He'd like to speak with you."

Reese was no longer weeping. It was as if he'd simply run out of tears and nothing was left but the unbearable ache inside him. He nodded to the doctor and numbly followed him out of the room. A tough-looking, heavyset man with bristly, close-cropped, gray hair and a beer belly hanging over his belt was leaning against the corridor wall. As Reese emerged, the man pushed himself away from the wall and approached.

"Detective Donovan," he said to Reese, flashing his ID, and the doctor drifted away. "Cambridge PD."

"John Reese."

"I'm sorry about what happened to your daughter, Mr. Reese, and I don't like disturbing you at this time, but I need to ask you a few questions. It won't take long, but would you like to go somewhere to sit down?"

"I'm okay." It was an effort just to speak, and Reese had to force himself to begin to think again. "What happened?"

"Vandals broke into the building in which your daughter was working tonight. They were in the process of wrecking one of the labs when she apparently surprised them. It appears that there was a scuffle, and she either tripped and fell or was knocked to the floor. Her head struck a piece of apparatus upended on the floor."

"Who did it?" Reese asked, visceral anger churning beneath his grief. Someone had done this to Allison. Someone had to pay.

"We don't know yet, Mr. Reese. That's why I'm here." Donovan took out a pen and notebook. "Let me get the preliminaries out of the way. I'll need your full name, your address and phone number, and your place of employment."

Reese gave him the information, and Donovan wrote it into his notebook.

"I understand that you were on the phone with your daughter while the break-in was in progress. I was hoping you might have heard something that might be useful."

"No," Reese said, struggling to think clearly. "She heard something and went to investigate. I heard crashing sounds, and then she cried out. That's all."

"Are you certain?"

"Yes," Reese snapped.

"Take it easy, Mr. Reese," Donovan said, eyeing him. "I can imagine how you feel, but we need your help."

"That's all I heard. You must have some idea of who did this."

"Well, there's the obvious explanation, of course. A coalition of antiabortion groups has been demonstrating against Professor Singer for the past week. It looks like some crazies in the group weren't satisfied with picketing and decided to wreck his laboratory. They broke in between Security rounds, and they probably thought the building was deserted. Your daughter was the only one inside. She caught them by surprise, and someone panicked."

"You said that's the obvious explanation," Reese said, determined not to miss the nuances. "Is there another?"

"Not at the moment," Donovan said, his expression closing up. "We have men out checking on the locals among the demonstrators right now. Harvard Security has some of their names and addresses."

"What are the chances of catching the bastards?" Reese asked, and his voice sounded unnatural to him.

Donovan eyed Reese again, and he didn't immediately answer. "I could feed you the usual pap," he said finally, "but you look like you can take it with the bark on. Unless the perps left prints or something else behind—or we find ourselves an informant—the chances aren't good. There were no witnesses, and most of the demonstrators were from out of state. The perps may have already blown town. There's always a problem when we're dealing with an irrational crime, and that's what this looks like."

Reese had wanted Donovan to be straight with him, but he couldn't accept the answer. Somehow the bastards had to be found. They had to be made to pay.

The detective looked down at his notebook and riffled through the pages.

"You didn't hear anything beyond the crashing noise and your daughter's cry," Donovan said, still looking for something in his notebook, "but did she say anything before she left the phone?"

"Only that she heard a noise. She had no idea what was happening." Reese blinked as fresh tears welled in his eyes.

Donovan found the page he was seeking, and he looked up at Reese. "Did your daughter ever mention a man named Kenji Hamada? Or talk about the work he was doing?"

"Yes," Reese said quickly. "Tonight, as a matter of fact. Why?"

"Just filling in some gaps." Reese tensed. The man was playing games with him. "Did she happen to mention an archaeological sample that was sent to Singer for a DNA analysis?"

"*Yes*. She said it was the basis of some important project that Hamada and Singer were working on. Why?"

"What else did she say?" Donovan asked, deliberately ignoring Reese's question, but this time Reese refused to be deflected. If there was a possibility of a lead, he wanted to know about it.

"Why do you ask?" he demanded.

"Please let me ask the questions, Mr. Reese," Donovan said in a tone that left no room for argument. "What else did she say?"

Reese stared at him in silence for a moment, fighting down the blind anger rising in him. It wasn't Donovan who'd struck down Allison, he told himself, but without a target, his anger was all the more difficult to control.

"She didn't tell me much. Just that they were excited about the project, but not talking about it. Why are you asking?"

"That's police business, Mr. Reese."

Now Reese's anger spilled over. *"Police* business? That's my daughter lying in there—not yours. I have a *right* to know."

"No," Donovan said coolly, returning Reese's stare. "As a matter of fact, you don't. Look, Mr. Reese, if you want us to nail the perps, let us do our job."

"But why won't you tell me?" Reese demanded. "What are you worried about? I won't shoot off my mouth and queer your investigation. I'm not that stupid."

Donovan bit off a reply and looked at Reese speculatively for several seconds. Finally he nodded. "All right. It's bound to get into the papers anyway, so you might as well know. Nothing else appears to be missing, but the archaeological sample has disappeared. Apparently the vandals took it, and thieves are easier to trace than vandals. That's why I asked about it."

"And?" Reese pressed.

"What you've told me only confirms what Hamada and Singer had to say. It looks like the theft was a random act—a fluke. Professor Singer insists that it has no value."

"But it was valuable to him," Reese objected. "Maybe the break-in wasn't vandalism at all. Maybe they were after that archaeological sample."

"It won't wash. At least not yet. Singer's interest in the

sample was purely scientific, and he's adamant that no one would want to steal it.''

''Then why was it taken, Donovan? For Christ's sake, who would think to take such a thing if it really has no value?''

''We're dealing with crazies, Mr. Reese. They don't have to make sense. The odds are, it's already in a trash bin somewhere.''

''But are you sure Singer is telling you the truth? Who sent the sample to Singer for analysis? Maybe he would know why—''

''Don't worry, Mr. Reese,'' Donovan cut in, closing his notebook. ''We'll be checking on that, and every other possible lead.''

Reese felt that there was something more he should do—ask more questions, make demands—something. But he could think of nothing. He felt unutterably weary, and as grief closed in again, it overwhelmed him. God, Allison . . .

Donovan held out his hand. ''Thank you for your cooperation, Mr. Reese. Get some rest. You look like you need it. I'll be in touch, and I assure you that we'll do everything possible to solve this case.''

''I'm counting on that,'' Reese said as he shook the detective's hand. Then he turned and walked toward the nurses' station to locate Dr. Kaplan. If nothing else, he could at least make sure that the doctors did everything possible.

As Donovan watched Reese walk away, he wondered how long it would be before Reese called Professor Singer to obtain the name of the man who'd sent him the archaeological sample. Donovan had no choice but to accept the inexplicable disappearance of the sample, but he wasn't the girl's father.

Anger, the flip side of grief, had already surfaced in Reese, and he had none of the softness Donovan associated with schoolteachers. The tall, rangy man was not heavily muscled, but he could have walked into the roughest bar in Boston tonight and no one would have hassled him.

His rough skin, broken nose, and thick, dark eyebrows gave his face a hard look, but it was his expression, not his face, that warned one off. Behind the shock and grief in Reese's eyes, Donovan had detected more than a hint of danger. Donovan had seen the same look in the eyes of a few other men in his career—men who wanted blood for blood.

Donovan doubted that Reese would be content to leave things to the police. He could accomplish nothing on his own, of course, but he would try. The perps, Donovan reflected with some regret, were lucky that they were beyond Reese's reach.

When Simon knew that his last days were upon him, he gathered his followers about him. And from among them he chose those whom he most loved, saying: Abide with me, that you may truly receive the Spirit. The Last Mystery shall I impart to you, and you shall hear all that has been and that which is yet to come. They remained with him six days and six nights, and in the seventh hour of the seventh day was it accomplished. Seeing it was so, thus spoke Simon: As you have heard it from my lips, so let it be written.

—SAMARIA SCROLL 1, COLUMN 1.1.2

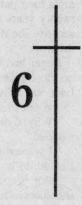

6

Lara Brooks looked forward to surprising her brother, and she was smiling as she knocked on the door to his office. Roger was hard of hearing, and there was no response to her knock. But she could see lamplight behind the door's frosted-glass panel, and as she opened the door, the smell of fresh pipe smoke confirmed his presence.

Her brother was a full professor at Georgetown University, and he'd been accorded a sizable office with an anteroom. Lara walked through and found him seated at his desk, which was piled high with books and manuscripts. Roger hadn't heard her enter, and he was staring fixedly at a pink message slip in his hand.

"Hi, Rog," she said, startling him, and then he grinned. He was a craggy-faced rock of a man, who looked more like a retired prizefighter than the Jesuit priest he'd been for twenty years.

"Lara!" he cried, coming out of his chair. "Where'd you come from?"

"I flew down for a DNA conference," she said as he hurried across to her with his arms outstretched. "I got in this morn—"

Her words were cut off as her brother seized her in a bear hug. She still remembered the first time he'd held her—the night their parents had died in the car crash. Roger had been twenty years old, but Lara only twelve, when the love and security she'd taken for granted had been swept away in an instant.

Roger had been the rock to which she'd clung. They had no close relatives, and he'd put his own life on hold until Lara was fully grown. Only then had he pursued his calling to the priesthood.

"Why didn't you *tell* me you were coming?" he demanded.

"I wanted to surprise you—and I wasn't absolutely sure I could do it. This is my first trip since . . ."

"But you did!" Roger exclaimed happily, gripping her shoulders in his powerful hands and stepping back to observe her. "You look terrific, Lara. It's over, isn't it. Really over."

"The Prozac works, all right," Lara said, smiling up at him. "No more panic attacks."

"That's great," Roger said fervently. "I prayed for you constantly."

"You did more than that," Lara said, reaching up and squeezing his hands. "You were my lifeline, Rog. You know that, don't you?"

"Don't be silly. You'd have made it on your own. You're a tough cookie."

Not so tough, Lara thought, and whatever strength she had, she'd drawn from her brother. Sometimes Lara thought that they were as different as a brother and sister could be, but the bond forged between them after their parents had died was indissoluble.

"How long will you be in Washington?" Roger asked. "Where are you staying?"

"At the conference hotel—the Hyatt Regency on Capitol Hill. It's a five-day conference, but I've booked the room through next weekend."

"Great, but what do you have on for today? Has the conference started?"

"Yes, but the first session that interests me doesn't start till two. Want to have lunch together?"

Roger glanced at his watch and then at the message slip he still held.

"Problem?" Lara prompted.

"No," Roger replied a little too quickly. "Just a call I'm waiting for. . . . But if it doesn't come by eleven-thirty, to heck with it. Okay if we wait here until then?"

"Sure. As a matter of fact, I need to sit for a while."

"Is your leg bothering you?" Roger asked with sudden concern.

"No big deal," Lara replied, going to a chair beside his desk and sitting down. "I've got a new prosthetic that's supposed to be an improvement, but something's not quite right and the stump's getting inflamed."

Her brother's face darkened, and he compressed his lips.

"Don't worry about it, Rog. I don't."

"God may forgive your husband," Roger growled, "but I'm still working on it."

"The accident wasn't Mark's fault. The road was slick and he misjudged the curve."

"He'd been drinking, Lara. And what he put you through afterward was unforgivable."

"Well, he's my ex-husband now. The divorce finally came through last month."

Lara had met Mark Brooks in her first year as an assistant professor of molecular biology at Dartmouth, where Mark was a middle-level administrator. The accident hadn't been the root cause of their divorce, but it had hastened it.

Mark had come through with only cuts and bruises, and Lara had lost her left leg below the knee. She hadn't blamed him, but perhaps he'd blamed himself. Either that, or he couldn't adjust to her disfigurement. She only knew that nothing had been the same afterward.

"You're well rid of him," Roger said.

Lara smiled faintly. "Mark dumped *me*, Rog."

In retrospect, Lara knew she should have seen it coming, for somewhere along the way she'd fallen out of love with him, as well. Yet for Lara, marriage was meant to be for life, and she'd been utterly unprepared when Mark had abruptly asked for a divorce. Bewildered and overcome with a sense of failure, she'd felt as if her life were crumbling around her.

"He did you a favor," Roger said, going back to his desk and sitting down.

"I know," Lara said as he began rummaging through the papers on his desk.

Now that everything was over, Lara felt relief more than anything else. But at the time, the breakup had hit her hard. *God, had it ever.* Though she'd fought against it, she had slipped into an ever deepening depression—and then had come the anxiety.

There was nothing rational about it, for she was financially independent and had her own career, but as time went on, she became increasingly subject to attacks of anxiety that were as severe as they were undefined. They would hit her at odd moments, wherever she happened to be. At first she could ride them out, but inexorably they grew in intensity and she began to lose control.

Now she knew that this was but a consequence of a clinical depression that had probably been with her in a mild form all her life, but she hadn't known it then. The sudden panic attacks could hit her anywhere at any time, and with little warning. Her palms would begin to sweat, she would find it difficult to breathe, and sometimes terrifying chest pains would seize her. As she became afraid of the attacks themselves, she began avoiding people, even her close friends.

At first she was only afraid to travel any distance, but eventually she had to force herself just to leave her apartment. Lara knew that she was in danger of losing her job, but what truly frightened her was the idea that she was losing her mind.

"Rog, your pipe is behind that pile to your left," Lara said, realizing what he was looking for, and she smiled fondly as he commenced a new search—presumably for his tobacco.

It was Roger, talking to her for hours on the phone, who had stopped her slide into the depths, and he'd come up to

Dartmouth to see that she got the medical help she needed. So unexpectedly and overwhelmingly had her symptoms developed that Lara had not had the self-possession to take this step herself.

The psychiatrist's diagnosis had been straightforward: mild clinical depression exacerbated by the crisis of divorce. He had prescribed Prozac, and the medication had proved completely effective. Over time, he had told her, the dosage would be reduced, and one day she might not need it at all.

Roger lit his pipe and began to fill the room with fresh clouds of aromatic smoke. Lara responded by taking out her cigarettes.

"I thought you were going to quit," Roger protested.

"I will when you do."

"Touché," he said, and smiled. Yet Lara sensed that something was not quite right. He was obviously happy to see her, but although he appeared relaxed, Lara had the feeling that he was working at it.

"Look what I found," Roger said abruptly, turning a framed photograph on his desk so she could see it. "I still had the negative of the snapshot, and I had the picture enlarged. I look a little goofy, but it's a great picture of you."

"And out of date," Lara said, looking at the slight-figured brunette in a college-graduation cap and gown smiling into the camera. "I was fifteen years younger then."

"And you don't look a day older now—and frankly, you're even more beautiful."

Lara laughed. "You don't need to boost my morale, Rog. I'm *okay* now."

"How's your research coming? Back on track?"

"Definitely. That's why I'm down here. I think I'm closing in on an Alzheimer's gene, and I want to hear what the competition is doing."

"And what about your sabbatical leave? Is Dartmouth granting it?"

"Yes, it's all set." Lara smiled. "As soon as classes are over, I'll be as free as a bird for a year. I'm just not sure where I want to go, and I've got to make up my mind soon.

Yale is the better bet, research-wise, but Oxford would be a lot more fun.''

"Well, for what it's worth, I recommend Oxford and fun.''

Despite the cheer in Roger's voice, Lara noticed his eyes strayed worriedly to the message slip now lying on his desk. "That call you're waiting for, can't you phone the person yourself?''

"I did earlier," Roger replied casually, but once again he seemed to be trying. "I was told he couldn't be reached.''

"What's wrong, Rog? Something's been bothering you ever since I came in.''

"Nothing," Roger replied, but when he saw her expression, he smiled slightly and shook his head. "Well, that's not absolutely true.''

"And?''

"I don't know. Maybe nothing's wrong, but a police detective in Cambridge, Massachusetts, wants to ask me some questions about an archaeological sample I sent up to Harvard for a DNA analysis. I don't know the man, or why he's calling, but—well, I just have this feeling.''

"Since when are Jesuits superstitious?''

"It's just that I hope nothing's happened to the sample.''

"Why? Because it's a cop who's calling?''

"I guess so. Silly.''

"Not really. Not if the sample is important. What is it?''

Roger's eyes slid away for a moment, and Lara could feel his hesitation. Why? she wondered.

"Some mummified human flesh and bone," Roger said.

"Yuck. Where'd you get it?''

"It was embedded in clay inside the spindle of two ancient scrolls I've been translating that date roughly from the time of Christ. I inherited them from a late colleague of mine, who found them in a cave in what used to be ancient Samaria.''

"Like the Dead Sea Scrolls?''

"Not really." Again Lara saw hesitation. She sensed that he didn't want to talk about it, but couldn't think of a reason to refuse.

"The two scrolls were rolled together, with the inner one elaborately sealed. Both were written in Aramaic, but the innermost scroll was obscured by one of the simple codes in fashion at the time. The first scroll appeared at first to be an early Christian text, but once I began to decipher the coded scroll, it became clear that we were dealing with a magical tract."

"Magic? Isn't that a bit out of your line?" Lara asked with a smile, trying to draw him out.

"Not in this case. The scrolls' authors were disciples of Simon Magus."

"Who?"

"Didn't the nuns teach you anything?" Roger responded with a wry smile, but the smile looked forced. "Simon the Magician was a contemporary of Jesus, who's mentioned in Acts. He was quite famous at the time, and indeed long afterward. His cult following survived him by at least a century, and we know that some Samaritans worshiped him as a God.

"In Acts, it appears that Simon converted to Christianity, and the writings in the first scroll suggested that might be true. Particularly this passage," he said, and he recited it: " 'As Simon went up to Sychar in Samaria, many came out to hear him, for they knew he was great among the Great Ones. And thus spoke Simon: Behold the miracles of God that you may know that I have received the Spirit of the Son of Man.' "

Lara could understand the importance of such a find to Roger, for he was a recognized biblical historian, yet she neither saw nor heard any of the excitement she would have expected. He had recited the passage as if he were reading from the phone book.

"The tone of the first scroll is apocalyptic and definitely influenced by early Christian teaching, but as I began to decipher the inner scroll, it became clear that Simon clung to his magic. Neither Simon nor his followers disputed Christ's miracles, but they ascribed them to magic. Simon must have considered Jesus his greatest competitor."

"But what about the yucky stuff in the scroll's spindle?"

"It was to be used in connection with the magical incantations contained in the coded scroll," Roger said with what struck Lara as deliberate vagueness. He looked away from her, and she could see his jaw muscles working. "If only I hadn't sent it out for analysis . . ."

"Who'd you send it to?" It wasn't the question Lara wanted to ask. Why did he care about some mummified skin and bone? Surely it was the scroll that was important.

"I sent it to Professor Singer."

Lara whistled. "The big time. I didn't know he did that sort of—"

The ringing of Roger's telephone cut her off, and her brother answered it in haste.

"Father Wilson here," he said, and after a few seconds silence, "yes, Detective Donovan, I got your message. How can I help you?"

Again there was a silence, and Lara saw Roger swallow hard. "Yes, an archaeological sample. No, it wasn't valuable—not in the normal sense. Why do you ask?"

The silence that followed seemed unbearably long to Lara, for almost at once Roger stiffened in his chair, and as she watched, the color drained from his face.

"Oh, no," he said in a shocked voice. "Oh, that's terrible—tragic. How could they—" He broke off, and again there was silence. "Yes," Roger said hoarsely. "Yes, I understand why it's important to you, but I have no idea. Are you sure it was taken?"

As the detective spoke again, Roger looked directly at Lara for the first time, but she had the feeling he wasn't seeing her.

"Yes, of course I'll get back to you if I can think of anything. Yes, you're very welcome. Good-bye, Detective Donovan."

"What's happened?" Lara gasped as her brother hung up. As gentle as her brother's spirit was, there was nothing weak about him. Inside he was as sturdy as his rough-hewn face and rocklike physique suggested, and she'd never seen him so shaken.

"A girl has been badly hurt," he said hoarsely, and he

swallowed hard. "She's in a coma. The doctors say she may not come out of it."

"What girl?"

"One of Professor Singer's Ph.D. students. Vandals broke in and wrecked his lab last night, and she happened to be there alone. They struck her down."

"But why, Rog?"

"I don't know," he said, shaking his head dazedly. "The police think they were antiabortion protesters. It makes no sense, Lara. They took the sample. It's gone—disappeared." Roger shook his head. "I had a premonition, but not this. That poor girl . . ."

"Rog," Lara said, unable to understand the depth of his shock and bewilderment. "It's not your fault."

"I should never have sent it out," Roger said, looking right through her.

"Rog, what is it you're not telling me?" The devastation she saw in his eyes took her breath away.

Roger blinked and visibly tried to pull himself together, but none of the color returned to his face. "I'm sorry, Lara. Really, it's nothing for you to worry about."

But it is, Lara wanted to cry. Her brother had always been there when she needed him. *Always.* She had thought him invincible, but not now—not after the look she'd seen in his eyes. She desperately wanted to help him, but she didn't know how.

"Do you want me to go?" she asked, sure that he'd say no; but he didn't.

"Maybe that would be best," he said apologetically. "I— well, there are some calls I have to make, and I'm afraid I wouldn't be good company just now."

He stood up, and Lara reluctantly rose with him.

"I'll give you a ring at your hotel when I have things cleaned up," Roger said, walking with her through the anteroom to the corridor door. "Lara, I'm really sorry," he said, gripping her shoulders. "I know I'm spoiling things."

"You *haven't*," she said, hugging him, "I just wish you'd . . ."

She felt him sigh, and she released him and looked up at him.

"It's a Church matter," he said, opening the door for her. "It's not your problem."

"If it's a problem for you, it's a problem for me. We've always been a team, haven't we?"

"Yes."

"Maybe I can't help," Lara pleaded, "but I wish you'd tell me what's wrong. I don't care about Church secrets, but I do care about you—and whatever you tell me would be just between us. You know that."

"Yes, I know."

"Then don't shut me out, Rog. Please. It's that thing you sent out for analysis, isn't it? Why is it so important to you?"

For a moment Lara thought he would answer, but then a heavy sigh escaped him and he shook his head. "Please, Lara, no more questions. Someday I may be able to explain, but not now."

That evening, Roger phoned Lara at her hotel to tell her that he was being called out of town. He didn't say why—or when he might return—and Lara didn't ask. The strain in his voice was too plain.

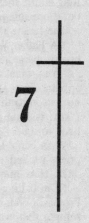

7

Reese shoved aside the exam papers he'd been trying to grade. Allison had been in a coma for six days, and although her doctors refused to deliver a final verdict, Reese knew what it was. She would never come out of it. Work was his only defense against the grief and rage that sometimes threatened to overwhelm him, and he burrowed into it each day. But now, waiting for his call, he couldn't concentrate.

He took out his cigarettes and willed himself to be patient. The Jesuit priest was supposed to call him between three and four, and it was already three-thirty. He had been trying to reach Father Wilson for three days; he could wait a little longer. Wait and hope. It was a forlorn hope, but all Reese had left—the hope for vengeance.

He lit a cigarette and dragged the smoke deep into his lungs. The pack he'd bought the morning after the break-in had been his first in more than twenty years. He was probably hooking himself again, but he couldn't have cared less.

When he'd lost Kathy, the agony had been no less, but the finality had been inescapable and Reese had finally come to terms with it. But there might be no end to this—not as long as the men who had taken Allison's life from her were out there somewhere.

The phone rang and Reese picked up.

"A Father Wilson is on the line," said the Baxter switchboard operator.

"Yes, thanks. Put him on," Reese said, preparing for disappointment. The police were getting nowhere, and there was no reason to think he could do any better; but he had to try. "This is John Reese, Father. Thanks very much for getting back to me."

"I'm sorry I couldn't return your call sooner," the Jesuit priest replied apologetically. "I've been away for several days. How may I help you?"

"I'm calling in connection with an archaeological sample Professor Singer tells me you discovered in Palestine—the sample that was stolen from his laboratory. I assume you know about that."

"Yes—yes, I know what happened. A terrible affair. Terrible. But I don't understand," Father Wilson said diffidently. "May I ask your interest?"

"The girl who was attacked—she's my daughter. She's in a coma, Father, and the doctors don't think she'll come out of it."

There was a momentary silence, and Reese heard the priest clear his throat. "I'm sorry, Mr. Reese," Father Wilson said hoarsely. "Deeply sorry."

"The police have told me very little, but it's pretty clear they have no leads. They're assuming that the break-in was an act of vandalism, but that doesn't explain the disappearance of your sample." Reese paused and took a breath, praying for a lead, however slim. "I was hoping you might know why someone would want to take it."

"I've already talked with the Cambridge police, and I'm afraid I can tell you no more than I told them. I have absolutely no idea why anyone would steal it. It had no monetary value at all."

It was just the answer Reese had expected, but that didn't lessen the impact. "Could you tell me a little more about the find, Father?'' he asked, though he knew it was hopeless.

"Certainly," Father Wilson replied patiently. "We were in the process of deciphering a scroll a late colleague of mine unearthed in Palestine when we discovered some mummified flesh and bone inside the scroll's spindle. I sent it to Professor Singer for a DNA analysis, in the hope that the results might be of interest to researchers outside our own narrow field—people who trace man's genetic history."

"But are you absolutely sure that it's of no value to anyone else—for any reason? I know I'm supposed to leave everything to the police, but . . . she's my daughter, Father, and they might as well have killed her."

"I understand, Mr. Reese," said Father Wilson, and again his voice became hoarse, "but there's nothing I can tell you. I can assure you that the police detective who questioned me on the phone was quite thorough. I had the distinct impression that they intend to do everything possible to solve the case."

"Which hasn't been enough, Father."

"I understand how you must feel, but . . . well, I'm not sure what more one can do. Have you considered hiring a private detective?"

"I can't afford it," Reese said, trying not to sound bitter. It wasn't the priest's fault that he was at a dead end.

"I see," Father Wilson said sympathetically. "I really can't tell you how sorry I am that I can be of no assistance. All I can say," he added with obviously heartfelt sincerity, "is that you and your daughter will be in my prayers."

"Thank you, Father." There was nothing more to say, and nothing more Reese could do. He was helpless. "Good-bye, Father, and thank you again."

"God be with you, Mr. Reese."

8

Lara saw the light behind Roger's office door and opened it. The message he'd left at her hotel, asking her to come to his office at four, had been the first word from him in five days, and impatience had brought her twenty minutes early. She hadn't bothered to knock, and she stopped short in the anteroom as she heard a stranger's voice. He had a soft voice, but there was no mistaking its cool tone of authority.

"You did well, Father," said the stranger. "I'm sure Reese believed you."

"And why not?" Lara heard Roger respond angrily. "No one expects a priest to lie."

"We have enough to worry about without Reese getting in our way, and I'm glad to know he won't be hiring a private detective. I appreciate your probing his intentions— as I appreciated your not returning his call until I'd had a chance to check up on him."

Lara was embarrassed to find herself eavesdropping. She knocked loudly on the open door, closed it behind her, and walked through the anteroom into Roger's office. Her brother and his visitor rose as she entered, and Lara was taken aback.

The dark, stocky, bearded man who smiled graciously at her wasn't dressed in clerical garb; he wore an expensively tailored business suit.

He appeared to be in his fifties, but there was little gray in his thick, jet hair and closely trimmed beard. His tailored suit disguised his somewhat excessive weight, and something in the way he carried himself gave him an imposing presence. He had a round, congenial face, but his dark eyes were alert and probing.

"I hope I'm not intruding," Lara said.

"Not at all," Roger replied, smiling and coming over to her, and there was no hint of the angry tension she'd heard in his voice only moments before. "Lara," he said, putting his arm around her shoulders, "this is Mr. Beretta, a New York attorney."

"A lawyer? Do you need one, Rog?"

"Not in the least," Beretta interjected with a good-natured grin, and he stepped forward and extended his hand. "I'm here as a friend—not in a legal capacity. A pleasure to meet you, Ms. Brooks. Father Wilson has told me quite a bit about you."

In contrast to her brother, Beretta exuded smooth sophistication, and he struck her as a man used to being in control.

"Nothing bad, I hope," Lara said as they shook hands, and she hoped her smile looked natural.

"Of course not." Beretta laughed, and his smile almost disguised the probing look in his dark eyes.

Lara was completely mystified. She'd heard the way Beretta had talked to her brother, and she couldn't imagine what power a layman could have over a Jesuit priest.

"Have you known my brother long, Mr. Beretta?"

"Call me Al. No, Father Wilson and I met only recently. When I said I was here as a friend, I meant it more in terms of the Church."

"Oh?"

"Mr. Beretta is a member of Opus Dei," Roger said in a decidedly neutral voice.

"Have you heard of us, Ms. Brooks?" Beretta asked.

"Only what my brother has told me."

"Nothing bad, I hope," Beretta said with wry amusement, and Lara realized that her tone had given more away than she'd intended. Opus Dei had tried to recruit Roger away from the Jesuits years ago, and his remarks at the time had not been entirely complimentary.

Certainly Roger had no great liking for Opus Dei—God's Work. Opus Dei was not a conventional religious order, and its membership numbered far more laymen than priests. The caliber and religious devotion of its recruits were undeniable, Roger had told her, and the rise of Opus Dei's influence in the Church had been nothing short of spectacular. Her brother had no quarrel with Opus Dei's precept that anyone, regardless of vocation, could aspire to a saintly life, but he was wary of Opus Dei's methods, which struck him as conspiratorial.

Lara didn't understand why her brother had to defer to Beretta, but she did know that Opus Dei was a power to be reckoned with.

Beretta was watching her. His appraising gaze reminded her of the subtle arrogance his cool tone had conveyed while speaking with Roger, and she felt a flash of resentment.

"Well, I'd better be on my way," he said. "Thanks for giving me your time, Father. Ms. Brooks, it's been a pleasure meeting you. If you'll permit me to say so," he added smoothly, "the photograph on Father Wilson's desk hardly does you justice."

Lara responded with a neutral smile, and Beretta left the office.

Roger smiled tiredly. "Sorry. I thought he'd be long gone by the time you got here."

"Who *is* he?"

"A man with clout."

"Rog . . . are you in some kind of trouble?"

"Trouble? What makes you think that?"

"Well, for one thing, I've never seen you as worried or upset as you were the last Monday. And then you disappear on me for five days . . ."

"I'm really sorry about that, Lara," Roger said, coming over to her, "but it's not something you should worry about.

And believe me, I'm *not* in any kind of trouble.''

"But you're not going to tell me what the problem is.''

Roger shook his head. "I can't, Lara. But I'll tell you this much. It's not my problem now; it's Mr. Beretta's.'' Then he smiled and put his arm around her shoulders. "Come on,'' he said briskly. "Let's get out of here and make up for lost time.''

It was nearly 11 P.M. when Lara returned to her hotel room, after a long and pleasant evening with her brother. Roger had seemed almost his old self again, and while she sensed that he was still troubled for some reason, he had at least recovered his equilibrium. That would have to be enough for her, she thought as she slipped off her shoes and settled onto the bed. Never before had the priesthood placed a barrier between them, but there was nothing she could do about it.

She lay back and closed her eyes, more tired than she'd thought. Her amputated leg throbbed dully, but she didn't have the energy to tend to it. She didn't realize she was drifting off to sleep until the phone rang and jolted her awake.

With a groan of irritation, Lara sat up and lifted the receiver. "Hello?'' she said, wondering who was calling. It couldn't be Roger, she thought, for he'd said good-bye to her in the lobby less than fifteen minutes ago.

"Good evening, Ms. Brooks. This is Al Beretta.''

"Yes?'' Lara responded, too surprised to add a polite phrase.

"Did I wake you?''

"No,'' Lara said, and cleared her throat. "No, I just got in.''

"I know it's late, but I was hoping I might still have a word with you this evening. I have to catch an early flight tomorrow, and there's something I think we should discuss.''

Lara grimaced in annoyance. She couldn't imagine what he wanted, but whatever it was, she was too tired. "Discuss what?''

"It's about your brother, Ms. Brooks. I gather that you

and Father Wilson are quite close, and it occurred to me that you're in a unique position to help him.''

Lara tensed. "Help him? In what way?"

"That will take some explaining, but let me say this: I represent the Church at the very highest level, and my mission has the blessing of the Holy Father himself."

"What mission?" Lara asked, taken aback.

"That's what I want to discuss with you."

Despite Roger's assurance that he was in no trouble with the Church, she couldn't forget the tone she'd heard Beretta use with him. "All right," she said, trying to hide her anxiety.

"Thank you. If it's agreeable to you, we could meet in your hotel's cocktail lounge in twenty minutes."

"Very well."

"Excellent. I really do appreciate your consideration. See you then."

9

The hotel's cocktail lounge was still doing brisk Saturday-night business, and Lara didn't see Beretta in the crowded, dimly lit room until he waved to her from a table in the far corner. He rose as she approached, smiled, and extended his hand.

"Thanks for coming."

"I'm here because of my brother," Lara replied without returning his smile. Her anxiety that her brother might be in trouble with the Church had her on edge, and if he was in trouble, she strongly suspected that Beretta had something to do with it.

"Of course," Beretta replied easily. "May I order you something?" he asked as they sat down.

"No, thanks. I'd like you to get to the point."

"I've come to ask a great service of you, Ms. Brooks," Beretta said, lowering his voice, and Lara could barely hear him above the chatter in the bar. "A service to us, but most of all a service to Father Wilson."

"What on earth are you talking about?"

"I understand that your brother told you about the scrolls

he's been translating—and what was found with them.''

"You don't have to ask," Lara said quickly. "I'm not interested in whatever secrets the Church may have, and I'm not a blabbermouth. I can assure you that what little Roger did tell me, I'll keep to myself.''

"You misunderstand. If I weren't convinced of your discretion, I wouldn't be here. And it's not the scrolls in themselves that concern us. It's what was found with them. You see, we have reason to believe that the mummified flesh and bone your brother sent out for analysis may be a relic of the earliest of the Christian martyrs, Saint Stephen.''

Lara blinked. "I don't understand. Roger told me that what was found in the spindle was to be used for some sort of magic. He said that the scrolls were written by followers of . . .''

"Simon Magus. That's correct, but as I understand Father Wilson also told you, Simon believed in Christ's powers, though he ascribed it to magic. The scrolls show that Simon Magus and his followers believed Christ's powers were transferred to the disciples, and from them to certain other Christians—and Simon sought to acquire those powers for himself.

"Magicians of the time worked their magic indirectly, Ms. Brooks, by conjuring the spirits of men who had died violently. And the most powerful spirits of all were thought to be the spirits of men who had worked magic. Apparently Simon considered Saint Stephen such a man, for the scroll that Father Wilson is in the process of deciphering contains instructions and incantations for conjuring his spirit.

"But incantations alone were thought to be insufficient. The magician required the dead man's body, or at least some part of it, for the incantations to work. Hence the flesh and bone preserved inside the coded scroll's spindle. According to the scrolls, it was cut from the body of Saint Stephen.''

"And you believe that?" Lara asked in wonder.

"We only know what Father Wilson has already established. The scrolls are clearly genuine, and the text is consistent with known historical facts and the magical practices of the time. Beyond that, scientific inquiry can tell us nothing, but how can we possibly ignore the possibility? I know you're not a practicing Catholic, Ms. Brooks, but surely you understand. If the scroll's claim is true, the relic is precious to the Church.''

"But how could you possibly ever know, one way or the other?"

"Such things are not mine to answer. I am not the Holy Father."

"But the question is moot," Lara said, completely mystified. "Whatever it is, it's lost to you."

"Gone," Beretta corrected with a peculiar intensity, "but not necessarily lost. And my mission is to get it back. I'm hoping you'll help me do just that."

For a moment Lara was too astonished to respond. "I don't have the slightest idea what you're talking about," she said, her earlier anxiety turning to annoyance, "but you've gotten me here under false pretenses. My brother isn't to blame for the relic's disappearance—if it really is a relic. It's not his problem, and it's certainly not mine."

"You're wrong, Ms. Brooks, it *is* a problem for Father Wilson. The burden of its loss weighs more heavily on your brother than you imagine. Of course he's not at fault, and we're not blaming him; but Father Wilson blames himself. And I happen to know that the pain he hides from you is excruciating."

"What pain? What are you talking about?"

"As I told you, no one can say if the relic is genuine or not, and frankly, I have my own doubts. But I am not your brother. God speaks to us all in different ways and at different times, and in Father Wilson's heart of hearts, he is already convinced that the scroll's claim is true."

"But he didn't . . ."

"Didn't tell you?" Beretta responded, finishing her thought. "He's a priest, Ms. Brooks, and there are some things he wouldn't share, even with you."

"What do you know about it?" Lara snapped.

"Enough," Beretta replied evenly. "I've learned a great deal about Father Wilson—and through him, much about you. I don't make a habit of prying into others' lives, but

I've been entrusted with a mission that I intend to fulfill.''

Beretta's self-justification didn't lessen Lara's anger.

"Whatever you think of me," Beretta said, reading her expression, "I think you already know that I'm telling you the truth. Whether or not Father Wilson is right, he believes the relic is genuine. Surely you can imagine what that means—what he must feel. I asked you here because I thought you'd want to help him. At the moment, at least, only one thing can set his mind at rest: recovering what has been lost.''

Lara knew she was being manipulated, and she rebelled against it, but she couldn't forget the look on Roger's face the morning the detective had called.

"We don't think the break-in was an act of vandalism," Beretta continued, "nor the relic's disappearance an accident. We have reason to believe that it was stolen deliberately, and we think we know by whom. If you're wondering why your brother didn't tell you, he wasn't authorized to.''

"Then why are *you* telling me? And why aren't you talking to the police?''

"Because we have no proof that would stand up in court. The relic, itself, is the only possible proof, and at the first hint of trouble, the thief would make sure it's never found. Beyond that, an unsupported accusation from us would be politically explosive. We're on our own, Ms. Brooks, and as Providence would have it, you are in a unique position to help us.''

"Does Roger know you're here?" Lara demanded.

"No.''

"Why not?''

Beretta smiled slightly. "He's quite protective of you, Ms. Brooks, and I don't imagine he would approve of what I'm going to ask of you. But more than anyone else, your brother—''

"You've made your point," Lara interrupted, her tension mounting as she stared at the smooth, calculating man before her. Whatever Beretta wanted, she knew she wouldn't like it, yet already she felt ensnared. Roger had always been there for her when she needed him—always.

"All I ask is that you hear me out. Whatever your decision, I know you'll keep what I tell you absolutely confidential."

"And you know I'll listen." Lara's voice was icy.

"No," Beretta replied evenly, "I didn't know. I *hoped*. Have you ever heard of the Reverend Bobby Jordan?"

"No."

"He's a televangelist based in Louisiana, but he has a large, national following. In many ways he's a more charismatic version of Oral Roberts. He shares Roberts's penchant for dramatic religious visions and claims that God speaks to him directly. And like Oral Roberts, Bobby Jordan has embraced modern medical science as an adjunct to his faith healing. Naturally that improves his success rate.

"What sets Jordan apart, however, is his fascination with DNA research, which seems to have developed after he built a fertility clinic on a private island off the coast of Maine. Born-again couples can go there for a heavy dose of prayer and the very latest medical treatments—including in vitro fertilization and DNA screening. Apparently that's what drew his attention to DNA research, and it seems to have captured his imagination.

"Frankly, I think the man's unbalanced. Judging by some of his sermons, Bobby Jordan appears to believe that decoding human DNA can unlock great religious mysteries. Two years ago, he announced a fund drive to build a full-fledged research lab on his island, claiming that he wanted to contribute to the Human Genome Project. Since then he's poured millions into the lab, and—"

"Not *Miracle Isle*," Lara interrupted, suddenly recalling the peculiar poster she'd seen on her department's bulletin board.

"Yes, that's it," Beretta said with satisfaction. "Jordan has been trying to recruit young scientists for his new laboratory. He hasn't had much success, but six months ago, he landed a very big fish to take over as his lab director—Dr. Richard Michaels."

"Michaels? Of NIH?" Lara asked incredulously.

"Yes."

It seemed incredible to Lara that a man of Michaels's stature would agree to direct a laboratory set up by a televangelist.

"Where's all this leading?" she asked, impatient to know exactly what Beretta wanted of her.

"To the break-in at Harvard. The antiabortion protests that preceded it were instigated by Bobby Jordan Ministries. We think Jordan organized the protests to cover his theft of the relic."

"What makes you think that?"

"Because we're almost certain that Jordan knew something of what the scrolls contain. As Father Wilson probably told you, the outer scroll was not obscured by code, and he was not the first to translate it. He gave it to a young man studying under him for a master's degree in biblical archaeology—a young man on temporary leave from the faculty of the Bobby Jordan Bible College outside Baton Rouge.

"Evangelical Christians don't make the most objective of scholars," Beretta noted dryly, "but this young man was bright and knowledgeable, so your brother took him on. The student could read Aramaic, and he made rapid progress with the outer scroll. But then he claimed to be having difficulty, and weeks passed with no progress reports.

"Then—abruptly—he announced that he was terminating his studies, claiming that 'personal problems' required his return to Baton Rouge. He disappeared the very next day, and to Father Wilson's surprise and annoyance, he took all his notes with him.

"Your brother then took up the task of translating the outer scroll himself. Too late, he discovered the scroll's claim that the mummified remains within the scrolls' spindle were a relic of Saint Stephen, and before he could recover the relic, the lab was ransacked.

"Consider the order of events," Beretta said grimly. "A devoted follower of Bobby Jordan inexplicably claims to be unable to complete a translation well within his capabilities and abruptly returns to the Bobby Jordan Bible College. Then, only weeks later, Bobby Jordan Ministries trumps up protest demonstrations and the relic is stolen. It's too much of a coincidence to swallow.''

''It may be difficult to swallow, but that doesn't mean it isn't a coincidence.''

Beretta smiled thinly. ''Which is precisely why we haven't gone to the police. Can you imagine the uproar if the Catholic Church accused a nationally known televangelist of conspiracy, theft, and a vicious assault that left a young woman in a coma?''

''But why would Jordan want to steal it? What motive could he possibly have? Fundamentalists have no interest in the Catholic Church's saints.''

''I can only guess what goes on in his twisted mind, but he can only know what is in the first scroll, and that is filled with apocalyptic prophecy that is similar in many ways to that found in Revelation. Without the benefit of the second scroll's text, the first scroll could be easily misconstrued as the writings of an early Christian sect.

''Bobby Jordan's preaching is laced with the belief that the Second Coming is imminent, and some of the passages in the first scroll would certainly excite him. Father Wilson pointed out one to me that would certainly get Jordan's attention: 'A thousand upon a thousand years shall pass before the coming of the Son of Man. Then shall the Nations fall, and all that was shall be swept away,' and so on and so forth.

''And there are repeated references to the Chosen One, who will presumably prepare the way for Christ's return. It wouldn't surprise me a bit if Jordan believes that could refer to him. Maybe he thinks he can verify the relic's authenticity in his own laboratory and in that way offer proof that the scroll's prophecies are true.''

''But DNA analysis can't tell him a thing.''

''Of course not. But Bobby Jordan isn't rational, and he thinks there's mystical power in knowledge of the genetic code. I don't know why he stole the relic, but I don't think he destroyed it. And given his fixation on DNA research, the place to look for it is on Miracle Isle.''

Beretta fell silent, and Lara finally understood.

''Just how thorough were you in your prying?'' she asked.

"Do you already know that Dartmouth has given me a leave of absence for the coming year?"

"Yes, and I'm hoping you'll modify whatever plans you've made. You may not realize it, but the laboratory on Miracle Isle is among the best equipped in the country. Jordan has spared no expense. It would be entirely plausible for you to apply for a position as a visiting scientist, and with your credentials, I'm sure you'd be accepted."

"And play Mata Hari on the side? Is that it?"

"Nothing so dramatic. All I'd ask is that you keep your eyes open. If one of Jordan's scientists is analyzing the relic's DNA, I think you'd discover that in short order. And if I'm wrong about Jordan—if you find nothing—you could stay on and complete the research you started there. As I said, the facilities there are first-rate."

"And if the relic *is* there?"

"Then we'd want you to leave. Recovering the relic would be our problem, not yours. You'd not be involved in any way. I can promise you this. Whatever should happen, no one besides myself need ever know why you applied for a position at Miracle Isle."

Lara had been sitting rigidly for too long, and she shifted position in an attempt to relieve her tension. Fatigue had caught up with her, and it was a struggle to think clearly, much less master the conflicting emotions coursing through her.

"Believe me," Beretta said, "I know how much I'm asking, and I wouldn't have approached you if we had a better choice. But we don't. Time may well be short, and although Opus Dei has considerable resources, you are our best hope of getting someone onto the island quickly. If you should choose to help us, we'd be grateful beyond words, and to compensate you—"

"Don't!" Lara snapped, cutting him off.

Every fiber of her being rebelled at being used, but she could find no easy excuse to refuse. Stripped of its distasteful deceit, Beretta's request would only cause her inconvenience and disappointment. It would ruin her sabbatical leave, but that wasn't reason enough to refuse to help Roger.

As much as she wanted to get up and leave Beretta flat, she couldn't without turning her back on her brother, as well. She couldn't understand how Roger could be so affected by the loss of the relic, even if it were genuine, but she had never fathomed his faith. If there was any chance at all of repaying her brother for all that he'd done for her, how could she refuse?

And Beretta had counted on that. *The bastard had counted on it.*

"I'll have to think about it," Lara said, getting up from the table. She knew she was caught—that there was no point in stalling—but suddenly she could abide his presence no longer.

"Of course," he said, rising with her. "Whatever you decide, we're very grateful that you gave it your consideration."

Lara couldn't read his expression, and she wondered if he knew how much he repelled her.

10

Kenji Hamada was nervous as he waited for his father's visitor to leave, but he was also determined. He had no idea how his father would react to his request, but he had to make it.

The politician climbing into the limousine outside was just another of the luminaries from the upper strata of Japanese society who found their way to Yoshiro Hamada in search of favors. Thereafter they returned at intervals to pay their respects, but few were willing to have their names linked with the leader of the Naguchi-gumi. The gestures of respect were as discreetly private as the favors the petitioners sought.

In the past, Kenji had viewed such visitors with a measure of contempt, but now he wondered if he was any different. He had chosen to live entirely outside his father's world, and now he, too, was coming to Yoshiro Hamada for help that only an *oyabun no oyabun* could provide. The only saving grace was that Kenji would not try to keep his own skirts clean.

He could smell the tantalizing odors drifting to him from the kitchen, where his mother was supervising the preparation of a special meal to welcome him home. She would be busy for some time, and this was an opportune moment to speak to his father without his mother's knowledge. If his mother got wind of his plan, Kenji knew, she'd put a stop to it.

The moment the politician's limousine pulled away, Kenji went through to the trophy room, where his father received all distinguished visitors. There, his father would almost certainly be enjoying an illicit smoke. Yoshiro Hamada ruled the Naguchi-gumi with an iron hand, but at home, Kenji's mother held sway and Kenji's father only lit up when he knew it was safe.

Kenji found him still seated at the ceremonial teak table, and as expected, he was smoking.

"Ah, Kenji," his father said warmly. "Come sit with me awhile. We have a lot of catching up to do."

Yoshiro Hamada was still sternly handsome, but age was taking its toll. His wiry, well-muscled body had stiffened with arthritis, and he was plagued with emphysema. As Kenji approached, a fit of coughing racked him. The doctor had ordered him not to smoke, but only Kenji's mother could enforce the edict.

As Kenji sat down and waited for the coughing to subside, his eyes strayed around the room. It held the finest of his father's private treasures. Kenji doubted that it was possible to count the prominent men and women who were indebted to Yoshiro Hamada for the power and influence he had wielded on their behalf, and all of them had presented him with gifts of gratitude.

The glass display cases and shelves lining the walls were filled with such gifts, and they served as a reminder to Yoshiro Hamada's visitors that he was a man to be reckoned with. He understood the importance of image, and the display contributed to the image he desired. But Kenji knew that the gifts were also a source of deep satisfaction. His father enjoyed viewing his treasures and reliving the memories they kindled.

In one corner stood the shining championship trophy won by a great sumo wrestler whose career his father had fostered. Nearby hung a magnificent ceremonial sword presented by a film actor his father had lifted from obscurity to stardom. His father's most prized possession was a priceless suit of ancient samurai armor that hung in a hermetically sealed glass case. The armor had been presented to him by a former Japanese prime minister.

"It's good to have you home again," said his father as his coughing subsided. "You don't come often enough."

"I always mean to, but somehow I never seem to find the time."

His father reached across the table and struck Kenji's chest gently with his fist. "*Make* time, Kenji. A man has to work hard to make his way in the world, but you should set limits. You're worn-out. I can see it."

"Jet lag."

Kenji could see that his father didn't accept the excuse, but his father nodded tolerantly. "All right, no lectures. You're not a boy anymore." His father smiled conspiratorially and inhaled another lungful of smoke. "So. Tell me about your work. Last time you called, you sounded excited, but you wouldn't tell us much."

"I've made a discovery in the lab, Pa," Kenji said, grateful that he could now get to the point quickly. Delay could only weaken his resolve. "It could be really important, and Professor Singer advised me not to talk about it until we were absolutely sure."

"And now?" his father asked eagerly, his eyes alight with interest and pride, and Kenji felt a stab of renewed chagrin.

"I've discovered a new gene, Pa," Kenji said, desperately wishing he could have come with news of success. "Quite by accident. It was just luck, but—"

"Don't put yourself down!" his father chided. "You've *always* underestimated yourself. But don't let me interrupt, Kenji. Go on."

"Some time ago, Professor Singer asked me to analyze the trace DNA in a sample of mummified human flesh and bone that had been sent to our lab. Neither of us expected to find anything of biological interest; it was just a professional courtesy to the archaeologist who sent us the sample."

"But?"

"But then I found this gene—a gene not listed in the data banks. It was on a fragment of surviving DNA from the Y chromosome. That's the—"

"Yes, yes, I know. I've been doing a lot of reading, Kenji. What good is it to have a brilliant scientist for a son if you don't understand what he does?"

"Well, it appears that the gene is entirely new—unknown in modern man," Kenji continued, hoping his nervousness didn't show. "On the off chance that I might learn something, I synthesized copies of the gene and inserted them into a lab culture of human somatic cells. When some of the cells incorporated the foreign gene into their chromosomes, the result was startling. The genetically altered cells ceased to exhibit cellular senescence."

"That I don't understand. What's 'cellular senescence'?"

"Aging on a cellular level, Pa. Somatic cells in culture divide and multiply, and the culture grows—up to a point. For reasons we don't understand, they eventually stop dividing and the culture dies. But the cells that accepted the foreign gene continued to live and multiply well beyond the senescence limit, and perhaps they would indefinitely. And they hadn't turned cancerous. In all other respects, they were completely normal. They—"

"Wait, Kenji!" his father broke in with an utterly uncharacteristic display of excitement. "Are you telling me that you've found an *antidote to aging?*"

"I can't say that, Pa. Some people believe that cellular senescence is the root cause of aging, but no one really knows."

"But it *could* be?"

Once again Kenji felt the stab of guilt and remorse. How he had longed to see just such an expression on his father's face!

"I don't know, but if I could have confirmed my initial results, it certainly would have been a discovery of major importance."

"Would have?" his father asked, crestfallen. "Do you mean you were mistaken?"

"No, Pa," Kenji replied, guilt washing over him. It was his fault that Allison Reese lay in a coma. It was his fault that his father was denied the pride Kenji had just seen so briefly in his eyes. "I think the effect was real, but I didn't get the chance to prove it. Before I could complete my experiments, vandals broke in and wrecked our lab. The cell cultures and most of my data were destroyed—and the sample itself was stolen."

Yoshiro Hamada's eyes flickered for a moment, then his visage darkened with anger. Kenji had never seen such controlled ferocity.

"*Stolen?* Who stole it from you?"

Kenji swallowed, hating the very idea of lying to his father, but he had no choice. As succinctly as possible, he related the events of the break-in, but with a crucial modification.

"I was coming back to the building just as two men were leaving, and the timing was such that they had to be the thieves. I was in shadow as they came out and they didn't notice me. But I saw them, and one I recognized—a scientist who'd visited our lab several weeks earlier. His name is Michaels."

"Did he know about your discovery?" Kenji's father asked sharply.

"Not at the time, but he must have found out somehow. Maybe someone in our lab read my—"

"Have the police arrested him?" Kenji's father interrupted impatiently.

"No, Pa." Kenji took a breath. "I haven't told them about Michaels."

Abruptly Yoshiro Hamada's expression closed, and he looked at Kenji for several seconds in silence. "Ah, so," he said finally. "That's why you've come home."

"Yes," Kenji said, relieved to have it over with. Whatever his father's reaction now, he'd done what he'd had to do. "I want the sample back, Pa, and the police might bungle it."

"Who is this Michaels?" his father asked tonelessly. His anger had slipped below the surface like a shark, and Kenji had no idea what he was thinking.

"He's currently the director of a private DNA lab funded by a religious sect. The lab is located on a small island off the coast of Maine."

"A religious sect?"

"Yes, Pa. It's a Christian sect run by a television preacher named Bobby Jordan. I have no idea why, but Jordan has built a full-scale laboratory on his island."

"Are you *sure* that you recognized this man, Michaels?"

"Yes, Pa. Absolutely sure. And there's something else. One of the newspaper accounts mentioned in passing that some of Jordan's people were involved in the protests that preceded the break-in."

"Then maybe the police will pursue that."

Kenji shook his head. "I don't think so. They have no reason to think the sample was deliberately taken, and they don't know about Michaels. I'm the only one who does."

"Where is the sample now?"

"It must be in the island laboratory," Kenji said, unable to stop himself from swallowing nervously. It was almost over, he told himself. Whatever the outcome, all he wanted now was it to be over. "Michaels wouldn't have taken it unless he intended to analyze it."

"That's only what you think, Kenji—not what you know."

"I might be able to find out for sure. I've made inquiries, and the computer system in Michaels's lab is hooked into a network I can access from Harvard. If I could break into their system, I could download Michaels's data files. If he's analyzing the sample's DNA, sooner or later I should find a match with the scraps of data I managed to salvage."

"*Can* you break into the system?"

"If I had the right password. But only someone on the inside could get it for me. A technician with computer expertise might be able to ferret it out . . . and Michaels's lab is still hiring people."

"What kind of technician?"

"A lab technician with experience in recombinant DNA research. There are many around, but . . . well, I don't know if such a thing could be arranged."

Kenji's father ignored the implied question. "Suppose you could verify that the sample actually is on this island. Then what?"

In spite of himself, Kenji hesitated as his father's eyes bored into him, but there was no point in retreating now. "I'd need men who could help me get the sample back," he heard himself say. "If I simply gave the information to the police, they might not act swiftly or surely enough—even if they believed me."

"You mean," his father said without inflection, "send men to raid the island and steal it back for you."

Kenji took a breath. "No, Pa. I'd need men to come *with* me."

For a moment Kenji's father looked as if he thought he'd heard incorrectly, but as Kenji continued to meet his gaze, his father's expression hardened. "No. Absolutely not!"

Kenji didn't wince at the sharp rebuff, for he'd half expected it. "I'm sorry," he said, bowing in acquiescence. "I had no right to ask for your help. I should never have—"

"You misunderstand me," his father cut in brusquely. "Of course I'll help you. You're my son! Do you really think I'd let these men steal your future from you?"

Kenji's father paused for a moment before continuing. "What you ask may be difficult," he said, half to himself, "but not necessarily impossible."

Abruptly, Yoshiro Hamada stiffened his back and planted his hands on his thighs in a gesture of decision. "I'll see what can be done, but understand this. I'll permit you to break into their computer, for I imagine you're an expert in such things. But beyond that, you'll not be involved. This is my sort of business, Kenji, not yours."

Kenji had never opposed his father's will before, nor had he ever felt the need, but now he braced himself and stubbornly shook his head. "I'm asking for your assistance, Pa, but that's all I can accept—assistance. Michaels stole from *me*. I'm the one who has to get the sample back."

"Don't talk nonsense, Kenji!"

"I've thought about this." Kenji drew a deep breath. "I'm

asking for men to go with me, not to go in my place. Pa—it's that, or nothing.''

Inwardly Kenji quailed before the storm he was sure was about to break, but he forced himself to meet his father's hard stare, determined to make it clear that he wouldn't yield.

''*Why?*'' his father burst out in frustration.

Kenji couldn't tell his father of his cowardice—or of the moment in which he'd resolved never to feel such shame again. Instead he gave the one answer he could, and as he spoke, he knew it was the right answer.

''Because that's what you would do, and I'm your son.''

11

We're comin' up on the island now, miss," called the
boozy old captain who was ferrying Lara out to Miracle
Isle in his converted lobster boat. They were practically his
first words to her since he'd picked her up from the dock in
the Maine coastal village of Lambeth Cove.

Lara rose from her seat and made her way forward to the
wheelhouse to have a look. She moved from handhold to
handhold, balancing against the boat's pitching and rolling
in the heavy swell. A stiff wind blew from the northeast, and
heavy gray clouds scudded across the sky. Lara was wearing
jeans and a windbreaker, but she wished she'd dressed even
more warmly.

Yet the chill invigorated her, and as she neared her des-
tination, she felt a sense of release. Lara had lost count of
the number of times she had almost backed out in the two
months since she'd agreed to Beretta's plan, and it was a
relief to have the inner struggle behind her. It no longer mattered whether she was on a fool's errand or not. She was on
her way.

"There she is," the captain said in his heavy Maine accent, pointing through the wheelhouse windscreen at a green, pine-forested island rising out of the gray sea. "Forty minutes," he added with pride. "The *Mary Jane* always makes good time."

Lara smiled and nodded out of politeness. From the sound of the *Mary Jane*'s engine, it seemed a minor miracle that they could make any speed at all. The boat sported a fresh coat of white paint, and a bright blue awning stretched over the rows of cushioned seats that had been built into the hold, but the new fittings couldn't disguise her age.

The *Mary Jane* looked even older than her captain, and the grizzled, rail-thin Mainer was at least sixty. Jarvis was his name, and he had the red-rimmed, watery eyes of an inveterate drinker. Lara had seen him nipping at the bottle he carried in his baggy, faded duck trousers, and the liquor had apparently loosened his tongue. By the taciturn standard he had set thus far, he was becoming positively garrulous.

The island looked even smaller than Lara had imagined, no more than a half a mile in length. They were approaching the southwestern side, where the shore curved inward to form a natural harbor. A high plateau extended across the entire island, which was thickly forested with pines. Some pines even clung to the island's clifflike sides, where the ground dropped sharply from the plateau to the rocky shore below. Only directly behind the harbor did the land rise more gently in a broad, grassy slope.

The slope led up to a cluster of ultramodern buildings on the edge of the plateau overlooking the harbor, which Lara took to be the Miracle Isle complex. Foremost was a dramatic structure that appeared to be built entirely of glass, surmounted by a great aluminum cross. Lara concluded that it was someone's idea of a church, but she couldn't guess the purpose of the slender, aluminum-skinned tower behind it, rising high into the sky and surmounted by a cylindrical, glass-enclosed platform.

"They told me you're a scientist?" Jarvis said, giving her a curious sidelong glance. "That right?"

"That's right. Why? Does that surprise you?"

Jarvis shrugged. "Just don't look like one, that's all."

"Thanks." Lara laughed. "I'll take that as a compliment."

"Aayuh."

Jarvis lapsed into a long silence again, but as they entered the harbor and headed for an old wooden dock, he pointed to a ramshackle, weather-beaten cottage built against the hillside off to the right of the dock. "That's my place."

"You live on the island?"

"Aayuh. All my life. They tried to buy me out—like they did the others—but I'm not sellin'."

A shiny red Jeep was parked on the shore road behind the dock, and two men climbed out and came walking out along the dock, apparently intending to meet the boat. The young man in the lead was short, overweight, and wearing a gaudy flowered shirt. He was followed by a tall, slim older man, in a conservative, lightweight suit, whose shiny bald head was thrust forward by curvature of the spine.

"Who are they?" Lara asked.

"The old guy is a scientist, too. Can't remember his name. The piggy little guy is Billy-Lee," Jarvis said disparagingly. "Billy-Lee Jordan. He's the preacher's son, and he likes to think he runs things."

12

Billy-Lee Jordan always made a point of greeting new recruits to the Miracle Isle staff. He lacked his father's inborn talent, but he was an assiduous student of Bobby Jordan's methods, both onstage and off. Bobby Jordan cultivated staff loyalty by showing interest in each and every one of his adherents, and Billy-Lee tried to do the same on Miracle Isle.

When his father had placed him in charge of the island complex, Billy-Lee had felt he was coming into his own at last. Here he enjoyed a measure of independence and was master of his own small flock, young people who looked up to him as Bobby Jordan's heir apparent. Miracle Isle was Billy-Lee's rehearsal stage. For fifteen years, he had toiled in his father's service with but one, consuming ambition—to inherit Bobby Jordan Ministries.

"What's the woman's name again?" he asked Michaels, the lab director, as the *Mary Jane* neared the dock.

"Dr. Brooks. Dr. Lara Brooks."

Undoubtedly she would be a frumpy, academic type, Billy-Lee thought irritably. Such women got on his nerves, and he was already in a bad mood. His father was coming tonight, and Bobby Jordan's infrequent visits always set him on edge.

Billy-Lee had been raised to fear the Lord, but as a child he had feared his father more. He was thirty-five now, and a preacher in his own right, but deep inside him the fear of his father's watchful eye and unpredictable moods lingered. Bobby Jordan was the gatekeeper to Billy-Lee's future.

"We're lucky to be getting her," Michaels added, "even if only for a year. Her credentials are first-rate."

Billy-Lee nodded perfunctorily. He found it increasingly difficult to hide his dislike of Michaels, but he was careful not to alienate his father's old friend. Bobby Jordan had already made it clear that he trusted Michaels more than he did his own son. Billy-Lee still shuddered when he thought of the risk he'd run for his father that night at Harvard, yet he still didn't know why God had commanded them to steal some dried-up scrap of flesh and bone.

But Michaels certainly knew. Bobby Jordan had told *him,* and Michaels was working day and night, doing something with the thing. But what? Michaels refused to say. *Damn the man's arrogance!* Billy-Lee caught himself grinding his teeth and stopped, concerned for his new set of caps.

Why was his father cutting him out? Sweet Jesus, his father hadn't even told him why he was coming secretly to Miracle Isle tonight. Not even the staff were to know. *Why? What's happening?*

The *Mary Jane* had almost reached the dock, and Billy-Lee could see Jarvis's dour face behind the wheelhouse windscreen. As always, the sight of him annoyed Billy-Lee, and he could almost smell the old lush's whiskey breath. He had employed Jarvis to carry passengers to and from the mainland to avoid having a penniless drunk lying about on their doorstep, but now he wished he hadn't. The man's insolence was insufferable.

Jarvis throttled back, spun the wheel, and reversed the engine, and the *Mary Jane* glided gently against the dock. Jarvis came out of the wheelhouse and tossed up the bowline to Michaels. As Billy-Lee went to catch the sternline, he glanced down at the newcomer, expecting to see a mousy, bespectacled woman with the appeal of a codfish.

Billy-Lee caught his breath, instantly captivated by the striking brunette smiling tentatively up at him. Her short, wavy hair and eyebrows were almost jet-black, setting off her clear, ivory skin and eyes that were a surprising deep blue. She was slight figured, and although she had to be in her thirties, she looked much younger.

Billy-Lee realized he was staring and belatedly put on his best TV smile. "Welcome to Miracle Isle." For once he didn't have to feign enthusiasm. "I'm Billy-Lee Jordan— Bobby Jordan's son. I'm the resident director."

"Hi," she replied, her smile fading slightly, and Billy-Lee's mind raced as he tried to think of something winning to say.

Without warning the sternline snapped against his chest.

"Wake up," Jarvis cackled as Billy-Lee hastily snatched at the line, and he felt his cheeks burn. How he'd like to thrash the old drunk! he thought.

Unable to think of a rebuke that wouldn't rob him of his dignity, Billy-Lee set about securing the line to a dock piling. As he tied off the line, he heard Michaels introducing himself to Lara Brooks. She was climbing the dock ladder as Billy-Lee turned back, and he hastened to give her a hand; but Michaels was there ahead of him.

"What a pleasure it is to have you join our staff, Dr. Brooks," Billy-Lee effused, but although she smiled and thanked him, her eyes returned immediately to Michaels.

Billy-Lee swallowed. Sweet Jesus, there was something about her. Just looking at Lara Brooks excited him.

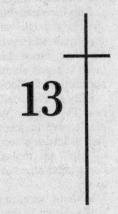

13

Lara tried not to wince as Michaels seized her hand too tightly and vigorously pumped her arm. Despite his age, which had hunched his narrow, rounded shoulders, Michaels was charged with a youngster's irrepressible energy.

"I've read several of your papers, Lara," he said. "I must say, we're lucky to have you, if only for a year."

"And I've been looking forward to meeting you, Dr. Michaels," Lara said truthfully, "and learning from you."

"Why, thank you," Michaels said, beaming, "but call me Dick—or Dr. Mike. That's what everyone around here calls me. I got my MD before I turned to research, and I've been filling in for our clinic's regular physician, who's on leave. Believe it or not," Michaels said with a laugh, "I'm still licensed to practice in Maine."

Lara smiled and nodded, uncomfortably aware of Billy-Lee Jordan's eyes upon her. As he'd stared down at her from the dock, those close-set eyes had been hot and hungry. Billy-Lee was no taller than Lara, but twice as heavy, and Jarvis's sobriquet was apt, she thought; Billy-Lee *was* a piggy, little man.

"Okay," Michaels said briskly, seizing the first of Lara's bags that Jarvis handed up. "Get the other one, Billy-Lee, and then you can give us a lift up the hill."

"Thanks for the ride, Captain," Lara called down to Jarvis, who had turned away to fetch her second bag.

"Aayuh," Jarvis grunted without turning around.

"He's a character," Michaels said jovially to Lara as he led the way off the dock. "Adds a bit of local color, but it's a shame he drinks so much. We haven't been able to bring him to Jesus yet, but we'll keep on trying. Are you a Christian, Lara?" he asked, catching her off guard.

"Not a practicing one," Lara said, hedging reflexively. "Is that a requirement?"

"Certainly not," Michaels laughed.

It was only logical that the lab director should turn out to be a born-again Christian, Lara told herself, but still she was surprised. Michaels was a leading scientist, and to her, science and fundamentalism seemed an impossible mix.

Behind them she heard Billy-Lee hurrying to catch up. As he came alongside, he pointed up to the complex of buildings on the edge of the plateau. "What do you think of our Crystal Chapel?" he asked Lara. "Magnificent, isn't it?"

"It's certainly striking," she said, glancing at him.

Billy-Lee clearly believed in adornment, she thought with distaste. A hairstylist had recently fluffed and coiffed his sandy hair to disguise its thinning, and a heavy gold chain hung around his thick neck. He wore two jeweled rings on his manicured fingers, and on his wrist was a Rolex watch.

"What's that behind the chapel?" Lara asked, hoping to overcome her disastrous first impression of Billy-Lee.

"The Prayer Tower," he replied as if that explained it.

As they neared the Jeep, Billy-Lee strode ahead and placed the bag he carried on the rear seat. "Why don't you ride in back, Dr. Mike," he said, and Lara grimaced inwardly. Michaels would undoubtedly have done so anyway, but Billy-Lee had wanted to be sure. God, she thought, he really is on the make.

They climbed into the Jeep, and Billy-Lee drove them along the macadam road that skirted the shoreline and then snaked up the long grassy slope to the plateau in a series of sharp switchbacks. Billy-Lee drove much faster than necessary, and Lara wondered if he thought he was impressing her.

Michaels leaned forward. "Do you want to get settled in first or would you like to have a look at our lab right away?"

Lara smiled at Michaels's eagerness. "The lab," she said, giving him the answer he obviously wanted.

"*Okay,*" Michaels responded enthusiastically. "I think you'll be impressed. We have the very latest equipment, and our technicians are top-notch. Lou Brown and Jeff Lessard are our two staff biologists, and they're looking forward to meeting you. They're both fresh out of grad school, but they're sharp and real go-getters."

"Are they Christians?" Lara asked over her shoulder, unable to resist, and Michaels laughed appreciatively.

"You bet!" he replied, clapping her on the shoulder. "But don't let that worry you. We're in a fellowship of science here, and I'm sure you'll feel right at home."

Billy-Lee glanced at Lara Brooks sitting beside him, and he tightened his grip on the steering wheel as he felt a fresh tingle of excitement. Certainly she was beautiful, but that hardly explained the strength of his reaction. He didn't know what it was about her that got to him so, and he didn't care. Billy-Lee didn't analyze his desires; he satisfied them.

He had noted her immediate reserve toward him, but he told himself that she didn't yet appreciate his position. One day soon, it would be Billy-Lee Jordan who moved millions of television viewers and brought them to Jesus. When she realized that, she'd come around, for power *was* an aphrodisiac.

The very sinfulness of the thought titillated him, and his loins stirred. God hated the sins of the flesh, but Billy-Lee knew that Jesus had saved him each time he'd fallen in the past. That was the glory of walking in the Lord. Even if one stumbled, repentance and Jesus' love would wash away the sin.

Still, Billy-Lee cautioned himself, he would have to be

careful. As his stepmother, Lurleen, had sharply reminded him when she'd caught him with a young staffer, God might forgive him, but the world would not. Nor would his father. "If you must cat around, Billy-Lee," she'd caustically admonished, "for God's sake, be discreet!"

Billy-Lee had taken her advice while he was in Baton Rouge, but cooped up on Miracle Isle, a discreet affair was almost impossible. So far, Billy-Lee had resisted temptation, but the pressure had been building inside him for months. He was a God-called preacher, but he was also a man—a man with needs.

"Pull up here," Michaels said, cutting through a tantalizing vision of Lara Brooks gasping with desire beneath him, and Billy-Lee braked more sharply than he'd intended. They had come up onto the plateau, where the road leveled out and circled the compound, and Billy-Lee pulled off onto the lawn to the left of the chapel.

"I'll show Lara the lab," Michaels said to Billy-Lee, "and you can take her bags over to the dormitory."

"Sure," Billy-Lee said, though he wanted to go with them. *Take your time, Billy-Lee.* "See you later," he said to Lara. Her smile as she replied was disappointingly neutral, but Billy-Lee refused to be discouraged.

So preoccupied was Billy-Lee with thoughts of Lara Brooks that nearly an hour passed before he remembered with a pang that his father was coming tonight.

Thus spoke Simon: Who is worthy to open the Second Book? It is he that is not, but will be. The One Chosen of God. Let none but the Chosen One loose the seal of the Second Book, for he alone shall know when the time is come. To him shall be given understanding, and he shall prepare the way for the Son of Man.

—SAMARIA SCROLL 1, COLUMN 1.4.3

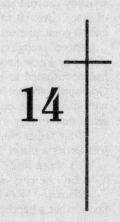

14

The hands of Billy-Lee's office clock crawled toward midnight as he sat alone at his desk, feeding his resentment and trying to dull the nagging anxiety that underlay it. A Bible and a bottle of Jack Daniel's were open on the desk before him, but he found the whiskey more comforting. He had drunk too much already, but he took another swallow. "It's not right," he muttered disconsolately into the silence.

His father and his stepmother, Lurleen, had slipped onto the island after dark, and although Billy-Lee had met them at the dock, their secret visit remained unexplained. His father had immediately gone up into the Prayer Tower, and Lurleen had repaired to her own quarters, telling Billy-Lee to wait for his father to send for him. Billy-Lee felt like a lackey.

It *wasn't* right. He wasn't a child. He was a God-called preacher in his own right. If his father truly intended to crown him his successor, why was he keeping secrets from him now?

Billy-Lee heard a knock on his door, and he hastily capped the whiskey bottle and slipped it into his bottom desk drawer.

The door opened, and Lurleen came in. As always, she was stylishly dressed and not a strand of her blond hair was out of place. Even at fifty, she was still a good-looking woman and as great an asset on camera as she was behind the scenes.

Lurleen's religion was heavily laced with pragmatism, and Billy-Lee knew how much her shrewd, steadying influence had contributed to his father's rise to national prominence. God spoke to Bobby Jordan, who delivered His messages with charismatic power, but Lurleen provided the business sense that a mega-ministry required.

"Your father wants to see us now," Lurleen said in her soft Georgia drawl.

"It's about time," Billy-Lee said, rising unsteadily.

"Don't be churlish, Billy-Lee."

"*Churlish?* Why is Daddy keeping me in the dark? I don't know what's happening!"

"I don't know either," Lurleen responded coolly.

"You *always* know."

Lurleen compressed her lips. "Not this time—not for months. Believe me, if I'd known about that escapade of yours in advance . . . Damn it, Billy-Lee, did you have to hit that girl?"

"It wasn't *my* fault!"

Lurleen shook her head grimly.

"It *wasn't*, Lurleen."

"All right," she said impatiently. "What's done is done, and your father is waitin' for us in the Prayer Tower. Whatever this is all about, it has somethin' to do with your father's revelation. Michaels was up there with him for a long time, but he's gone now."

"And why does Michaels know why God sent us to get that disgusting thing when we don't?" Billy-Lee burst out.

"I don't *know,*" Lurleen replied curtly, "but I think we're about to find out. And for your information, jealousy doesn't become you."

"I'm not jealous of Michaels."

"Yes, you are," Lurleen said in a softer tone, "but you don't have to worry about him—or anyone else. You are your father's son, Billy-Lee—his only child—and in the end that's all that matters.''

In spite of himself, Billy-Lee smiled, for he always drew comfort from Lurleen's reassurances. She had married Bobby Jordan when Billy-Lee was ten years old and still yearning for a mother, but that was not to be. Billy-Lee still remembered the day his father had heard him call her "Mama."

"Your mother's in heaven, Billy-Lee," his father had sternly admonished. "Lurleen is *not* your mother."

Billy-Lee had been raised in a world of holy absolutes dictated by his father, and he'd accepted Bobby Jordan's injunction without question. It had never occurred to him that Lurleen might have ignored it herself, and it was enough for him that she had tempered his father's severity.

Bobby Jordan was the self-taught son of an itinerant Louisiana preacher, and he'd retained his own father's harsh ways. It was Lurleen who had put a stop to his practice of smothering Billy-Lee with a pillow when Billy-Lee was too slow in learning his Bible passages.

"Come on, Billy-Lee," Lurleen said. "Let's find out what your father has to say to us."

As they left the office, Lurleen tucked Billy-Lee's hand under her arm, as if to remind him that she was his ally. Of late, his father was increasingly subject to caprice and disturbing mood swings, and Billy-Lee suspected that Lurleen was warily looking to the future and the means to secure it. He preferred to think that her fostering of his own ambition sprang from more than practical considerations, but either way, he was grateful for her support.

The Miracle Isle staff went early to bed, and the dormitory was silent as he and Lurleen walked through the passage to the front entrance. Outside, the compound's central quadrangle was lit by the glare of floodlights, and high atop the Prayer Tower the Prayer Room's window glowed like a giant beacon against the black sky.

As Billy-Lee and Lurleen entered the tower's base, she released his hand and Billy-Lee preceded her up the narrow spiral staircase. He secretly disliked the Prayer Tower, for he detested exertion and the climb always winded him. Once inside the Prayer Room, he had to avoid the windows. If he ventured too near, he was invariably seized by vertigo.

Billy-Lee was panting by the time he reached the top, and he paused to catch his breath as Lurleen came up behind him. His father was standing at a window, looking out into the night. The soft light from the room's table lamps reflected off the floor-to-ceiling plate glass, and Billy-Lee could see nothing beyond but black emptiness.

Billy-Lee's angry resentment had given way to reflexive anxiety as he'd climbed the stairs. He remained in awe of Bobby Jordan's spiritual powers, and he'd never quite overcome his childhood fear of his father. As his father turned, Billy-Lee looked anxiously for a clue to his mood, and relief flooded through him as he saw Bobby Jordan's ebullient expression.

"Billy-Lee—Lurleen," Bobby Jordan exclaimed ecstatically, striding toward them with outstretched arms. "Praise God, what a night this is!"

To Billy-Lee, as to millions of television viewers, Bobby Jordan looked the very image of a man of God—a tall, commanding figure with thick, graying dark hair and a patrician visage with chiseled, Nordic features. He had a presence on camera that Billy-Lee could never hope to match, but that thought was only fleeting as Bobby Jordan embraced him, and he basked in the unexpected effusion of affection.

Everything *was* going to be all right, he thought joyfully as his father released him and embraced Lurleen. It was just as she'd told him. He was Bobby Jordan's son, and that was all that mattered.

"Come," Bobby Jordan said, putting his arms about Billy-Lee and Lurleen and guiding them to a circle of chairs in the center of the room. "Let's sit together. This is a joyous night, and my legs are weak from the wonder of it."

"The wonder of what, Bobby?" Lurleen asked coolly as they sat down.

" 'A thousand upon a thousand years shall pass,' " Bobby Jordan intoned, " "The sea shall give up its dead, and there shall be a new heaven and a new earth. Then shall the Kingdom of God be established on earth for a thousand years of Glory.' ''

''I don't recognize that passage,'' Lurleen said.

''It isn't in the Bible, darling. I'm quoting from the prophetic text young Brother Richards translated. It's a treasure of divine prophecy, and as God in His Grace has revealed to me, it is the completion of the Word.''

''What does that mean, Daddy?'' Billy-Lee asked.

''That God has given us new understanding!'' Bobby Jordan exclaimed in a transported voice. ''The two thousand years will soon have passed, and the new millennium shall be the Millennium of Glory! Christ is coming at last, Billy-Lee, and we have been chosen to prepare the way!''

''And what has all this got to do with that *thing* you had your son risk everything to steal?'' Lurleen asked sharply, and her tone jolted Billy-Lee. He'd never heard her speak to his father that way before.

''Don't be afraid, darling.'' Bobby Jordan's eyes glowed with luminous intensity. ''It's God's precious gift to the world! I know you don't understand, but you will when God grants that I reveal the Divine Plan.

''When Brother Richards first came to me with news of the ancient scroll he had translated,'' Bobby Jordan bubbled on, ''I thought it might be blasphemy. I prayed to the Lord for guidance that very night, for I was sure He had brought me the news for a purpose. And that night He laid a command on my heart—to wrest from the Catholics that which was found with those most holy scrolls.''

''We know that, Bobby,'' Lurleen interjected tartly, ''but we don't know why.''

''Nor did I, darling. Not at the time. Please believe me, I know how you've been worrying. I know it's been difficult for you—and for you, Billy-Lee. I'm so proud of you, my boy. The Lord commanded, and though you understood no more than I, you obeyed.''

Billy-Lee felt a warm glow spreading through him as his father beamed at him.

''Billy-Lee, the night you phoned and told me that you and Dr. Mike had succeeded, I prayed again for guidance. I prayed as I've never prayed before, and the Lord spoke to me again.''

Bobby Jordan's eyes filled with tears, and Billy-Lee shivered. Tears came easily to his father onstage, but Billy-Lee knew the difference. He saw the Spirit coming upon his father now, and he sensed the power, like electricity in the air.

His father closed his eyes and tears spilled down his cheeks as he raised his face to heaven. ''And this is what the Lord told me,'' Bobby Jordan said, his rich baritone filling the room. '' 'Give my gift to thy servant, Michaels, so that he may discover its secret, for you are the one I have chosen.' ''

Billy-Lee shivered again, for it seemed as if God were speaking directly through his father.

'' 'Rejoice!' the Lord said to me,'' Bobby Jordan cried ecstatically, '' 'for My Son is coming soon, and I have chosen you to prepare the way.'''

Bobby Jordan said nothing more, but his lips continued to move silently.

''We don't understand what that means, Bobby,'' Lurleen said, and Bobby Jordan opened his eyes.

''Nor did I, at first,'' he said hoarsely, tears still streaming down his cheeks, ''and when I did, I didn't dare believe. But tonight, when Dr. Mike gave me the glorious news, I knew with absolute certainty that it was true. Oh, the wonder of it!'' Bobby Jordan exclaimed, throwing back his head in exultation. ''Oh, how I wish I could reveal all to you, but soon—very soon—your questions will be answered.''

Abruptly Bobby Jordan's expression darkened, and he fixed his eyes upon Billy-Lee. ''My son, you have a sacred duty. You must secure this island to keep God's precious gift safe until the time has come. Hire men for that purpose, and pay them well. Can I rely on you for that?''

''Yes, Daddy,'' Billy-Lee said automatically. ''You can rely on me.''

''Make no mistake, Billy-Lee. There are those who will never understand God's purpose. Certainly not the Catholics,'' Bobby Jordan added venomously. ''Listen well to what is written in the scroll: 'The deceiver shall cry out against the Chosen One and those who are deceived shall war against him.' So be strong in the Lord, my son, and ever vigilant.''

"I will be,'' Billy-Lee replied quickly, though he had no idea what his father was talking about, and Bobby Jordan's answering smile warmed him again.

"Come my faithful wife and son,'' Jordan said, reaching out to Lurleen and Billy-Lee and drawing them from their chairs onto their knees. "Pray with me now.''

As Bobby Jordan bowed his head, Billy-Lee glanced at Lurleen, but her expression was unreadable.

Hours later, Billy-Lee was lying exhausted on his bed, but unable to sleep, when he heard a soft knock on his door. It opened silently and a shadowy figure slipped into the room. Stray light filtering through the window curtains faintly illuminated Lurleen's blond hair.

"Billy-Lee,'' she whispered. "Are you awake?''

"Yes.'' He sat up. "What is it? What's wrong?''

"Did you believe what your father told us tonight?''

"Of course,'' Billy-Lee responded automatically.

"Billy-Lee!'' Lurleen whispered urgently. "I'm askin' you a serious question! Did you believe it? Did you even *understand* it?''

"Don't you?'' he croaked, shocked and frightened by her question. If she had doubts, how could he overcome his own? Billy-Lee's belief in his father's powers had made him a lifelong prisoner of Bobby Jordan's will, and he couldn't imagine a life outside those walls. Just the thought unmanned him.

"I have a bad feelin' about this. I don't know what's in your father's mind, and frankly I don't care. It's what he made you do that I care about. A young woman lies in a coma by your hand, Billy-Lee. Is that how God would have us 'prepare the way'?''

Billy-Lee felt his lips tremble. "What are you going to do?'' he whispered.

"Nothin' but hope and pray, Billy-Lee. I hitched my wagon to your father's star long ago—for better or for worse.

But you're young. You could leave and go your own way."

"No!" Billy-Lee gasped as his stomach churned. "This is my life, Lurleen. I don't know anything else."

For a moment Lurleen was silent, and then he heard her sigh. "Then listen to me, Billy-Lee. Do as your father said and be vigilant, for I'll tell you what I *do* believe. If that wretched thing you stole should fall into the wrong hands— we're finished. Finished."

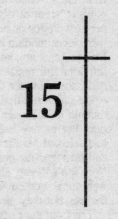

15

Reese arrived an hour later than usual at Manor Oaks, the nursing home where Allison's body languished. The nursing home was a converted, rambling country house on a rural road ten miles from Baxter Academy, and Reese visited each night. Allison had been in a coma for over two months. Reese had tried telling himself that oblivion was oblivion, but somehow the unending coma seemed worse than death. Each time he came to the nursing home, a part of him hung back.

As he walked up the long wheelchair ramp to the lighted entrance, he felt an uneasy sense of expectancy he couldn't explain. Reese didn't believe in premonitions, and even later, when he considered this night in retrospect, he would ascribe the feeling to the approaching thunderstorm.

The leaves of the great oaks surrounding the old house rustled in response to a freshening breeze, and thunder muttered somewhere in the muggy night. A storm was definitely on the way, and Reese hoped it would break the late-July heat wave that had lain for days across New England like a steamy blanket.

He opened the glass front door and felt a puff of cool air from the air-conditioned interior. The air was laced with the pungent scent of disinfectant that never quite eradicated the pervasive odor of urine from the incontinent patients. There were more modern nursing homes within driving distance of Baxter Academy, with scrupulously clean, brightly decorated interiors and registered nurses in crisp uniforms, but Reese had chosen Manor Oaks.

He suspected that his colleagues, and some of his friends, thought he'd chosen Manor Oaks because of its low monthly rate, but money had nothing to do with his choice. Reese had selected Manor Oaks because of the woman who owned and managed the home. Mrs. Filbert actually cared about her "residents," and she hired staff accordingly. Mostly they were local women who worked part-time and had learned on the job, but they also cared.

The front door opened directly into the common room, the far corner of which doubled as a dining room for the few patients who were ambulatory and mentally competent. Four old women were there now, quietly playing cards. Last week, there had been five.

"Good evening, Mr. Reese," chirped one of them, and her companions looked up and smiled at Reese.

"Good evening, ladies," Reese replied with practiced cheerfulness. It wasn't easy, for he knew that none of the cardplayers would leave Manor Oaks alive, and they knew it, too.

The old flooring creaked softly beneath the industrial carpet as Reese walked across to the corridor into the annex where Allison and the Alzheimer's patients were housed. Aside from the cardplayers, Manor Oaks' inmates were all tucked or tied into their beds. The house was quite still, and the skeleton night staff was apparently occupied upstairs.

Reese walked down the corridor to Allison's room. He should have been used to it by now, he thought, but he wasn't. Persistent coma was the doctors' verdict—as final as it was terrible. Yet each time he came into her room, he felt an irrational stab of disappointment as he saw no change in her condition.

Allison lay on her side in a fetal position beneath a thin blanket. Over time, the random movements of her head and hands had subsided, and her body was often inert—breathing on its own and slowly wasting in a living death.

Reese approached the bed and gazed down at her, trying to remember how she had looked—how she looked in the photographs he had at home. But her pale, unnaturally pinched face and shorn hair blotted out the memory. At least Kathy had been spared this, he thought, but it was a bitter consolation.

"Hi, honey," Reese said, drawing up a chair beside her and sitting down. "It's Dad."

Then, as he always did, Reese began to talk to her. He knew she couldn't hear him, but he talked anyway—telling her about his day. He talked to pass the time, but deep down there was another reason. Reese knew it was utterly irrational, but he couldn't quite escape the nightmarish idea that Allison might be able to hear, but simply couldn't answer.

He talked softly in unconscious response to the stillness in the house. The mutter of thunder he had heard outside had grown loud enough to detect through the sealed windows, but as yet it did not disturb the coffinlike atmosphere that pervaded Manor Oaks at night. He talked about the little things that had happened during the day, but not how he felt inside.

Reese had come to terms with his grief, and time had finally dulled his futile, vengeful anger and encapsulated it somewhere deep inside him. Determined not to withdraw into himself, he sought out his friends and never refused a social invitation, and he found satisfaction in the work he'd begun with the coming of Baxter's summer vacation. For years he had intended to write a high-school math text, and now he spent long days in his school office working on the manuscript.

But each time he returned to his empty house, he felt the emptiness inside him—the void left by the loss of the two people he'd so loved. Emptiness laced with guilt.

The dreams came almost every night. The dreams were always different and always the same. Allison or Kathy, and sometimes both, were in danger, and Reese was helpless. He could do nothing to save them. Invariably Reese awoke with a cry, and long after the details of the dream had faded, the guilt clung to him. They were dead, and he was alive.

Reese's back was to the door of Allison's room, and he didn't hear Mrs. Filbert until she spoke to him from the doorway.

"Mr. Reese, there's a phone call for you."

"What?" he responded in surprise. No one had ever called him at the nursing home.

"It's a gentleman." Mrs. Filbert was a trim woman in her forties with dyed-blond hair and a tired face, but she bore her wearing job with matter-of-fact good humor. "He says his name is Alfons Beretta."

Reese frowned in puzzlement. "Never heard of him," he said, rising from his chair.

"I don't know what he wants, Mr. Reese, but he says it's important. You can take the call in my office."

"Thanks," Reese said, mystified. "Sorry for the trouble."

"It's no trouble."

Reese leaned over the bed, kissed Allison's sunken cheek, and followed Mrs. Filbert to her office. As Reese answered the phone, she left and closed the door behind her.

"Good evening, Mr. Reese. My name is Alfons Beretta." The stranger had a smooth, cultivated voice that carried a trace of a New York accent. "I'm an attorney with the firm of Morton, Benedict and Joy in Manhattan. I'm sorry to call you at this hour, but I tried earlier in the day and apparently your home phone was out of order."

"Yes, it was," Reese said, frowning. "How did you know to call me here?"

"I inquired at your school. I have something rather important to discuss with you as soon as possible. It's in connection with your call to Father Wilson at Georgetown some months ago."

"What about it?" Reese had heard nothing from the police for months, and he'd given up hope for a break in the case.

"Father Wilson could tell you very little at the time, but the situation has changed. Are you still interested?"

"Of course," Reese said, his pulse quickening. "But I don't understand. You say you're a lawyer, Mr. Beretta. How do you come into this?"

"I'm acting as a representative of the Catholic Church, but not in a legal capacity. I'll be happy to explain, but I'd prefer to do it in person."

"And I'd prefer to know what this is all about."

Static from the approaching storm crackled on the line, and Beretta waited until it subsided.

"It's about justice, Mr. Reese. Will you meet with me?"

"When and where?"

"There's a small restaurant a few miles north of you on Route One Twenty-five. It's called Maxie's Café. Could you meet me there in twenty minutes?"

"Yes," Reese said, feeling a cold tingle of anticipation. He was wary of this stranger who knew so much about him, but for a break in the case, he would have met with the devil himself.

"Excellent. In twenty minutes, then."

"How will I know you?"

"I'll know you, Mr. Reese."

16

The thunderstorm overtook Reese en route to the rendez-
vous. Brilliant lightning flashes lit the sky, and the deep
rumble of rolling thunder was punctuated by the sharp crack
of ground strikes. The storm matched Reese's mood. It had
taken months for him to submerge his corrosive, frustrated
hatred of Allison's unknown attackers. Now it bubbled up in
him again like vitriol, and with it, the need to strike back—
for himself and for Allison.

Wind-whipped torrents of rain blurred the windshield of
Reese's old Chevy, and he almost missed the restaurant.
Squinting against the glare of oncoming headlights, Reese
cut left across the highway and pulled into the small parking
lot in front of Maxie's Café. A Mercedes sedan with New
York plates was parked near the entrance, and Reese drew
up beside it. Apparently Alfons Beretta had already arrived.

Reese dashed through the downpour into the café, a stuffy,
run-down little restaurant with a counter and a half dozen
booths. Three locals in work clothes sat at the counter, talking to the lone waitress, and all the booths save one were
empty. A stocky, prosperous-looking man in his fifties, with

black hair and a closely trimmed black beard, was seated in the corner booth. He nodded to Reese and rose to shake hands as Reese approached.

"Mr. Beretta," Reese said, shaking hands.

"Mr. Reese," Beretta responded with a disarming smile. "Thank you for coming."

Beretta was shorter than Reese, but there was something physically imposing about the man. He appeared solid rather than fat, and he carried himself with unassumed confidence. The smile on his round, congenial face was friendly and easygoing, but it didn't quite touch his dark, probing eyes.

"I'm glad you agreed to meet me on such short notice," Beretta said, resuming his seat.

"You caught my interest." Reese took off his wet windbreaker and slid into the booth, opposite Beretta.

Beretta had a mug of coffee before him, and as the waitress started to come out from behind the counter, Reese looked over and ordered the same. Beretta produced a business card and handed it to Reese. The embossed card declared Beretta to be a partner in the firm of Morton, Benedict and Joy and listed the firm's address and a telephone number.

"I've penciled a number on the back of the card," Beretta said, "along with the foreign access code. What I'm about to tell you will undoubtedly strike you as bizarre, Mr. Reese, so it's important for you to know that I actually do represent the interests of the Catholic Church in this matter. That number is a direct line to Monsignor Alvarez in the Vatican. He will confirm my bona fides."

Reese nodded but said nothing. As anxious as he was to hear what Beretta had to say, his instinct made him cautious. There was something a shade too smooth about this stranger, and Reese sensed that Beretta hadn't looked him up simply to give him information. Beretta wanted something.

Judging from the ashtray on the table, Maxie's Café was still a haven for smokers, and Reese took out his cigarettes and lit up. Beretta smiled slightly, as if he understood Reese's silence.

"I'll get straight to the point," he said, but he broke off as the waitress came over with Reese's coffee. He waited until she returned to pick up her conversation with the men at the counter.

"As I indicated on the phone, Father Wilson was unable to be as forthright with you as he would have liked. What was stolen from your daughter's laboratory was no ordinary archaeological sample. I say 'stolen' because we believe we know who took it."

"Who?" Reese asked, and although he managed to keep his voice level, he could feel his pulse begin to beat at his temple. The long-suppressed anger in him was burning in his gut.

Beretta shook his head. "We'll have to take this in stages, Mr. Reese. I have a proposition for you, and how much I reveal to you depends upon your willingness to accept that proposition."

Reese frowned. "If you know something, why haven't you given the information to the police?"

"Our evidence is circumstantial, and as compelling as it is to us, it wouldn't stand up in court. Given the prominence of the man we suspect, an unsupported accusation would be politically explosive. And at the first hint of trouble, the item that was stolen—the only real proof of his guilt—would certainly disappear."

"Then why are you telling me?"

"We want you to help us recover what was stolen. Help us retrieve it, and we'll help you jail the men responsible for your daughter's tragic condition. That's our proposition. Are you interested?"

"If you didn't think so, you wouldn't be here," Reese said, fighting his rising tension. He could almost taste the bitter lust for vengeance Beretta had loosed in him, and it was at war with his suspicion of the man and his mysterious approach. "What exactly do you want from me? You're going to have to put your cards on the table."

"All right, but first I'll need an absolute assurance that what I tell you will remain strictly between us."

"I can't give you such a sweeping assurance. I don't know what you're going to tell me."

"Then let me modify the condition," Beretta said

smoothly. "Will you agree to keep it confidential within the requirements of the law and the demands of your conscience?"

"Yes," Reese said, and Beretta smiled. "But if I don't like what I hear, what's to prevent me from going to the police and telling them that you know who did it?"

Beretta's smile became less cordial. "Nothing, but I'll deny it—along with the suggestion that you're still distressed by your daughter's tragic condition."

Reese dragged deeply on his cigarette and exhaled slowly. "I *am* distressed, and I wouldn't forget it if I were you."

"Let's not talk at cross-purposes," Beretta said, quickly backpedaling. "You want justice, and we want to retrieve what was stolen from us. That's the basis on which we can work together. And as far as confidentiality is concerned, your word is good enough for me."

"How do you know?"

Beretta smiled slightly. "I've made it my business to learn quite a bit about you, Mr. Reese."

"For instance?" Reese responded with deliberate coldness.

Beretta was unfazed. "John Wharton Reese," he said as if he were reciting from a dossier. "Forty-eight years old. Three years in the army immediately after high school. Volunteered for Special Forces and decorated for valor in Vietnam. Entered the University of Connecticut upon discharge. Married Katherine Gray four years later. Master's degree from U. Conn. in applied mathematics and computer science. Upon receiving the degree, you joined the faculty of Baxter Academy. One child, Allison.

"Army records indicate a stable psychological profile. Highly regarded by colleagues at Baxter. No criminal record. No problems with the IRS. Insurance records indicate good health . . ." Beretta paused and cocked an eyebrow. "But you're listed as a nonsmoker. I assume you recently took up the habit."

Reese wasn't amused. "How did you manage to pry into my life?"

"It wasn't prying," Beretta replied evenly. "It was necessary research."

"Necessary for what?"

"To be sure that you were the man to help us."

" 'Us'? You said you represent the Catholic Church, but you're not a priest, are you?"

"No. Have you ever heard of Opus Dei?"

Reese shook his head.

"Opus Dei has the official status of a Personal Prelature, though I imagine that means little to you. Suffice it to say that we are an organization dedicated to God's work. Our membership numbers many laymen, and we have many lay friends. As a result, we have resources beyond the reach of the conventional religious orders."

"Resources for spying on people?"

"I assure you, Mr. Reese, there's nothing sinister about our activities."

The storm was at its height. Thunder rolled, and the gusting wind drove the rain against the café's windows in rattling bursts. Lightning struck nearby with a deafening bang that shook the windowpanes, but Beretta didn't even blink.

"I've given you my word on confidentiality," Reese said, "so let's get down to it. Who attacked my daughter?"

"That, we don't know, but we do know who engineered the break-in."

"Who?" Reese demanded, drawing reflexively on his cigarette. The smoke tasted as acrid as his hate—hate for men he didn't know.

"The Reverend Bobby Jordan. He's a nationally known televangelist."

"A *preacher?*"

Beretta smiled humorlessly. "Difficult to believe, isn't it. That's one reason we haven't gone to the police. But we firmly believe that he engineered the break-in for the express purpose of stealing the archaeological sample that was taken."

"Why? Why would he do such a thing?"

"That need not concern you, Mr. Reese—nor our reasons for suspecting him. As I said, this is a highly sensitive affair for us, and I'm afraid I can tell you no more than you need to know."

"Then why should I believe you?"

"Because I'm a serious man, Mr. Reese—sent by serious men at the very highest level of the Church. That's why I gave you my card—to verify that for yourself."

"You're going to have to do better than that, and you can start by telling me what that archaeological sample actually is."

Beretta did not respond at once, but then he nodded. "It may be a holy relic, Mr. Reese, preserved in clay inside the spindle of an ancient scroll Father Wilson deciphered. Unfortunately, he sent it out for scientific analysis before he discovered what the scroll claims it to be. According to the text, that mummified flesh and bone was cut from the body of Saint Stephen, the first Christian martyr. If the claim is true, the relic is precious to us, and we intend to get it back."

The term *relic* conjured in Reese's mind an image of yellowed bones in an ornate case secreted in a dark recess of some European cathedral. The concept reeked of medieval superstition and seemed wholly at odds with the crisply intelligent man before him. Yet there was no denying the intensity he'd seen in Beretta's eyes when the lawyer had said they intended to get the relic back.

"I don't get it," Reese said. "Why have you come to me? What do you think I can do?"

"We know where to look for the relic, Mr. Reese, and as it happens, you are in a unique position to help us locate it. To understand why, you have to know something about the Reverend Bobby Jordan. He's not your run-of-the-mill televangelist.

"Years back, a wealthy widow among his followers bequeathed him most of the real estate on a private island off the coast of Maine. On the charts, it's listed as Hansen's Island; but five years ago, Jordan rechristened it Miracle Isle and constructed a fertility clinic on the island. Born-again couples go there for a heavy dose of 'healing' prayer and the latest medical treatments, including DNA screening and in vitro fertilization.

"Like some other evangelists, Jordan has embraced modern medical science as an adjunct to his faith healing, and the construction of a fertility clinic—while perhaps a little odd for a fundamentalist preacher—is not what sets him apart. What does is a fetish he's developed for DNA research. By some twisted logic, he's come to believe that genetic research can unlock great religious mysteries.

"Two years ago, he announced that he was going to add a full-blown DNA research laboratory to the Miracle Isle complex, in order to contribute to the Human Genome Project. That's a worldwide cooperative effort to read out the entire human genetic code. That lab is now operational, and I believe the relic's DNA is being analyzed there."

"Analyzed? For what purpose?"

"As I said before, Mr. Reese, there are aspects to the situation that I'm not at liberty to discuss. This is a take-it-or-leave-it proposition. I'm telling you who we think was responsible for the break-in, and where to seek the proof. For your purposes, that should be sufficient."

Reese's cigarette had burned down close to his fingers, and he hastily ground it out. Beretta had told him too little to make sense of the situation, or his proposition, but if there was any chance at all . . .

"What is it you would expect me to do?" Reese asked, anxious to get to the punch line.

"Infiltrate the laboratory and locate the relic."

If Reese hadn't been wound up inside, he would have laughed. "Oh, is that all. I assume you'll give me a white lab coat for disguise."

"We're not fools," Beretta snapped, giving Reese a momentary glimpse of the tension hidden beneath the man's smooth exterior. "We don't intend you to pose as a scientist or technician. Do you know the Compstar company?"

Reese nodded. "It's a small firm north of Boston that builds customized computer systems with advanced parallel processing."

"Well, Mr. Reese, Jordan's laboratory already has a Compstar computer, and a second unit is about to be installed. It so happens that Compstar executives are willing to cooperate with us. The company will be sending a field rep to Miracle Isle to get the new system up and running. If you're willing, you could be that man.''

''Are you serious?''

''Perfectly. The Compstar operating system is a version of UNIX, and given your background, they estimate that three weeks of intensive training would enable you to pose as their field rep. You could be ready to go by the end of August, with plenty of time to finish the job and get back to your school for the fall term.''

In spite of himself, Reese was impressed. ''How did you get Compstar to go along? What was your explanation?''

''As I told you, Opus Dei has many friends, and we were lucky that Jordan has a Compstar system. You'd be in a perfect position to search for the relic, Mr. Reese. While installing and checking out the software for the new computer, you'd be at the center of the laboratory's activity, and no one would be surprised if you asked questions and looked around. But we're dealing with a fairly narrow time window. If you're willing, you must say so tonight.''

Reese took out a second cigarette and lit it, drawing the smoke deep into his lungs. Without the information Beretta was withholding, there was no reason to believe his claims, much less to trust him. But Reese's distrust was no match for the hatred Beretta had rekindled. He *wanted* to believe.

''So, you can get me into the laboratory, but how would I know what questions to ask? How would I know what to look for—or where to look?''

''We'll prep you. By the time you go in, you'll be familiar with Jordan's operation, the lab setup, and what you need to look for.''

''How much time would I have?''

''Enough. One of Compstar's selling points is full on-site support, and once you've installed the new software, you can string out your stay by finding a few fictitious bugs in the system.''

''Assuming I can master their operating system in only three weeks' time.''

''You will,'' Beretta said with complete assurance, ''but

you'll have backup in case of difficulty. The laboratory's computer is hooked via satellite into a network that accesses the major DNA data banks, and a Compstar engineer will be on call who can access your computer through the network.

"And if I can locate the relic—what then?"

"We'll cross that bridge when we come to it. We have resources I can draw on if the need arises, and I want you to keep in touch with me every step of the way. I can arrange for an E-mail drop at Compstar, and that's how I'd want us to communicate. A simple open code should do. I'd also give you a telephone number—but just for eventualities."

Reese looked at Beretta for a moment in silence. "Open code? The last time I heard that phrase, it didn't come from a lawyer."

Beretta smiled thinly. "You're right, Mr. Reese. I wasn't always an attorney. While you were on the ground in Nam, I was at war in a more oblique capacity."

"And now you're a spook for the Vatican."

Beretta smiled again, but Reese didn't smile with him. He'd only had one experience with CIA operatives in Vietnam, but one was enough.

"Suppose you're right about Jordan," Reese said. "If I use my own name, someone might make the connection with Allison."

"You wouldn't use your own name," Beretta said immediately. "I can provide you with a full ID set—driver's license, social security card, credit cards—in any name you choose."

Reese could see that Beretta was sure he was hooked—and maybe he was—but suspicion continued to gnaw at him.

"I don't get it. You obviously have your own 'resources,' as you put it. Why have you come to me?"

"I have access to information, and help of various kinds, but I need a reliable operative, Mr. Reese, and that's not so easy to come by. You asked me what will happen if you do find the relic, but I think you know the answer. If it's possible for you to bring it out with you, we'll want you to do so. Not the least of my reasons for coming to you is your demonstrated capacity for direct and forcible action."

"And what does that mean? Do you imagine you're getting a poor man's Rambo?"

"Hardly. Rambo wasn't very bright."

"Just how far *are* you willing to go to get your relic back?"

Once again, Reese thought he saw a flash of passionate intensity in Beretta's eyes, but the look vanished, as if a shutter had closed. "As far as you're willing to go."

Reese didn't respond, and the silence stretched out.

"Well?" Beretta prompted. "I'd like your answer now. Are you in or out?"

Despite the warning bells sounding in Reese's head, he knew he had no choice. Avenging Allison wouldn't bring her back, but it was the only thing he could do for her now. Call it justice, or call it vengeance, Reese wanted it more than life itself.

"I'm in."

17

Lara lit her first cigarette of the day and tried to derive some pleasure from the idyllic morning. As usual, she was among the first to leave the dining hall after breakfast, and the sunlit quadrangle at the center of the Miracle Isle complex was serenely silent. White clouds dotted the bright blue sky like cotton puffs, and a soft breeze carried the scent of the surrounding pine forest.

But the beauty of the morning couldn't still Lara's edgy impatience. Beretta had been right about Jordan, after all. She was virtually certain the supposed relic was on the island, and now she had but one desire. She wanted out.

Behind her a laughing group of young men and women emerged from the dining hall, and as they passed her, carrying their study Bibles, she received the inevitable invitation to join them. Lara returned their smiles and gave her stock reply: "I've got to get to work."

Most of the staff were in their twenties, and to Lara they looked even younger. All were clean-cut, fresh-faced, and friendly, and all were cheerful proselytizers. They accepted Lara's rebuffs without rancor, but they never stopped trying.

The Miracle Isle staff were happy in their work, and even happier in their religion.

As Lara watched them cross the manicured lawn and settle in the grass in the shade of the Prayer Tower to discuss Bible passages, she wondered how they would react if they knew. Probably they wouldn't believe it; Lara could hardly believe it herself. Nor would the thousands and thousands of faithful whose money had built the Miracle Isle complex, now as familiar to Lara as prison walls to an inmate.

The early-morning sun lit the Crystal Chapel's expanses of plate glass and shone on the slender, aluminum Prayer Tower. The tower was at the center of the quadrangle framed by the chapel, the dormitory behind Lara, the DNA laboratory facing it on the opposite side, and the fertility clinic on her right, facing the rear of the chapel. The dormitory, laboratory, and clinic had been constructed in similar style, modern, two-story buildings with sandstone facades and tinted plate-glass windows.

Lara dropped her half-smoked cigarette and ground it out. She knew she was smoking more and enjoying it less, but she was too edgy to quit. Why hadn't Beretta responded to her E-mail message? She'd done her bit. What was he waiting for?

She got to her feet and headed for the DNA lab. As she walked up the asphalt path that led past the clinic to the DNA lab, Michaels emerged from the clinic's far door and locked it behind him. As far as Lara knew, it was the only locked door in the entire complex. She hadn't seen him at breakfast, and he'd obviously worked through the night again.

As Michaels walked in Lara's direction, heading for the dormitory, his bald head was thrust forward even farther than usual and his eyes remained fixed on the ground in front of him. Even from a distance he looked worn-out, but when one of the youngsters in the study group called out to him with a cheery "Morning, Dr. Mike!" he responded with a smile and straightened up.

"And a beautiful morning it is!" he called back.

Good old Dr. Mike, Lara thought grimly. She, too, had been fooled by his seemingly open, outgoing manner—as well as his scientific reputation. God, she thought, it had taken her nearly a month to accept what should have been obvious much sooner.

"Morning, Lara," Michaels said with a smile as they met on the walkway.

"Hi," Lara responded with forced cheerfulness. "Another all-nighter?"

Michaels laughed. "You know us senior citizens. Can't sleep, so we might as well work. How's your research coming?"

"Fine," Lara replied, knowing the question was empty courtesy. He never asked for details. "Are you sure you don't have something hot going? You've really been burning the midnight oil."

Michaels grinned and shook his head dismissively. "Just the same old, same old."

Same old, same old bull. Michaels had to be lying.

"It's young go-getters like you who'll make the breakthroughs," Michaels said, clapping her on the shoulder as he walked on.

As brief as their meeting had been, Lara was glad to have it over with. Billy-Lee was no longer the only one who gave her the creeps. Ever since her suspicion had hardened, it had been difficult to act naturally with Michaels. Although she couldn't prove he was analyzing the relic's DNA, all the signs pointed that way. And the men who'd stolen the relic had thought nothing of snuffing out a woman's life.

She quickened her pace. It was too early to expect to find an E-mail response from Beretta waiting for her, but she allowed herself to hope. If it didn't come soon, she resolved, she'd leave the island anyway. Behind her she heard footsteps hurrying to catch up, and she knew who it was without looking around.

"Good morning, Dr. Brooks," said her technician, drawing alongside and falling into step with her.

"Hi, Kiru," Lara said, wishing that she liked him more. Kiru Kuroda was a nondescript, bespectacled Japanese in his thirties. He was hardworking, thoroughly competent, and his command of English was perfect, but Lara found him irritatingly anxious to please.

"I didn't get a chance to run that last batch yesterday," he apologized as they entered the lab, "but I'll have the printouts for you this morning."

"No hurry. As it is, you're generating data faster than I can analyze it."

Kuroda walked over to the laser-fluorescence sequencer he was using and began turning on the electronics. As DNA fragments passed through the machine, the sequence of molecular subunits, called bases, that were strung together like beads to form the DNA strand were recorded electronically and stored. The bases were the alphabet of the genetic code, and the sequence in which they appeared on the DNA strand spelled out the DNA's genetic instructions.

The capacity of the laboratory's computerized equipment for high-speed DNA analysis outstripped anything Lara had seen before, and she'd taken full advantage of it. That was the one saving grace of her month on Miracle Isle, and in that time she had accomplished more than she could have in six months in her own laboratory.

"I'll be glad when the new computer comes on-line," Kuroda said, airing his recent frustration.

For the past week, he'd been unable to use the state-of-the-art autorad sequencers that were integrated into the lab's central computer system. Michaels's work was always given priority, and he'd been bogging down the system. The laser sequencer Kuroda was now using was adequate for Lara's purposes, but she knew he'd have preferred the faster machine.

"I hear that Compstar is sending out a man next week to bring it on-line," Kuroda huffed. "We could have had it on-line weeks ago if they'd let me install the software."

"What you really mean," Lara responded with a smile, "is that you wanted a chance to fool around with the new system."

Kuroda was a dyed-in-the-wool computer geek, and he'd been filling in as part-time system operator when Lara had arrived on Miracle Isle.

"That's true, too," Kuroda admitted with a smile.

"Maybe you should switch to computers full-time," Lara said, walking toward the door to the corridor that led to her office.

Kuroda didn't reply, and Lara wondered why he didn't switch fields. There was a lot more money in computers, and Kuroda was forever talking about expensive sports cars.

Lara's office was at the far end of the corridor, and as she sat down at her desk and logged on to the central computer, she heard her fellow scientists, Jeff Lessard and Lou Brown, arriving. They were friendly enough, but their research didn't overlap Lara's, and their born-again religion made for even less common ground.

"Hey, Lara," she heard Lou call as she turned on her computer terminal. "We're making coffee. Decaf or regular?"

"Either one," she called back distractedly.

On her terminal screen, the computer system had printed its opening message to her: YOU HAVE NEW MAIL.

Hastily Lara called up her E-mail, hoping the message was from Beretta, and not from one of her friends at Dartmouth. The island's computer was hooked into two networks via a satellite link, and Beretta had arranged for them to exchange messages through an E-mail address at Compstar. Lara didn't know Beretta's connection to the company that had supplied Miracle Isle's computer system, and she hadn't asked.

Two messages were logged in, and the first had come from Dartmouth late last night. It was a short message from Ellen, Lara's friend and coresearcher, and Lara was about to pass it by when the first line caught her eye.

News flash, Brooks! You're ex is leaving town.
I just heard through the grapevine that he's landed a job at Brown, so he won't be around by the time you get back. Good news, right?

Right, Lara thought fleetingly, and scanned the rest of the message.

Now—hang on to your hat! Guess who our resourceful colleague, Ted, is sleeping with. Claire Richards! If shacking up with the dean won't get you tenure, what will?

Well, that's the latest from here. I'll be sending you a draft of our paper soon. Do you want to submit it to *Science*?

Lara tapped the keyboard to call up the second E-mail message and crossed her fingers. "Yes!" she whispered joyfully as she saw that the message was from Beretta:

Well done, Lara! I agree with your assessment, and I'm immeasurably grateful. Sorry to hear about your brother's deteriorating health, and that you'll have to interrupt your research and leave the island, but at least that will give me the chance to thank you in person.

So far, so good, Lara thought, but as she read the second part of the message, she wished Beretta hadn't insisted on using impromptu code. E-mail wasn't secure, but the youngster who was running Miracle Isle's computer system was not the type to snoop, and Lara had to read Beretta's cryptic message twice before she was sure she understood.

Incidentally, I hear that a friend of mine at Compstar, John Reed, is coming to Miracle Isle on the 25th to get the new computer up and running. I insist that you make time to get acquainted. I haven't told him about you, but I know you have a lot in common. He's interested in the same puzzle we've been working on, and if you convey the relevant facts to him, he's sure to reach the same conclusion we have. But don't spell out the solution for him—or let him know that you've been working on it with me. That would spoil his fun.

Lara erased the message and sat back with a sigh of relief. She would have to wait at least until the twenty-fifth before she could leave, but a few days hardly mattered. It was all but over.

Somehow Beretta had managed to slip an Opus Dei man in as the Compstar rep, and Lara wondered if he would try to steal the relic from Michaels's lab. She was glad that Beretta was sticking to their agreement, but surely he could have briefed his man without telling him how he'd come by the information. Lara wasn't sure how she was going to point the stranger in the right direction without giving herself away.

Don't worry about it, she told herself with a buoyant sense of release. She'd find a way, and then she'd finally be free and clear. And to hell with work. It was a beautiful day outside, and for the first time since coming to Miracle Isle, she was in a mood to appreciate it.

The King of Kings shall sit upon a white throne, and beside him shall sit the Chosen One, who prepared the way, together with his servants. Then shall the dead, both great and small, stand before the throne to be judged according to their deeds. And those who know His name and believe shall have no part of the Second Death, but shall live forever in the Kingdom of God.

—SAMARIA SCROLL 1, COLUMN 2.9.4

18

Billy-Lee sped along the macadam drive that circled the compound, heading for the road down to the harbor to meet the ferry coming in on its weekly supply run. Miracle Isle had a contract with a ferry service out of Lambeth Cove, and Billy-Lee, who had inherited his father's fear of being cheated, personally checked each consignment. But as he rounded the curve where the road ran along the brow of the hill in front of the Crystal Chapel, he forgot about the ferry.

Lara Brooks was walking alongside the road, and as always when he came upon her unexpectedly, he felt an immediate tightening in his chest. She certainly heard him coming and knew it was his Jeep, and she didn't even glance back. Sweet Jesus, he thought with sour frustration, when was she going to stop playing hard to get?

"Hey, Lara," he called, and pulled up beside her. "Where're you headed?"

"Down to the dock," she said, and as always, her tone was as maddeningly neutral as her expression. "I felt like a break, and I thought I'd shoot the breeze with Steve for a while," she added, almost as if she knew it would annoy him. She had no time for him, but she spent plenty of free time with Jarvis. And the man was a drunken bum!

"Hop in," Billy-Lee offered, trying to sound breezy. "I'll give you a lift."

"Thanks," Lara replied coolly, "but I need the exercise."

The cell phone Billy-Lee carried in his Jeep chirped, but he ignored it as he tried to think of another approach.

"Your phone's ringing," Lara said with a saccharine smile. "Don't let me hold you up."

Billy-Lee grimaced as she turned her back on him and walked on, and he snatched angrily at the phone. "Billy-Lee Jordan," he snapped.

"Billy-Lee!" came his father's resonant baritone over the satellite link. "Praise God, the time has come!"

"What?" Billy-Lee responded distractedly. Even his habitual wariness when he spoke to his father didn't immediately quell the frustration and resentment bubbling inside him.

"The time has come, Billy-Lee! I'll be coming to Miracle Isle weekend after next. I've just gotten off the phone with Dr. Mike, and he's assured me that all will be in readiness. Glory to God! And now that the time is upon us, you and Lurleen will be the first to hear the wondrous details of God's revelation."

The first after Michaels, Billy-Lee thought sourly. Michaels had been working feverishly in his laboratory for weeks, and Billy-Lee still had no idea why. He only knew that it had something to do with the thing they had stolen from the Harvard laboratory. *God's precious gift.* What had his father meant by that?

"Last time, Lurleen and I came in secret, but not this time," Bobby Jordan crowed. "This is a time for celebration! I want your people to share in our joy. Oh, how I wish we could tell them everything, but that's not possible yet. What is coming is simply too overwhelming to be grasped without preparation.

"We must begin that preparation now—for our own followers and for Christians around the world. Billy-Lee, I'll be taping a special broadcast for that purpose in the Crystal

Chapel, and your staff will be the first to hear my message to the world.''

Abruptly Bobby Jordan's tone sharpened. ''You've seen to security, haven't you, Billy-Lee?''

Once gain, Lurleen's warning stabbed Billy-Lee: *I have a bad feelin' about this, Billy-Lee. If that wretched thing you stole should fall into the wrong hands—we're finished. Finished.*

''Yes,'' Billy-Lee replied, consoling himself with the thought that he'd brought in the toughest security team he could find. The staff had been astonished, but they'd accepted his explanation. Neither Billy-Lee nor his father had worried about the year-old threats Bobby Jordan had received from the leader of the Aaronites, an obscure fringe cult, but they had provided the excuse for security guards.

''Excellent. You've been my strong right arm, Billy-Lee, and I know you'll dwell with us in Glory.''

''Thank you, Daddy.''

''God bless you, Billy-Lee,'' his father said, and abruptly hung up.

For several seconds Billy-Lee didn't move as he strove to rationalize away the apprehension Lurleen's warning kindled in him each time he was reminded of it. Whether he believed in his father's revelation or not didn't really matter, he told himself. What mattered was getting rid of the only evidence that could tie them to the break-in.

Billy-Lee took a deep breath. He was glad that ''the time'' was at hand. The sooner the better. Whatever Michaels was doing with that scrap of mummified flesh and bone, he was almost finished. Without that evidence, no one could ever prove a thing, and Billy-Lee intended to see to its destruction himself.

19

It was nearly midnight, and the knock on Kenji Hamada's apartment door startled him. He was about to break into the Miracle Isle computer system again, and as always, he was as nervous as a cat. One slip and he might be discovered and traced. He grimaced in annoyance at the interruption and cleared the screen of his personal computer.

Cambridge was in the grip of another heat wave, and Kenji mopped his brow with his handkerchief as he went to the door. His landlady refused to allow him an air conditioner, and even this late, the room he rented on the top floor of her old frame house was still too hot.

Kenji irritably opened the door, expecting to find one of the students who occupied the rooms on the floor below, and he tensed as he saw the lithe, slim-hipped Japanese in the hallway. It was Tanaka.

"I thought we agreed that you'd never come here," Kenji said in Japanese.

"Your phone line has been busy, Hamada-san," Tanaka replied, stepping past Kenji into the room, "and I had to speak to you."

"I'm using it for my computer." Kenji quickly shut the door. Kenji's PC was connected by a telephone modem to the Harvard computer system, through which he entered the network to access the Miracle Isle system.

"Maybe you should put in another line."

Although Tanaka's clipped tone was respectful, Kenji took the comment as a rebuke. He was always ill at ease in Tanaka's presence. The *yakuza* enforcer Kenji's father had placed at his disposal was no older than Kenji, but he was tough, intelligent, and experienced beyond his years.

Kenji couldn't believe that Tanaka relished his assignment, for he certainly knew that Kenji was out of his depth. Yet it was impossible to know for certain what Tanaka actually thought. Even without the sunglasses that usually masked Tanaka's eyes, his expression was unreadable.

In contrast, Kenji had the feeling that Tanaka could see right through him, and the *yakuza* missed nothing. When they'd first met, Kenji had surreptitiously glanced at Tanaka's hands, and as fleeting as the glance had been, Tanaka had noticed. "No fingers missing," he'd commented with a thin smile. "I've never failed my *oyabun*."

"What's wrong?" Kenji asked, once again failing to strike the right tone. Nominally he was in command, but it was a role he found impossible to carry off.

"I've just received a message from Kuroda," Tanaka replied, walking across the room to look at Kenji's computer. "He's afraid your access will be cut off soon."

"Why?" Kenji asked, trying not to betray his sudden anxiety. He couldn't emulate his father, but he could try not to embarrass him.

"A second computer is about to be added to the Miracle Isle system," Tanaka said, turning back to him. "The company is sending a man to complete the installation, and Kuroda thinks he may change all the passwords. New software will be installed—with improved security."

"Can't Kuroda get us a new password after the change?"

"He's lost his access, Hamada-san. Of course," Tanaka added without enthusiasm, "I could ask him to look for the sample himself."

"No," Kenji said immediately. Kuroda was a hireling who had no idea why he'd been bribed to slip them a password, and Kenji didn't want him to know. "When is the Compstar man due to arrive?"

"Five days from now."

Kenji swore softly, unable to suppress his frustration. "I need more time."

"How much more?"

"I don't know. I've scanned all their data files, and if anyone is analyzing the sample's DNA, it's the lab director. It's clear that he's analyzing short, disconnected DNA fragments. That's just what you'd expect. But I still haven't found a match with the scraps of my own data that I managed to salvage, and without a match, I can't be absolutely sure."

"If we could arrange for a few days' delay, would that make any difference?"

"Why? How could you do that?"

"Would it make a difference, Hamada-san?"

"It might. Their lab director adds new data to his files every day, and I want every bit he has. Even if he *is* analyzing the ancient DNA, I have so little data of my own that the chance of finding a match is small."

"And if you don't find a match?"

It was the first time Tanaka had posed the obvious question directly, and Kenji shied away from it. "We'll cross that bridge when we come to it," he said, finding it difficult to meet Tanaka's steady gaze.

Kenji saw himself as he imagined Tanaka saw him—a weakling. Kenji still didn't know if he'd have the nerve to raid the island without knowing for certain the sample was there.

"If you want me to try and delay the installation of the new computer," Tanaka said, "you'll have to tell me now. That's why I'm here. We have very little time to make arrangements."

"What arrangements? How could you delay it?"

"Leave that to me, Hamada-san. There'd be no risk. We wouldn't be involved directly."

Kenji couldn't miss the implication of Tanaka's deliberate

vagueness, and his father's words came back to him. *This is my sort of business, Kenji, not yours.* Kenji knew that Tanaka would have to explain if he insisted, but he couldn't bring himself to ask. He wanted the extra time too much.

"Do what you can."

Tanaka bowed slightly in response and left without another word.

20

Reese was hungry and tired after the long drive up to Lambeth Cove on the Maine coast, and he asked the motel desk clerk where he could get a good steak dinner. The clerk recommended an upscale country restaurant three miles inland. Although the dinner Reese ordered there was even more expensive than he'd expected, it was first-rate. Reese left the restaurant feeling that he'd eaten too much and drunk one Bass ale too many.

As he passed through the vestibule, he caught his reflection in the mirror on the wall, and he briefly assessed his appearance. Reese hadn't owned a suit for decades, and he was slightly uncomfortable in the lightweight business suit he'd bought for his role. He was a little too old to be a computer field rep, he thought, but the suit and a fresh haircut helped make him look the part. And Compstar had certainly trained him well enough to pass muster. Max, the Compstar engineer who had tutored him, had worked him like a slave.

Reese stepped outside and paused on the flagstone path that led to the parking lot, feeling the need for a nicotine jolt. He lit up, inhaled gratefully, and looked around. The restaurant was in a converted farmhouse in a grassy field surrounded by pine woods. The sun had just set, and the pines on the western edge of the field appeared as black, one-dimensional silhouettes against a brilliant band of red sky. The beauty of the scene seemed surreal, but no more surreal than the quest on which he'd embarked.

In the three weeks Reese had spent at Compstar, he'd had no time to reflect, and now it was too late for second thoughts. Tomorrow morning he would be picked up in Lambeth Cove and ferried out to Jordan's Miracle Isle. He had no idea of what he was walking into—perhaps just a wild-goose chase—but for better or for worse, he was going. Reese dragged deeply on his cigarette, shoved his doubts aside, and headed for the parking lot. There was only one way to find out if Beretta's belief in Jordan's guilt was fact or fantasy, and Reese would know soon enough.

A tall, thick hedge screened the parking lot from view, and Reese didn't see the bikers until he walked through the gap in the hedge. Three leather-clad toughs lounged on their gleaming Harley hogs, which were parked beside Reese's Chevy. The three men were swigging from cans of Budweiser, and they looked dramatically out of place.

The restaurant catered to the affluent, and Reese's car was the only one in the lot worth less than forty thousand dollars. Reese dismissed the idea that the bikers were waiting for one of the restaurant's workers. The trio could have posed for a magazine photograph captioned "Outlaw bikers," and the manager would certainly have frowned on their presence.

All three were big men, wearing faded bandannas, weathered black boots, and riding leathers. Their motorcycle jackets hung open, revealing grubby T-shirts stretched over hefty beer bellies. Their waists were girdled by heavy steel chains, and their mustachioed faces were stamped with bullying expressions.

As Reese approached, the largest of the three, who looked like an aging linebacker gone to seed, said something Reese didn't catch. The other two laughed derisively, apparently at Reese's expense. He returned their stares with a deliberately neutral glance and walked past them to his car.

"Hey, jerk-off," the big man said. "What're you staring at?"

Reese opened his car door, looked over his shoulder, and said, "Nice bikes."

"Mind your own fuckin' business."

"Sure," Reese responded, and slipped in behind the wheel and closed the door.

The trio laughed as they heard the click of the electronic door lock, and Reese felt his cheeks flush. He started the engine and backed up. As he turned the car, one of the bikers hurled his beer can, and it bounced off the right rear door. Reese ignored it and drove out of the lot. He didn't like being spooked, but even as a young man, he'd never gotten into a fight unless he was cornered.

The bikers were clearly looking for trouble, and Reese half expected them to crank up their Harleys and follow him, but they stayed where they were. He turned left onto the narrow country road that led to Lambeth Cove and switched on his headlights. The sky overhead was darkening, and the pine forest hemming in the road cut down the available light, but it was not yet dark enough for the headlight beams to be effective.

He had driven about a mile when he came over a rise and saw a dusty minivan parked beside the road, canted to the side on the steep shoulder. A buxom, miniskirted girl with flame red hair was leaning against the side of the van, and she stepped into the road and frantically waved him down.

Reese was tired and in no mood to play the Good Samaritan, but there was no traffic on the road and it was getting dark. He sighed resignedly and pulled off the road behind the minivan. It had California plates.

Reese rolled down his window as the girl clattered up to him on spiked heels, and he saw that she was older than he'd thought. Her once attractive face looked used, and her bottle-red hair and garish makeup didn't help. She looked like a cheap hooker on the skids.

"I've got a flat, mister," she said breathlessly.

"So I see," Reese said, eyeing the minivan's squashed

left rear tire. "Hop in. I'll give you a lift into Lambeth Cove, and we'll find a garage with road service."

"But I'm late already, mister!" she pleaded. "Can't you put on the spare for me?"

"I don't know," Reese said, recoiling from the prospect of sweating and straining to loosen frozen wheel nuts. He wanted to get back to the motel, watch a little TV, and go to sleep.

"Please try," she begged, her voice rising in apparent desperation. "Please." Reese gritted his teeth and switched off his engine. "I'll pay you for the work."

"That won't be necessary," Reese said, opening the door and climbing out. "I'll see what I can do. Where's the spare hidden?"

"I don't know. I'll get the keys to open the back." She clattered back to the minivan. "Thanks, mister," she called over her shoulder. "You're real nice."

And real stupid, Reese thought dispiritedly, removing his tie and suit jacket and tossing them in through the car window. Marauding mosquitoes from the woods were already homing in, and he lit a cigarette in the forlorn hope of discouraging them. The girl came clattering back to him, smiling brightly and jangling her car keys.

Just then, Reese heard a muted rumble from the road behind him, and as it quickly rose in intensity, he recognized the unmistakable sound of Harley V-twin engines. The girl was staring past Reese, and as he turned to look, the three bikers from the restaurant roared over the rise in the road. Before Reese had a chance to hope that they wouldn't stop, the motorcycles began to backfire as the riders slowed their machines.

"Jesus, mister," the girl said anxiously, moving closer to Reese. "Look at those guys. I'm glad you're here."

It was a sentiment Reese didn't share, and he tensed as the bikers drew up in line on the edge of the road in front of him and stopped. One by one they switched off their engines, and they leered at Reese and the girl in silence.

Reese drew on his cigarette and nodded to the big man in the middle, who continued to leer at him, displaying a chipped set of dirty teeth. A mosquito hummed in Reese's ear, but he barely registered the annoyance.

"Need help, jerk-off?" asked the big man, and his two companions cackled appreciatively.

"The lady does," Reese replied. If he was lucky, he thought, the three would be satisfied with humiliating him, but he had the sinking feeling that this was not a lucky evening. There was something too deliberate in the way the big man lowered his bike's kickstand and dismounted. The other two followed suit, and Reese felt his mouth go dry.

"The *lady?*" the big man jeered. "She looks like a bimbo to me." His companions cackled, and the girl took hold of Reese's arm.

"She has a flat," Reese replied, sensing that it didn't matter what he said. He swallowed what little saliva he had left and sized up his opponents. The big man outweighed him by at least eighty pounds, and the other two were only slightly smaller. Any one of the three was more than a match for Reese in size and weight.

The man on the leader's right looked like Charles Bronson in need of a haircut. The one on the left was blond and wore his hair even longer, tied in a ponytail. Blondie looked weaker than the big man or Bronson, but just as mean. Blondie, Reese suspected, was the type to carry a knife.

"The lady has a flat, boys," mocked the big man, "but there's nothing wrong with her chest. Hey, bitch, why don't you show us your tits?"

The girl tightened her grip on Reese's arm, but she wasn't as afraid as she should have been. "Mister," she demanded, "are you going to let him talk to me like that?"

The dryness in Reese's mouth was spreading down into his throat, and he felt a cold trickle of sweat run down over his ribs. Three against one, he was forty-eight and out of condition, and he hadn't been in a brawl since he'd left the army. Reese saw a fight coming, and he was scared.

"Well, jerk-off?" the big man prodded. "*Are* you going to let me talk like that? What's the matter, cat got your tongue?"

"I could use some help changing the tire," Reese said.

The big man scowled theatrically. "What do you think we are—fuckin' mechanics? I don't like your attitude, boy."

"Yeah, Manny," Bronson growled. "Maybe we should teach him some manners."

"That's right," Blondie chimed in. "Let's teach the jerk-off some manners."

The big man said nothing. He just stared coldly at Reese and unhooked the chain at his waist. Grinning, Blondie and Bronson immediately followed suit. The big man let his chain dangle quietly from his right hand, but Blondie and Bronson began to rattle theirs menacingly. Reese didn't think they were bluffing.

His pulse pounded in response to the adrenaline pouring into his bloodstream, and his breathing quickened. The big man noted the change, and he smiled derisively. Reese was scared, and the big man knew it. But now that Reese was cornered, anger was rapidly displacing his fear.

"I'm not looking for trouble," he said.

The big man just stared at him as Blondie and Bronson moved a bit farther to the left and right. Rattling their chains, they moved forward onto the dirt shoulder, hemming Reese in between his car and the big man.

The girl's fingers were digging into Reese's arm, and he shook her off.

"Ooh," sneered the big man, shaking his head. "Don't you like her anymore, jerk-off?"

Reese knew what he had to do now, and he let his anger take over. "I don't like *you,*" he said to the big man, taking a last drag on his cigarette and flicking off the ash, and he positioned his middle finger behind it at its midpoint. "I don't like fat-assed faggots who need their friends to do their fighting for them."

Until now, the big man had been coolly deliberate, and Reese was afraid that he might be too smart to be suckered. But he wasn't that smart. "He's *mine,*" the big man snarled, waving off Blondie and Bronson, and he took a step toward Reese.

"You even walk like a fairy," Reese said to keep him coming, and Blondie and Bronson added their own prods.

"Go get him, Manny!"

"Whip his ass!"

One more step brought the big man near enough to smell, and Reese braced himself, watching the big man's eyes. They widened fractionally an instant before he swung his chain at Reese's head, and Reese flicked the burning cigarette into his face.

The big man flinched, and Reese lunged forward and drove his knee into the big man's crotch with every ounce of his strength. Reese had a fleeting glimpse of bulging eyes and a gaping mouth before he bolted past the big man and up the shoulder's slope. Bronson was closer to Reese than Blondie and reacted more swiftly, but as he tried to snare Reese's arm, he became entangled with the big man, who was collapsing with a whistling gasp of agony.

"Manny!" Reese heard the girl cry shrilly, her voice rising above Blondie's and Bronson's angry bellows, and he realized with a shock that he'd been set up. But the thought was only fleeting as he sprinted across the road and plunged into the woods on the other side. Behind him he heard the thud of boots on the roadway and then the racket as Blondie and Bronson crashed, cursing, through the undergrowth in pursuit.

Reese's lungs were pumping like a steam engine, and almost at once he felt warning pains in his thighs and chest. He was hopelessly out of condition, and he knew he couldn't run far at full speed. But he wasn't trying to escape the two men, who were only a second or two behind him.

As his strength faded, he glanced back over his shoulder, as if in fear, and Bronson, who was in the lead, bellowed like a hound scenting blood. Blondie trailed Bronson by several steps, and for Reese that would be enough. Flailing his arms in feigned desperation, he deliberately slowed his run. He heard Bronson closing the gap between them, and when Bronson's footfalls were almost on his heels, Reese made his move.

Abruptly he broke his run by twisting his body and digging in his lead foot. He grunted from the jolt as his stiffened right leg brought him to a jarring stop, and he dropped to his hands and knees an instant before the surprised Bronson crashed into him. Bronson's momentum carried him over Reese, and he fell headlong to the ground.

Blondie was right behind, with no chance to stop, but he had a half second to react. As Reese rose to a crouch, Blondie flew straight at him, swinging his chain. Reese could barely see it flash toward him in the gloom, and he made no attempt to dodge or deflect it.

He ignored the chain's stunning blow as it struck his left shoulder, and he concentrated on maintaining his balance as Blondie slammed into him. They went to earth in a tangle of arms and legs, and Reese had but one objective. As Blondie tried to grapple with him, Reese plunged his thumb into the corner of Blondie's right eye.

With a shriek, Blondie rolled away from Reese, his hands clapped over his savaged eye, and Reese seized the chain he'd dropped. With sweat running into his eyes, Reese whirled about and rose to face Bronson, who had already gotten to his feet. "If you want some of the same," Reese panted at Bronson, "come and get it."

Blondie was screaming like an animal as he writhed and thrashed on the ground, and Bronson was clearly unnerved. "What'll it be?" Reese bellowed, his chest heaving. "Lose one of your own eyes, or help your buddy?"

"Fuck you!" Bronson snarled, but he made no move as Reese slowly backed away. Reese was soaked with sweat and his arms and legs trembled from his brief but desperate exertion. He continued to back away until he was sure the fight had gone out of Bronson, and then he turned and ran in a direction parallel to the road. To his relief, Bronson didn't follow.

Behind him, Blondie's shrieks had turned to anguished wails, and as Reese turned left toward the road, he heard the big man shouting. "Bob! Mike! What the fuck's happening?"

"Bob's down!" Bronson yelled back. "His eye! The bastard gouged his eye!"

Still panting, and weak from exhaustion, Reese reached the edge of the woods and crept forward to peer cautiously up the road to his left. His car was thirty yards away. The big man was limping across the road with one arm about the redhead's shoulders and his free hand cupped over his crotch.

"I'm coming!" the big man yelled, releasing the redhead. "Goddamnit, where *is* the bastard?"

"I don't know!" Bronson yelled back, and Reese could hear that he was close to the road. "We're coming! Give me a hand with Bob!"

"Be careful, Manny," called the redhead as she watched the big man hobble down the shoulder into the woods. Reese willed her to follow her boyfriend, but she remained standing in the middle of the road.

Reese was too tired for another fight, and his left shoulder throbbed viciously, but he decided to make a break for his car. If they caught him now, they would make short work of him, but he was not about to give them the chance to trash his car. As he heard Manny and Bronson meet up, he rose from cover and ran for his car.

"Manny!" the redhead shrieked. "He's here! The bastard's here!"

Reese almost wished the biker bitch would try to stop him, but she stayed clear of him, jumping up and down in frustration and yelling for Manny. Reese reached his car, yanked open the door, and jumped inside. Out of the corner of his eye, he saw Bronson and Manny break from the woods across the road, with Blondie stumbling blindly after them, his hands clutching his face.

Reese hit the ignition switch as he pulled the door closed, and mercifully the engine sprang to life. He threw the gear lever into reverse and popped the clutch. Wheels spinning, the car shot backward up onto the road. He jammed on the brake and shifted gears just as Manny and Bronson reached the car. Reese floored the accelerator and shot past them before they could open the doors.

Reese was still fighting mad, and he had no qualms about scarring the side of his old Chevy. He swerved right and sideswiped the Harleys as he went by, and the sight of the motorcycles in his rearview mirror, sliding down the shoulder, brought a smile of satisfaction to his lips. It was all the satisfaction he would get. He would have liked to sic the police on the foursome, but he wanted no complications. He hadn't come to Maine to clear Vacationland of biker scum.

As Reese drove away, he wondered briefly how the bikers had signaled the girl to flag him down. Maybe they had a transceiver he hadn't seen. Despite the neatness of the setup, he thought they were either idiots or strung out on drugs. If they'd had a working brain between them, he thought, they wouldn't have set a trap to mug a man driving a Chevy.

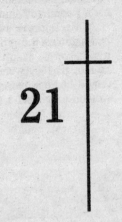

21

The motel desk clerk looked up as Reese entered the lobby, and he stared at Reese's sweat-stained shirt and dirt-smeared trousers.

"Have you got any aspirin?" Reese asked. Every muscle in his body seemed to be aching, and his left shoulder still throbbed angrily.

"No, sir, but I can have some sent to your room. Are you all right?"

"I had a flat on the way back. Hell of a time fixing it, and the damned car rolled off the jack."

"Weren't your friends there to help?"

Reese blinked. "What friends?"

"The ones who were looking for you. A woman asked me if you'd checked in yet—not long after I told you about the Red Robin Restaurant. As she was asking, I saw you driving out of the parking lot. I pointed out your car and told her where you were going."

Reese realized he was staring, and he deliberately smoothed his expression. "She wasn't a redhead, by any chance?"

"Yes, sir, she was."

"And she asked for me? By name?"

"Yes, sir. Is anything wrong?"

"No," Reese said, feeling a chill ripple up his spine. "They found me."

Reese had been waiting impatiently in his motel room for over an hour before Beretta finally returned his call. The phone rang, and he snatched up the receiver. "Reed," he said, using the alias Beretta had provided.

"Sorry I couldn't get back to you earlier. Is there a problem?"

"You bet there is. I was waylaid tonight. Some cheap hoods tried to put me in the hospital, and it was no accident."

"What?"

"Someone doesn't want me going out to Miracle Isle tomorrow."

"What happened?" Beretta asked tensely, and Reese told him as succinctly as possible.

"Are you sure it wasn't just a random mugging?" For the first time since Reese had met him, Beretta sounded off balance.

"A mugging on a country road in *Maine?*" Reese responded angrily. "Weren't you listening? I was set up, Goddamnit! The bimbo who flagged me down asked for me by name at the motel desk."

"Reed or Reese?"

"Reed. That's how I checked in. Listen, Al, those bikers must have been tipped off by someone on Miracle Isle. No one at Compstar knew where I planned to stay the night, but Jordan's people did. I told them when I called to make arrangements to get out to the island."

Beretta didn't immediately respond, and when he did, he sounded uncharacteristically uncertain. "It doesn't make sense. Jordan can't possibly know about you. And even if he did, they wouldn't try to stop you. They'd let you come and simply make sure that you didn't find anything."

"No kidding," Reese snapped. "I figured that out myself.

There has to be someone else in this game. Who is it, Al?"

"I don't know."

"Don't give me that! You've held out on me from the start, but now I want to know what the hell is going on."

"I told you, Reese, I don't know," Beretta said worriedly. "I'll have to do some checking."

"Checking on what?" Reese's hand tightened on the receiver. "What do you know that you're not telling me?"

"Nothing. It's obvious there's something we've missed. Where are you right now?"

"In my motel in Lambeth Cove."

"If you think someone is trying to stop you, why didn't you change motels?"

"Because I don't want them to know I tumbled to the setup. Until I know what's going on, it's the only edge I have. How long will this checking of yours take? I'm due to be picked up tomorrow morning."

Beretta didn't answer for several seconds. "Do you want to back out?"

"I want answers, damn it!"

"And I don't have them. Maybe . . . maybe we should put this on hold."

"No," Reese snapped. "I'm going."

"I don't understand. If you don't trust me, why are you still willing to go?"

"Because now I'm convinced there *is* something to find on Miracle Isle. Unless you tell me that it isn't your relic, I'm going."

"All I can tell you, Reese, is that I'm convinced Jordan was behind the break-in. The details I've withheld don't affect you."

"Then I'm going. If someone else is after the relic, I want to get to it first."

"Okay," Beretta said with a reluctance that didn't quite ring true, "but watch your back."

"Thanks for the sterling advice."

"I'll do my best to find out what's going on."

"I want more than your best. I want you to do it."

22

Lambeth Cove was a quaint, picture-postcard coastal fishing village, unspoiled by tourism. As Reese walked out along the harbor's main dock, the cool sea breeze balanced the warmth of the sun. The harbor waters sparkled, and gulls wheeled overhead, their white wings etched against the cloudless blue. The air was crystal clear, and one could see to the horizon where the ocean met the sky in a sharp line.

The perfect Maine morning helped clear Reese's head and dissipate the angry tension that had disturbed his sleep throughout the night. He was sure Beretta was holding out on him. He was being used and sent in with blinders on.

But at least the biker ambush had proved he wasn't on a wild-goose chase, and that was more important than anything else. Reese wanted vengeance, and the only risk he really feared was failure. In his own mind, he had nothing left in life to lose.

A converted lobster boat, christened the *Mary Jane,* was moored at the end of the dock, and a grizzled, rail-thin man in a greasy captain's cap stood beside the boat, watching Reese approach. Save for the tan on his weather-beaten face, the man looked like a skid-row bum.

"Captain Jarvis?" Reese inquired, setting down his overnight bag and the oversize attaché case he'd brought from Compstar.

"Aayuh." Jarvis looked at Reese with bleary, red-rimmed eyes, and Reese caught a whiff of alcohol breath.

"I'm John Reed. I understand you're to take me out to Miracle Isle."

"Aayuh."

Reese briefly wondered if Jarvis was putting him on with the dialect.

"Climb aboard, and we'll shove off," Jarvis said, and Reese decided that the old Mainer's accent was genuine.

As Jarvis moved to the sternline and untied it, Reese picked up his bags again, climbed across the gunwale, and settled onto one of the padded passenger seats that had been built into the boat's hold. A bright blue canvas awning on aluminum stanchions stretched from the wheelhouse to the stern to shield the seats from sun and rain, but neither the *Mary Jane*'s new fittings nor the fresh coat of gleaming white paint could disguise her age.

Jarvis loosed the bowline and climbed aboard. He went into the wheelhouse and started what sounded like an antique diesel on its last legs. The engine coughed twice and rumbled reluctantly to life. For a moment before the boat gathered way, exhaust fumes drifted back over the seats, and almost at once Reese began to feel queasy.

"How long a trip is it?" Reese called up to Jarvis.

"Forty minutes," Jarvis replied, and Reese cursed himself for not buying seasickness pills. The sea looked completely calm, but already the barely perceptible motion of the *Mary Jane* was unsettling him.

As the boat cleared the harbor and turned northeast at a slight seaward angle to the coast, he knew he'd made a serious mistake. The pitch and roll of the deck was slight in the light swell, but it was enough. Saliva began collecting in Reese's mouth, and he swallowed repeatedly. He focused his eyes on the horizon, as someone had once advised him to do, and tried to ignore his protesting stomach.

Half an hour later, Reese was on the verge of vomiting.

Far ahead, the low outline of an island was visible, but even if it was Miracle Isle, they wouldn't reach it soon enough. He stood up and moved to the rail, taking hold of one of the stanchions and bracing for the inevitable spasm from his stomach.

"Yuh don't look so good," Jarvis called back to him from the wheelhouse. Reese turned his head and saw Jarvis fish a pint bottle from the seat pocket of his faded white ducks. "Come on up here and have a snort."

"No, thanks," Reese replied through gritted teeth. The last thing he wanted was the old Mainer's hooch.

"Come on. It'll be good for what ails yuh."

Reese swallowed back more saliva and started to shake his head, but then he changed his mind. What the hell, he thought. If it made him throw up, he'd at least have it over with. He made his way forward, and Jarvis unscrewed the cap and handed him the bottle.

Reese looked dubiously at the pint of Old Grand-Dad and then took a swallow. He grimaced as the bourbon burned all the way down, but to his surprise it didn't make him retch. In fact, he slowly convinced himself, the whiskey actually did settle his stomach.

Reese handed back the pint, and Jarvis gave him a yellow-toothed grin. "What'd I tell yuh." Jarvis put the bottle to his lips. His Adam's apple bobbed in his scrawny neck as he took several gurgling swallows in quick succession. "Aa-yuh. Good for what ails yuh," he affirmed with another grin, and he rubbed his gnarled hand over his gray-stubbled chin in satisfaction.

"Is that Miracle Isle?" Reese asked, peering through the wheelhouse windscreen at the forest-green island ahead.

"Don't see no other island, do yuh?"

From a chart Reese had found in a library, he knew that Miracle Isle was kidney shaped. The southwestern shore curved inward, and a further indentation formed a natural harbor. They were heading toward the harbor, and as they came closer, the island's detail became clear.

Behind the harbor, a grassy slope rose to a plateau that extended across the island. Someone, Reese thought, must have planted pines on the island, for the plateau was thickly forested with them. Pines also clung to the much steeper slopes ringing the island, where the plateau ended abruptly and the ground dropped sharply to the rocky shore below.

Overlooking the harbor atop the plateau was a large clearing with a cluster of modern buildings. The foremost structure was a modernistic concoction of steel and plate glass that was basically a huge, embellished A-frame, surmounted by a great aluminum cross. Apparently it was Jordan's idea of a church.

To the left and right of the church and farther back, two long, rectangular, two-story buildings faced each other. They were built in a similar style, with tinted-glass windows set in sandstone facades. Directly behind the church and rising high above it, a tower jutted into the sky. To Reese it looked like a futuristic aircraft control tower.

"What's that tower?" he asked Jarvis.

"They call it the Prayer Tower," Jarvis said disparagingly. "And that thing in front is their 'Crystal Chapel.' Ain't like no chapel I've ever seen."

"I'm going to be working in a research lab. Which building is that?"

"I think it's the one up there on the left. The one on the right is where they all live, and there's a clinic in a building you can't see—behind the chapel and the Prayer Tower."

"Do you make the trip out here often?"

"I live on the island. When this preacher, Jordan, got the Widow Purvis's land, he bought out everyone else on the island. Everyone except me. I grew up on Hansen's Island, and by God, that's where I'll die."

"I take it you don't like Jordan much."

"Never seen him, and maybe I shouldn't complain. His people fixed up the *Mary Jane*, and they pay me a fair wage to carry passengers back and forth from the mainland when the ferry ain't runnin'. But they sure fucked up my island. Cleared away all the cottages and built that shit up there."

"What ferry?" Beretta had solved the problem of getting Reese onto the island, but if he ran into trouble, getting off might not be so easy.

''It comes out from Lambeth Cove once a week—carrying supplies and equipment, mostly. Jordan foots the bill. These people sure have money to burn. I'd like a penny for every dollar they spent puttin' up those fancy buildings way out here.''

As a means of escape, the ferry would be useless, and Reese wondered if Beretta had deliberately neglected to arrange a pickup for him as a means of control. If Reese did locate Beretta's relic, he couldn't try to steal it before securing his escape. Reese looked speculatively at the *Mary Jane*'s captain, wondering which way Jarvis's relationship to Jordan's operation would cut.

The old Mainer was in Jordan's pay, but his antipathy to Jordan was obvious. Given the right incentive, he might be willing to spirit Reese off Miracle Isle. It was a possibility worth considering, Reese thought, for he was wary of depending entirely on Beretta.

Jarvis throttled back as the *Mary Jane* entered the harbor, and Reese breathed a sigh of relief as the deck steadied. Two stone jetties extended into the sea on both sides of the natural indentation in the shoreline, adding to the natural harbor's effectiveness. Near the jetty on the left was the ferry slip, with a large prefab storage shed on the shore behind it, but Jarvis was making for an old wooden dock on the opposite side of the harbor.

Behind the wooden dock was an old boathouse, and beyond that, a weather-beaten cottage with a sagging roof was built against the grassy slope rising to the plateau. It was the only cottage in sight, and Reese concluded that it belonged to Jarvis.

A girl in jeans and a man's white shirt was sitting on the end of the dock, her legs dangling over the edge. She waved to the *Mary Jane* and called across the water, ''Got my cigs, Steve?''

Jarvis picked up a carton of Marlboros lying on the binnacle and held it up to the windscreen. The girl grinned and gave him the thumbs-up sign.

A man in a shiny red Jeep had pulled up on the shore road, and he climbed out and came striding out along the dock. A short, overfed man with sandy hair, he wore sharply creased white trousers and a bright, flowered shirt. The girl continued to watch the *Mary Jane*'s approach, and she didn't look around as the man came up behind her.

He leaned over and said something to her, and as he did so, he laid his hand familiarly on her shoulder. The girl immediately slid back from the edge and got hastily to her feet. Reese had the clear impression that she'd recoiled from the man's touch.

From a distance, she'd looked like a teenager, but as Jarvis brought the *Mary Jane* alongside the dock, Reese saw that she was a woman, not a girl—and an extraordinarily attractive woman at that. She was a striking brunette with short, wavy hair, ivory skin, and surprising, deep blue eyes. Her lips were delicately sculpted, and her smile as she returned his look almost made him forget his seasickness.

"I'm Billy-Lee Jordan," said the short, chubby man to Reese in a voice tinged with a Louisiana accent.

"John Reed." The man looked to be in his early thirties, and Reese wondered if he was speaking to the preacher's son.

"We've been waiting for you," Billy-Lee said with a trace of petulance. "My daddy paid a lot of money for that new computer, and we'd like to start using it."

So, he *was* the son.

"Sorry for the delay," Reese said in a placating tone that he thought a company rep would use. "I'll have it up and running as quickly as possible."

"I hope so," Billy-Lee huffed.

Reese noted the heavy gold chain around Billy-Lee's thick neck, the shoes with the built-up heels to increase his height, and his blow-dried, thinning hair. If Jordan was anything like his son, Reese thought, it was hard to imagine that Jordan had had anything to do with the break-in at Harvard. Billy-Lee impressed Reese as a vain little man who was probably as ineffectual as he was pompous.

But if either one had been involved, Reese thought implacably, they would rue the day he came to Miracle Isle.

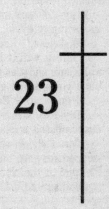

23

Lara looked with interest at the man Beretta had sent to take over from her. He was tall, with dark hair and wide, dark eyebrows. He was older than the usual company rep, and his rough, furrowed skin and broken nose gave his face a tough, lived-in look. Lara couldn't have said exactly what she'd expected, but John Reed wasn't it.

Jarvis had moved up onto the foredeck, and as he handed Lara her Marlboros and the foreline, she could smell the whiskey on him. "Thanks, Steve."

"Aayuh," he replied, and turned away.

"Toss up the sternline, will you, son?" Billy-Lee said to Reed, and Lara glanced at the Compstar rep.

Billy-Lee was at least ten years Reed's junior, and the way he'd said *son* was only a notch up from *boy*.

Reed nodded and did as he was asked, but the look Lara saw flash briefly in his eyes was a warning that only Billy-Lee could miss.

As Lara and Billy-Lee secured the lines to the dock pilings, Reed lifted his luggage onto the dock and climbed out of the boat. He turned toward Billy-Lee, who came over to him and extended a pudgy, manicured hand.

"You don't look so good, ol' buddy," said Billy-Lee with surface joviality. "Don't tell me you're seasick?"

Billy-Lee was smiling, but Lara caught a glint of ridicule in his piggy eyes.

"It'll pass," Reed said.

"Sure it will," Billy-Lee said, looking past Reed at Lara to be sure she was listening. "It's like a lake out there today, but I guess some guys get sick just looking at a boat."

"I guess so," Reed said without inflection.

Billy-Lee was running true to form, Lara thought. He never missed a chance to cut others down.

"Mr. Reed," she said, and as Reed turned around, she stepped forward and extended her hand. "I'm Lara Brooks. I'm one of the researchers here."

Reed smiled. "Hi," he said, shaking hands. "Nice to meet you."

Lara liked his easy smile, and she found herself holding his hand a trifle longer than necessary. *God,* she thought, *I've been on this damned island too long.*

"Dr. Brooks is a professor at Dartmouth," Billy-Lee hastened to say, obviously anxious not to be left out. "She's taken a year's leave of absence to work in our laboratory."

"Will you have to shut down our system?" Lara asked Reed.

"Yes, but not for long."

"It'll be nice to have the increased capacity," Lara said, trying to ignore Billy-Lee's avid gaze. "The system has been overloaded lately."

"So, Reed," Billy-Lee interjected in an irritated let's-get-going tone. "I'll give you a lift up to our dormitory. We'll get you settled in, and then you can go right to work. Want a ride up, Lara?"

"No, thanks," she said reflexively. "I'll walk."

As anxious as she was to get to know Reed and pass on her information, she couldn't endure Billy-Lee's company one second longer than necessary. Jarvis had disappeared into the *Mary Jane*'s engine compartment, and Lara called down to him, "Thanks again for the cigarettes, Steve."

"Aayuh," came the disembodied reply.

"See you later," she said to Reed, ignoring Billy-Lee, and turned and started to walk away.

"I'll go with you, Dr. Brooks," Reed said, and she turned back to him. "Lara," she corrected with a smile.

"Look, Reed," Billy-Lee said hastily, "if you're still feeling sick, you should ride up in the Jeep."

Reed shook his head. "Walking will do me good." He picked up his attaché case. "But take my bag up to the dormitory, will you?" Without giving Billy-Lee a chance to reply, he turned away and walked with Lara off the dock.

Lara almost laughed aloud at the expression on Billy-Lee's face. Reed had spoken as if to a footman, and she had no doubt that the tone was intentional. She instinctively liked the tall, rangy man walking beside her with a long, loose-limbed stride. It was too bad, she thought, glancing up at him, that she wouldn't get the chance to know him better.

Reese had asked to walk with Lara Brooks on impulse, but he quickly convinced himself that it was strictly business. The sooner he got to know the staff, he told himself, the sooner he could start asking the right questions. That she'd struck a chord in him had nothing to do with it.

They walked off the dock onto the macadam road that ran along the shore, past the ferry slip and storage shed, and then curved around in a hairpin turn to ascend the broad, grassy slope in a series of switchbacks to the compound above.

Behind them he heard Billy-Lee start up his Jeep. "That was Bobby Jordan's son, right?"

"Right," Lara said, and her distaste was crystal clear. "The heir apparent. They tell me he's quite a preacher, but I wouldn't know."

As Billy-Lee's Jeep came up behind them, they moved aside, and he tooted and waved as he drove by. Billy-Lee's interest in Lara Brooks was pathetically obvious, Reese thought, but at least he had good taste. Reese would give him that.

"How long have you been on the island?"

Lara sighed. "Only a month. It just seems longer. Most of the people here are nice enough, but the incessant Jesus talk can wear you down. Sometimes—'' She glanced quickly at Reese. "I hope I didn't offend you—I mean, if you're religious.''

"Nope"—Reese laughed—"and I guess you aren't either. What brought you here?''

Lara gave him a wry smile. "It seemed like a good idea at the time.''

Reese had noticed that she walked with an uneven gait, and as they started up the hill, her limp became more pronounced. "Anything wrong?" he asked, looking down at the foot she seemed to be favoring.

"It's just my prosthetic," she said, startling Reese. "It's bothering me again. Car accident," she added lightly. "They had to amputate below the knee.''

"I'm sorry," Reese said, feeling awkward.

"Don't be. I'm fine.''

Reese stopped casting around for the right thing to say and came back on track. "You said your computer system is overloaded right now. How many users are there?''

"Only four. It's Michaels, the lab director, who's been bogging down the system with his data crunching.''

"Only four?" Reese responded, secretly pleased. With only four to investigate, his search would be that much easier. "I thought Jordan had built a major facility.''

"Oh, the facility is first-rate, and it could accommodate another half dozen researchers. But I guess there aren't that many people interested in working here. So, once the new computer is up and running, we shouldn't have any more overload problems.''

Lara had a solid working knowledge of data-processing systems, and they talked computers until they reached the top of the hill. The road came up onto the plateau to the left of the Crystal Chapel and circled the cluster of buildings, and as Lara led the way across the road onto the compound's manicured lawns, she began to point out the buildings.

"This is the Crystal Chapel," she said as they walked past it into the quadrangle at the compound's center. "And that's the Prayer Tower. I have no idea what it's for.''

The shining aluminum tower behind the chapel was cylin-

drical and it tapered inward as it rose, flaring out at the top
to support a round, glass-enclosed platform. The tower stood
in the center of a quadrangle framed by the chapel and three
rectangular, two-storied buildings with large tinted-glass
windows set in sandstone facades.

"That's the main DNA laboratory," Lara said, pointing
to the building to their left. "You'll find the computer room
through that side entrance facing the ocean. And over there
is the dormitory," she said, indicating the building directly
across the quadrangle from the laboratory.

"We all have our own rooms, complete with private bath
and a TV hooked into the satellite system. At the far end on
the ground floor is the dining hall. Meals are served at fixed
times, and we all eat together there. And that's the fertility
clinic," she said pointing to the building at the rear of the
quadrangle.

"Is that a communications center behind it?" Reese asked,
looking at the large microwave dish mounted on the roof of
a building hidden by the clinic.

"They call it the maintenance building. The communications center is there, but also the power generators, a repair
shop, and storage and supply rooms. This place is pretty self-
sufficient. And—you can't see it from here—but there's a
helicopter pad back there, to the right of the maintenance
building. It's for Bobby Jordan's use, and they tell me he's
flying in next weekend."

Several clean-cut, cheerful-looking young men and women
were walking on the flagstone pathways that crisscrossed the
quadrangle's lawn, and all appeared to be in their late teens
or early twenties. Several of them waved to Lara.

"Are college kids here for the summer?"

"Young, aren't they," Lara said with a wry smile. "But
they're the regular staff. As Billy-Lee likes to say, 'Young
people are the backbone of Bobby Jordan Ministries, and—
praise God—they have energy and enthusiasm that just
won't quit.' "

Lara looked at her watch. "It'll be lunchtime soon, but I
can give you a quick tour of the buildings if you'd like."

"Thanks, but I think I'll find my room, wash up, and then

have a look at the computers. I'm going to skip lunch.''

"Still not feeling well?''

"Just no appetite.''

"Okay. Just go into the dormitory through the main entrance there, and you'll find a young woman—Margaret—in the office inside. She'll tell you which room is yours. How long will you be staying?''

"That depends. I should have your new computer booted up and loaded with the new software sometime this afternoon, and then I'll run the diagnostics. Barring difficulties, I'll be finished by this evening. But I'll stay on for a while, in case you people turn up some bugs we missed.''

"That's nice,'' Lara said with a warm smile. "It'll be a relief having someone to talk to who hasn't come to Jesus.''

24

Once Reese had found his room and unpacked, he reconsidered going to the dining hall for lunch, despite his lack of appetite. He didn't want to waste any time in getting to know the staff. But meeting Lara Brooks had given him a head start, and he had the technical job to do for Compstar. Reese decided to get it out of the way.

As he crossed from the dormitory to the DNA laboratory on the opposite side of the quadrangle, he passed a number of smiling young people, all of whom made a point of stopping to introduce themselves and welcome him to Miracle Isle. The girls wore demure summer dresses, and the boys were dressed in neatly pressed slacks and clean, carefully ironed short-sleeved shirts.

All seemed cast in the same mold—clean-cut, fresh-faced, and cheerful—and the young man whom Reese found at the console of the laboratory's computer system was no exception. As Reese came through the research building's seaward entrance, he found himself in a vestibule that served as a buffer between the outside world and the humidity-controlled atmosphere protecting the computer system. The door in front of him had a glass panel, and the young man seated at the console smiled at him and waved him inside. "You're the man from Compstar, I take it," the young man said with an infectious smile as Reese entered, and he rose to shake hands.

"That's right. John Reed."

"Bill Fletcher." The young man brushed back a recalcitrant shock of thick blond hair that immediately fell across his forehead again. "Everyone calls me Fletch."

Fletch was a sturdy youngster with the stamp of Middle America on his lightly freckled face. He could have posed for a Norman Rockwell painting, Reese thought, and he certainly didn't look like a computer geek. "Are you the system manager?" Reese asked, wondering if Fletch was just filling in.

"Yes, sir. In fact, I'm the only operator. One of our technicians helped me out while I was learning the ropes, but now he's fully occupied in the lab."

"You don't run twenty-four hours a day?" Reese asked in surprise.

"Well, there's usually not much activity at night, and we let the system run on its own. There's never been a problem."

Reese glanced at a list of UNIX operator commands taped to the wall above the console—commands no operator should have to look up. Fletch, he concluded, was an amateur, and evidently not too worried about it. An oversize Bible lay open on the table beside the control terminal, but Compstar's operating manuals were stacked on a shelf across the room.

Reese was astonished, but pleased. Without a pro looking over his shoulder, he would have no difficulty prolonging his stay as long as necessary. He could invent bogus software problems at will.

"So," he said, setting down his attaché case and walking to the glass panel at the back of the control room. "I might as well get to work." In the larger room beyond were the two mainframes and associated storage units. "They installed your new computer as a stand-alone machine, but once I've loaded in the new software and run the diagnostics, I'll integrate it into your system. Did you say that you haven't had any problems with your current system at all?''

"Not a one," Fletch said, resuming his seat. "Praise the Lord."

Reese drew up a second swivel chair and sat down. "The software I'll install has some new features, but it won't take long for me to bring you up to speed."

"How long will you be here, Mr. Reed?"

"Call me John. I'll stay until I'm sure that everything is working right. A day or so, at any rate."

Fletch grinned. "Great. Then you'll be here tomorrow morning, and you'll have a chance to hear Billy-Lee. Are you a Christian, John?"

"Atheist."

Fletch was unfazed. "No, you're not," he said earnestly, brushing back the shock of blond hair, and it immediately fell back across his forehead. "No one is. Not really. I once thought I was an unbeliever, too. I was doing drugs and making a mess of my life, and then one day I heard Bobby Jordan preach. That changed my life, John. I came to Jesus, and nothing has been the same since. Jesus' love can change your life, too."

"I doubt it," Reese said with a smile, but Fletch was not to be deflected.

"But He *can*—if you open your heart to Him. And this is the place to discover God's Grace, John. Miracle Isle. It's not just a name, it's the truth. Come to chapel tomorrow and hear Billy-Lee."

"Tomorrow is Wednesday, not Sunday."

"Billy-Lee conducts a sunrise service every day, and it's really beautiful in the chapel when the sun comes up. I'll admit Billy-Lee isn't quite up to his father yet, but he's still a powerful preacher of the Word. I know it will be a blessing to you."

"We'll see," Reese said, dodging the issue. "Right now, though, I'd better get to work. It may be a long day."

"But it's almost lunchtime."

"I'm not hungry. I'd appreciate it if you'd set up an account for me on your system now and give me Super-User status. I'll need it when it's time to hook in the new computer and change the software. Make the password *Patton*.''

With Super-User status, Reese would have system-manager privileges. He could alter, add to, or delete any file in the computer, including those of the operating system.

Fletch nodded, and as he began typing in the necessary commands, Reese had an inspiration. Running diagnostics on the new computer would be tedious enough without being cooped up with an eager Evangelical anxious to bring him to Jesus.

"If there aren't going to be any tapes to mount, I can keep an eye on the system for you. There's no reason why you can't knock off for the afternoon.''

"Oh, that would be great," Fletch said, much to Reese's relief. "I've been having trouble with some Scripture I've been working on, and there's a study group meeting after lunch. I'll check with Dr. Mike to be sure it's okay.''

"Who?''

"Dr. Michaels, the lab director. Everyone calls him Dr. Mike. He has an MD from way back, and he's been filling in while the clinic's regular doctor is away. There's a dispensary in the clinic, with nurses on duty, but if you have a real problem while you're here, Dr. Mike will take care of it.''

"That's nice, but I'll try not to get sick.''

Fletch laughed. "Don't worry, I'm sure he's competent. And he's a terrific guy.''

Fletch finished setting up an account for Reese and pushed back his chair. "Okay. You're all set.''

"Then you might as well take off.''

"Thanks, John.'' Fletch picked up his Bible. "I really appreciate it.''

"Incidentally''—Reese looked at the telephone on a stand beside the door to the vestibule—"can I dial the mainland from that phone? I may have to call the company.''

"Sure. Just dial nine and then one. The call will go through the satellite link. Oh—which reminds me. If you do call Compstar, could you ask them something for me? Or maybe you know the answer.''

"To what?''

Fletch picked up a batch of computer printouts and handed them to Reese. ''I've been trying to familiarize myself with all the system's capabilities—even the ones we don't use. These are printouts of the usage log and the billing program. We don't bill our users, of course, but just for the heck of it, I ran the billing program.

"When I checked it against the usage log, the results didn't quite match. The billing total for last month is short by thirteen cents. I know they're separate programs, but I figured they should give the same results.''

Reese frowned. "Are you sure they don't?''

"Yes. You can see for yourself.''

"Okay," Reese said, trying to remember what he'd once heard about the same kind of discrepancy. "I'll look into it.''

Fletch smiled and stood up. "Thanks. And once again— welcome to Miracle Isle. I really do hope you can come to chapel tomorrow morning.''

"See you later," Reese said, looking at the printouts Fletch had given him.

Fletch left, and Reese continued to study the printouts. To his surprise, he concluded that Fletch was right. The totals from the two different programs didn't match, and that should have been impossible. Somewhere, Reese was sure, he had heard, or read, of a similar discrepancy . . .

Suddenly the elusive memory popped to the surface, and as the full implication hit him, he felt a thrill of anticipation. Hastily he went to the phone and dialed Compstar, hoping he was right.

Here is wisdom, initiate of holy magic. Beware the evil demon that comes upon you as a thief. Keep watch, and by the mysteries revealed to you, divine the demon's name, that you may have power over it.

—SAMARIA SCROLL II, COLUMN 3.7.4

25

"Don't tell me you've got problems already, Reed," said the deep voice of Max Larson, the Compstar engineer who had tutored Reese.

"You tell me," Reese said, cradling the phone on his shoulder. "The system manager here has noticed something odd. The output totals from the billing program and the usage log don't quite match. I've checked, and he's right."

"No way," Max declared with his usual air of authority. "Computers don't make mistakes in addition."

"They don't match, Max."

"They *have* to."

Reese didn't argue, and he didn't ask the question burning in his mind. He just let the silence stretch out. He wanted Max to reach his own conclusion.

"They have to match," Max said, "unless . . ."

"Unless what?"

"Can't be," Max snorted.

"Can't be what?"

"It can't be a hacker breaking into the system," Max said, and Reese smiled in satisfaction. "Our security is airtight."

"Then give me another explanation."

"Maybe your system manager has fiddled with the operating system and screwed things up."

"Try again, Max. He's a rank amateur, and he hasn't touched the operating system. I'll bet money on that. Someone with Super-User privileges has been messing around, but not him."

"A hacker could log into your guest account over Bionet, but he couldn't grab Super-User status," Max asserted flatly. "We've plugged all the holes. Goddamnit, I worked on our security myself. It's hacker-proof."

"Suppose the system manager here has been careless. What if someone here has stolen a Super-User password and given it to the hacker?"

"Hell, Reed, that wouldn't be *my* fault."

"I never said it was. I just wanted to know if the account discrepancy meant what I thought it did."

"Of course," Max responded, reversing himself. "What else could it be?" Now that his security measures weren't being challenged, his resistance had evaporated. "A hacker is breaking in and altering the usage log to cover his tracks. Change the password and shut the bastard out."

"Not just yet. I want to run a trace on him. Can you set it up?"

"Starting when?"

"I think he breaks in at night. Can you set it up by this evening?"

"No sweat. I'll call Bionet, set it up, and E-mail the name and number for you to call to initiate the trace."

"Thanks." For the first time Reese felt a step ahead of the game.

Whoever was breaking into the system was secretly interested in the research being conducted on Miracle Isle, and he'd had help from the inside. Reese was willing to bet that the same informant had tipped off the outlaw bikers. With a little luck, a trace might lead him to the people who'd tried to stop him from reaching Miracle Isle.

"Just be careful how you monitor the hacker if he does break in again," Max warned. "He'll be watching his back.

You could modify the daemons to direct his input to your terminal, but if he's savvy, he'll check for changes in the operating system. And he'll be checking who's logged on to the system. Have you integrated the new computer into your system?''

"Max, I just got here."

"Well, get it hooked in, and rig it so that it reads what's going on in the rest of the system, but rejects all log-in attempts. That way, you can monitor the hacker's activity, and he won't know you're watching him. Can you do that?''

"I think so. I've got all afternoon."

"Good." After a pause Max added, "Maybe someday you'll tell me who you are and what this is all about."

In the three weeks Reese had trained at Compstar, Max had not asked a single question, though he must have been consumed with curiosity. It was an impressive demonstration of Beretta's influence. "Maybe someday."

"Okay. I'll call Bionet right now," Max said, and the line went dead.

Reese was smiling as he hung up. Fletch's curiosity had given him his first break. Tracking down the hacker wouldn't help him find the relic, but it might lessen the risk of being sandbagged by the people who'd tried to stop him. He was still smiling as he returned to the computer console and set to work.

"Praise the Lord," he said to the empty room.

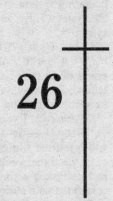

26

Reese leaned back in his chair and rubbed his tired eyes, which were bleary from staring at the video monitor. He'd booted up the new computer, loaded in the software, and run most of the diagnostics. All that remained was to integrate the new computer into the existing system and set it up to monitor the hacker.

"Hey," called a woman's voice from the vestibule, startling him. He hadn't heard the outside door open. "Are you working or sleeping?"

He opened his eyes and saw Lara Brooks smiling at him through the inner door's glass panel.

"Working," he said as she opened the door, and he glanced at his watch. "But it's time for a break," he added, more pleased to see her than he cared to admit.

It was only a little after three, he told himself. He still had plenty of time to set his trap, and he couldn't locate Beretta's relic without getting to know the staff and asking questions.

"I'm taking a break, too," Lara said, raising the paper lunch bag she was carrying. "Come on outside. I thought you might be hungry by now, so I brought along some coffee and a sandwich."

"Thanks," Reese said, smiling and getting stiffly to his feet. "Thanks very much."

As Reese followed her outside, he had to squint against the bright afternoon sun, but it was a relief to be in natural light and breathing the fresh salt air.

"Let's sit where we can look at the ocean," Lara suggested, and they walked across the road and settled into the dry, wild grass on the brow of the hill overlooking the harbor.

The ocean breeze ruffled her dark, wavy hair, and the sun shone on her ivory skin and lit her deep blue eyes. Reese was struck afresh by her beauty.

"I hope ham and cheese is okay," she said, fishing out his sandwich and handing it to him.

"That's fine."

"I brought coffee regular, and black. Which do you prefer?"

"Black." She handed him a covered styrofoam cup. "First-class service," he said with a smile. "Thanks again. Aren't you having anything?"

"Just a smoke."

Reese took out his pack. "Have one of mine."

Lara grinned. "So you're hooked, too," she said, taking a cigarette. "I knew we were going to get along."

Reese flicked his lighter, and as she cupped her hand alongside his to shield the flame, he found himself keenly aware of her touch. She was undeniably attractive, but still the feeling surprised him. In the months since Allison had been taken from him, he'd felt that his thirst for vengeance was the only spark of life left in him.

As John Reed began to eat his sandwich, it was immediately clear that he'd been hungry. He was probably grateful for her apparent thoughtfulness, Lara thought guiltily. She was just doing what Beretta had told her to do, but the deception still bothered her. She wondered if it would have been any easier had she not taken an immediate liking to Reed.

"Has Fletch tried to bring you to Jesus yet?" she asked, and even as she asked, she wondered why she was stalling.

She'd sought Reed out for a purpose. Why didn't she get on with it?

"Mmh," Reed responded with his mouth full, and he nodded in affirmation.

"He's a good kid, but terribly persistent. I warn you, he won't give up easily. I can vouch for that personally."

Reese nodded but didn't reply, and Lara turned and looked out to sea. "This place is really beautiful, but I don't think I'll be staying much longer. I feel like a fish out of water."

"Why *did* you come here?" Reed asked, responding to her cue.

"Well, it seemed a good idea at the time," Lara lied. "I wanted to take a leave to push through a special research project I've been working on. I could have tried for a fellowship to work somewhere else, but Jordan pays a top salary, and the facilities and technicians here are better than you'd find almost anywhere else.

"I had my doubts about the born-again angle, but when I learned that Dick Michaels was the lab director, that sold me. He was a really big gun at NIH, and he gave up his post to run Jordan's laboratory. I figured that if he was here, I couldn't go wrong by coming."

"But?"

"Well, he's something of a disappointment. It turns out that he's born-again himself, and a close, personal friend of Bobby Jordan. I'd hoped to learn from him while I was here, but as a research colleague, he's a complete washout. When he isn't quoting Scripture, he's talking sports. For all practical purposes, I'm on my own."

"But what about the other scientists?" Reed asked, again as if on cue.

Filling Reed in was going to be as easy as falling off a log, Lara realized. She was only feeding him what he was here to find out, but somehow that didn't make her feel any better.

"There are only two other researchers besides Michaels and me, Jeff Lessard and Lou Brown. They're bright young guys, but their work doesn't overlap mine. I'm getting things done, but I can't say it's much fun. Both Jeff and Lou are born-again types, and as I said before, the Jesus talk wears you down.''

''You said Michaels is a washout. Does that mean he does no research?''

''Oh, no. He works like a beaver, but he never discusses his research. I have no idea what he's doing because he doesn't work in the main lab. He's set up his own, very private lab in the fertility clinic, and no one but his technician is allowed inside.''

''No one?'' Reed asked, and although he sounded merely curious, he could hardly miss the point.

''Well, it's not that explicit, but when I went across to the clinic a few times to ask Michaels a question, the outer door was locked. One time, I found it open, but the technician intercepted me with some excuse for not allowing me into the lab itself. I got the drift pretty quickly, and so have Jeff and Lou.''

''Isn't that a little odd?''

''More than a little,'' Lara replied, forcing a laugh she hoped sounded natural. ''I don't know, maybe Michaels thinks he has a potential Nobel Prize in the works. Or maybe he's one of those strange birds who's secretive for no good reason. But whatever he's doing, he keeps his technician hopping. And lately, he's really been bogging down the computer.''

''Are the other two secretive?'' Reed asked immediately.

''Jeff and Lou? Not in the least. We're doing basic research. There's nothing to be secretive about.''

Reed didn't respond and his expression didn't change, but Lara hadn't expected him to react visibly. He now knew as much as she did, and he could hardly miss the implication. She lay back in the grass with a sense of relief. She had fulfilled her last obligation to Beretta. She was free.

She slipped her hands behind her head and closed her eyes, luxuriating in her release. ''How do you like working for Compstar?'' she asked, glad that she no longer had to choreograph the conversation. It was a trivial, small-talk question, but at least it was genuine.

"I only moonlight for Compstar. I'm a prep-school math teacher."

"Really?" Lara responded, opening her eyes in surprise. "You don't look like a teacher."

"Oh?" Reed laughed. "Why not?"

"I don't know," Lara said with a shrug and a dismissive smile, wishing she hadn't made the impulsive remark.

It *was* hard for her to picture Reed in a classroom, but she didn't want to explain. Despite his soft voice and easy smile, there was something about him . . . the toughness in his face and the hint of danger in his eyes when Billy-Lee had angered him—even the way he moved. Lara could picture him as a hunter, or . . . or what?

Reese didn't like the drift of the conversation. Next she might ask where he taught, or some other question he'd prefer not to answer, and he liked Lara Brooks too much to lie to her. As much as he would have liked to stay with her, it was time to pocket his winnings and leave.

He could hardly believe his luck. He had only been on the island for a matter of hours, and already he had scored twice. Fletch had unwittingly exposed an intruder breaking into the system, and Lara had just directed him to his main target. If anyone on the island was working with Beretta's relic, it had to be Michaels. Dr. Mike, the terrific guy.

"Well," Reese said, balling up the sandwich wrapping and stuffing it into the lunch bag, "I think I'd better get back to work."

"What's the rush? You haven't even finished your coffee."

She sounded genuinely disappointed, and Reese almost changed his mind. But the temptation to linger with her was a warning in itself. *Keep your eye on the ball, Reese.*

"No rush, really, but what I'm doing now is pretty boring and I'd like to get it over with."

"Okay, but I think I'll stay here for a while."

"Thanks for the sandwich and coffee." Reese stood up. "I really appreciate it."

"You're welcome," Lara replied with a warm smile. "See you at supper."

"See you," Reese said, refusing to read anything into her smile. As he turned and walked away, he told himself to ignore the feelings she awoke in him. Lara Brooks was a distraction he didn't need.

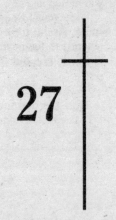

27

It took Reese longer than he'd expected to modify the computer's operating system so that he could safely monitor the hacker if he broke in again. It was almost 6 P.M. when he finished. Tired though he was, he set himself one last task. He called up the lab director's data files.

Reese didn't expect to understand the data Michaels's files contained, but he wanted to have a look anyway. To his surprise, he found something significant without even having to read them. Each of the system's users had protection codes on their files that prevented other users from deleting or altering the files, but Michaels's files had more stringent protection.

The other users' files could be read by anyone logged on to the system, but Michaels's files could only be read by Michaels himself—or by someone with Super-User privileges. Reese had had no reason to disbelieve Lara, but the protection code Michaels had chosen for his files confirmed what she'd told him. Michaels was keeping his research strictly secret.

Reese was about to override the read-protect code when

he heard someone enter the vestibule, and he quickly flushed the terminal screen.

"Hi," Fletch said cheerfully, coming into the control room. "Still at it?"

"I just finished."

"Good, because it's suppertime. Come on, I'll walk you over."

Meals in the dormitory's dining hall were served cafeteria style, and Fletch and Reese were among the last through the serving line. Forty or so wholesome-looking young men and women were already seated at round, cloth-covered tables, and their laughter and chatter filled the dining room. In spite of himself, Reese found himself looking for Lara. She was seated at a table across the room, and she smiled at him and waved him over.

Fletch grinned. "So, you've already met Lara Brooks. Fast work, John," he said with a good-natured wink. "See you later."

Two academic-looking young men and a much older, bald-headed man were seated at the table with Lara, and as Reese approached, he reminded himself to keep his mind on the business at hand. It wouldn't be that easy, he thought wryly. The moment Lara had smiled at him, he'd felt a flutter deep inside him.

The older man bounced up and stretched out his hand. "Ah, the man from Compstar," he boomed, seizing Reese's hand in an iron grip and pumping his arm. "Welcome to Miracle Isle! I'm Dick Michaels, the lab director."

"John Reed. Pleased to meet you, Dr. Michaels."

"Call me Dr. Mike, John. Everyone does."

Michaels was a tall man in his sixties, with a shiny bald head thrust forward on narrow, hunched shoulders, but he seemed to be bursting with energy.

"Sit down, sit down," Michaels urged, and Reese took the empty chair beside Lara.

"John, this is Jeff Lessard and Lou Brown," she said, introducing her younger colleagues. Like Lara, they were untanned by the sun, but unlike her they could have used some color. They both had a pasty-faced, mousy look. Each reached across the table to shake hands with Reese, but their brief smiles were diffident. Reese couldn't tell if they were shy or standoffish.

"Okay, folks," Michaels boomed, "let's not let the chow get cold."

Reese started to pick up his silverware, and he felt Lara's foot nudge his ankle. Michaels bowed his head, and Jeff and Lou followed suit. "Thank you for your bounty, Lord," Michaels intoned. "In Jesus' name, amen."

"Amen," echoed Jeff and Lou.

Michaels raised his head and dug eagerly into his meal. "Tell me, John," he asked between mouthfuls, "what denomination are you?"

"Lutheran," Reese replied, choosing at random, "but I don't go to church."

"Ha!" Michaels responded with a laugh and a vigorous nod. "Can't say I blame you. No life in the churches these days. Dry as dust. Come to chapel tomorrow morning, John, and you'll see the difference. Our Billy-Lee is a mighty fine preacher. Takes after his dad, he does, and when the Spirit moves him, he can shake the old devil by the tail!"

Across the room, the mighty fine preacher was holding court at a table twice as large as the rest, and he was clearly enjoying himself. Several of the prettiest girls in the room were seated with him, and he appeared to be the center of attention. Even at a distance, Reese could see that when Billy-Lee talked, everyone listened, and when he laughed, they all laughed.

Four of Billy-Lee's dinner companions, however, looked distinctly out of place. They were powerful men with military haircuts and tough, cynical faces. Bodyguard types, Reese thought, and he wondered what four wolves were doing among Jordan's innocent flock.

"How soon will we have that new computer to play with?" Michaels asked, forking in more food.

"Soon, I hope, but I've run into a snag. I've booted her up, loaded in the software, and hooked her into your system, but I've rigged it so you can't log in yet. I keep getting indications of a bad data block, and I'm not yet sure if the problem is in the software or hardware. I'll tackle it again tonight."

"Good man," Michaels said, chewing vigorously. "The sooner we can take advantage of the increased capacity, the better." Jeff and Lou nodded in agreement. "Too bad, though. You'll miss the fun tonight. We're having a bonfire and a sing-along."

Again Jeff and Lou nodded, and Reese began to wonder if they ever talked. Lara, too, was quiet, but that didn't make Reese any less aware of her.

"I'm told your laboratory is contributing to the Human Genome Project," Reese said to Michaels. "What is that, exactly?"

Lara had already targeted Michaels for him, but Reese wanted to do some probing of his own.

"A worldwide effort to read God's Book of Life," Michaels replied enthusiastically. "Bit by bit, piece by piece, we're transcribing that book into computer data banks."

"Book of Life?"

"Inside each cell of your body, John, are long strands of DNA packaged in the chromosomes. That DNA is a molecular book of instructions for the chemical reactions that developed your body and now maintain its functions. You see, each DNA molecule is like an incredibly long necklace of beads of four different colors, strung together in endlessly varying order.

"The beads are actually molecular subunits called bases, and the order in which they're strung together determines our genetic characteristics. Those four bases are the four letters of the genetic alphabet, and the sequences in which they appear on the DNA chain spell out the countless instructions in God's Book of Life.

"Our task is to transcribe that book and then decipher it. Just transcribing it is a mighty undertaking, for the Book is ten billion letters long. And deciphering it—correlating the genes we find with the characteristics they produce—will take even longer."

"How much are you able to do here?" Reese asked.

"Don't be fooled by our size," Michaels said with a good-natured smile. "Machines do most of the work these days, and our equipment is the very latest. Our sequencers—the devices that read out the sequence of the bases appearing on the DNA molecules—can process DNA at an unprecedented rate. And our DNA synthesizers are also state-of-the-art. We can create fragments of DNA of our own design, containing any code sequence we desire, with the touch of a switch."

"What for?" Reese asked.

"For many reasons. For instance, synthesis is crucial to Lou's experiments. Having identified the genetic defects that produce inherited diseases, we'd like to do something about them by modifying the victim's cellular DNA. Gene therapy is still in its infancy, but Lou is developing new retroviruses that can 'infect' human cells and carry the DNA segments into their chromosomes. By synthesizing and then inserting the proper gene into carrier cells, we can cure genetic defects.

"We're all approaching the general problem from different angles, John—according to our particular interests. Lara, for example, is sequencing a stretch of DNA in chromosome twenty-one that appears to be implicated in Alzheimer's. With luck, she'll find a gene that codes for the production of a protein associated with the disease.

"Jeff, on the other hand, isn't sequencing DNA. He's doing genetic linkage studies that tell researchers like Lara where to look for genes governing certain inherited characteristics—on which chromosome, and approximately where along the DNA chain."

Michaels paused to swallow another mouthful of food and nodded enthusiastically. "I'm really excited about what we're accomplishing here, John, and as our results start flowing into the literature, I'm sure our staff will grow."

"But what about you?" Reese prompted. "You haven't said what you're working on."

Michaels shrugged and smiled deprecatingly. "I keep my hand in, but I'm afraid my own work is not very imaginative. I'm simply grinding out sequences on long stretches of DNA that no one has looked at yet—creating a database for future use by other workers. These three young go-getters are our laboratory's strength," he said, beaming at Lara, Jeff, and Lou, "and I hope to recruit more of their caliber."

Michaels made it sound convincing, but the prodigious amount of computer time Michaels was burning up didn't square with just "keeping his hand in." And neither did his secrecy.

"Where do you hail from, John?" Michaels asked, and Reese wondered if he was changing the subject deliberately.

"I've lived in New Hampshire for the past twenty years."

"But Compstar is in Massachusetts. Do you commute?"

"Mostly I work out of my home."

"Do you have a family, John?"

The harmless question caught Reese off guard, and he didn't trust himself to speak. He simply shook his head.

Michaels had cleared his plate, and he looked at it for a moment, as if wondering whether to refill it. Apparently he decided he'd had enough. "Well, even if you live in New Hampshire, you must be a Red Sox fan. How 'bout those Sox! I think they'll really make it this year."

"I don't know. I'm not much of a baseball fan."

But to Reese's surprise, Jeff and Lou were, and they suddenly came to life.

"The Sox will fade," Jeff asserted forcefully, and Lou nodded in agreement. "They always do," he chimed in.

Michaels countered and a heated debate ensued. Lara had been silent throughout the meal, but now she leaned close to Reese and said, "I'm working this evening, too. If you'd like, I could give you a quick tour of the lab."

Reese caught the light scent of her perfume, and it affected him as had the touch of her hand that afternoon. It was pointless to try to deny his attraction to her, he realized. Even while he'd been concentrating on Michaels, he had felt her nearness.

"Yes, I would," he said, trying not to embarrass himself by betraying his eagerness to be alone with her. The chemistry he felt might be strictly one-sided, he thought, but as he looked at Lara and returned her smile, he knew he wanted to find out.

Across the room, Billy-Lee's high-pitched laughter rang

out, and Reese looked over. Billy-Lee was still laughing, but his piggy eyes were focused on Lara. As he noticed Reese watching, his smile froze and he looked away.

Billy-Lee's cheeks burned as he saw Lara lean toward Reed again and say something to him. Her smile and the casual familiarity of her body language seemed a deliberate affront to Billy-Lee, as if she knew he was watching. It *had* to be deliberate. She couldn't possibly see anything in Reed. Sweet Jesus, he was only a company rep—a nobody—a complete zero.

Billy-Lee saw Reed staring across the room at him and looked away. *Insolent bastard.* Billy-Lee had disliked him at once. If Reed didn't show more respect, he resolved angrily, Compstar would get a strong letter of complaint from Billy-Lee Jordan.

One of the girls at his table asked him a question, and he answered it with a joke that provoked a fresh round of laughter. He was in top form this evening, he congratulated himself. Even the stolid security men he'd hired had smiled and occasionally laughed at his wit.

He'd come to dinner in a buoyant mood. Billy-Lee had begun to count the days until his father arrived, and earlier this evening, Michaels had intimated that his work in the laboratory was almost completed. Everything seemed to be on schedule. For what, exactly, Billy-Lee really didn't care. All that mattered was that he would finally be able to destroy the only evidence that could tie them to the break-in.

Yet as the evening meal had progressed, Lara Brooks had once again contrived to sour his mood. Each time one of his witticisms had triggered an outburst of laughter at his table, he'd glanced in her direction, expecting to see her look his way. And each time he'd been disappointed.

And now she was pretending to be oh-so-chummy with the Compstar rep. Why? Was she trying to make him jealous? As the idea took hold, Billy-Lee found comfort in it; and when he saw Lara get up from her table with Reed and watched them leave together, he refused to let it bother him.

She *was* trying to make him jealous, he told himself, and there'd be no point if she weren't interested. When she did finally yield to him, he thought with a surge of sexual excitement, he'd make her regret playing hard to get.

28

The sun was about to set as Lara left the dining hall with Reed. The yellow-orange light of the sun's slanting rays cast long, deep shadows on the lawn, and the quiet in the deserted quadrangle was nearly absolute. The silence emphasized their solitude, and Lara suddenly felt self-conscious.

Had Reed guessed why she'd offered him a tour of the lab? She'd done it on impulse, and only afterward had she acknowledged the reason to herself. She'd wanted an excuse to be alone with him. What was it that so attracted her to him? she wondered.

Reed was striking rather than handsome, and besides, a man's looks had never swept her off her feet. Was it just that he was so different from the men who populated academe? Despite Reed's quiet voice and easy smile, she sensed a hard core hidden inside him. Yet, paradoxically, she didn't find it threatening. Rarely had she felt so immediately comfortable with a man.

They started walking across the quadrangle toward the lab, but then Reed paused and offered her a cigarette. Lara looked into his eyes as he lit it and he smiled tentatively.

"I'm not really all that anxious to get to work," he said. "Are you?"

"No, not really," Lara replied, smiling in return, and in the long second that they held each other's eyes, she felt an unspoken question pass between them. A question asked and answered. "It's going to be a beautiful sunset," she added lightly to cover her flutter of anticipation. She'd wanted an excuse to be alone with him, and now she knew that he felt the same way.

"Right," Reed said, his smile broadening, "but let's not watch it from up here. I'd hate to get roped into that sing-along. Care for a walk down to the shore?"

"Yes, let's." As they turned and walked toward the front of the compound, Lara was suddenly glad that she'd come to Miracle Isle.

As he and Lara reached the road at the front of the compound, Reese took one last drag on his cigarette and then discarded it. For the first time in months he felt no need to smoke, and as he glanced at the beautiful young woman beside him, he could almost forget why he was on the island.

"Too bad we're not on the Pacific," Lara said, looking toward the red sun sinking behind the dark outline of Maine's distant coast. "I've always wanted to see the green flash."

"The what?"

"The green flash. It has something to do with the refraction of light in the atmosphere, but you can't see it when the sun sets over land. Sailors see it sometimes when they're on the open seas—a bright flash of green a few seconds after the sun sets. When my brother was nineteen, he shipped out on a tramp steamer for the summer, and he saw it more than once. Roger told me it was spectacular."

"How many brothers and sisters do you have?"

"Just Roger. In fact, he's my only family. My parents died when I was twelve and Rog was twenty. He took care of me until I was grown, and—well, let's just say I owe him a lot. What about you, John? I heard you tell Michaels that you had no family. None at all?"

"My wife, Kathy, died two years ago of cancer."

"Oh—I'm sorry."

"It happens," Reese said, shying away from the memory, "but you never think it will happen to you. I didn't have any brothers or sisters and my parents are gone, so I'm on my own," he added, hoping the implication would forestall a question about children. "I take it you're not married either."

"Divorced," Lara replied in a decidedly neutral tone, and Reese looked at her.

"Recently?"

Lara nodded and smiled wryly. "I'm over it, if that's what you're wondering. Looking back, I'd say the marriage died long before the divorce. I'm relieved, and I know Mark is."

The man had to be a fool, Reese thought, but he made no comment.

The air was still, and the soft rustle of the surf only emphasized the quiet of the beautiful evening as they descended the hill to the shore. They said little as they walked up the shore road and out along the old wooden dock, and to Reese the silence between them seemed comfortably intimate.

As they settled themselves at the very end of the dock, they began to talk again. Reese could never remember clearly what they talked about that evening as the light died and darkness crept over the sea. What he would remember was the music of Lara's infectious laughter, and how—for the first time in months—he, too, was able to laugh.

Reese skirted the tricky areas of his past, and had he not been so absorbed by Lara herself, he might have noticed her own occasional reticence. But he didn't notice; and despite the gaps in what they told each other about themselves, by the time the moon rose and carpeted the ocean with quicksilver, they were no longer strangers.

But for Reese, the coming of darkness was an unavoidable reminder that time was passing. As much as he hated to end their evening together, he couldn't stay with Lara much longer. If the unknown intruder broke into the system earlier than he anticipated, he might miss his chance to trap him.

The air had turned colder and the sea breeze was stiffening. Reese saw Lara shiver, and that decided him. He had delayed the moment as long as possible, but now it was time to go.

"You're cold," he said, and as she looked at him, her face softly lit by the moon, he ached to take her in his arms. Instead he got to his feet, slipped off his jacket, and offered it to her.

"Thanks," Lara said, smiling up at Reed as he draped his jacket over her shoulders. She could feel the warmth it carried from his body, and she pulled it tightly around her. "I'm fine now," she added, anxious not to break the spell of a magical evening. "Really."

"But it's getting colder by the moment, and I'm afraid I have to get to work. I have a long night ahead of me."

The regret in his voice was unmistakable, and it took some of the edge off Lara's wrenching disappointment. The last few hours *had* been magical, she thought. There was no other word for it, and she hadn't wanted it to end.

Reed took her hands and helped her up, and Lara was keenly aware that this was the first time they'd touched all evening. How easy it would be for him to kiss me, she thought as he drew her gently to her feet, yet despite her desire, she wasn't entirely sorry when he released her hands and stepped back. Perhaps he, too, was reluctant to rush things—to seize everything at once, as if there were no tomorrow.

There *was* tomorrow, she consoled herself, and . . . With a pang, Lara realized that she didn't know how long he would stay—or what he intended to do. If only she'd told him why she was here! At some point she had intended to, but then, incredibly, she'd completely forgotten Beretta and the relic. And now just didn't seem the moment to tell him. She felt she couldn't just blurt it out.

I'll tell him tomorrow, Lara promised herself as they left the dock and headed back up to the compound. She didn't understand how Reed could be connected to Beretta and Opus Dei; he didn't appear religious in the least. But, she reminded herself, it was hardly surprising that he would disguise his faith.

There was much she still didn't know about him, yet already something deep inside her whispered, "This could be the man for you." The suddenness with which it had happened only intensified the feeling, for Lara knew herself too well by now to believe she could be swept off her feet.

"Still interested in seeing the lab?" Lara asked as they neared the research building.

"Sure, but then I really will have to get to work."

From the rear of the compound, orange sparks were rising into the night from the bonfire Michaels had talked about, and Lara could hear singing. They reached the entrance to the laboratory, and Lara opened the door and flipped on the lights.

"Voilà. The best little lab that money can buy."

"Looks impressive," Reed said, looking around him.

In fact, the laboratory was anything but small, and the principal room was unusually large. It was at least fifty feet long and crammed with lab benches and equipment. In addition to the laser sequencers on the benches, two massive pieces of computer-controlled apparatus took up a third of the floor space. These, too, were sequencers, but of a type found in only the most up-to-date laboratories.

Imagining how the lab looked to a visitor, Lara suspected that the dominant impression was one of clutter. Shelves along the walls and mounted on the benches were crammed with bottled chemicals and solvents. Glass flasks and beakers were everywhere. They hung on the pegs of drying racks and were scattered over the benches in the spaces between large pieces of electronic equipment, around which snaked translucent plastic tubing.

As Reed's eyes scanned the laboratory, Lara noticed that his expression didn't betray the usual layman's lack of comprehension of what he saw, and that made sense, she thought. Beretta had sent him, after all. But something else she saw in his eyes she didn't understand. A hint of sorrow.

"This is where our technicians work," Lara said. "They

run the routine production end of our experiments. Lou, Jeff, and I have offices and small labs through that doorway on the left.''

Lara saw Reed glance at his watch, and she felt a stab of disappointment. ''You've got to get to work,'' she said, producing a smile.

''Yeah, I really do.''

''I could drop by with some coffee later on,'' Lara said, and instantly she regretted the impulse.

She could see that the offer caught Reed off guard, and he seemed to fumble for a way to decline. ''Thanks,'' he said awkwardly, ''but once I get going, I like to push things through in one go.''

''That's okay,'' Lara said quickly. ''I know what you mean. See you tomorrow then.''

Reed smiled at her. ''You can bet on that.''

29

Reese was asleep in his chair and dreaming when the intruder broke into Miracle Isle's computer. In Reese's dream, he was standing beside a hospital bed, staring helplessly at Allison's pale face. Her eyes were open, but vacant, and her lips moved spasmodically. Suddenly he thought he heard a whisper, and he bent over her, putting his ear close to her lips. The sound came again, barely more than a faint sigh, but this time Reese heard it clearly: "Daddy. Daddy, help me."

Reese spun away and rushed to the door. "Get me a doctor!" he shouted into the deserted corridor. "A doctor!" he shouted again and again, but the corridor remained silent and empty.

"Hush!" commanded a woman's voice behind him, and he whirled around. A nurse stood beside Allison's bed, glowering at him. "Be quiet, Mr. Reese! You're causing a disturbance."

"But she spoke to me!" Reese cried. "I heard her!"

"Nonsense," said the nurse, shaking her head and pointing to a machine beside Allison's bed that was emitting a beeping tone from an audio speaker. "Can't you hear the monitor, Mr. Reese? Don't you know what it means? Your daughter is brain-dead. She's brain-dead, Mr. Reese. Brain-dead."

"No!" Reese cried. "No!"

He awoke suddenly with the cry in his throat, and for a moment he was disoriented. The dream clung to him, and he did not immediately realize that the beeping tone was the audio alarm he'd set to alert him if anyone logged on to the system.

Abruptly he straightened in his chair, rubbed his eyes, and peered at the video monitor. A remote user had just entered the computer through Bionet and logged into the guest account. It was six minutes past midnight.

Reese waited tensely to see what the user would do. The guest account log showed occasional use by outsiders, presumably colleagues at other laboratories who were in communication with the Miracle Isle scientists, and this might be a false alarm. Then the guest user typed in his first command, and Reese smiled with cold satisfaction.

The UNIX command was "WHO," and the computer promptly responded by listing all the users logged on to the system. The "guest" was checking to see who else was on. Reese's presence on the system was screened from the operating system, and as soon as the intruder saw that he was apparently alone on the computer, he logged off.

"That's right," Reese muttered aloud, "the coast is clear. Now, come on back."

The console's audio prompt sounded again, and this time the intruder logged in on the UUCP account, using the proper password. The UUCP account permitted rapid transfer of files from one UNIX system to another, and it came with system-manager privileges.

The computer responded with a prompt that told the intruder he had successfully logged on. Now that he had Super-User status he could go anywhere in the system and do anything he desired—including wiping out records of his activity. Reese slid his chair across to the telephone and hastily punched in the Bionet number Max had sent him.

"Bionet," a woman's voice answered. "Renfrew speaking."

"This is John Reed," Reese said quickly. "I'm the—"

"Yes, I know," the Bionet engineer cut in. "Max alerted me. Is the hacker on your system now?"

"He just logged on. Can you give me a trace?"

"Sure. What's your node address?"

Reese gave it to her and looked over at the video monitor. The intruder's commands from the remote terminal were scrolling over the video screen. The hacker repeated his request for a list of users and then looked for any changes in the operating system. Max had been right. The intruder was being careful.

Finding no changes, the intruder proceeded. A system message informed all users that the new computer was online, and the hacker attempted to log on. This proved he was curious, but nothing more. Reese wanted confirmation that he was after Beretta's relic.

"I'm setting up a trace now," Renfrew said, and Reese could hear the clicking as she typed instructions into her own computer terminal. "It shouldn't take long, John. Stay on the line."

The intruder tried to log on to the new computer several more times, but finally he gave up. His next command erased Reese's last doubt, for the hacker went directly to Michaels's data files. Reese restlessly drummed his fingers on the arm of his chair, willing the Bionet engineer to complete the trace. There was no telling how long the intruder would stay on the system.

Reese was about to ask the Bionet engineer how much longer the trace would take when he heard the outer door to the vestibule open. He twisted around, fearing it would be Lara. To his relief, he saw one of Billy-Lee's bodyguards coming in. The man had appeared at the worst possible moment, but at least he was unlikely to understand what was on the video screen.

"Evening, sir. My name's Johnson. Chief of security."

Johnson was bigger and older than his three buddies. He was a swarthy, hawk-faced man in his midthirties, with a military bearing and the build of a football running back. He was carrying a heavy police flashlight and a transceiver on his hip.

"John Reed," Reese responded, trying to appear relaxed. "What can I do for you?"

"Nothing," Johnson replied, glancing without interest at the terminal screen. "Just checking. I saw the lights, and no one's usually here this late. You're the man from the computer company, right?"

"That's right. I'm talking to one of my people right now," he added, hoping Johnson would take the hint.

"You guys get paid overtime?"

"I'm afraid not."

"But I'll bet the pay's good," Johnson said conversationally.

"I can't complain." Reese glanced at the terminal screen. The intruder had cranked up the UUCP program and was preparing to transfer Michaels's data files to his own distant computer.

"Me neither," Johnson said, leaning against the wall. "Between you and me, this is a pretty cushy job. Boring as hell, but cushy."

Reese smiled and nodded, but inwardly he chafed at the need to humor the security man.

"How's it going?" he said into the phone, but there was no response. Renfrew must have put down the phone while she worked on the trace. *Hurry up!* he urged silently. It wouldn't take the intruder long to copy Michaels's files, and he was likely to log off as soon as the task was completed.

"What's this place need security for?" Reese asked Johnson, though he itched to get rid of him. "We're all alone here."

"Jordan has received some death threats. Apparently there's some wacko cult that doesn't like the fertility clinic he's running here. Call themselves Aaronites. That's what I'm told, at any rate. We've got shotguns, just in case."

And Johnson and his men undoubtedly knew how to use them, Reese thought.

Abruptly the Bionet engineer came back on the line. "John?"

"Yes," Reese said quickly. "What have you got?"

"I've traced him to the computer system at Harvard University."

"What? Are you sure?"

"That's where he's entering our network, but he could be entering the Harvard system from somewhere else and dialing out again from there."

Reese fervently hoped not.

"If you want," Renfrew said, "I can give you the Harvard system manager's phone number."

"Please." Reese pulled a pen from his pocket. Renfrew read him the number and Reese noted it on the back of the telephone directory beside the phone. "Great job," he said gratefully. "Thanks!"

"No thanks are necessary. These renegades are a plague on all of us. Good hunting, John."

Reese hung up and looked at Johnson. The security man was clearly in no hurry to leave, but Reese could no longer indulge him. "Sorry to be inhospitable, but I'd like to finish up here and hit the sack."

"Sure. I didn't mean to disturb you. Have a good night."

"Thanks. See you later."

As Johnson left, Reese checked the terminal screen. The intruder was still copying data from Michaels's files, but he wasn't likely to be much longer. Reese dialed Harvard.

The system manager who answered sounded young and bored, but as soon as Reese explained the situation, the young man's boredom evaporated. "One of *our* users?" he responded angrily. "Son of a bitch! Any idea who?"

"No. That's why I'm calling you. He's on your system right now."

"That's not much help. A lot of users are still on here."

"Well, this guy isn't going to be on my system much longer. He's copying our DNA data files, so he's probably biology faculty, a grad student or a postdoc. Can you pin him down on that basis?"

"Maybe, but it may take time."

"We don't have time. Can you slip me a list of the users who are on your system right now? Maybe one of my people here would recognize a name."

The brief silence that followed indicated the system manager's reluctance, but his hesitancy gave way to the imperative of all system managers to run down outlaw hackers. "Okay. I'm listing all the current log-ins to file right now."

"Shit, there he goes! He's just logged off here."

"Well, everyone is still on at my end. No log-offs." There was a long silence before the system manager came back on the line. "Okay, I've got all the current users in the file. I'll go over the list and narrow it down to those connected to the Biology Department. What's your E-mail address?" Reese gave it to him. "I'll get right on it, and I'll send you the short list as soon as I can. Okay?"

"Great. I appreciate it."

"No problem, John. But let me know if you figure out who the bastard is."

"Sure thing," Reese lied, and said good-bye.

In the twenty minutes Reese had to wait for the E-mail message, he killed the log-in disable on the new computer and ran a last few checks to be sure it was integrated properly into the system. With that, his job for Compstar was completed, but he would have no difficulty prolonging his stay as long as necessary. He could fake whatever imaginary problems he liked, and Fletch wouldn't catch on.

Then the E-mail message from Harvard came through, and the moment he saw the list he'd been sent, he knew he'd struck pay dirt. He recognized the fourth name on the list at once: Kenji Hamada. The people who'd tried to stop Reese knew about Beretta's relic, all right, and now Reese knew where they'd gotten their information. He couldn't guess their interest in the relic or how they'd come to suspect it was on Miracle Isle, but that was secondary.

Reese would have liked to try to reach Beretta by phone, but the man from Opus Dei had urged him to communicate via E-mail through Compstar once he was on the island. Reese didn't trust Beretta or his judgment, but as long as there was any chance the man could help him, he would play by Beretta's rules. He didn't expect Beretta to receive his E-mail message before morning, but he drafted and sent it at once:

I've identified a kibitzer in our network poker game. He's penetrated the computer here to look at the cards. His name is Kenji Hamada, and he works at Harvard for Professor Singer. Check it out. I want to hear from you ASAP.

30

Reese rarely needed an alarm clock, but to his annoyance he overslept the next morning. He had gone to bed, his head buzzing with fatigue and unanswerable questions about Kenji Hamada, but when he awoke, his first thoughts were of Lara. He arrived late for breakfast, and as he went to the serving counter, he saw to his disappointment that Lara and her companions were already rising from their table.

She smiled as he caught her eye, and instead of heading for the exit, she came his way. Each time he saw her, Reese thought, she looked more beautiful to him.

"Hi," Lara said as she came up to him. "How did it go last night?"

"Not so good. There's still a problem with the system I can't get a handle on."

"Does that mean you'll be here for a while yet?"

"Looks like it. But . . . I can't say I'm sorry."

Lara gave him a slow smile. "Me neither."

"Any chance you could knock off for a while today?" Reese asked quickly.

"Well," Lara responded in a cheerfully conspiratorial

whisper, "a morning's work would be enough to keep up appearances."

"Would you like to get together this afternoon?"

At that moment the young woman behind the serving counter came over and informed Reese that they were about to close up. As he turned and asked for two sweet rolls and coffee, he heard Lara's voice behind him.

"It's a date," she said in a stage whisper, and then she was gone.

Reese collected himself along with his breakfast, and as he turned away from the counter, he saw Fletch gesturing for him to sit at his table.

"You didn't come to chapel," Fletch greeted Reese, and he seemed genuinely disappointed.

"Too early for me," Reese said, sitting down. "I was up late last night."

"Tomorrow, then," Fletch insisted, and he introduced Reese to his smiling, fresh-faced companions at the table, beginning with a pretty blond girl beside him. "This is my friend, Kimberly." From the way Fletch and the girl looked at each other, Reese concluded that she was more than a friend. Apparently Fletch's happiness was not entirely due to Jesus' love.

"Are you still having problems with the system?" Fletch asked Reese.

"Yes and no. Your new computer is on-line, but there's still a glitch somewhere. I've asked for advice from the company and I should get an answer soon. In the meantime, I'll put a warning message on the system, so your users can avoid the problem until I cure it.

"And by the way, you were right about the billing program. It had a bug."

"Really?" Fletch responded with a grin, clearly pleased to have caught a software error.

"That's what they told me when I called yesterday, but the version that came with the new software should be okay."

As Reese began to eat, Fletch and his young friends picked up the conversation he'd interrupted. It was Bible talk, and

Reese didn't try to follow it. The warm glow from his brief exchange with Lara quickly dissipated as he reconsidered the situation. He had come to Miracle Isle with nothing to lose, but Lara had changed that literally overnight.

He still didn't know who had tipped off the bikers—or why—and that presented a risk he couldn't possibly assess. What would he do if Beretta didn't come through for him? Before last night, he would have pressed on, regardless, but now . . . However innocent Lara's involvement with him, how could he be sure that she wouldn't be hurt if things blew up in his face?

"What's that mean?" Fletch asked, peering over Reese's shoulder at the veiled E-mail message from Beretta that came through just before noon. Reese was surprised by the speed of Beretta's response, and he was astonished by the message. Beretta was pulling him off the island:

> The problem is not in the software. It's a faulty board. Please return *immediately* to consult further and pick up new components for on-site installation.

"It's what I was afraid of. There's a hardware defect in the new computer. I'll have to take it off-line and go pick up a new circuit board."

"All the way back to Massachusetts?" Fletch asked in surprise. "Why don't they just send it up by express delivery?"

"Ours not to reason why," Reese replied with a shrug that was far more casual than he felt. He couldn't imagine why Beretta was insisting that he leave the island at once, but the demand for haste was too clear to ignore.

"But the ferry won't be coming until tomorrow morning," Fletch said.

"Damn, that's not good enough." Reese felt the urgency of Beretta's message all the more because he didn't understand it. Beretta's surprisingly quick response confirmed Reese's belief that he knew more than he'd been willing to say, and Reese made himself a promise. He wouldn't be coming back with blinders on.

"This was a big order for the company," he said to explain the agitation he'd betrayed, "and my boss wants things fixed in a hurry. I'll get Jarvis to take me across on his boat."

"Jeez, you may have missed your chance," Fletch said worriedly, looking at his watch. "I overheard Billy-Lee saying that he was sending Captain Jarvis down to Lambeth Cove for something or other, and he usually leaves around noon."

Reese came out of his chair. "Do me a favor," he said hurriedly. "If I don't come back, let Lara Brooks know I caught the boat and why."

Reese arrived home in the early evening. His legs and back were stiff from the long drive down from Lambeth Cove, but he ignored the pain as he hurried into the house. He had tried to reach Beretta by phone from Lambeth Cove, and once again without success on the way down from Maine, and he was anxious to check his answering machine.

As Reese entered the kitchen, he was greeted by musty air and a scurrying sound. He'd have to buy some mousetraps, he thought distractedly as he strode through the kitchen and down the hall to the living room. The digital readout on his answering machine indicated one message, and he stabbed the play button. Beretta's voice emerged from the speaker:

"If you've been trying to call me, you know I'm not available. I flew to Washington to follow up on some inquiries, and I won't be able to meet you until tomorrow evening. Meet me at the office I rented near Compstar at ten P.M. tomorrow. Take Exit Thirty-two off Route Four Ninety-five and take a right. The office park is two miles farther on. Two-twenty Ridge Road. You'll find my name on the directory at the entrance."

There was a short silence, and then Beretta added, "I still have some checking to do, but it looks like the man whose name you sent me is mixed up with some very nasty types. I'll fill you in tomorrow evening, but I think I should warn you. If I'm right, his friends are far more dangerous than those bikers you tangled with. Watch yourself—just in case.''

In case of *what?* Reese wondered as the message ended, and he cursed Beretta's continuing secretiveness. Watch himself? Where? When?

Reese turned on his heel and went upstairs. Hidden away in his bedroom closet was the Browning nine-millimeter automatic he'd brought back from Vietnam. He pulled out the box containing the automatic and a supply of hollow-point ammunition. The gun had been oiled and sealed in a plastic bag, but Reese decided to fieldstrip it and clean it just to be sure.

Although the Browning design was outdated, the gun had once saved his life in Vietnam, and he trusted it. Reese hadn't fired the pistol in years, but he hadn't forgotten how to use it.

31

The ringing of Kenji Hamada's telephone dragged him from a deep sleep. Groggily he looked at the illuminated digits of his bedside clock, but without his glasses they were an indecipherable blur. Still half-asleep, but prodded by the undefined anxiety of an unexpected call in the dead of night, he climbed out of bed and stumbled across the room to the phone.

"Hello," he croaked.

"Kenji, wake up!" commanded his father's deep voice in Japanese, and it cleared his head like a dash of ice water in the face. Never before had his father called him from Japan.

"I'm awake, Pa."

"Kenji, I've just been warned that inquiries are being made about you. An American with influence in Washington has been asking questions through diplomatic channels. Do you know why?"

"No," Kenji said, his throat constricting, and his mind raced. *What has happened?* "I have no idea, Pa."

He didn't have to ask how his father had received the warning. Many men in the Japanese government were beholden to Yoshiro Hamada.

"I was hoping you might," his father said, "but since you don't, we must assume the worst."

Kenji shivered. In spite of his care, he must have been discovered and traced. After the fact, Tanaka had had to tell him what he'd tried to do to delay the Compstar field rep, and Kenji had secretly been relieved that nothing had happened to the man.

Yet the failure had forced Kenji's hand. He'd abandoned his usual caution and stayed inside the Miracle Isle system long enough to download all of the lab director's data files at once. Too long.

"What do you want me to do?" he asked his father.

"What I wanted in the first place, Kenji. Come home and leave things to us."

The temptation to cut and run was almost overwhelming; but Kenji still had nightmares about the night of the break-in, and his secret shame continued to haunt him by day. The need to redeem himself had become more important to him than the ancient flesh sample itself.

"I can't do that," he heard himself say. "This is something I have to do for myself, Pa."

For several seconds there was silence on the line. "I haven't forgotten what you said when you were here," his father finally replied. "A man makes his own choices and accepts the outcome as his karma. I'll not forbid you."

Again there was silence, and Kenji knew that his father still hoped he'd change his mind.

"I've decided. I'm staying."

"Then I have some information for you," his father immediately responded, and now his voice was crisply detached. "But this is an open line. I've already dispatched it to Tanaka. Be guided by him, Kenji. He has the experience you lack."

As Kenji said good-bye, he felt a strange mixture of dread and relief. Until this moment, he hadn't been absolutely sure that he would carry through no matter what. Now he knew.

Kenji met Tanaka for lunch the next day in a student hangout on Brattle Street, a block from Harvard Square. Tanaka arrived wearing the sunglasses and hip-hugging suit that were virtually a *yakuza* uniform, and he drew several curious glances as he made his way to Kenji's table.

Tanaka wasted no time getting down to business. "Your father has sent me the name of the man who has been asking about you," he said in Japanese as he sat down. "Alfons Beretta. Do you know him?"

"I've never even heard of him," Kenji said, satisfied that he'd matched Tanaka's dry, matter-of-fact tone.

"He's an attorney in New York, but he requested that answers to his inquiry be faxed to an office he's renting at a Massachusetts address northwest of us."

"Do we have any clue to what he's after?"

Tanaka shook his head. "I called his law firm in New York and asked for him. They told me he's on temporary leave. I asked why, but they wouldn't say, and I didn't think it wise to press."

"I don't get it. If I—" Kenji broke off as a waitress appeared, and he hastily glanced at the menu and selected an item at random.

The waitress looked at Tanaka and he shook his head. "I'm not staying," he said, surprising Kenji.

"Would you like a glass of water, sir?"

"No, thank you."

"Why aren't you eating?" Kenji asked, reverting to Japanese as the waitress left.

"I already have. You were saying . . . ?"

"If I was traced while I was connected to the island's computer, I would have expected Harvard to be alerted—or federal agents. Why should some unknown lawyer from New York be making inquiries about me?"

"Unknown to us," Tanaka corrected. "He has good connections in Washington."

Tanaka fell silent and looked at Kenji impassively from behind his dark glasses. Kenji knew what he was waiting for.

"We've obviously run out of time," Kenji said. "I can't be certain the sample is on the island, but I think it is. Unless you tell me it's too late to go after it, that's what I want to do. What's your advice?"

"Break in and search the lawyer's office," Tanaka said coolly. "He seems to be proceeding cautiously, so the Christian sect may not realize what you're after. But I'd like to try and find out more. If they've been forewarned, there's no point in a raid.

"As you said, time is running out, so we should act at once. And this time we won't rely on hirelings; we'll do this ourselves. That entails some risk, but we can't afford another bungled job. I'd try to slip in after hours this evening—early enough to avoid immediate suspicion if we're seen entering or leaving the building."

Despite Kenji's resolve, he found himself shrinking once again from the responsibility of committing his father's men to direct, illegal action. Yet if he didn't have the nerve to break into an office, he might as well give up now.

"All right," Kenji said. "We'll try tonight, as you suggest. I'll be going with you."

"That's not necessary," Tanaka said quickly, and Kenji wondered what orders his father had given him.

"I'm *going,* Tanaka-san."

Kenji thought that Tanaka started to frown, but the change in his expression was too fleeting to be sure. Tanaka bowed fractionally in acknowledgment. "I'll notify my men and get back to you." He pushed back his chair, preparing to leave. "Please wait for my call in your apartment."

"But what if the search yields nothing?" Kenji asked, instantly regretting the useless question.

"Then you'll have another decision to make, Hamada-san."

Thus spoke Simon: I heard a voice saying, As you have called me, so am I here. And I turned to see the voice, who stood like unto the Son of Man. He that lives, and was dead, and shall live forever more. And the voice spoke to me again, saying, Behold I hold the keys of hell and death.

—SAMARIA SCROLL 1, COLUMN 1.8.3

32

Shortly before 10 P.M., Reese pulled into the parking lot of the two-story brick building in which Beretta had rented an office. Beretta's Mercedes was parked to the left of the entrance, but the building looked deserted. Although the entrance hallway was illuminated, no lights showed in the office windows, and Reese concluded that Beretta's office faced the rear.

The office building Beretta had chosen surprised Reese, for it was clearly a cheap rental. The lawn surrounding the building was overgrown with weeds and needed mowing, and the vacant lots bracketing the office park had peeling for-sale signs. The only other commercial site in view was a convenience store on the opposite side of the highway.

Reese parked his Chevy beside Beretta's car and got out. The only other vehicle in the lot was a minivan with tinted windows, parked in the far corner and apparently left overnight. Whoever had left it wasn't worried about theft or vandalism, but Reese still locked the door of his own car behind him.

Under the driver's seat was his Browning with a fully

loaded magazine. If he was caught with it in Massachusetts, he would face a mandatory one-year jail sentence, but he was willing to take the risk. Cryptic though Beretta's warning had been, Reese took it seriously.

As he walked toward the building's front entrance, he pulled away his shirt where it had stuck to his back. Although summer was almost over, one last mass of hot, muggy air had edged up from the south, and the night was only beginning to cool.

Beside the plate-glass door at the entrance was a double row of buzzer buttons with the names of the offices' occupants beside them. Most of the offices were vacant. Reese found Beretta's name, pressed the button beside it, and waited. There was no response, and Reese tried the door. It was locked, and he pressed the button twice more.

Finally he heard the buzz and click as the electronic lock opened, and he entered and climbed the stairs to the second floor. Apparently there was no central air-conditioning, and the stale air had retained the heat of the day. Reese began to perspire.

Although the entrance hallway and stairs were lighted, the corridor at the top of the stairs was dark. It ran the length of the building, and light glowed behind the frosted-glass panel of a door at the end of the hallway to Reese's left. As he walked down the silent corridor, Reese half expected Beretta to open the door to greet him, but the door remained closed.

Two doors faced him at the end of the hall, both to corner offices, and the lighted one on the left bore the number Reese had read beside Beretta's nameplate. He was fifteen feet from it when he suddenly felt gooseflesh rise on his arms—an instinctive reaction that came an instant before he registered the reason. The office behind the lighted door was bound to have a window overlooking the parking lot, yet all the front windows had been dark.

Reese halted and listened. The building was completely silent, and the only sound he heard was his own breathing. He was spooking himself, he thought, for there was probably an innocent explanation. Perhaps Beretta had been napping in the dark—or maybe he had arrived just ahead of Reese and entered his office as Reese buzzed him at the entrance. Maybe—but Reese didn't move.

Feeling slightly foolish, he turned and retreated quietly to the stairwell. He slipped down the stairs and out through the entrance. As he walked to his car, he looked up over his shoulder and verified that light now shone from the corner window on the second floor. He still felt overly cautious, but he unlocked his car, reached into the back, and pulled out a lightweight windbreaker that had been lying on the rear seat.

He slipped it on and fished his Browning out from under the driver's seat. He chambered a round and put on the safety. With a final glance around him, he straightened up and shoved the automatic into his waistband behind his right hip, making sure that the gun butt was hidden beneath the windbreaker.

As he walked back to the entrance, he watched the lighted window, but he saw no one inside. Beretta had let him into the building, and Reese hadn't arrived at his door. Why hadn't Beretta checked to see why? Wouldn't he take a look out his front window? Reese reached the entrance and was about to press the buzzer when he saw feet coming down the stairs.

He tensed as two slim-hipped, broad-shouldered young men in identical dark, tailored suits came fully into view. They wore snap-brimmed hats and sunglasses that partially masked their faces, but they were clearly Asians. They didn't need those sunglasses, and they didn't look like businessmen. As they came down the stairs to the entrance, they moved with the aggressive, fluid grace of tigers. *Hamada has dangerous friends.*

Reese took a step back from the door and moved to one side. Neither of the men coming toward him had a visible weapon, but Reese took another step back and braced himself as they came out the door.

"Good evening," he said, forcing a casual smile as he looked into the stone-faced stare of the man in the lead. Both men nodded to him but said nothing as they strode past him into the parking lot. Reese caught the door before it closed and watched them walk toward the minivan.

As the man in the lead reached the van and opened the door on the passenger side, he looked back over his shoulder. Reese turned and entered the building, but not before the minivan's dome light had revealed a third man sitting in the driver's seat.

Kenji Hamada released his white-knuckled grip on the steering wheel and reached for the ignition switch as Tanaka opened the van's door. The two strangers arriving unexpectedly one after the other had given him a fright, and he was anxious to be gone.

"Not yet," Tanaka snapped, reaching across and seizing Kenji's wrist before he could turn the key. "We're not finished."

"What?"

"Beretta showed up." Tanaka reached into the van's backseat. "Shigeta sapped him as he came in, so he never saw us; but that second man just did."

Tanaka pulled a laundry sack from the backseat and handed it to his taciturn partner, Shigeta. The sack was heavy, and Kenji heard the clink of steel on steel. His stomach muscles knotted. "What's that?" Kenji asked, afraid he already knew. "What are you doing?"

"He *saw* us, Hamada-san—enough to guess we're Japanese. That could make trouble for you."

"No!" Kenji protested, but Tanaka cut him off.

"Our *oyabun* gave me strict instructions," Tanaka said curtly. "You may tell us *what* to do—but not how to do it."

As Reese reached the second floor, he pulled his automatic and slipped off the safety. He was sweating profusely as he strode the length of the dark corridor to Beretta's office door, and it was not just from the heat in the hall. He knocked sharply and stepped aside with his gun at the ready. There was no response.

Reese waited three seconds and twisted the doorknob. The door was unlocked, and he threw it open. "Al!" he called, still keeping clear of the open doorway, but again there was no response. Reese took a deep breath, crouched, and sprang inside, sweeping his gun in an arc as he scanned the office.

Beretta's body lay facedown on the floor of the empty room, and for a moment Reese thought he was dead. But as he went to one knee and started to roll him over, Beretta twitched and groaned. "Al!" Reese said loudly in Beretta's ear. "It's Reese. Al!"

Reese rolled Beretta onto his back, and the attorney jerked spasmodically and his eyes flew open. He gave Reese a wild, unseeing look, growled unintelligibly, and snorted fresh gobs of blood from an already bloodied nose.

"Aarcha-gargh," Beretta yelled, his glazed eyes rolling, and Reese held him fast as he started to struggle.

"Take it easy, Al. You're going to be okay."

"Mama," Beretta moaned, snorting more blood and twisting his head from side to side. Gradually his struggling became less violent, and his wild eyes finally focused Reese.

"That's it, Al. Take it easy."

"Oh," Beretta moaned weakly. "Oh, my head."

"What happened?" Reese asked loudly, trying to get through to him.

"Oh, my head. This *sucks!*" Beretta groaned, and he closed his eyes.

"You've got that right, but what happened? I just saw two Asians leaving the building. Were they in here?"

Beretta opened his eyes again. "I don't know," he moaned. "I came in . . . It was dark. That's all I remember. Christ, I'm seeing double."

"They must have been in here when you arrived. How did they get in? Who are they? Al, what the hell is going on?"

"Yakuza," Beretta said weakly. "Must be."

"What?"

"Yakuza. Hamada is involved with a Japanese crime syndicate. . . . Oh, my head hurts!"

"Stay still," Reese said as Beretta raised his head. "I'm going to call an ambulance."

Beretta was looking past Reese toward the open doorway, and suddenly his eyes went wide. He jerked upright, and Reese turned to look. Two dark silhouettes were outlined in the hallway against the light from the stairwell, and Reese reacted reflexively. An instant before two muzzle flashes flared in the corridor's darkness, he flung himself backward out of the line of fire.

A staccato popping like a string of small firecrackers erupted from the hallway, and a hail of bullets chewed up the carpet and slapped into the wall opposite the door. Reese hit the floor and skidded on his back. His convulsive backward leap had carried him to safety, but Beretta was a sitting target.

Beretta cried out, jerked twice, and fell backward, and the gunmen immediately shifted their aim. Bullets splintered the doorjamb nearest Reese. He rolled to the wall, scrambled to a crouch, and reached up and switched off the overhead light. For a moment after the office was plunged into darkness, the shooting stopped, but then the gunmen began firing again. They were squeezing off controlled, three- to five-shot bursts from submachine guns that were clearly equipped with silencers.

Whether or not they'd spotted the gun in Reese's hand, the two gunmen were taking no chances. They were advancing in tandem, raking the doorway to keep him at bay as they closed in. As soon as one man had to change magazines, the other began to fire, and Reese knew that if they reached the doorway he was dead.

Gritting his teeth against the roiling in his gut, he flattened himself on the floor and slid forward on his stomach to the edge of the doorway, where bullets splintered the doorjamb only inches from his head. His breath came in quick, short gasps, and his palm was slick with sweat as he tightened his grip on the Browning.

Reese had only thirteen rounds in the gun, so he couldn't afford to waste shots. He waited until the last possible moment, when he sensed that the nearest gunman was almost at the door. Then he angled up the barrel of the automatic, thrust his gun hand around the doorjamb, and fired blindly into the corridor.

The Browning's muzzle blasts were deafening, blotting out all other sound. Reese fired as rapidly as the bucking pistol allowed, but he counted his shots and stopped at eight. Ears ringing, he pulled back from the door, and only then did he realize that the gunmen were no longer firing.

He thought he heard a groan from the corridor, but the sound was covered by a fresh burst of automatic fire that raked the doorway. Reese scrabbled backward on his stomach as far from the door as he could go and steadied the Browning in a two-handed grip. His heart hammered, and stinging sweat ran down into his eyes, blurring his vision as he aimed at the doorway. His throat was raw from gasping, and his nostrils were filled with the stench of cordite hanging in the air.

A second short burst poured through the doorway and slapped into the opposite wall, but this time the firing seemed to be coming from farther down the corridor. Before the next burst, Reese heard panting and a dull groan, and his lips drew back from his teeth. He had hit one of the bastards!

The man still shooting was dragging his wounded partner back down the hall and firing sporadically to cover their retreat. Awash with adrenaline, Reese had to suppress the urge to try to get a shot at the man he'd missed. Abruptly the firing ceased, and Reese heard a thumping from the stairwell as the wounded man was dragged down the stairs.

Reese wiped the sweat from his eyes and, chest heaving, crawled to where Beretta lay. He couldn't see Beretta clearly in the darkness, but he could hear his breathing. He scrambled to his feet and went to the desk, which was in front of the window overlooking the parking lot. There was just enough stray light from outside to see the telephone. Still breathing hard, Reese lifted the receiver and dialed 911.

As Reese waited, he peered out the front window and saw that the minivan had been drawn up in front of the entrance. The driver might not have heard the silenced machine guns, but he'd certainly heard the Browning. The 911 dispatcher came on the line.

"A man's been shot," Reese said. "Two-twenty Ridge Road off Four Ninety-five's Exit Thirty-two. It's an office building, and he's in the corner office on the second floor. Number two-thirteen."

"What's your name, sir?" asked the dispatcher, and Reese hung up.

The minivan's driver was helping bundle the wounded man into the vehicle. The wounded man's partner, who carried two silenced Uzis, glanced up at the window and then climbed in. The driver jumped in behind the wheel and slammed the door. The minivan shot forward, wheels squealing, and sped out of the parking lot onto the deserted highway.

Reese strode to the doorway and flipped on the light to have a look at Beretta. Bright blood had soaked Beretta's shirt across the abdomen and was forming a spreading stain on the carpet. Beretta had also been hit in his right leg and high on the left arm, but there was no arterial spurting. It was the gut shot that was likely to kill him.

Reese was glad Beretta was unconscious. He'd seen too many men writhing in agony from a stomach wound. Quickly Reese scanned the room, looking for something that might have dropped from his pockets. He would have liked to have picked up his spent shells, in case there were readable fingerprints on them, but it would take too much time to find them all.

He looked at Beretta one last time and left the office. There was nothing he could do for the man. That was up to Beretta's god and the paramedics.

33

"Slow down!" Tanaka warned Kenji. "We don't want to be pulled over for speeding."

Kenji drew a ragged breath and tried to stop shaking. His hands were ice-cold and sticky with the blood that had soaked Shigeta's shirt. He'd never seen so much blood. In the rear of the van Shigeta was gasping and groaning horribly. ·

"Take Four Ninety-five south," Tanaka said as a sign appeared ahead.

"Can we get him to the doctor?" Kenji croaked, knowing that Tanaka had included a physician in his team.

"He can't help Shigeta," Tanaka said tonelessly. Then he added, "This is my fault, Hamada-san. Please accept my apology."

No, Kenji thought, shaking his head, *it's my own doing. The man in the office already dead, and Shigeta dying . . . My doing. Mine.*

Behind them, Shigeta cried out sharply, and Kenji almost missed the turnoff. The cry turned to a gurgle, and then there was silence. Tanaka turned in his seat and looked back. "He's dead."

Kenji felt he should say something, but he found no words. Intensifying his guilt was his relief that the horrifying groans had stopped. Out of the corner of his eye he saw Tanaka shift in his seat and pull something from his pocket. Slowly Tanaka extended his left arm and placed his hand flat against the dashboard, and Kenji caught the gleam of a knife blade.

"Don't!" Kenji cried as he realized what Tanaka was about to do, but Tanaka ignored him and placed the blade against the second joint of his little finger. True to *yakuza* tradition, Tanaka was going to slice off his finger in atonement.

"No!" Kenji barked, the pent-up strain and horror bursting out of him as anger. "I *forbid* it! You're still working for me, Tanaka. Cut off your finger on your own time."

For a long second, Tanaka continued to press the blade against his finger, but then he sat back and slipped the knife back into his pocket. "My apologies again, Hamada-san," Tanaka said with a deference that took Kenji aback. But then he understood. For the very first time, Kenji had given Tanaka a command.

"Did you find anything in Beretta's office?" Kenji asked, still struggling to master his shock.

"There was no paperwork, but we found a discarded envelope with a return address in the Vatican. That only confirms that he's working for the Christians on the island."

"The *Vatican?*" Are you sure?"

"Yes."

"But the Vatican is Catholic, Tanaka. Bobby Jordan's sect is entirely different. Why would Beretta be in contact with . . ." Kenji's voice trailed off as a possibility occurred to him.

"What are you thinking, Hamada-san?"

"That we may not be the only ones trying to get the sample back," Kenji said, amazed that he could think at all with Shigeta's agonized groans still ringing in his ears. "The sample was sent to us by a Catholic priest," he said, willing himself to concentrate, "and maybe they want it back. Suppose it has some religious significance. Maybe *that's* why

Jordan stole it. I never did understand how he could have found out about my experiments."

"Then why would he want to analyze the sample's DNA?"

"I don't know," Kenji said, trying to make sense of the puzzle, "but if Beretta *is* working for the Vatican, they must think the sample is on the island. How could they find out about me, except through a network trace? They must have broken into Jordan's computer and discovered I was doing the same."

Kenji lapsed into silence as conflicting possibilities darted randomly through his head. He could find no order in them, and he was too exhausted to continue to try.

"The man who came to see Beretta is still alive," Tanaka said, and Kenji knew he was being prompted. Beretta was dead and a witness had been left behind. Kenji had the police to reckon with now.

"I won't return to my apartment," he said, astonished by the steadiness of his voice, "in case someone comes looking for me. We'll have to move quickly now."

"To leave the country, or raid the island?"

For Kenji, there was nothing to decide. Two deaths had propelled him beyond the point of return. "There's no indication that Jordan has been forewarned. We'll raid. How soon can we go?"

"My men are ready, and I've arranged for a helicopter. But Shigeta was to be our pilot," Tanaka said with audible chagrin. "I didn't expect serious trouble tonight. It may take a few days to get a replacement."

"Do it."

34

All was quiet as Reese ran from the office building to his car. No cars were parked in front of the convenience store across the road, and although Reese couldn't see the clerk inside, he doubted the man had heard the shots. Still, he wasted no time in getting clear.

The adrenaline was draining from his system as he drove away, leaving him shaky and exhausted. A mile down the road, he pulled off into the parking lot of a shopping plaza and switched off the engine. His dry throat ached, and his body itched and tingled from drying sweat as he leaned back in his seat and briefly closed his eyes.

"Jesus," he breathed aloud, and looked at his watch. Twenty minutes past ten. It didn't seem possible that so little time had passed. Was Beretta still alive? No ambulance had passed Reese, and he hoped the paramedics were coming from the other direction. If they didn't get to Beretta soon, it would be too late.

Reese shoved the thought aside. He was on his own now, and time had to be running out. Hamada and his gangster friends were clearly after the relic, and now that they knew

Beretta was on to them, they were bound to act swiftly.

Yakuza was the word Beretta had used, and Reese had heard it before. Some sort of Japanese Mafia. That much Reese could believe, for the hoods he'd just seen in action were pros. But why were they after the relic? How far would they go to get it?

Beretta must have known, Reese thought bitterly. He must have known all along. Reese slammed his fist against the steering wheel. *Damn the man for holding out on me!*

Reese had hit the steering wheel too hard, and the pain cut through his useless anger. With Beretta out of the picture, only one person might give him a clue to Hamada's interest in the relic. Professor Singer.

Quickly Reese scanned the line of storefronts in the shopping plaza, seeking a pay phone. He spotted one at the far end and started up the car. He was going back to the island, no matter what, but if Singer could give him a better idea of what he was up against, Reese was determined to extract it.

As he pulled up in front of the pay phone and climbed stiffly out of his car, he heard a siren approaching. A police car raced past the shopping plaza, followed almost immediately by an ambulance. Late, Reese thought grimly. Too damned late.

He got Singer's number from information, dialed, and waited. Three rings . . . four . . . five . . . Reese's fingers drummed restlessly on the phone counter. *Be there, Singer. Damn it, be there!* He was about to give up when Singer finally answered. "Hello," came a hoarse, sleep-drugged voice.

"Professor Singer, this is John Reese."

"Who?"

"John *Reese*. Allison's father."

"Oh—Mr. Reese. What do you . . . ? What time is it?"

"Almost ten-thirty."

Reese heard Singer clear his throat. "Allison," Singer said, his tone becoming sympathetic. "How is she?"

"Still in a coma."

Two more police cars raced past the shopping center in the direction of the office building.

"I'm sorry," Singer said, embarrassment creeping into his voice. "I meant to stay in touch with you, but somehow—"

"I apologize for waking you up," Reese cut in, "but what I have to ask you is urgent."

"Urgent? I don't understand."

"When we spoke months ago, you told me about the archaeological sample you were analyzing. You said the results were interesting from a scientific point of view, but that they didn't make the sample valuable in any way."

"Yes, that's right."

"Are you absolutely sure of that?"

Perhaps because Reese was listening for it, he thought he caught the barest hesitation before Singer answered. "Yes, I'm sure. Why do you ask?"

Reese had met Singer only a few times, a cheerful man with a smiling, cherubic face that belied his age. Reese had liked him, and he tried to be patient.

"Is it possible that your postdoc Kenji Hamada knew something about those results that you didn't?"

This time the pause before Singer responded was measurable. "Why are you asking, Mr. Reese?"

"I'm not in a position to explain, Professor Singer." Reese was finding it hard to remain civil. Singer was trying to dodge. "But I have good reason to think that Doctor Hamada *did* consider the sample valuable."

"Mr. Reese, I . . . Believe me, I can imagine how troubled you must have been all this time, but please see things from my point of view. You call me in the middle of the night and ask me questions I've already answered, and you won't tell me why. With this air of mystery, you can't expect—"

Reese ran out of patience. "The air will be cleared quickly enough if I have to go to the police." He was sure that he heard an intake of breath at the other end of the line. "There's something about that sample that they haven't been told, and I don't think they'll be amused. *Obstruction of justice* is the phrase that comes to mind."

"Has Kenji talked to you?" Singer asked, suddenly sounding unsure of himself.

"I'm interested in what *you* know," Reese said, his voice rising. "My daughter is in a coma! The *least* you can do is be straight with me."

"But the theft was a fluke. It *had* to be. No one knew about . . ."

Reese's fingers tightened on the receiver. "No one knew about *what?*"

"You have to understand," Singer said hastily. "I wasn't lying when I said that the archaeological sample wasn't valuable to the fanatics who wrecked our lab. It couldn't be, because no one besides myself knew of Kenji's discovery."

"What discovery?"

Singer was still intent on defending himself. "I didn't give the information to the police," he rushed on, "because I knew it wouldn't help their investigation. And at the time, I thought Kenji might still salvage something from his experiments. It could have been a real scientific breakthrough, and I wanted him to have a chance to follow through."

Reese took a deep breath. "Water under the bridge," he said, forcing a calmer tone. "Please tell me what he discovered."

"A genetic anomaly in the DNA he extracted," Singer said in a low voice. "A gene was present that's not found in modern DNA. Kenji has considerable experience in creating hybrid DNA, and he incorporated copies of the foreign DNA segment into a culture of human somatic cells.

"The result was extraordinary. Somatic cells in culture have a limited life, Mr. Reese. They cannot grow and divide indefinitely. It's called cellular senescence, and it may be a cause of aging. But the cell culture with the hybrid DNA didn't die; it continued to grow. The cells were normal in all other respects, but they exhibited no senescence."

"Are you saying that the gene prevents aging?" Reese asked, taken aback.

"In cell cultures, yes, but the aging of an organism may depend on many other factors. Now, unfortunately, we'll never know. The cell cultures—and all of Kenji's records— were destroyed by those vandals. . . . Maybe I should tell the police," Singer added nervously.

"No, you're right. There'd be no point." Reese felt his anger slip away. Even if Singer had told the police originally, it wouldn't have led to Jordan. "But thank you for telling me."

"You're welcome," Singer said with audible relief.

"And I wouldn't mention this to Hamada. There's no point in getting him upset."

"No, of course not," Singer said quickly. "I quite understand."

Singer didn't understand a thing, of course, but as Reese terminated the conversation, the professor sounded too relieved to care.

Reese returned to his car and dropped into the seat behind the wheel, exhaustion at war with his need to return to the island. Now he knew why Hamada's gangster friends were willing to kill for Beretta's relic, and if their plant on the island was there to steal it, surely he would have made his move before now. No, they were going to raid Miracle Isle. He could feel it in his bones, and it chilled him.

Lara . . .

Again Reese heard a siren, and the ambulance he'd seen returned at high speed with its lights still flashing. It could only mean that Beretta was still alive. Reese hit the ignition switch and drove out of the parking lot in pursuit.

Beretta had questions to answer, and if he somehow managed to survive, the answers might yet give Reese an edge. Time was running out, but driving back up to Lambeth Cove tonight would gain him no more than a few hours, and besides, he desperately needed rest.

35

The early-morning sun slanted through a gap in the drapes screening the window of Beretta's hospital room. The man from Opus Dei lay inert with his eyes closed. A thin plastic tube snaked out of his left nostril, and an intravenous glucose drip fed into one arm. His eyes didn't flutter open until he heard the nurse warn Reese that he couldn't stay long.

"I wondered where you were," Beretta said weakly to Reese, "but I knew you'd come." He tried to smile as he spoke, but all he managed was a feeble grimace. His closely trimmed black beard emphasized his pallor, and dark circles were under his eyes. His fleshy cheeks were now sunken, as if someone had let the air out.

"Don't tire him," the nurse sternly warned Reese. "The doctors did a marvelous job and he's incredibly lucky, but you can't stay for more than a few minutes."

Beretta's eyes rolled toward the nurse with obvious dislike as she left the room. "How did you get past the dragon?" he asked when the door closed behind her.

"I lied. If anyone asks, I'm your half brother. I saw them

let the cops in to see you, so they couldn't refuse me."

Beretta's eyelids drooped and then closed. "Doped up," he said groggily. "You're a lucky bastard, Reese. How did you get away?"

"I was carrying."

"Carrying? Carrying what?"

"A pistol. If I hadn't had it with me, we'd both be in the morgue. What did you tell the police?"

"Nothing," Beretta said, his voice barely above a whisper, but he opened his eyes again. "They didn't mention you, so neither did I. Told them I didn't know what happened."

"And they bought that—with your office riddled with bullets?"

"No, but what can they do?" Beretta's lips twitched into another feeble smile. "Who was it, Reese? *Yakuza?*"

"Who else? How long have you known about them, you bastard?"

Beretta weakly shook his head in protest. "I didn't have a clue. Only just found out. Hamada's father is a crime boss, Reese—big one. Who'd have figured that? Don't know why they . . ."

Beretta's voice drifted off, and his breathing deepened.

"Al!" Reese said sharply. "Al, do your people know what's happened to you?"

"People?"

"Opus Dei. Do they know?"

"Yes . . . Moving me to a private clinic soon. But you can still reach me by phone at the number I gave you before," Beretta breathed. "Beeper service will get through to me."

"Your kidding yourself."

"Down, but not out," Beretta whispered, and he closed his eyes again. "What are you going to do now, Reese? I've got to know."

"I'm going back. But from here on out, Al, I'm on my own. You're out of it."

"No," Beretta protested feebly. "I can help you."

"How?"

"Listen!" Beretta whispered fiercely, and the effort silenced him for several seconds. "I've made arrangements.

You can call for a helicopter pickup if you have to get off the island fast. Don't need to contact me. Just call the number—anytime. Pilot's good. He'll take you out no matter what.''

"Do you remember the number?'' Reese asked quickly. He still didn't trust Beretta, but it was an offer he couldn't refuse.

To Reese's amazement, Beretta recited the phone number, and Reese committed it to memory.

"There's a cellular phone in my car,'' Beretta added, his voice again barely above a whisper. "Still parked outside the office. Take it, in case you can't use a phone on the island. Car keys on the nightstand. Take them. I knew you'd come, Reese. I knew . . .''

Reese went to the nightstand and scooped up the keys, and as he turned back, he heard Beretta whisper something he didn't catch.

"What?''

"Wasn't going to tell you,'' Beretta croaked, "but now I think I must.''

"Tell me what?''

"Lara Brooks, Reese. She's working for me.''

For a moment Reese was too surprised to respond. "What do you mean, she's working for you?''

Beretta coughed and groaned with pain at the spasm. He raised his hand and feebly waved off the question. "She'll tell you . . .'' he muttered, closing his eyes.

"Damn it, Al, wake up,'' Reese snapped in anger. He could see that Beretta wouldn't be able to talk much longer. "What else haven't you told me? What about the *yakuza?*'' he demanded, sure now that Beretta was holding out on him. And as much as he wanted to know about Lara, there was a more vital question. "I have to find out who they planted on the island.''

"No idea,'' Beretta protested weakly as his eyes fluttered open. "I don't even know what they're after.''

"No?'' Reese responded, unwilling to believe him. "Even I know that much. The secret of eternal life.''

"What?''

"I already know Hamada found something in your relic's DNA that may prevent aging, so you can stop playing dumb."

Beretta's eyes widened, and Reese heard his sharp intake of breath. "Reese!" he gasped. "Is that true?"

Reese was taken aback by the strength of Beretta's reaction, and for once Reese believed him. Beretta hadn't known.

"Al, are you all right?"

"Is it *true?*"

"How do I know?"

"Reese, please. You *must* retrieve the finger."

"Finger? The relic is a finger?"

"Yes," Beretta hissed in an exhausted sigh. His eyes closed again, and he barely managed to speak. "I have to tell you now. You've got to know how important . . ."

"Tell me what?" Reese pressed as Beretta started to slide under again.

"Not a relic of Saint Stephen. Scrolls say it's the finger of Christ."

36

Something went wrong," Lara said to her technician, looking at the developed film Kuroda had brought her. "These bands here just aren't sharp enough."

"I'm sorry," he said with chagrin. "I'll do another run right away."

"Don't worry about it. It just happens sometimes."

But Kuroda apologized again and slunk from her office, leaving Lara feeling guilty. She should have done the work herself, she thought. Lara still used the outdated Maxim-Gilbert method to spot-check the results from the automated sequencers, but Kuroda was unfamiliar with the procedure, which was as tedious as it was accurate.

Restless, she took her cigarettes from her handbag and rose to go outside for a smoke. Ever since Reed had left, he'd hovered in her thoughts, and she'd found it increasingly difficult to concentrate on her work as she awaited his return. Why had he left so abruptly? she wondered.

Was there a genuine problem with the computer, or had something gone wrong with Beretta's plans? Only three days ago, that possibility wouldn't have worried her, but it did now. She couldn't be sure that Beretta had sent Reed to steal the relic, but why else had he come? And if so, she worried, what risks was he prepared to run? Reed was nothing like Beretta, yet he had to be an Opus Dei operative, and he might be as driven.

As she walked through the corridor toward the lab's main room, she heard Jeff and Lou in Lou's office, enthusing over Bobby Jordan's imminent arrival. Rumor had it that the great man was going to preach a special televised message from Miracle Isle. Lara couldn't have cared less, but she was aware of the change that had come over her.

The born-again fervor of the Miracle Isle staff no longer got on her nerves. She even thought more charitably of Beretta, for however unwittingly, he had brought her and Reed together. Over and over, Lara's head told her that she still hardly knew Reed, but her heart told her otherwise. That evening on the dock, something inside them had seemed to meld, and Lara couldn't believe it had been an illusion.

A half dozen technicians were hard at work in the main room, and every sequencer was in operation. Michaels's own technician was there, too, processing another batch of DNA for the lab director. Michaels's technician was a squirrelly, officious young man with beady eyes behind rimless spectacles. In contrast to the others on Miracle Isle, he wore a permanently earnest expression.

At the moment, he was at the lab bench reserved for him, writing in his notebook. As Lara approached, he closed the book and left the bench, giving her a perfunctory smile as he walked past. Lara was about to turn toward the exit when her eyes caught a flash of metal on his bench that stopped her in her tracks. Lying beside his notebook were his keys.

The technician was heading for the chemical storage room, and in a moment he would be out of sight. Lara warned herself not to overreach, but the temptation was too great to resist. At most, she told herself, she risked embarrassment— nothing compared to the risk Reed would run by breaking into Michaels's lab. And with a key, Reed could slip in at will.

How long would the technician be inside the storage

room? Thirty seconds? At least that, and probably longer.
But how to copy the key? Lara had seen it done in movies,
but she had no clay to make an impression. Maybe she could
trace its outline.

Still hesitant, she moved to the technician's bench, trying
to appear casual as she looked around her. All the other technicians were concentrating on their own work, and no one
was looking her way. As Michaels's technician disappeared
into the storage room, temptation overcame caution, and Lara
slipped out the pen and pocket notebook she carried in her
lab coat.

One key on the technician's ring looked like the key to
the main lab, which Lara carried but never needed to use.
That seemed the best bet, and she didn't have the nerve to
try to trace more than one. She took a deep breath and a last,
nervous look around and reached for the keys.

She continued to tell herself that all she risked was embarrassment, but still her heart pounded as she hastily traced
the key's outline into the notebook. She was finished in seconds, and as she pocketed the notebook and looked around,
she sighed silently in relief. No one appeared to have noticed.

With a secret smile of satisfaction, she left the laboratory.
Several youngsters were out and about in the quadrangle, and
Lara headed for the front of the compound. As soon as she
was out of sight of them, she settled into the grass to the
right of the Crystal Chapel. Crossing her fingers, she compared her own lab key to the outline she had traced, and she
grinned in triumph.

As she'd hoped, the key she'd traced appeared to be a
master that opened the main lab, as well. It had fewer teeth
than hers, and to duplicate it, all she had to do was file down
bits of her own key to match. Still grinning, she got up and
headed for the machine shop in the maintenance building. It
wouldn't be difficult to make up an excuse to borrow a file.

Lara still couldn't be sure that she'd selected the right key
from the technician's ring, but she was feeling lucky.

In the season of wind, before the earth quakes and the fire comes, shall the Second Book be opened. Then shall the Chosen One speak to the Nations: Fear Him that made heaven and earth, for the hour of His judgment is come.

—SAMARIA SCROLL I, FRAGMENT 32

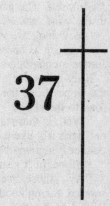

37

The summer's final spate of muggy weather had pushed up into Maine, and as the *Mary Jane* entered Miracle Isle's harbor, the sticky heat seemed to close in. Reese rose from his seat and moved up to the wheelhouse.

"Yuh don't look so bad this time," Jarvis said, eyeing Reese.

"I took a pill," Reese responded distractedly.

He had called Miracle Isle immediately after leaving Beretta, and he'd made it up to Lambeth Cove in record time, but he could almost hear the clock ticking. Not even twenty-four hours had passed since the *yakuza* had gunned down Beretta, but how much time did he have?

Squinting against the hazy sun's glare off the glassy waters, he looked toward the dock, half expecting to find Lara waiting, but the dock was deserted. He would have been disappointed in any event, but his desire to see her again was shot through with anxious urgency.

He would have to set things straight with her and get her off the island at once. Reese didn't even try to guess how she was connected with Beretta; he would find out soon enough.

"Want a snort?" Jarvis asked, pulling out his pint bottle. Reese shook his head, and Jarvis took a long, gurgling swig for himself. The gaunt, old Mainer was already four sheets to the wind, and Reese wondered if he was on a binge.

"How long are yuh stayin' this time?"

"As long as necessary," Reese replied, looking up toward Jordan's compound.

Billy-Lee's Jeep had appeared on the road at the top of the slope above the harbor, and it started down the winding road to the shore.

"Well, if yuh stay too long tomorrow, you're gonna find out what it's like to be on an island in the middle of a hurricane. It's gonna be a big blow."

"I thought it's supposed to hit land much farther south."

"Aw, those weather guys don't know shit," Jarvis snorted, taking another swig of whiskey. "That's what I told Billy-Lee, but the stupid bastard didn't listen. I told him, this ain't no time for a shindig."

"What shindig?"

Jarvis shrugged. "I dunno, but the ferry's comin' this afternoon with a mess of people for some celebration tomorrow. And Billy-Lee's old man is flyin' in today."

"*Jordan* is coming?"

"Aayuh. And if that whirlybird of his is still here when the hurricane hits, he won't have nothin' left to fly."

Belatedly, Reese recalled Lara telling him that Bobby Jordan would be coming to Miracle Isle, and he could hardly believe he'd forgotten.

Billy-Lee had reached the bottom of the slope by the ferry slip, and he sped up the shore road. As the *Mary Jane* pulled in, Billy-Lee braked sharply in front of the dock and got out of the Jeep. Jarvis climbed onto the dock, and Reese tossed up the sternline and then lifted out the small overnight bag he'd picked up at home.

In addition to the Browning, ammunition, and the cellular phone Reese had retrieved from Beretta's car, he'd brought a set of rough clothing and boots. It had been an afterthought that he couldn't have explained, but he wanted to be prepared for any eventuality.

As Jarvis tied up the boat, Reese climbed out and turned to face Billy-Lee, who came striding out along the dock atop his elevator shoes. Even considering the muggy weather, Billy-Lee seemed overheated. Sweat glistened in the creases of his thick neck and dampened his thinning, sandy hair, ruining its blow-dried look.

"It's about time you got back," he huffed at Reese.

"Why? What's the problem?"

"Our new computer isn't on-line," Billy-Lee snapped. "That's the problem."

"It will be soon."

"I hope so! My daddy's flying in today, and he's expecting to see results."

"Well, in that case, I'll get right on it. I wouldn't want to get you into trouble with your daddy."

As anxious as Reese was to speak to Lara, he had to keep up appearances. And besides, the sooner he pumped Fletch, the better. He had yet to identify the *yakuza* informant on the island, and Fletch might help. There couldn't be many staffers who'd had the opportunity to steal a Super-User password.

"Hey, welcome back!" Fletch exclaimed with a broad, freckle-faced grin as Reese came into the computer room. He brushed back the recalcitrant shock of blond hair from his forehead and extended his hand.

"Thanks," Reese said, smiling in return. Fletch might be a religious zealot, but it was impossible not to like him.

"Where's the new hardware?"

Reese put on a grimace. "Trip was a complete waste of time. It *was* a problem in the software, after all. A small one, but well hidden. They didn't find out until I got down there."

"Gee, that's a shame."

"Well, we're all set now, so no harm done. Any problems crop up while I was gone?" Reese took a seat before the console and checked the system status.

"Nothing the new computer won't fix. Dr. Mike has really been loading down the system."

"I'll say he is. What's going on?"

"He's trying to finish up some special project in time for Brother Jordan's arrival. Did you know Bobby Jordan is flying in today?"

"Yeah, I heard."

"There'll be a party tonight and a special service in the Crystal Chapel tomorrow morning." Fletch took a seat beside Reese. His eyes were bright with excitement. "You got back just in time."

"Why?"

"For the service tomorrow! It's going to be really terrific," Fletch said excitedly. "Bobby Jordan has had a revelation, and tomorrow he's going to deliver God's message right from Miracle Isle! They'll be taping the service for a special television broadcast."

"What message?"

"We don't know yet, but, John, you've got to come! I'm sure there'll never be a better opportunity to feel the Spirit move you. Bobby Jordan is something *else,* and if you let him, I know he can change your life forever."

He already has, Reese thought bitterly, but he managed a neutral smile. "How much longer is Dr. Michaels going to be running all these programs?"

"Well, he asked for priority until five-thirty."

"Okay, I guess I can hold off, but Billy-Lee wants the new computer on-line today. Why don't you put a message on the system that we'll be shutting down for half an hour at five-thirty."

"Sure." Fletch immediately began typing in the necessary commands.

Reese decided it was time to probe. "So," he said casually, "no troubles at all with the new software?"

"Nope, but I do have some questions when you have the time."

"What about that technician you mentioned? The one who filled in as an operator. Do you think I should have a session with him?"

Fletch shook his head. "I could explain the changes myself, but he's not going to be available anyway. He's working for Lara full-time."

"Has anyone else helped you run the system?"

"No. Only Kiru Kuroda."

Reese blinked, hardly believing it could be that easy. "Lara's technician is Japanese?"

"That's right," Fletch said, finishing up and turning away from the keyboard. "You probably noticed him in the dining hall. He's our only Asian."

"No, I didn't."

But from now on, he thought with grim satisfaction, it was Kiru Kuroda who would have to watch his back.

"Well," Reese said, pushing back his chair and getting up to leave, "I guess there's no point in my hanging around. I'll be back at five-thirty."

"Why don't you look up Lara? She was in here a couple of times, asking when you'd be back. If you ask me," Fletch added with a grin and a good-natured wink, "she has more than a passing interest in you."

"Is that right?"

Fletch's grin widened. "And I'm not the only one who thinks so."

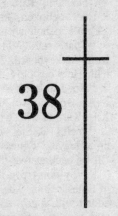

38

Lara watched the multicolored tracery of graph lines on the video screen as her technician changed the readout parameters of the laser sequencer he was using. Kuroda had seemed nervously preoccupied all day, and she wondered what was on his mind. She heard a man's footsteps behind her, and a voice said, "Hi."

"John!" Lara exclaimed, turning eagerly. Too eagerly, she thought, self-consciously aware of Kuroda listening. "When did you get in?"

"Just now," Reed said, returning her smile, and then he looked past her at Kuroda.

Lara introduced them, and Kuroda hastened to his feet and extended his hand. "Pleased to meet you, Mr. Reed."

"Same here. Don't let me disturb you."

Reed was smiling as he spoke, but as Kuroda sat back down and turned away, Lara thought she caught a puzzling flicker of hostility in Reed's expression.

"What's the story with the computer?" she asked, clinging to the banal to cover her flush of pleasure at Reed's return; and she immediately chided herself. Why should she care what her technician might or might not think?

"I should have it back on-line by late this afternoon. Dr. Michaels has a mess of programs running right now, so I decided to hold off shutting down the system. I guess I'm at loose ends for a while . . .''

Lara smiled happily at the obvious hint. "Want some company?''

"Sure. Care for a walk? I'm still a little woozy from the *Mary Jane*.''

"Okay," Lara said, slipping off her lab coat.

As they left the laboratory she resolved to tell Reed about her involvement with Beretta at once. From now on, she wanted no barriers between them.

In contrast to the air-conditioned lab, the atmosphere outside seemed positively steamy. "Why don't we go down to the shore?'' Lara suggested, but Reed shook his head.

"Let's take a walk into the woods,'' he said, and to Lara's surprise, he suddenly seemed tense.

"All right. There's a path behind the maintenance building that leads out to the northeastern end of the island.''

"Good.'' Reed turned toward the rear of the compound, and as Lara fell into step beside him, he quickened their pace.

"John . . . is something wrong?''

"I just don't want people seeing us together more often than necessary. Tongues are beginning to wag.''

Lara laughed. "Is there something wrong with that?''

"I don't want us seen together any more than necessary,'' Reed said tensely. "Things are about to pop, and the aftermath could be messy. So far, you're probably in the clear, but I don't want anyone ever to suspect that you've been working for Beretta.''

"You *know?*'' Lara exclaimed, stopping short.

"I do now.'' Reed took her arm and tugged her into motion again. "Beretta told me this morning.''

"John, I was going to tell you, but I—''

"It doesn't matter,'' Reed cut in, walking her past the end of the clinic building and out of sight of the quadrangle. "What does matter is that we get things straight now. What are you doing here?''

"Didn't he tell you?"

"No," Reed said curtly. "All I know is that you're working for him."

"I'm *not* 'working' for him. I only came here for my brother's sake. Roger is a Jesuit priest who teaches at Georgetown, and—"

"Not Father Roger Wilson?"

"Yes."

"But your name is Brooks."

"That was my married name, and I didn't bother changing it. How do you know my brother?"

"I don't, really, but I spoke with him on the phone once," Reed said, staring at her. "Are you telling me that you're here just because your brother *asked you?*"

"No!" Lara exclaimed. "John, he would *never* have asked this of me. Roger has no idea I'm here. Beretta approached me on his own. It was he who persuaded me to come."

"What hook did he use?" Reed asked grimly.

"I told you—my brother. You see, Roger believes the relic is genuine, and apparently he blames himself for its loss. I can't begin to understand why he took it so hard, but I know it was tearing him up inside. When Beretta asked me to help get the relic back, I just couldn't refuse."

"Why not? You just told me that your brother wouldn't have asked."

They had skirted the maintenance building behind the clinic, and Reed spotted the gap in the pines bordering the rear of the compound and headed for it.

"I . . . It's not easy to put into words. John, all my life, Roger has been there for me when I needed him. And there were times . . . Look, I don't expect you to understand, but this was my first chance to do something for him, and I had to take it.

"What Beretta proposed was easy enough for me to do. I'd already been granted a sabbatical leave, so I was free to take a position anywhere I wanted. And Beretta was only asking me to apply for a job here and to keep my eyes open."

"Only?" Reed responded incredulously.

"Yes, only," Lara replied defensively. "Beretta promised that I wouldn't be involved further—and that the reason for my coming would be a secret strictly between him and me. That's why he didn't tell you about me—and why I followed Beretta's suggestion that I tell you about Michaels indirectly."

"I see." Reed looked away. "And that's why you were on the dock when I arrived—and why you went out of your way to be friendly."

"Yes, at first . . ." Lara halted and caught Reed's arm. "But that wasn't why I walked down to the harbor with you that evening, John—or why I'm with you now."

Reed looked at her questioningly for a moment, and then he smiled slowly. "I'm glad."

"Me, too," Lara replied, returning his smile. "Even if you are an Opus Dei man."

"Is *that* what you think?" Reed responded in obvious surprise. "Lara, I'm strictly Opus Atheist. Didn't Beretta tell you about me?"

"No, John, nothing. All I knew was that a Compstar rep was coming who was working for him. I just assumed . . ."

Reese saw Lara's confusion, and he realized that he wasn't the only one Beretta had kept in the dark. "What did he tell you about the relic we're after?"

"That it might be a relic of Saint Stephen preserved by a magician's cult. They thought they could work magic by conjuring the saint's spirit, and for the incantations to be effective, they had to possess a part of his body."

"That's more than he told me," Reese said grimly, "but he didn't level with you, either. It isn't a relic of Saint Stephen. It's supposedly the finger of Christ."

Lara stared at him in disbelief. "You can't be serious."

"Beretta was."

For a moment Lara continued to stare at him incredulously, but then Reese saw the disbelief fade from her eyes. "My God," she whispered, half to herself. "Now I understand. No wonder Roger was so shaken."

"Understand what?" Reese asked, mystified. "How could

a Catholic priest possibly accept the idea that Jesus' body was stolen from the tomb?''

"He wouldn't, John. That can't be what the scrolls claim. Maybe they simply say that a finger was cut from the body. That wouldn't necessarily violate the faith. And suppose it were true. For the Church, the finger would be a holy relic beyond any price. That makes sense, doesn't it?''

"I don't know, and at this point I don't much care. Lara, I'm here for my own reasons, and I want to get things straight between us.

"My name is Reese, not Reed, and I don't moonlight as a Compstar rep. Beretta put in the fix with the company, and they gave me a crash course for the role. Beretta approached me only last month, but he had the right bait. The relic, Lara. That's the proof I need to put Bobby Jordan behind bars.''

"I'm not sure I understand.''

"You don't recognize my name, do you?''

"No . . . Should I?''

"There was a graduate student in Singer's lab when Jordan's goons broke in.'' Reese felt his face harden into a mask. "Her name is Allison Reese. She's my daughter.''

"Oh, no!'' Lara gasped.

"She's in a coma,'' Reese said, and in spite of himself his voice grated hoarsely. "She'll never come out of it.''

"Oh, God, John,'' Lara whispered, reaching out to touch him. "I'm so sorry. It's . . . It must be horrible for you.''

Something in her voice uncannily reflected the anguish Reese still felt when he awoke in the middle of the night, and he blinked and looked away.

"You're going to try to steal the relic back yourself, aren't you,'' he heard Lara say in a hollow voice.

"I'll bring the bastard down, if it's the last—''

Reese felt Lara's fingers tighten anxiously about his arm, and he caught himself.

"Lara, you don't have to worry,'' he said, turning back to her. "You're leaving. I want you to leave here today.''

"What?'' Lara was taken aback. "Today?''

"Yes, you have to leave right away. Make any excuse you

like. Tell them your brother has had a heart attack—
anything. It doesn't matter.''

''But *why?*'' Lara asked, blinking in confusion.

''Believe me, the less you know the better. Please just trust
me. It isn't safe for you to stay here.''

''Not safe for me? What about *you?*''

''Lara, this is something I have to do. It's my problem,
not yours.''

''How can you *say* that? Not after we . . . John, you can't
expect me to just pack up and leave now that I know why
you're here. I can help you. I *want* to help you!''

''You don't understand. You *can't* stay.''

Lara stared at him for a moment. ''You don't think I can
help, do you?'' She dug into her pocket. ''Think again.'' She
pulled out a ring of keys. ''This one is a key to Michaels's
lab.''

''But how did you get it?'' Reese asked, completely dis-
tracted by the unexpected stroke of luck.

Lara grinned. ''I copied the key his technician had. And
don't worry, it works. I've tried it.''

''That's terrific! You've solved my biggest problem.''

''But not your only one,'' Lara said quickly. ''Even if you
get into Michaels's lab, how will you know where to look?
God knows how long it would take you to search the whole
lab. But *I'd* know, John. We could slip in together and—''

''No!'' Reese cut in sharply. ''As of right now, you're out
of this. You're leaving today.''

''Wait a minute,'' Lara protested, bridling. ''You can't
just shoo me away.''

''That's not what I'm—'' Reese broke off, floundering. It
hadn't occurred to him that Lara might resist leaving. ''Lara,
please. You can't stay. There's too much risk.''

''And even more for you, if you go it alone,'' Lara replied
insistently. ''Those guards Billy-Lee hired aren't going to let
you waltz off the island if you're caught—and Jordan has
plenty of influence. John, you could be the one who ends up
in jail.''

''But I'm not just worried about Jordan. You don't know
the half of it.''

"No? Then why don't you tell me?"

For a moment, Reese hesitated. He had wanted to tell her as little as possible—to limit her involvement in every way—but nothing was more important to him now than getting her off the island and out of harm's way.

"Okay," he said, taking her arm, "but we've been standing here too long as it is."

By the time Reese finished talking, they had nearly reached the tip of the island. Coming at Lara all at once, she found it almost too much to absorb, and the new fears Reese had conjured tore at her two ways at once. The shooting of Beretta had shocked her, and if there was chance at all that Reese was right about the *yakuza,* Lara wanted to leave—but not without Reese.

Her own anxiety only intensified her concern for him as she recalled the hatred in his voice as he'd spoken of Jordan. He didn't seem to care about the risk to himself, but she did—and she knew she could help him.

Reese was watching her, waiting for her response. But she didn't know . . . God, she had to try to think.

"How did Beretta react when you told him about Hamada's discovery?" she asked just to give herself time.

"It seemed to shake him up," Reese replied, barely able to contain his impatience, "but what difference does it make?"

Why was she asking irrelevant questions? Hadn't he gotten through to her? "The *yakuza,* Lara. That's what we have to worry about."

"I know," she replied, but her eyes slid away and she moved ahead of him to the end of the forest path.

Her silence as Reese followed her out to the edge of the plateau filled him with foreboding. What was there to think about? Didn't she see why she had to leave?

They halted on a rock ledge overlooking the sea. Below them the surf broke languidly against the shore's black rocks, and the only other sound was an occasional cry from the gulls wheeling overhead. The vista's serenity seemed to mock Reese's anxiety. If Lara refused, there was no way to force her to go.

"Lara, we don't have all that much time. We have to make sure that Jarvis will take you off today."

She turned and looked up at him questioningly. "Do you really expect them to raid the island—pirate style?"

"Yes," Reese snapped in exasperation. "That's exactly what I think. If they were going to rely on Kuroda to swipe the finger, he'd have made his move long before now."

Lara stiffened. "And what else do you think? That I'm too ditsy to understand the situation?"

"No, but . . . Lara, these guys are deadly serious, and they know they're running out of time. You've got to leave now."

"Will you come with me?"

Her question caught Reese off guard. "You know why I have to stay."

"Yes," Lara said, and took a deep breath, "and I know you want me to go. But do you know that Bobby Jordan is flying in this evening?"

"What does that matter?"

"Because there's going to be a big celebration tonight and tomorrow, and Jordan is bringing an entourage. Kuroda knows that, and if the *yakuza* do intend to raid the island, don't you think they'll at least wait until it's over and all the extra people have left?"

"Maybe," Reese said, feeling forced to answer, "but I wouldn't count on it."

"But you *know* it's a good bet, and that means tonight is the time to go for the finger. With my help—"

"I don't *want* your help, Lara," Reese burst out. "I want you to leave!"

Under any other circumstances, Reese would have admired her nerve, but not now. She might understand the danger, but he was sure she didn't *feel* it. How could she? To her, violence was only a word.

"Calm down, John, and give me a chance. Think about it. I'll know where to look for the finger. We can slip into Michaels's lab tonight—quick in, and quick out—and leave immediately on Jarvis's boat."

"How? What do you mean?"

"I'm sure I could set it up," Lara said hastily. "Steve's an odd character, but we get along. He likes me, John, and with a little cash as an incentive, I think he'd be willing to take us off the island—even in the small hours of the morning.

"And what if worse comes to worst?" Lara rushed on. "Suppose the *yakuza* do come tonight. We won't be asleep, and we'll be on our guard. We can slip off into the woods."

Reese saw he was losing, and he felt fear settle in his gut like a cold stone. For the first time, he was afraid of what might happen on Miracle Isle.

"Please, Lara. I don't want to have to worry about you!"

"But I'm not a child you have to protect. And you know you have a better chance with me than without me."

"Maybe so," Reese lashed out before he could stop himself, "but it's my daughter they turned into a vegetable— *not yours.*"

Lara reacted as if she'd been slapped, and for a moment she stared wordlessly at Reese. But then she took a deep breath and said evenly, "That was a cheap shot, but it won't work. I know it makes sense for me to help you, and so do you. You're stuck with me, John Reese—whether you like it or not."

"*Shit!*"

To Reese's surprise, Lara laughed, and with that laugh he knew with absolute certainty that he'd lost.

"Well? Do you want me to speak to Jarvis?"

Despite Reese's gnawing anxiety, he recognized that her impromptu plan might work, and falling in with it—at least initially—might be the best way to keep her under his wing. He would have to play the rest by ear.

"If you're sure he won't go running to Billy-Lee," he said reluctantly, and Lara grinned.

"He won't. He *hates* Billy-Lee."

At that moment, they heard the distant drone of an aircraft engine. It grew steadily in intensity until it was overlaid by the *whap-whap-whap* of helicopter blades. "That must be Bobby Jordan," Lara said. "He's early."

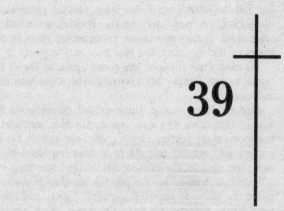

39

A welcoming supper party was being held for Bobby Jordan, and the dining hall was filled to capacity. Crowded in with the Miracle Isle staff were the musicians, gospel singers, and TV technicians Jordan had ferried in to tape tomorrow morning's service in the Crystal Chapel. The room reverberated with excited chatter and laughter, and Reese immediately picked up an electric undercurrent of excitement.

As he moved along the fringes of the crowd, he heard the same phrases repeated again and again. *Bobby Jordan has had a revelation. Bobby Jordan is bringing a special message from God.* The crowd awaited Jordan's appearance like overgrown children at a Christmas party waiting for Santa Claus, and Reese noted only five of the staff who appeared immune to the excitement.

Johnson, the burly, hawk-faced security chief, stood apart from the crowd with his three muscular, crew-cut men. All four looked bored, and they obviously wished they were elsewhere. And then there was Kiru Kuroda. He stood with an animated group of young people, smiling with polite disinterest.

Did he know what was going to happen? Or when? As Lara had suggested, the *yakuza* might not raid until the extras had left the island, but Reese wasn't taking chances. Beneath his jacket, he was carrying the Browning tucked into his waistband. If they did come, he expected them in the small hours of the morning, but that was only a guess.

Worriedly he scanned the room again to see if Lara had come in yet. Simply not knowing where she was made him nervous.

Minutes later, Reese glimpsed her entering on the other side of the room. She was looking for him, too, and through the momentary parting in the crowd she caught his eye. She smiled and started toward him, drawing sidelong glances from the men as she passed. She looked stunning.

Lara had dressed for the party in an elegant pants suit that made the most of her slight, girlish figure, and for the first time Reese was seeing her in makeup. With her dark eyebrows and lashes and clear, ivory skin, she hardly needed it, but the effect was still dramatic. A touch of eyeshadow highlighted her deep blue eyes, and lipstick drew attention to the delicate curve of her lips.

At any other time, in any other place, she would have taken Reese's breath away, but not here. Not now.

"Gee, don't look so happy to see me," Lara chided as she came up to him.

"Have you talked to Jarvis?"

"Yes," Lara said, her eyes alight with conspiratorial excitement, "and the fix is in. He'll take us off the island as soon as we're ready, and it only cost me a hundred bucks. Not bad, right?"

"What did you tell him?"

"Don't *worry,* I was very discreet." Lara arched an eyebrow. "What's the matter? Don't tell me I'm still in the doghouse."

"You're still on the island. That's what's the matter."

"Stop complaining. We're going tonight, aren't we? Into Michaels's lab and right back out again—and then down to the *Mary Jane.*"

"Sure. As easy as falling off a log."

Lara ignored his tone. "When shall I come by your room with the key? Late, right? Uh-oh, here comes Fletch. Where's your room?" she asked hurriedly.

"Second floor. Two-ten."

"Hey, you two!" Fletch called over the noise of the crowd, and they turned toward him.

"Great party, isn't it?" Fletch enthused. His freckled cheeks were flushed and his blond hair was damp, and Reese wondered if the punch was spiked.

"It would be better with booze," Lara responded, answering the question.

"No way!" Fletch said gaily. "We've got something better. We've got the Holy Spirit. Listen, you two. You've got to come to chapel tomorrow. You've *got* to hear Bobby Jordan."

"In a sunrise service?" Reese asked.

"You won't have that as an excuse." Fletch laughed. "Breakfast will be late, and the service won't begin until ten. Will you come?"

"Sure," Reese said, taking the line of least resistance.

"Great," Fletch said, turning to Lara. "What about you?"

At that moment there was a stir at the far end of the room, and the crowd burst into excited applause as a grinning Billy-Lee ushered in Bobby Jordan and his entourage. Jordan was holding hands with a blond woman Reese assumed was his wife, and they were followed by a shy, young couple barely out of their teens. An ecstatically smiling Dr. Michaels brought up the rear.

Lara leaned close to Reese and nudged him in the ribs. "Lighten up," she warned under cover of the applause.

Reese realized that he was staring fixedly at Jordan, and he deliberately relaxed his facial muscles.

In contrast to Billy-Lee, Bobby Jordan was tall, slim, and vigorously handsome, with a patrician visage that reminded Reese of Billy Graham in his younger days. He had commanding eyes, a high, broad forehead, and wavy, dark hair, gone gray at the temples. Despite his wife's spiked heels, Jordan towered over her.

She was a curvaceous, attractive woman still young

enough to get away with bottle-blond hair and flashy makeup, and she exuded a cool, controlled sexiness. Although she looked up at her husband with apparent devotion, Reese had the immediate impression that she had the dominant personality.

"Folks!" cried Billy-Lee, clearly basking in his father's reflected glory. "You all know my daddy and Lurleen!"

This provoked intensified applause, and Jordan beamed.

His wife's smile was less effusive, and rather than reveling in the crowd's reaction, she seemed to be assessing it. Even from a distance, her eyes had a steely look. Reese suspected that she was the one who counted the money.

As the applause subsided, Jordan raised his arms. "Praise the Lord!" he called out in a rich baritone. "I can feel the power of the Holy Spirit here right now! Can you?"

"Yes!" cried a girl in the crowd, and throughout the dining hall arms stretched heavenward, accompanied by a chorus of hallelujahs and fervent shouts of "Praise God!"

"Friends!" Jordan called, stretching out his arms to still the crowd. "I thank you for your welcome. Lurleen and I sure do appreciate it. Don't we, honey?" he said, turning to his wife.

"Yes, we do," Lurleen Jordan responded with canned enthusiasm, and her southern drawl was far more pronounced than her husband's light, Louisiana accent.

"And . . ." Jordan added loudly, cutting off the renewed applause, "we'd like you to extend your welcome to our young friends here, Mary and Tom Joplin."

Jordan looked back at the couple behind him, and the pair received a gentle push forward from Michaels. They moved up beside Jordan and smiled shyly at the gathering.

"Mary and Tom have come all the way from Texarkana to receive the Lord's miraculous blessing," Jordan announced portentously. "Give them a big hand, folks!"

The crowd responded, and Jordan allowed the applause to roll on until it finally died of its own accord. He let the ensuing silence stretch out until he'd milked it for dramatic effect.

"These two young friends of ours are mighty special,"

Jordan continued, "for the blessing they're about to receive here on Miracle Isle is part of God's grand design. I know Billy-Lee has told you all that I'll be delivering a special message in the Crystal Chapel tomorrow morning, and I can hardly wait.

"The Lord has called upon me, his humble servant, to deliver joyful news—and he's laid it on my heart to deliver that message from Miracle Isle. Joyful news, brothers and sisters!" Jordan exclaimed, throwing back his head and laughing exultantly. "Praise God, I can hardly wait!"

"What news, Brother Jordan?" cried a young man ecstatically.

"Patience," Jordan responded with a good-natured laugh. "All in the Lord's good time. God has called upon me to speak to the world, and tomorrow morning I will. But tonight, I must prepare. I'll be going up to the Prayer Tower later on, and that's where I'll remain until dawn—praying in the Spirit. When I speak tomorrow, the Spirit will flow out of my mouth to unstop the ears of those who have not yet come to Jesus."

This was greeted by more hallelujahs and a chorus of "Praise God" 's, and Jordan smiled beneficently. Then he leaned over to say something to Lurleen and moved into the crowd, shaking the men's hands and giving the women brotherly hugs. A puffed-up Billy-Lee and a coolly smiling Lurleen followed in his wake, trailed by Dr. Mike and the Joplin couple, who looked slightly dazed.

Reese saw Billy-Lee look in their direction, and his piggy eyes fixed on Lara. Reese glanced at her just as she noticed Billy-Lee staring at her, and he saw her stiffen.

"I think I'm going to have to leave," Lara said to Reese's surprise.

"What?" Fletch protested. "You can't leave, Lara—not without meeting Brother Jordan."

"I'm not feeling so good, Fletch. I've felt something coming on all day, and now I'm getting the chills. I'd better go up to bed."

Fletch was instantly concerned. "Really?" he asked worriedly. "I'll go get Dr. Mike."

"No," Lara said quickly. "It's just some sort of bug. I'll be okay after a good night's sleep. Maybe I'll get a chance to meet Brother Jordan tomorrow."

"Sure," Fletch responded solicitously. "I'm sure you can, but maybe Dr. Mike should—"

"It's *okay,*" Lara interrupted with a smile. "Sleep is all I need. Have fun, guys," she said, and turned and slipped away.

"Gee, that's too bad," Fletch said, and Reese nodded distractedly, wondering at Lara's abrupt departure.

Across the room, Billy-Lee was still watching Lara, and his eyes followed her all the way to the exit. Reese could understand her distaste for the man, but he found it hard to believe that Billy-Lee's mere presence could drive her away.

Reese saw Fletch looking in the direction of the pretty girl Reese had seen him with the morning Reese had left. "Hey," Reese said, "don't waste time hanging around with me. It's not a good idea to leave a girl alone too long at a party."

"Right." Fletch laughed, and he needed no further prodding. "See you later," he said happily, and headed in his girl's direction.

Bobby Jordan clearly intended to greet everyone in the room, and his progress through the crowd was slow, but Reese waited patiently. He was looking forward to meeting him. Ten minutes later, Jordan and his entourage neared Reese's position. The Joplin couple, Reese noticed, had become detached somewhere along the way. Michaels caught sight of Reese and grinned.

"John!" Michaels boomed, bounding forward and seizing Reese's arm. "Come say hello to Bobby Jordan."

Michaels's bald head gleamed with perspiration, and he seemed to be sweating as much from excitement as from the heat in the room.

"Bobby," Michaels said to Jordan, "this is John Reed, the Compstar rep who's been working overtime to get our new computer up and running."

"Good to meet you, John," Jordan said, shaking Reese's hand in a hearty grip as Lurleen and Billy-Lee looked on. Jordan looked older at close range, with the beginnings of jowls beneath his camera-ready Billy Graham visage.

"The pleasure's mine," Reese said, smiling and looking steadily into Jordan's eyes. He wanted the man to remember that smile when he brought him down. Jordan blinked, and his eyes slid away.

"What's the story, John?" Michaels asked Reese. "Fletch told me the new computer is up and running. Is that right?"

"Yes, you're all set. There don't seem to be any problems, but I'll stick around a little longer just to be sure nothing crops up."

Reese noticed that Lurleen Jordan was eyeing him with a curiously appraising half smile.

"Great," Michaels said, clapping Reese on the shoulder and looking to Jordan to second his approval.

"I admire a man who takes pride in his work," Jordan said, clearly preparing to move on. "Too little of that these days."

"Amen," Lurleen drawled, and as Jordan turned away and moved off with Michaels and Billy-Lee to greet more of his flock, she stepped closer to Reese.

"I'm Lurleen," she purred, holding out her hand, and as Reese shook hands with her, she asked, "Are you a Christian, Mr. Reed?"

"I'm an atheist."

Lurleen laughed and shook her head. "So you say, Mr. Reed, but I declare, I don't believe you."

"Trust me."

"But you believe in love, don't you?" she asked with a slow smile that was far sexier than a smile from a preacher's wife was supposed to be.

"I'm all for it."

"Well, then, you're a Christian at heart," Lurleen drawled, moving yet closer, and Reese caught a whiff of alcohol beneath the heavy scent of her perfume. "Love, Mr. Reed. That's what bein' a Christian is all about. Love is the mornin' an' the evenin' star."

The flirtatious look in Lurleen's eyes was as obvious as a neon sign, and it took Reese aback. Here she was in public, hitting on a perfect stranger. But as he recovered from his surprise, he realized that she wasn't being all that reckless. Everyone's attention was riveted on Jordan, and her husband was fully occupied. Perhaps from her point of view, Reese reflected, he was a safe target. He wasn't a believer.

"I see you're not married," she said, looking up at him through lowered false eyelashes. "Or don't atheists wear weddin' rings?"

"I'm single."

"Why, that's a shame—a vig'rous, handsome man like you."

Reese decided it was time to extricate himself. He didn't know if the restless Mrs. Jordan simply found harmless release in flirting with strangers or if she took more serious chances, but he had no wish to find out. "It's been a pleasure meeting you, Mrs. Jordan, but I—"

"Call me Lurleen," she purred.

"Well, I've enjoyed talking to you, Lurleen, but the fact is, I'm a pretty heavy smoker, and I'm in desperate need of a cigarette right now. I'm going to have to excuse myself."

Reese considered the excuse insultingly thin, but Lurleen was unfazed. "I understand," she said, reaching out and patting him playfully on the chest. "I used to smoke myself. But you will be comin' back, won't you? For a woman in my position," she added in a smiling stage whisper, "keepin' company with an atheist is a nice change of pace."

40

The evening had been perfect, Billy-Lee thought as he walked with his father, Lurleen, and Michaels to the Prayer Tower. His father had been in a rare mood, treating him almost as an equal, and Billy-Lee had savored every moment. Even Lara Brooks's abrupt departure from the party hadn't spoiled the evening. Billy-Lee had overheard young Fletcher telling Michaels that Lara wasn't feeling well, so she hadn't snubbed him, after all.

And to cap things off, Billy-Lee and Lurleen were finally to learn the details of his father's revelation. No longer would Billy-Lee have to endure the humiliation of Michaels's knowing what he did not. And whatever Michaels had been doing in his laboratory, the work was apparently finished. Soon now, Billy-Lee told himself, he could destroy that dangerous scrap of flesh and bone.

As they neared the Prayer Tower, Bobby Jordan quickened his pace, and as they entered and climbed the spiral stairs, Billy-Lee sensed a rising excitement in his father. Bobby Jordan mounted the stairs with the energy of a man half his age, and only Michaels could keep up with him.

"Oh, how I've longed for this moment!" Bobby Jordan exclaimed as Lurleen and Billy-Lee came up into the Prayer Room.

Billy-Lee was panting for breath, but for once he hadn't minded the climb. Everything was going his way, he thought. *Everything*.

"How it hurt me to withhold from you the details of God's grand design," Bobby Jordan said, "yet that was His command. But now, at last, I can share with you both the full glory of His revelation."

Michaels was looking on with an expression Billy-Lee hadn't seen on his face before. He was grinning as ebulliently as Bobby Jordan, but an uncharacteristic tranquillity was also in his eyes, as if his joy was one of fulfillment. For once, he wasn't shifting from foot to foot like a restless teenager.

"Come," Bobby Jordan said, leading them to the chairs in the center of the Prayer Room, "and I'll tell you of God's precious gift to the world and the wonders to come."

"Just what is this gift?" Lurleen asked tonelessly.

"Praise God, exactly what the scroll says it is!" Bobby Jordan proclaimed joyously. "Lurleen—Billy-Lee—it is a finger from the right hand of our Savior, Christ Jesus!"

For a moment Billy-Lee couldn't believe his ears, and then a wave of nausea swept over him. "How can you *say* such a thing, Daddy?" he choked out.

"Don't be afraid, Billy-Lee!" Bobby Jordan responded, his eyes aglow. "Christ's finger is God's precious gift to the world, and it points the way to Glory. 'Give my gift to thy servant Michaels, so that he may discover its secret,' the Lord said to me, and praise God, he discovered it!"

Through the roaring in his ears, Billy-Lee dimly heard Lurleen's voice, and it was astonishingly calm. "What secret, Bobby? We don't understand."

"Tell them, Dr. Mike," Bobby Jordan urged, turning to Michaels. "Tell them what you've found."

"Yes, of course," Michaels said eagerly, grinning at Billy-Lee and Lurleen with the same strange mixture of excitement and tranquillity Billy-Lee had seen earlier. "I've been analyzing the finger's surviving DNA and comparing it with the DNA we find in modern man. It was as clear to me as to your father that the Lord intended me to do so, for DNA is God's Book of Life. Where else would we find the finger's secret?

"What struck me at once was that the DNA I extracted and amplified by PCR was amazingly rich in fragments from the Y chromosome—the chromosome inherited exclusively from the father. And among these fragments I've discovered two genes that are completely unknown to us—two genes that simply do not exist in modern man."

Michaels paused, apparently expecting a reaction, but Billy-Lee's mind was reeling with confusion and he hadn't understood a word Michaels had said.

"Don't you *see?*" Bobby Jordan exhorted, looking from Billy-Lee to Lurleen. "Two genes from the chromosome inherited from the *father*. Two genes that no mortal possesses. *They* are the secret God bade us discover. They prove that it *is* the finger of Christ Jesus, and that the scroll is truly the completion of the Word of God. The completion witheld from the world until the Millennium of Glory was at hand."

"It's true," Michaels pronounced. "Those two genes are surely the physical essence of our Lord."

"But how can you *know* that?" Lurleen demanded of Michaels.

"Because I know that God spoke to Bobby Jordan," Michaels replied fervently. "It was Bobby who first affirmed my own conviction that science is an integral part of God's grand design, and I know he understands God's revelation. Christ is coming, Lurleen. We've all known it, for the signs are all around us. And now, at last, I see how science will meld with faith to fulfill God's greatest promise to the world.

"Lurleen, can you really believe it's coincidence that these two genes have been preserved for us to find after two thousand years? Is it coincidence that the scroll's secret was conveyed to Bobby just in time to rescue the finger from those who would not understand?"

Michaels paused and drew a deep, shuddering breath. "I believe in Bobby Jordan, Lurleen. He's more than a God-called preacher. Bobby Jordan is a prophet!"

"And now you must hear the rest," Bobby Jordan interjected excitedly. "Words God spoke to me that I couldn't reveal until tonight. 'My Son is coming, born of Mary,' He said to me, 'and on the island of miracles shall it come to pass.'"

"Bobby," Lurleen responded, her voice barely above a whisper, "did you say 'born of Mary'?"

"Yes," Bobby Jordan replied ecstatically, reaching out and seizing Lurleen's hands. "Right here, on Miracle Isle! Praise God, now I know why God laid it on my heart to build a fertility clinic, for we are to prepare the way. God has chosen me to prepare the way for the coming of our Savior, just as the scroll prophesied. 'It is he that is not, but will be. The One Chosen of God. To him shall be given understanding, and he shall prepare the way for the Son of Man.'"

"Bobby," Lurleen said hoarsely, "you can't mean . . . Surely you're not talking about that young woman you brought with us. You're not saying that she is the Mary of your revelation."

"Yes!" Bobby Jordan cried. "I knew the Lord would send her to me, but I didn't know when. And the moment I spoke to Mary Joplin, I knew that she was to be the Holy Mother. Her innocence and simplicity—the depth of her faith . . . Oh, how we've been blessed to prepare the way for the coming of Our Lord!"

"But Bobby," Lurleen said, and for a moment her voice shook, "Revelation tells us that Christ will come with clouds."

"And a hurricane is coming," Michaels interjected, but Lurleen ignored him.

"'In the season of the wind,'" Bobby Jordan intoned incomprehensibly, and Billy-Lee could feel his head spinning.

"Does Mary Joplin know about any of this?" Lurleen asked sharply.

"She will when God reveals Himself to her," Bobby Jordan replied.

"I see," Lurleen said.

"Yes, of course, you do!" Bobby Jordan exulted, oblivious to Lurleen's tone.

It was all too much for Billy-Lee to absorb, and a fresh wave of nausea swept over him. The joy he saw in the faces of Michaels and his father couldn't overcome his gnawing uncertainty. God *did* speak to his father. He'd known that all his life, but this . . .

His father started to speak again, but then a shudder passed over him and his lips trembled. "Oh," he cried loudly, and rose from his chair. "I feel the Spirit. I feel it now! Come, Billy-Lee. Come, Lurleen! Kneel and receive the Spirit and the blessing of the Lord!"

Still dazed and feeling ill, Billy-Lee slipped off his chair and went to his knees beside Lurleen. And as his father stretched out his hands, seized their bowed heads, and began to pray, Billy-Lee gave himself up to what he sensed was about to come.

He felt his father's arm begin to quiver, and he gasped as he felt the power of the Spirit rippling down through his father's arm like lightning. Jolt after jolt coursed through Billy-Lee, taking his breath away.

"How much do you know about those security men you hired?" Lurleen asked tensely as she left the Prayer Tower with Billy-Lee. Although the floodlit quadrangle was deserted, she kept her voice low.

"They were highly recommended," Billy-Lee said, trying not to be infected by Lurleen's edginess.

"But do you trust them?"

"They're paid to do what I tell them, and they didn't come cheap. Yes, I think we can trust them to do their job."

"That's not what I mean. Do they mind their own business?"

"Yes. What are you worried about?"

"Talk, Billy-Lee. That—and that damned thing your father thinks is the finger of Christ."

"Lurleen," Billy-Lee protested, desperately trying to suppress his own doubts, "I know you don't believe in Daddy's revelation, but how do you know it isn't true? I felt the power of the Spirit tonight. I *felt* it."

"Hold that thought, Billy-Lee," Lurleen replied caustically. "What I feel is the need for a drink. Your father is communin' with the Lord, and I think I'll do a little communin' of my own."

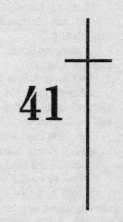

41

Midnight was approaching when Lara knocked softly on Reese's door. His room lay in semidarkness, lit only by the stray light from the floodlamps illuminating the quadrangle. He crushed out his cigarette in an already overflowing ashtray and rose from his chair in the corner.

"Michaels is still in his lab," Lara whispered in frustration as he let her into the room. She had changed into jeans and a black turtleneck.

"I know."

"Why do you have the lights out?"

"So I can see the harbor."

"Are you still worried about the *yakuza?*"

"If they come by boat, the harbor's the only place they can land," Reese said, trying not to let her tone annoy him.

Lara moved to the window overlooking the quadrangle and sucked her teeth in continuing frustration. "God, I hope he isn't going to work all night again."

"Is he likely to?" Reese asked, unsure of what he wanted. He knew he'd have a better chance of finding the finger with her along, and they just might pull it off. Quick in and out, and off on the *Mary Jane,* if nothing went wrong. *If.*

"I don't know . . ." Lara said, her voice trailing off. "What can he possibly be doing with the finger? *Why* did they steal it?"

"I have no idea," Reese said, too wound up inside for idle speculation.

"But there *has* to be a reason, and I can't get the question out of my mind. Maybe it's something to do with that 'special message' Jordan says he's going to deliver tomorrow. I just wish I knew . . ."

"Are you sure Jarvis is prepared to take us off the island tonight?" Reese asked impatiently.

"Yes," Lara said, coming back to him. "Absolutely."

"What story did you give him?"

"I told him that I'm fed up with this place, which Steve already knew is true—but that Billy-Lee won't let me leave with my lab notes. Steve agreed to help me skip out with my notebooks. In fact, he got a kick out of the idea—especially when I slipped him the hundred bucks."

"Isn't he worried about repercussions?"

Lara laughed. "I asked him that, John, and if I remember the quote correctly, it was 'Fuck the bastard.' "

"How did you explain my going along?"

"Oh, that was easy," Lara said with a slow smile. "I just told him that you and I—"

She broke off as they both caught the tap tap tap of a woman's high heels in the corridor. The footsteps were coming their way. Quickly Lara went to the clothes closet and opened it.

"That's not necessary," Reese whispered, moving to the door and flipping on the room light. "Whoever it is, I won't—"

Lara waved him into silence as the footsteps halted outside, and she slipped into the closet. The woman in the corridor knocked softly.

Reese opened the door to find Lurleen Jordan smiling at him. She had a bottle of champagne in one hand and two glasses in the other. "Well?" she prompted, arching an eyebrow. "Aren't you goin' to invite me in?"

Before Reese could respond, she stepped past him into the room, brushing against him with casual sensuality. "Close the door shugah," she purred. "You wouldn't want to get me into trouble, would you?"

Keenly aware of Lara in the closet, Reese felt his cheeks redden.

"Why, shugah," Lurleen said approvingly, "you're blushin'."

"You're taking a big chance, aren't you?" Reese asked, seeing no point in pretending that he didn't know why she'd come.

"Not really." Lurleen walked to the room's writing table and set down the bottle and glasses. "No one saw me in the hall."

"But what about your husband?"

"Bobby has other things on his mind. He's gone up to the Prayer Tower, and he'll be there all night."

Lurleen walked back to Reese and ran a hot hand over his chest. "He's doin' his bit for the Lord," she said huskily, "and I'll do mine. Call it ministerin' to the heathen."

She slipped her hand upward and around the back of his neck, and Reese tensed as she pulled his lips down to hers. The Browning was still tucked in behind his hip, and if her hands strayed . . . Lurleen kissed him lightly and stepped back half a step.

"How was that?" she asked with a languid smile. "Why don't we try again—but with a little more feelin' this time."

"I'd rather not," Reese said, casting about for the surest way to head her off. "No offense, but . . ."

"But what, shugah?" she asked, coming close again.

"I'm afraid I'm not the right sort of man for you," Reese said hastily.

"Why don't you let me be the judge of that," Lurleen said, slipping her arms around him again before he could retreat, and pressing her breasts against his chest. She closed her eyes and raised her face to his.

"I'm sorry, Lurleen, but I'm gay."

Lurleen's eyes flew open, and she pulled back as if she'd received an electric shock. For a moment she stared at Reese in disbelief, and then her expression turned to one of angry disgust.

"Well, I'm sorry for *you*," she snapped, her eyes flashing, "I surely am," and she turned away and marched out of the room.

The moment the door closed behind her, Reese heard what sounded like a strangled cough from the closet. He opened the door and found Lara collapsed on the floor, choking with laughter. "Shugah," she mimicked with tears streaming down her cheeks, "that was downright *mean.*"

"What did you expect me to do?"

"I don't know," Lara said, wiping away her tears, but then she started to laugh again.

"I declare, shugah," she drawled, "you must have been the life of the party after I left—at least for li'l ol' Lurleen. What *did* you do?" she added, looking up at him.

"Nothing. She has a problem, that's all."

"You mean her husband has a problem," Lara said as Reese reached down to help her get up.

As Lara rose, her prosthetic foot betrayed her and she slipped on the polished closet floor. Reese had to catch her to prevent her from falling, and she reflexively threw her arms around his shoulders for support. As he drew her to her feet, her scent and the warmth of her body seemed to envelop him, and his pulse began to throb.

Lara's face was raised to his, and he could feel her breath on his cheek. For a moment he hesitated, prepared to release her. But then she closed her eyes and her arms tightened about him, and Reese stopped thinking. As his lips found hers, he was aware of nothing but the treasure in his arms and his own pounding desire.

Lara felt as if a dam had given way inside her, and she responded to Reese's tender passion with an eagerness she had never known. *With him it feels so right,* was her last coherent thought before she lost herself in his embrace. *So right.* And then she thought no more.

Too late, Reese remembered his gun, and as Lara's hand brushed against it and he felt her stiffen in his arms, he al-most groaned aloud. She didn't pull away from him, but he knew it wouldn't be the same. Reality had crashed in on them. Aching with unspent passion, he drew a ragged breath and started to release her.

"It's okay," Lara whispered, still holding him. "It just startled me, that's all."

But Reese knew it wasn't okay, and he shook his head. For a few ecstatic moments he had forgotten everything, but already he felt the cold in the pit of his stomach again. Nothing would be okay until she was safely gone. "I'm sorry," he said, his pulse still pounding, and he gently disengaged. "I forgot about the gun."

Lara's cheeks were flushed, and when she spoke, she had to clear her throat. "Where did you get it?" she asked huskily.

"I've had it for a long time," Reese said, glad that she would never know the things he'd had to do in Nam. What would she think of him if she knew what he was still capable of doing?

Reese shook off the thought and moved to turn off the lights. He plunged the room into darkness again and crossed to the windows to check the harbor.

"Is Michaels still in his lab?"

"Yes." As Reese turned and looked at her, he knew it no longer mattered. He wasn't going to take the risk. And if Lara wouldn't leave on her own, he'd take her off the island himself. He would keep her safe, even if that meant letting Jordan go unpunished.

"Forget about Michaels," he said, coming back to her. "I'm calling it off."

"But he may not work all night," Lara protested. "And we agreed!"

"That was my mistake," Reese replied, impulsively pulling the Browning and cradling it in his palm. "This is all I have with me, Lara, and it may not be enough if things go wrong. I'm not going to take that chance with you here."

The weapon looked old and used to Lara, and it gleamed evilly in the half-light where the finish had worn off. Yet Reese handled the deadly thing so casually—as if it were nothing more than a tool, like a hammer or a wrench.

"This is no game," Reese said, slipping the weapon back under his jacket, and his voice sounded as cold to Lara as the gun.

"I know that," she said, dismayed by the sudden change in him. God, she didn't want to argue. Only minutes before she'd been aglow, and now . . .

"Then don't tie my hands," Reese said intensely. "Lara, you've *got* to promise me to leave tomorrow."

Don't tie my hands. The words cut Lara to the quick, for suddenly she thought she understood. It had been there all along, right in front of her. Why hadn't she realized it sooner? Rightly or wrongly, to Reese, she was in the way.

Again she heard the implacable hatred in his voice that afternoon as he'd said, "I'll bring the bastard down." That was what was driving him, she thought. It blotted out everything else—and she was in the way. She knew she could help him, but insisting on remaining on the island might be the surest way to lose him.

"All right," she heard herself say. "If that's what you want."

A sigh escaped Reese, and she could almost feel his relief. "Lara, I . . ."

"It's okay," she said, fighting back tears as she stepped back. She wanted to stay, but somehow she couldn't. "Just take care, John," she said before turning away. "That's all I ask."

Reese stared at the door that had closed behind Lara, listening regretfully to her receding footsteps. He hadn't intended to hurt her, but somehow he had. He'd heard it in her voice, and it all but displaced his relief. Disconsolately he lit a cigarette and returned to his chair by the windows to wait out the night.

For hours, nothing stirred in the floodlit compound, though lights still burned in Michaels's laboratory and atop the Prayer Tower. Then, around 3 A.M., a security guard passed by on his rounds again, and moments after he walked out of sight, another man suddenly appeared, coming from the dormitory's front entrance. Reese had no trouble recognizing the man. It was Lara's technician.

Kuroda had clearly timed his exit to avoid the security guard, and he walked hurriedly across the quadrangle. He was carrying a leather satchel, about the size of a physician's medical bag. At first, Reese thought he was heading for the entrance to the research laboratory, but as Kuroda reached the far corner of the clinic, he turned toward the rear of the compound and disappeared.

Forty minutes later, the technician reappeared, still carrying the leather satchel, and returned swiftly to the dormitory. Reese had no idea what Kuroda had been doing, but he had no doubt that it was *yakuza* work. Time was definitely running out.

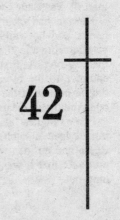

42

Day was breaking in a bloodred dawn as Reese approached Jarvis's weather-beaten Cape across the shore road from the dock and boathouse. Despite the early hour, smoke was rising from the metal stovepipe poking up through the sagging roof of Jarvis's cottage. It seemed a good time to have a private word with the *Mary Jane*'s captain.

Reese wanted to make sure that Lara would have no trouble getting off the island in advance of the hurricane, and possibly to make a deal for himself with Jarvis. Reese didn't want to rely entirely on Beretta's helicopter pickup.

He rapped on the weathered side door and heard muttering inside, followed by the scrape of a chair. The door opened to reveal Jarvis, half-dressed and disheveled, and behind him, an unappetizing kitchen. He was holding a cracked mug of coffee, and a dribble of egg clung to the gray stubble on his chin. The old Mainer stared at Reese with bleary, bloodshot eyes.

Reese smiled. "Good morning, Captain."

"A little late, ain't yuh?" Jarvis said, breathing alcohol fumes into Reese's face. "Where's Lara? I thought she wanted to leave last night."

"We changed our plans. She'll be leaving today."

Jarvis frowned. "Does that mean she wants her hundred bucks back?"

"No, you can keep it—as a consideration for your continued discretion."

"Right," Jarvis said, laying his finger alongside his nose and giving Reese an inebriated, yellow-toothed grin. "Won't say a word about it."

"I stopped by because I want to be sure Lara does get off the island today."

"That's up to her." Jarvis belched. "See that sky? Red sky at mornin', sailor take warnin'. I ain't gonna take no chances with my *Mary Jane*. We'll be goin' down to Lambeth Cove before the hurricane hits, and that's for sure."

"When?"

Jarvis looked at the sky and shrugged. "Dunno exactly. Noon . . . maybe a little later. Depends on how fast that hurricane is movin' in. And there may be other folks goin'. Ain't gonna be no fun on this island when that storm hits."

"How soon after the storm do you think you could make it back here?"

Jarvis frowned. "Depends. Seas'll be runnin' high for some time. What do yuh have in mind?"

"Could you come back late tonight, say, around midnight?"

Jarvis's frown deepened. "Maybe. Maybe not. Why?"

Reese took out his wallet and removed two fifty-dollar bills. "This is why, and another hundred if you're willing to take me down to Lambeth Cove as soon as I'm ready. I'd certainly want to leave before dawn."

"I could try, but I ain't makin' no promises."

"Good enough." Reese extended the money.

Jarvis eyed the cash in Reese's hand, but he didn't take it. "Ain't my business why you're askin', but is this gonna make trouble for me?"

"I don't know. Does Billy-Lee tell you when you can take the *Mary Jane* out and when you can't—or who you take on board?"

Jarvis grimaced and spat. "That'll be the day."

"Well, then? Two hundred bucks is two hundred bucks, but if you're afraid of pissing off Billy-Lee . . ."

Jarvis snorted. "Fuck the bastard." He reached out and took the money from Reese. "It's a deal."

The late-Sunday-morning breakfast was over, and the dining room was nearly empty. Those who remained were getting up to join the rest of the staff in the Crystal Chapel. Reese drained the tepid remains of his third cup of coffee and irritably glanced at his watch. Apparently Lara wasn't coming to breakfast. He couldn't blame her for catching up on her sleep, he told himself, but her absence made him uneasy.

Fletch, who had been sitting at another table with his girlfriend, came over to Reese. "If you're waiting for Lara," Fletch said, "you'll find her at the service in the Crystal Chapel."

"How do you know?" Reese asked in surprise.

"I knocked on her door on the way down from my room. I wanted to see how she's doing. She said she was skipping breakfast, but she told me she'd be going to chapel. I guess she's feeling better, but I did mention it to Dr. Mike. He promised to have a look at her this morning."

"That's good," Reese said, wondering why Lara was still pretending to be sick. Maybe she thought she could work it into an excuse to leave. Apparently she hoped that Jordan's special message from God would throw light on his theft of the finger. Reese could think of no other reason for her attending chapel.

"You're coming, aren't you, John?" Fletch asked. "We don't want to be late."

"I guess so." Reese was in no mood to sit through Jordan's service, but since Lara would be there, he'd go.

43

The sky to the south was becoming progressively hazier, but the sun still shone, flooding the Crystal Chapel with light. Surrounded by towering walls of plate glass, the chapel's interior had the feel of an outdoor amphitheater. Comfortable, cushioned theater seats were arranged in curved rows, with a scarlet carpet running down the central aisle to a raised, flower-bedecked stage. BOBBY JORDAN MINISTRIES was written in giant gilt letters across the stage's blue backdrop.

Reese, Fletch, and his girlfriend were among the last to enter, and they took seats near the aisle in one of the back rows. Reese scanned the audience, looking for Lara, but he didn't see her. Everyone else was swaying and clapping to the beat of a rousing gospel tune that blared from the speakers of a five-piece band playing on the stage. The young musicians were rock-style loud, but scrupulously clean-cut.

Bobby Jordan was seated center stage, between the band on the left and the gospel choir on the right. He was beaming at his followers and tapping his foot to the band's beat. Jordan was flanked by a smiling Lurleen and Billy-Lee on one side, and the young Joplin couple on the other. The pair smiled shyly at the audience and cast nervous glances at the three TV cameras in front of the stage.

The gospel choir consisted of six handsome boys paired with six demurely pretty girls. They all looked eager to burst into song, but at the moment, they were merely swaying and clapping to the band's music. As the band wound up its song, one of the cameras swung around to pan the audience, and Billy-Lee stood up and walked across the stage to stand in front of the gospel choir.

Gone were Billy-Lee's flowered shirt and thick gold chain. Like his father, he now wore a conservatively tailored suit and tie. The band finished playing, and Billy-Lee smiled into the nearest camera and launched into his spiel.

"Praise God!" he exclaimed. "Praise God, and expect a miracle today! Right now! Right in your own home!"

Billy-Lee's delivery was practiced and assured, but his reedy voice couldn't match his father's authoritative baritone. "I *believe* in miracles," he enthused. "I *believe* in the anointing of the Holy Spirit, and I expect you to feel the mighty power of God today!"

As Bobby Jordan and Lurleen looked on with expressions of pride, Billy-Lee beamed into the camera and declared, "That's what Bobby Jordan's ministry is all about—the healing, delivering touch of Jesus Christ."

On cue, the band struck up again and the gospel singers broke into song. To Reese's surprise, Billy-Lee appeared to be singing with them, but his contribution was inaudible. As the swelling music filled the chapel, the TV camera panned the audience again.

Some clapped to the beat and others raised their arms to heaven, and everyone in the chapel, save Reese, swayed in time with the music. Again Reese looked for Lara, and he felt a flash of annoyance as he ascertained that she wasn't in the chapel. She had ducked the service, and he was stuck with it.

The song ended, and Billy-Lee looked into the camera with a searching, earnest expression. "I know there are some of you watching this program now who are burdened with trouble. Some of you have financial problems—some of you are ill—some are having difficulties with loved ones. But whatever is troubling you, friend, *Jesus* can lift your burden, if only you believe.''

Billy-Lee paused and closed his eyes. ''Pray with me now and *expect* a miracle,'' he said, furrowing his brow in apparent concentration on the heavenly connection. ''Father, we ask in the name of Jesus that you work miracles today.''

Billy-Lee frowned harder, took a deep breath, and raised a clenched fist. ''In the name of *Jesus,*'' he said fervently, ''I speak to the devil and *command* him to take his hands off your life. I pray for your financial burden to be lifted. I pray for you to be reconciled with your loved ones. I pray for you to be *healed!* Every sickness—every fear—every tribulation—in Jesus' name, come out! Come *out!*''

Billy-Lee paused again, and Reese thought he had finished, but then he took another deep breath and went on, ''Satan—take your hands off God's property! By the power of the Living God, I command you to loose every man and every woman watching this program. Oh, Glory to God! Amen and amen.''

Billy-Lee opened his eyes and smiled into the camera, his look conveying utter confidence that his prayer had been answered. Reese shifted restlessly in his seat and looked at his watch, wondering how he was going to take an hour of this.

''Friends,'' Billy-Lee continued in a more conversational tone, ''today we are broadcasting direct from Miracle Isle. Here on Miracle Isle, countless young couples have been freed of the devil's hold. Here they have been able to conceive the Christian children the devil sought to deny them.

''And it is from here—Miracle Isle—that my dad has been called by God to deliver a very special message. In a few moments, my dad will tell you of a wondrous revelation. He will tell you how God spoke to him and what the message was. I know you will want to hear it.''

Yes, yes, Reese thought irritably. *Just get on with it.*

''But first I want to urge you to call us and tell us of your own special prayer needs—to let us help you know God's great healing power. Our Prayer Partners are standing by right now to take your call. So call the number that appears on your screen.

"And when you call," Billy-Lee said, producing what appeared to be a hand calculator and holding it up for the camera, "be sure to ask for our special offer."

Oh, Christ, a commercial.

"You see it right here in my hand, friends—the Parsons Electronic Bible. Friends, this electronic Bible contains the entire text of both the Old and New Testaments, and it will transform the way you study the Word of the Lord.

"Punch in *salvation*, for instance, and every verse from Genesis to Revelation will appear on the easy-to-read screen. The possibilities of this invention are endless! No one should be without this marvel, and it's compact enough to carry with you anywhere.

"Friends," Billy-Lee enthused, winding up his commercial, "this incredible offer costs only one hundred ninety-nine dollars. Call now, and use your credit card. Our Prayer Partners are standing by to hear your needs and to take your order."

Immediately the band and choir went to work on another gospel song, and Billy-Lee returned to his seat. Jordan smiled approvingly at his son, and then he looked at Lurleen. He took her hand, and they rose and walked together to the front of the stage.

Jordan put his arm around Lurleen, and they gazed adoringly at each other for a moment before looking into the central TV camera. In contrast to the previous evening, Lurleen now looked almost as chaste as the girls in the choir. An expectant hush fell over the audience. Apparently the time had finally come for God's special message.

"Lurleen," Jordan said, his rich baritone filling the chapel, "this is a wonderful day—a day we've all been waiting for."

"Yes, it is, Bobby," Lurleen replied in an excited, girlish voice full of innocence and wonder.

Jordan threw back his head and laughed, as if seized with the joy of the moment. "Oh, I feel so *good*!" he cried. "I feel charged with the Holy Spirit!"

"I feel it, too, Bobby," Lurleen gushed. "Praise the Lord,

this is a wonderful day. Tell them, Bobby," she said, detaching herself from his side. "Tell all our friends the glorious news."

"That I will," Jordan said, and Lurleen returned to her chair. Jordan grasped the Bible he carried in both hands and held it out toward the camera. "Friends," he began in a low-key, folksy tone, "you know this book. You know what's in it—the Word and the Promise. And you all know me—a minister of God who's preached the Word for almost forty years.

"Ours is a healing ministry, and we believe in God's miraculous power in our lives. But we don't ignore the miracles He works through modern science. Science, brothers and sisters, is one of God's greatest gifts to us, and that's why I built a clinic here on Miracle Isle—to help God-fearing couples conceive the children God wants them to have."

Jordan paused and turned to look toward the shy couple behind him. "God-fearing couples like our friends, Tom and Mary Joplin," he said as a camera focused on the pair. "But Tom and Mary are special, and that's why I brought them to Miracle Isle today—to be here when I broadcast God's glorious message.

"Let me tell you how the Lord came to me," Jordan said, smiling and shaking his head as if he still couldn't believe it. "The very night before these two young people contacted our ministry and told us of their need, I was lying awake. I was tossing and turning. I just couldn't sleep, and I didn't know why.

"Then—quite suddenly—I *knew* I had to pray. I just *had* to open up that channel to God. I didn't ask why. I just climbed out of bed, fell to my knees, and began to pray. And the channel opened!"

Abruptly Jordan shifted into high gear, giving full voice to his quickening emotion. "I felt the Holy Spirit welling up from my belly like a mighty river of living waters!" His baritone resonated throughout the chapel. "The Spirit filled me like it never had before, *and I heard the Lord speak to me!*

"Not like in the movies, friends." Jordan began to stride

up and down the stage. "Not an actor's voice, with music in the background. This was *real!* God's words were suddenly there in my mind, and I *knew* He was speaking to me."

The audience, responding to Jordan, stirred like trees swaying in a shifting wind as he paced the stage. "And these were the words He spoke: 'A young man and wife shall come unto you, seeking to conceive a child, and they shall be a sign unto you.' "

Abruptly Jordan halted in midstride and turned to his audience. "Of course, I didn't understand, and I asked aloud, 'What sign?' At once, more words flashed into my mind like lightning: 'A sign of a new beginning,' the Lord said, 'for they shall conceive in the dawning of the Millennium of Glory. My Son is coming, and He shall reign for a thousand years.' "

This was greeted by a scattered chorus of "Praise God" 's, and throughout the chapel, hands stretched heavenward.

Jordan paused, and although he was smiling, his eyes filled with tears. "Those were the words the Lord spoke to me, and I felt such a stirring in my soul that I cried—just as I'm crying now. 'When?' I asked, but no answer came. I prayed and I prayed, but no answer came.

"And then," Jordan cried, sweeping his arms upward in a gesture of holy triumph, "the Lord spoke to me again: 'Open your eyes, Bobby, and look around you. Bobby, open your eyes and *see!*'

"And I did, brothers and sisters." Tears were streaming down Jordan's cheeks. "Oh, praise God, I did! It was right there in front of me, and it's right in front of you—just as the Bible promised."

"Tell us, Brother Jordan!" cried someone in the audience.

Jordan held out his Bible, let it fall open, and clapped his hand on it for emphasis. "It's in this book, friends. It's all in here! Christ *is* coming! Just as the Bible promises. *That was the Lord's message to me,* and the signs are all around us!

"Read Isaiah, thirty-five, one," Jordan said excitedly, and again he began to pace the stage. 'The desert shall rejoice and blossom as a rose.' That's *exactly* what's happened in Israel! The Jews with their genius have made the desert bloom.

"Read the newspapers!" Jordan exclaimed in the same rapid-fire cadence. "We've just sold new fighter jets to Israel for the defense of the Holy Land. That was predicted by the prophets! 'As the birds flying, so will the Lord defend Jerusalem'—Isaiah, thirty-one, five. *Fighter jets,* brothers and sisters—*just as the prophets foretold.*

"Oh, my friends, Jesus is coming soon!" Jordan cried above the rising fervor of his audience. He fed the excitement in the chapel, and the audience fed it back to him, amplifying his histrionics. His cheeks had flushed, and beads of perspiration dotted his forehead.

"Every sign of Jesus' coming is here! Read Revelation. There the Bible tells us that the Antichrist will precede Him, and we can see the preparations for the False One. Study Revelation, thirteen, eleven! 'This Lamb that has two horns but speaks as a dragon'—that's the false religious prophet who rises with the Antichrist. And this fake prophet sits on seven hills in Rome—Revelation, seventeen, nine. In *Rome,* friends!

"Read your newspaper! So many bishops no longer declare that Christ is God that the pope is afraid his successor could be a defector. I admire the pope for speaking out. He speaks against the false prophet who will sit on seven hills in Rome."

Jordan paused for breath and pulled out a handkerchief to mop his brow as the noisy stir in his audience continued unabated. Jordan looked out at them and grinned. "Praise God"—he laughed—"that's good preaching! Oh, I do feel the power of the Lord."

The audience laughed, too, and a young man shouted happily, "Keep it coming, Brother Jordan!"

"The signs are here! Only last week, I read of a new global digital navigation system. A precision spotting tool developed in military research—an instrument for locating anyone on the face of the earth! And the Bible told us this would come to pass in the final days.

"The Good Book tells us that the Antichrist will give everyone a mark. It's right there in Revelation, thirteen, verses sixteen to eighteen: 'He causes all—both small and great, rich and poor, free and bond—to receive a mark in the right hand or forehead, that no man might buy or sell save that he have the mark, or the name of the beast, or the number of the name. His number is six six six.'

"Jesus *is* coming!" Bobby Jordan cried ecstatically, closing his eyes and raising his arms to heaven. "Oh, God, our Savior is coming!"

"Praise God!" rang through the chapel as even more arms reached heavenward. Many young men and women had closed their eyes, and their lips were moving in fervent, silent prayer. Others were grinning and bouncing in their chairs. Still others sat transfixed with tears streaming down their cheeks.

Of all the people Reese could see, only Billy-Lee and Lurleen seemed to have complete possession of themselves. Billy-Lee had the look of an eager apprentice watching the master in action, and Lurleen wore the discreetly satisfied smile of a businesswoman listening to the ring of a cash register.

"Oh, it's joyous news I'm bringing you today," Jordan cried, laughing and crying at the same time. "Jesus is coming. Oh, what a day it will be, and *it's almost upon us*!"

Jordan mopped his perspiring brow again, but he wasn't running out of steam. He seemed to draw more and more energy from the crowd. As he launched into another series of news stories that he contrived to twist into portents of the Second Coming, Reese shifted restlessly in his seat. How much longer would this go on?

Reese had learned nothing. If there was a connection between Jordan's hackneyed apocalyptic message and the theft of the relic, Reese didn't see it. Jordan wasn't claiming the discovery of a mummified finger as a biblical sign.

As Reese let Jordan's preaching roll over him, he wondered why Lara had told Fletch she was coming and then ducked out. For that matter, why had she skipped breakfast? It was as if Lara were deliberately avoiding him.

Suddenly an explanation occurred to him, and he stiffened in alarm.

Loose not the seal of the Second Book. Let no man seek to know that which shall be revealed to the Chosen One, for he who breaks this covenant shall be accursed in the eyes of God and tormented unto death.

—SAMARIA SCROLL 1, COLUMN 1.2.1

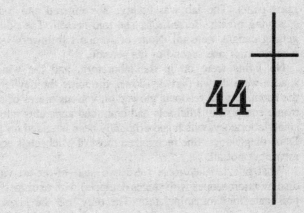

44

Lara cast one last look around the deserted compound and took out her key to the outside door to Michaels's lab. She was as nervous as a cat, and she fumbled with the key as she inserted it in the lock. *Calm down,* she told herself as she slipped inside. Everyone was in the chapel listening to Jordan. She should have at least an hour to search the lab.

Yet the moment the door closed behind her, Lara's tension mounted. Now that she was inside, she felt an unreasoning urge to get out again. God, she thought, she'd never make a burglar.

For several seconds she listened in the hallway to be sure the lab was deserted, and she almost wished that Fletch hadn't stopped by her room. Everyone was going to be in chapel, he'd reminded her, and that's when the idea had popped into her head.

Even though she'd told Fletch she'd try to make it, her supposed illness was a ready-made excuse not to show. God, Reese would have a fit if he knew, she thought guiltily. Yet she hadn't really deceived him, she rationalized. She *would* leave today, just as she'd promised.

The clinic was silent, but Lara remained cautious. She crept to the laboratory's inner door and peered through the glass panel. The lab was empty. She entered and took a steadying breath. *Be sensible,* she told herself. The odds of getting caught were nil. None of Jordan's followers would want to miss one second of his sermon.

No lights were on in the laboratory, and the window shades were drawn partway down, dimming the daylight in the room. Digital readouts glowed on various pieces of electronic equipment. Michaels had crammed apparatus into the small laboratory, which had originally been intended for fetal DNA diagnostics. She recognized most of Michaels's equipment, but not all.

What puzzled her most were two state-of-the-art video-display microscopes with stages equipped with extremely sophisticated micromanipulators. The only use she knew for such equipment was for cell cloning, and the mechanical injection of foreign DNA into individual cells. Older video microscopes were set up nearby, and they appeared to be part of the clinic laboratory's original equipment for in vitro fertilization.

Instead of making her feel secure, the silence in the lab got on Lara's nerves. Her hands were cold from nervousness, and she again urged herself to stay calm. *Use your head, Brooks. Narrow the search, and don't disturb anything.*

Lara moved into the center of the room and scanned the laboratory, looking for a small, individual storage unit that might conceivably contain the mummified finger. Nothing on the lab benches looked promising, nor anything standing against the walls. But perhaps Michaels hadn't stored the finger in a special location.

Quickly Lara crossed the lab and opened the insulated door of a general storage room for biological materials. Along both sides of the narrow room were refrigerated cabinets, and against the rear wall was a liquid-nitrogen freezer unit. She doubted that Michaels would store the finger at liquid-nitrogen temperatures, but she looked into the cryogenic freezer anyway. She wasn't sure what was in the test tubes she found inside—perhaps frozen embryos—but the finger wasn't there.

She turned to the refrigerated wall cabinets and opened them one by one, carefully searching each shelf. She found nothing but clone libraries for DNA analysis and bottles of chemicals that required refrigerated storage. Frustrated, she considered searching the shelves again, but she knew she couldn't have missed the finger. It simply wasn't there.

Lara left the storage room and scanned the laboratory again, thinking she must have overlooked something. She expected Michaels to keep the finger in a temperature- and atmosphere-controlled environment, but what if he'd just put it in a simple, sealed container somewhere?

She looked nervously at her watch, acutely aware of the time ticking by, and she had to stifle the urge to start opening cabinets at random. That would be her last resort. *Think, damn it! It has to be in here somewhere, and it's precious to Michaels.*

A partition in the corner of the cramped laboratory partially screened what appeared to be an improvised office. Lara could see shelves of books and the edge of a computer terminal. Mentally crossing her fingers, she went to look. It was Michaels's paperwork area, all right, and beside the table bearing the terminal was his desk, cluttered with computer printouts and several lab notebooks.

And against the wall was what Lara had sought—a compact, steel storage cabinet equipped with a digital temperature readout. The cabinet sat atop a small refrigeration unit, and a cylinder of compressed argon gas beside it provided an inert atmosphere for the cabinet's interior.

Lara grinned in triumph, but her grin vanished as she noticed the combination lock securing the cabinet's door handle. The presence of the lock virtually guaranteed that the finger was inside, but she couldn't get at it. The lock looked strong enough to withstand a bolt cutter, even if she'd had one. The weak point, if one could call it that, was the handle itself; and even that would have to be attacked with a sledgehammer.

Biting her lip in frustration, Lara rose and looked again at her watch. She still had plenty of time, she thought, but the creepy silence in the lab was preying on her nerves. Every passing minute intensified the urge to get out of Michaels's lab while she had the chance, yet she rebelled against fleeing prematurely and accomplishing nothing. Her eyes strayed to the notebooks on Michaels's desk. Reese didn't care why Michaels was analyzing the finger's DNA, but the information *might* prove useful in some way, and she still had time.

Lara sat down at the desk and hastily gathered Michaels's notebooks, checking the dates on the covers and arranging them in chronological order. She opened the most recent notebook first and began scanning the entries. As she'd hoped, Michaels's notes commented briefly on the results of each completed experiment, what he concluded, and what should be done next. If she was lucky, she might discover his goal.

She checked her watch and settled back in Michaels's chair, reading his lengthier entries as quickly as she could and skipping completely the many pages where his remarks were terse or nonexistent. Such was her concentration that she failed to notice the momentary break in the hum from the refrigeration unit beneath the storage cabinet. She heard the soft thunk of the motor starting up again, but she didn't register its significance.

45

Reese sat rigidly in his seat, hoping he was wrong, but growing more certain that he was right. He no longer believed that Lara had simply decided to skip breakfast. She had deliberately avoided him. She'd had a bright idea, and she'd known what his reaction would be.

Jordan had finally exhausted his list of portents heralding the Second Coming, and now he was about to lead a prayer of salvation. Reese glanced at his watch, hoping Lara was out of Michaels's lab by now. He was afraid the service was about to end.

"Lord Jesus," Jordan intoned, "I *believe*. I trust in you and in your shed blood to wash away my sins. I receive you now as my Savior. In your name, I pray this. Amen and amen."

Jordan opened his eyes, and Billy-Lee rose from his seat and walked forward to take his father's place before the camera. "Is that it?" Reese tensely asked Fletch.

The boy was too caught up in the holy fervor suffusing the audience to respond immediately, but then he turned and smiled at Reese reassuringly. "No, I'm sure Bobby is going to have more to say to us. Isn't this terrific?"

Reese produced a smile and nodded, and Fletch instantly returned his attention to the stage. Reese couldn't just sit and sweat it out. Whether or not he attracted attention, he had to make sure Lara got out of Michaels's lab in time. He would leave as unobtrusively as possible, but he was going.

Bobby Jordan had returned to his seat, and Billy-Lee took over. "You've just heard my dad's glorious news," he said, smiling into the camera. "Jesus is coming soon, and if you want to be saved—if you want to be ready—make your decision for Christ today! I know you want to be saved. I know you want to be cleansed by the Lamb's blood. Friends, we all must have the cleansing of the blood before we can receive the anointing of the oil."

A hint of the huckster had crept into Billy-Lee's reedy voice again, and Reese realized that another commercial was coming.

"That's why I hope you will call the number on your screen and ask for my dad's wonderful brochure on how to release the power of the Blood Covenant. On the day of Pentecost, only those cleansed by the blood received the Holy Spirit. As the brochure enumerates for you, Jesus shed his blood seven times, and seven is the number of completion.

"It is complete salvation, friends, and that's why my dad's brochure is so important to you. He will have more to say to you in a few moments, but while the Bobby Jordan Singers give voice to our hope for salvation, I want you to go to your phone right now and call the number on your screen."

The band and choir launched into another gospel song, and as the audience began to sway and clap, Reese started to rise from his seat. He wouldn't have a better opportunity to slip out, and he wasn't willing to wait any longer.

Abruptly the band's loudspeakers died and the television lights winked out. The sudden electrical failure brought a momentary hush to the chapel. Then the power came back on, and with it, chattering confusion. Reese saw Michaels leave his seat in the front row and signal to an odd-looking young man with small, rimless spectacles to come with him.

Reese took the man to be Michaels's technician. Farther back in the audience, two other men rose and made their way toward the center aisle.

"Folks!" Billy-Lee called out, raising his arms. "There's no need to worry. Just a momentary power failure. You see Dr. Mike and Don there, leaving, and I guess they're going to check on the lab equipment. And I see that our maintenance engineers are also leaving to find out what happened."

Michaels was striding up the aisle with his technician and the two maintenance men a few seconds behind him.

"I'll check the computers," Reese said quickly to Fletch.

"Want me to come?"

"No need," Reese said, stepping into the aisle. "I'll take care of it."

Reese turned toward the exit, and as Michaels came abreast, Reese fell into step beside him.

"Let's get on with our service to the Lord, folks," Billy-Lee called, quieting the audience. "I guess my dad's preaching has been so powerful this morning that the devil is frustrated. He's tried to twist our tail, but he sure can't stop a God-called preacher!"

The audience laughed approvingly, and the band and choir picked up their song again.

"What happened?" Reese asked Michaels as they came out of the chapel.

"I don't know." Michaels rounded on the maintenance men emerging from the chapel. "What the hell happened?" he demanded of the elder man.

"I don't know, Dr. Mike," the engineer said, "but if a breaker had tripped, the power wouldn't have come back on. I think the generator failed, and the alternate one kicked in."

"Failed? How could that happen?"

"I don't know," the maintenance man replied defensively. "We'll have to have a look."

"Do that," Michaels said irritably and walked on. "Don," he said to his technician, "you check the main lab and see if any of the control equipment has been thrown out of whack. I'll check ours. And, John, you're going to check the computers, right?"

"Right," Reese said, having no choice. If Lara hadn't made it out of Michaels's lab yet, he couldn't prevent her being caught. As he left Michaels's side and headed for the computer room, he tried to convince himself that there was nothing to worry about.

Lara was smart. Even if she'd still been in Michaels's lab when the power failed, she must have realized that someone would come to check the equipment. And maybe she hadn't gone into Michaels's lab at all. Maybe she was in her room asleep—or down at the dock, talking to Jarvis. Maybe—but Reese couldn't quell the sinking feeling in his stomach.

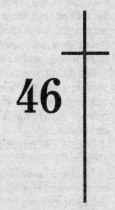

46

Lara stared in disbelief at the notebook she'd been reading. *My God,* she thought, *the man's deranged.* If she hadn't seen the evidence with her own eyes, she would not have believed it, for despite Michaels's religious fanaticism, he was a first-rate scientist. It seemed incredible that he believed his experiment might succeed, but what horrified her was his willingness to try. The risk to his subjects was unconscionable and perverted.

Shaken, Lara got to her feet and replaced the notebooks on the desk as close to the way she had found them as she could remember. She was desperately anxious to leave no trace of her intrusion. Before discovering Michaels's purpose, she'd been merely nervous. Now she was frightened. Michaels wasn't sane.

She took one last look at the desktop to be sure it looked all right and hurried through the lab toward the exit. As she neared the door to the hallway, the door's glass panel brightened suddenly as light spilled into the hallway from outside. Lara stopped short and her breath caught in her throat. Someone was coming in.

She spun around and raced back through the lab to a door that led to the clinic's medical area. She was sure it would be locked, but there was no other way out. Desperately she seized the door-knob, but it refused to turn. Behind her she heard someone entering the laboratory. She turned, her heart hammering, and saw Michaels.

He didn't see her at once, and as he reached for the light switch, Lara did her best to slow her breathing and smooth her features. She was caught, and she'd have to make the best of it. Michaels flipped on the lights and turned in her direction.

"Hi," she heard herself say lightly. "Is the service over already?"

Michaels started, reacting for an instant as if he'd trodden on a snake. But he recovered immediately. "What are you doing here, Lara?" he asked coolly.

Lara shrugged. "I was bored, and . . . Well, I've always been curious to see what sort of equipment you have in here. I found the door open, so I just wandered in. You don't have to worry. I didn't disturb anything."

"I'm not worried."

"Is the service over already?" Lara asked again, just managing to keep her voice from quavering. Michaels's notes were a window into the black pit of his unbalanced mind, and she had no idea what he might do if he realized she knew his secret.

"There was a power failure," he said, staring at her. "If you'd turned on the lights, you would have noticed. Why didn't you?"

"I don't know, I . . ."

"And how did you get in here?"

Lara's throat had gone dry, and she tried to swallow. "I told you. The door was open."

Michaels just stared at her.

"It *was* open."

"You're lying," Michaels said too quietly. "It's always locked when we're not around."

Michaels was staring at her coldly, and Lara realized that she'd never seen him when he wasn't smiling. His mouth was set in a grim line, and with his bald head thrust forward on his hunched shoulders, he reminded her of a vulture.

"Well, it was open when *I* tried it," she said, managing to summon a note of indignation, and she started walking toward Michaels. "I've never understood why you keep your lab locked. We're colleagues, after all."

"That's my business," Michaels said in the same ominously soft tone. "It would have been better if you'd minded yours."

Lara felt her throat constrict, and despite her efforts to control herself, her chest was visibly rising and falling. She was scared, and she was sure Michaels saw it. "I'm sorry to have intruded," she said, trying to move past him, but he sidestepped and blocked her way.

The smile he gave her then was worse than his icy stare. "Don't be in such a hurry, Lara. Now that you're here, it would be rude for me not to show you some of my toys. The micromanipulator stages over there, for instance—with the video-display microscopes. What did you make of them?"

"I didn't. Unless they're for in vitro fertilization."

"No. I've been using them to transfer cell nuclei from fertilized eggs to denucleated eggs—for cloning purposes. I'm getting rather good at it."

"Why?" Lara asked, feigning surprise. "That's hardly in your line."

"I'm trying to broaden my horizons," Michaels said, and she sensed that he saw right through her. "What's the point of decoding human DNA if we don't exploit our knowledge? Gene therapy remains in its infancy because of outdated taboos that hold us back from attempting germ-line modification. Yet the only way to eliminate genetic imperfection is to modify the genetic inheritance of the human embryo.

"I've been following up on Lou Brown's work with retroviruses, but I've had more success with mechanical insertion. Just between us, I can now insert a twenty-kilobase segment of foreign DNA into an embryo's chromosome with a success rate approaching five percent. Still, one needs to clone a four-celled embryo a hundredfold prior to modification to allow for the failures."

"What are you working with?" Lara asked, still trying hard to feign ignorance. "Mouse embryos?"

Michaels's smile vanished. "Let's not play games, Lara. You know what I've been doing. You've looked at my notebooks, haven't you? You know I'm working with human embryos, and you know why."

Lara shook her head, not trusting herself to speak.

"The door *was* locked," Michaels said softly but venomously, "and that means you must have a key. Give it to me, Lara. Don't make me search you."

Michaels's cold, controlled anger frightened her more than if he'd raged at her, and her fingers were stiff and clumsy as she dug into the pocket of her jeans and pulled out the key. She had to get out of the lab. She *had to!* As Michaels reached to take the key, she let it drop.

Michaels looked down, and she tried to lunge past him; but her artificial leg betrayed her and she slipped. Before she could recover, Michaels snared her arm and his fingers closed like a vise. "No!" she cried as he pulled her backward, but her next cry was cut off as he clamped his other hand over her mouth and held her fast.

"Easy," he said softly with his mouth obscenely close to her ear. "Don't be afraid. I won't hurt you."

Lara refused to listen, and she thrashed in his grip, trying with all her strength to pull free.

"All *right,*" he snarled. "That's enough! Come with me quietly or be dragged. It's your choice, and if you give me trouble, I'll have to slip you a hypo. Do you understand?" he cried, shaking her so hard her teeth rattled. *"Do you?"*

Lara understood, and she knew it was useless to fight him. He was simply too strong for her. She ceased struggling and tried not to give way to panic. But silently her mind screamed.

47

The computer system was equipped with battery backup power, and it didn't take Reese long to determine that the system had survived the brief power outage. As soon as he'd run his checks, he left the computer room and headed for the clinic building. He was desperate to know if Lara had been caught inside Michaels's lab. As he crossed the quadrangle, Michaels's technician emerged from the main laboratory and also walked toward the clinic.

Reese reached the outside entrance to Michaels's lab ahead of the technician, and to his surprise, the door was unlocked. But when he started to open it, the technician shouted at him and broke into a run.

"You can't go in there!" the technician yelled breathlessly, running up to Reese. Behind his rimless spectacles, his eyes were blinking furiously.

"I just wanted to tell Dr. Michaels that the computer system is okay."

"*I'll* tell him," the technician said officiously, pushing past Reese and opening the door.

"But he asked me to report back to him," Reese lied.

"I'll tell him," the technician repeated, stepping into the hallway. "Dr. Michaels allows no one inside."

"I'm also supposed to see Lara Brooks. Was she in the DNA lab?"

"No," the technician replied, and he closed the door in Reese's face and locked it from the inside.

Reese was about to pound on the door to attract Michaels's attention when he heard voices from the direction of the chapel. He turned and saw people streaming outside. They were clearly excited. Fletch emerged from the crowd and started running toward the computer room. Reese called to him, and as the boy veered in his direction, Reese went to meet him.

"John!" Fletch exclaimed. "We've got to shut down the system!"

"Why? It's running fine."

"We're about to lose power completely," Fletch said breathlessly, hurrying on toward the computer room, and Reese fell into step beside him.

"What's wrong?"

"I don't know exactly, but one generator is totally out of commission, and the maintenance men think the backup generator is about to fail. Something's wrong with the lubrication, and bearings are burning out. That's what I was told, at any rate."

"*Both* generators are down? How could that happen?" Reese asked, but he already knew. Kiru Kuroda's brief excursion in the small hours of the morning suddenly looked like sabotage.

"I don't know," Fletch replied excitedly. "It's really weird. Billy-Lee is having a fit."

"Have you seen Lara?"

"No. She must still be in her room. I hope she isn't really sick, because we're going to evacuate the island."

"What?"

"Not everybody. Billy-Lee and a skeleton crew are staying, but the ferry will be coming across to pick up everybody else. It looks like we're going to catch the brunt of the hurricane, after all, and there's no telling when the generators will be fixed. With this many people and no power—''

''None at all?''

''I think they have a small emergency generator for the communications equipment, but that's it.''

Kiru Kuroda had done his job well, Reese thought grimly. Nature had conspired with the *yakuza* to clear the island, giving them the perfect opportunity to raid. Most likely they'd be coming on the heels of the hurricane.

''Well, you don't need me to shut down the system,'' Reese said. ''I want to find out how Lara is doing. What's her room number?''

''One oh seven.''

''Thanks,'' Reese said, turning back toward the dormitory. ''See you later.''

Reese knocked on Lara's door, and when he received no response, he turned the knob. The door was unlocked, and he stepped inside. The faintest trace of her perfume hung in the air, but the room was empty.

People were returning to their rooms to pack for the evacuation, and as Reese went back down the corridor, he stopped at open doors along the way to ask if anyone had seen Lara. No one had. He went through to the dining hall, where some of the staff had already gathered, and asked the same question. No one had seen her.

Reese had one last hope. He left the dining hall and walked out to the brow of the hill overlooking the harbor. To the south, the hazy sky was taking on a leaden hue, and Jarvis was at work below, closing up the storm shutters on his cottage. The dock and ferry slip were deserted, and Reese saw no one besides Jarvis anywhere along the shore.

Lara was nowhere to be found, and Reese had little doubt what that meant. He felt his hands grow cold. She had taken a chance, and it had been one chance too many. He turned on his heel and strode back into the compound. He could no longer hope to retrieve the finger, he realized, but the thought was fleeting. He had only one imperative now.

As he neared the dormitory, he saw Fletch coming from the clinic's dispensary, and the boy waved and trotted toward him. "I just spoke to Dr. Mike," Fletch said as he came up to Reese. "He's put Lara to bed in one of the clinic's rooms. She really has a bad case of the flu."

"Did you see her?"

Fletch shook his head. "Dr. Mike thought it best to let her sleep."

"What about the evacuation?"

"I guess he's going to keep her here in bed, but she'll be okay, John. Dr. Mike will take good care of her."

To Reese, the reassuring phrase was chilling. Clearly Lara had given herself away, or they wouldn't be holding her. Reese had no idea what they would do with her, but Jordan might be capable of anything.

"Maybe Dr. Mike will let me see her before we leave," Reese said, trying to ignore his fear. He had to ignore it, lest it cripple him.

"There's plenty of time yet," Fletch said, walking with Reese toward the dormitory. "We'll be having lunch in the dining hall before the ferry comes to pick us up."

But there wasn't plenty of time. Reese couldn't leave Lara behind, and he was sure he couldn't take her off the island without using force. He had few options, and too little time to decide.

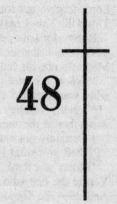

48

"Calm down, Billy-Lee," Michaels said.

"Calm down? She knows about the finger—and what you intended to do with it—and you say *calm down?*"

"Billy-Lee!" Bobby Jordan barked, his voice overpowering in the confines of Billy-Lee's office. "Ours is a *holy* mission, Billy-Lee. Trust in God, and know that we shall prevail."

Billy-Lee swallowed painfully, and he clawed at his tie and pulled it loose. He felt as if he were strangling. Lurleen had warned him. Sweet Jesus, why hadn't he listened?

"Everything's under control for the moment," Michaels said. "I've got the girl on ice, and the finger is still in the safe."

"We've got to get rid of it," Billy-Lee burst out. "Right now! Without the finger, no one can prove a thing."

"No!" Bobby Jordan thundered, glaring at Billy-Lee. "Would you do the devil's work for him?"

For the first time in his life, Billy-Lee wasn't cowed by his father. He was too determined to survive. "It's the Brooks woman who's doing the devil's work, Daddy, and I won't let her finish it."

For a moment Billy-Lee thought his father might strike him, but instead Bobby Jordan lifted his face to heaven. "Oh, Lord, forgive my son his weakness. Give him strength to do Thy will. This I pray in Jesus' name. Amen."

Bobby Jordan opened his eyes and gave Billy-Lee a man-of-God look that only added to Billy-Lee's anxiety. Neither Michaels nor his father seemed to understand the danger.

"Where's Lurleen?" Billy-Lee asked. "Have you told her what you intended to do with that finger?"

"I will," Bobby Jordan said, "but there's no need to worry her at the moment."

"Certainly not until we know more," Michaels chimed in. "I'll tell you what I think, Billy-Lee. I—"

"What *you* think? You're the one who brought her here! You're the one who said she'd be an asset to the laboratory. And now she knows all about everything!"

"But the Lord thwarted her!" Bobby Jordan exulted. "Do you think that power failure was an accident, Billy-Lee? Oh, hear the word of the scrolls! 'The deceiver shall cry out against the Chosen One and those who are deceived shall war against him. But he and his servants shall overcome all, for he is the One Chosen of God to prepare the way. And the King of Kings shall sit upon a white throne, and beside him shall sit the Chosen One, who prepared the way, together with his servants.' "

"Listen to your father, Billy-Lee," Michaels said, grasping Billy-Lee's arm. "No one can stop us if we keep faith. Surely you know that."

Billy-Lee only knew that he wanted to keep what was his—what he'd slaved for his entire adult life.

"No one is going to steal God's precious gift from us, Billy-Lee," Michaels said with calm certainty. "Brooks failed, and she won't have a second chance."

"But how did she get a key?" Billy-Lee demanded. "She must have had help. There could be others."

"Of course there are," his father said, his voice turning venomous. "Catholics, no doubt."

"But probably not here," Michaels said. "Lara Brooks is an outsider, and besides your security guards—men you chose yourself—there are only one or two others.''

"And what about them?''

"Even if she has confederates among us, they won't be a problem,'' Bobby Jordan interjected confidently. "We're clearing the island, Billy-Lee, and until the Lord's work is done, we'll let no stranger set foot on Miracle Isle.''

"But what about the Brooks woman?'' Billy-Lee asked. "We can't hold her indefinitely.''

"I think I can deal with that,'' Michaels said, and this time he didn't smile.

"Amen and amen,'' Bobby Jordan said, and he surprised Billy-Lee by putting his arm around his shoulders and pulling him close. "You must be my strong right arm,'' he commanded. "Trust in the Lord, Billy-Lee. We *shall* prevail. And if the Catholics try to interfere with God's grand design, you and your men must stop them.''

49

Lara couldn't see her hand in front of her face. She could hardly move, and she felt she was suffocating in her pitch-dark improvised cell. Michaels had forced her into a janitor's closet and locked her in. Lara hadn't thought she was prone to claustrophobia, but she was hyperventilating.

The closet was crammed with cleaning equipment, and she barely had room to sit. She was sick to her stomach with dread, and the stench of disinfectant and industrial solvents saturating the stuffy air added to her nausea. She was desperate to get out, but terrified of what might happen when Michaels returned. Jordan was probably as crazy as Michaels, and now that she knew their secret, she had no idea what they might do to her.

She had closed her eyes and was sitting with her legs drawn up, hugging her knees to her chest. The position made it easier to control her nausea, and with her eyes shut, the closet's walls did not seem to press in on her so much. But there was no escape from her fear. She had to fight it, she told herself over and over. She mustn't give way to panic.

How long had she been locked in the closet? An hour?

Longer? If only her watch had a luminous dial. The loss of her sense of time added to her feeling of utter helplessness. *God, what is going to happen?* Lara gritted her teeth, fighting against the fresh spasm of icy fear.

Hang on, Brooks, hang on. Reese was bound to realize what had happened. He would come for her and free her. He'd come—he *had* to come. But what if he couldn't get to her? What if . . .

Footsteps sounded in the hall outside, and Lara went rigid. A key turned in the lock, and the door opened. "Come out," said Michaels. "Bobby Jordan wants to talk to you."

Lara got stiffly to her feet and stepped out of the closet. Michaels immediately clamped his hand on her arm, but he didn't warn her against crying out. The building was silent and apparently deserted. Michaels led Lara down the dim hallway and up the stairs to an inpatient room on the clinic's second floor.

Simply being liberated from the pitch-dark, suffocating closet bolstered Lara's nerve, but she knew she was still helpless. No one outside would hear her if she cried for help. The room's single window faced the rear of the building and was closed.

The pressure on Lara's bladder was acute, and the room had an adjoining bathroom. "I'd like to use the bathroom."

"Go ahead," Michaels said tonelessly, releasing her arm. He no longer looked angry, but his expression was remote and implacable.

The bathroom was windowless, and Lara found nothing she might use as a weapon, but at least the physical relief steadied her nerve a little more. When she emerged from the bathroom, Jordan was waiting for her.

"I'm Bobby Jordan." He was even taller than she'd thought. He towered over her, and his smile was more intimidating than overt anger would have been. "We haven't met, but Dr. Mike has told me a good deal about you. Sit down, my dear."

Jordan gestured toward the room's only chair, and Lara sat.

"I regret that we meet under such awkward circumstances," Jordan said. "I'm afraid you've created a problem for us."

"I don't know what you're talking about."

"No? We've had a look at the key you used to break into Dr. Mike's laboratory. Very clever. Why did you go to the trouble of making it?"

"Just for the hell of it. Keeping his lab locked was—well, mysterious. I was curious, and I guess I took it as a challenge."

"Something of a prank? Is that it?"

"Something like that. I don't know what the big deal is, but if I'd known I'd cause all this upset, I wouldn't have done it."

"No?" Jordan responded archly. "Well, we *are* upset, Lara. What Dr. Mike has been doing in the service of the Lord wasn't your business, and now, unfortunately, you know about it."

"I only know what *he* told me," Lara said, glancing at Michaels, who was staring at her coldly. "His sub-rosa experimentation on human embryos borders on the unethical, and I'll tell you straight out, I don't like it."

"But you know a lot more than that. Dr. Mike thinks so, and so do I. There's no point in denying it."

"I have no idea what you're talking about," Lara said, trying to sound indignant.

Abruptly, Jordan dropped his mock civility. "Don't play games with me," he snapped. "You came to Miracle Isle to spy on us. Who sent you?"

"No one sent me!"

"Don't lie to me, woman!" Jordan thundered. "I can't abide liars. *Who sent you to spy on us?*"

"No one," Lara protested.

Jordan took a threatening step toward Lara, and she flinched, thinking he was about to hit her. "I don't know what you're talking about," she insisted again, but the small, frightened voice she heard was unconvincing.

Jordan's face contorted, and he lunged forward and seized Lara's shoulders. "It was the Catholics," he shouted into her face, and he began to shake her viciously. "Tell me!" he yelled. "The Catholics sent you, didn't they? Tell me! Tell me!"

"Yes!" Lara cried in self-defense, and Jordan abruptly released her. Dizzy and gasping, Lara fell back in the chair.

"I knew it." Jordan threw back his head. "I knew it, Lord!" he cried, gazing heavenward. "They sent this woman to spy on us and steal Your precious gift. Oh, they're clever, Lord—so clever to have discovered Your divine plan . . . *but they shall not prevail!*"

Jordan closed his eyes, and for several seconds he didn't move. Then he looked down at Lara and fixed her with a piercing glare.

"You Catholics," he hissed. "You play with your beads and light candles to your saints, but you don't heed the Word of God. Your pope is blind, but I have seen and understood. Jesus is coming, and God has called me to prepare the way."

Jordan took a ragged breath and shook his head. "Why? Why did your pope send you to steal God's precious gift to the world? What would he do with it? *What?*"

"I've stolen nothing!" Lara exclaimed. "And I've done nothing!"

"But you *have*, woman. You've discovered God's holy plan. I can see it in your eyes. And I know your kind. You'd try to twist our purpose and deceive the people. You'd raise a cry against us and our holy mission."

Jordan paused and shook his head again. "I can't permit that, Lara. We are so close! Soon our own blessed Mary will receive the holy seed, just as God has ordained."

"Mary?" Lara gasped. "That young woman Mary Joplin? My God, are you going to experiment with *her*?"

Jordan wasn't listening. His eyes had filled with tears and again he raised his face to heaven. "Oh, Glory to God!" he cried. "Thy will be done!"

Suddenly something inside Lara snapped, and she came up out of her chair. "Glory to Jordan, you mean," she hurled at him in fury. "You pathetic egomaniac! Do you really think your twisted Dr. Mike can *clone Christ?* Do you actually believe that God needs *you* to bring about the Second Coming?"

Lara was standing almost toe-to-toe with Jordan, and as he tried to thrust her back into the chair, she brought up her good leg and kneed him in the groin. Jordan bellowed and crumpled, and as Michaels reached for Lara, she struck him in the face. She managed to reach the door, but before she could open it, Michaels snared her shirt collar and yanked her off her feet.

He seized Lara as she fell, and she began to yell at the top of her lungs. Michaels clamped his hand over her mouth. "Shut up!" he growled. "No one can hear you."

Still groaning, Jordan was getting to his feet. "Bobby!" Michaels demanded. "Help me get her on the bed."

Together they lifted Lara, thrashing and twisting, onto the hospital bed. She started to bite Michaels's hand and he released her mouth, but she wasted no more breath crying out.

"Keep hold of her," Michaels said to Jordan, reaching into his jacket pocket and pulling out a hypodermic syringe.

"You bastards!" Lara cried, struggling harder in Jordan's grip. "You goddamn bastards!"

"Sticks and stones," Michaels said, holding up the syringe and depressing the plunger. He pushed up her sleeve and seized her arm in a viselike grip. "Keep still or you'll snap the needle."

"No, you son of a bitch!" Lara snarled, thrashing futilely, but as she felt the needle slip in, she stopped fighting. Struggling would only speed the drug's course through her veins.

Michaels withdrew the needle and looked at Jordan. "Are you okay, Bobby?"

"Yes," Jordan grunted, glaring at Lara. "I'll leave the bitch in your hands."

As Jordan left the room, Michaels loosened his grip on Lara, holding her just firmly enough to maintain control. "There's no point in resisting us. You can't resist God's will."

"You're crazy," Lara said, gasping to catch her breath. "You know that, don't you? *You can't clone Christ.*"

"*Committed* is the word—committed to a holy mission."

"You're going to use an in vitro embryo from that unsuspecting couple, aren't you? You want to modify its DNA and implant it in that poor woman."

"That's right, Lara."

"But even if the mummified finger *was* cut from Jesus' body, you can't clone Him," Lara said, hoping against hope that she could reason with Michaels. "At best you could only transplant a tiny fragment of the finger's DNA—less than a millionth of the dead man's genetic code. What would that accomplish?"

"We don't have to clone the entire man." Michaels's voice sounded distorted, and Lara's vision was blurring. "God is more subtle than that. What I'll transmit to the babe is the heaven-sent essence of Christ's natural body."

Lara struggled to hold on to consciousness, but she was slipping . . . slipping.

"In all the fragments I sequenced, I found only two genes not present in modern man. Two genes from the Y chromosome—the chromosome our Lord received from His Father. Mary Joplin's child will be born with those genes, Lara—genes that will make the child the perfect vessel for our Savior's spirit."

"How can you possibly know that?" Lara mumbled faintly as her eyes closed.

"Because, Lara, that's what God told Bobby Jordan."

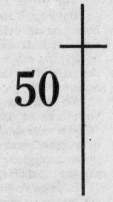

50

As Reese approached the entrance to the dispensary at the side of the clinic building, Bobby Jordan was coming out. His expression was grim, but the moment he spotted Reese, the look vanished and he flashed a smile.

"Ah, Mr. Reed. I assume you've heard we're evacuating."

"Yes, I heard."

"But we'll be riding out the storm in style in the best hotel in Portland, and you're certainly invited. I hope you'll join us there as our guest."

"Thanks. Maybe I will."

"Good! See you there," Jordan said, and he walked briskly away.

Reese entered the clinic and looked into the dispensary. Finding no one, he rang the bell beside the door several times. Finally he heard footsteps on the stairs down the hall, and Michaels appeared and strode to meet him.

"You look healthy," Michaels said with a smile, "so I assume you've come because you heard about Lara."

"I hear she's sick."

"And no doubt you're worried. I gather you two have hit it off. She's not sick, exactly," Michaels said, surprising Reese, "but she certainly isn't feeling well."

"What's wrong with her?"

"Well, I've been telling folks it's a flu bug, but since you have a special interest in Lara, you should probably know about her condition."

"What condition?" Reese asked, wondering what game Michaels was playing.

"She suffers from mild clinical depression, John, and one aspect of that is anxiety disorder—panic attacks. She had one last night. That story she made up to leave the party was just an excuse. And she had another attack this morning."

"I'm afraid I don't understand. What's she afraid of?"

"A panic attack doesn't require a reason. It's caused by a serotonin deficiency that produces acute anxiety, even when there is no objective reason for it. The patient has little, if any, control over the anxiety as it builds, and the body begins to react to it.

"The patient experiences sweaty palms, extreme shortness of breath, and even severe chest pains, and that only heightens the anxiety. It's a vicious cycle that can spiral out of control, threatening a person's hold on reality and sometimes reducing one to hysteria. That's what happened to Lara this morning. She was hysterical when I found her in the dispensary—shortly after I left you."

"But she's entirely normal," Reese objected, knowing Michaels would expect him to.

"Yes, of course she's normal," Michaels said smoothly. "As long as the condition is under control. According to her medical record, she's been under a psychiatrist's care, and he prescribed Prozac. Obviously the dose isn't quite right, and she's had a relapse."

"I'd like to see her."

"Of course you would," Michaels responded in a placating bedside manner, "but I've sedated her. She was hysterical and needed immediate relief."

"Aren't you going to bring her to the mainland?"

Michaels shook his head. "I think it best that she stay

here, despite the hurricane. Don't worry, John, I'll take good care of her. And of course I'll be in touch with the psychiatrist who treated her.''

"I'd still like to see her."

"All right," Michaels replied without hesitation, "but as I said, she's sedated and fast asleep.''

Lara didn't stir as Michaels and Reese entered her room. She was lying on her back, fully clothed and covered by a light blanket. Reese went to the bed and looked at her carefully. Her color was normal, and her breathing was deep and regular. She simply looked asleep.

"Lara," Reese said, taking her hand and squeezing it. Her head moved slightly, but her fingers remained slack and the momentary change in the rhythm of her breathing was slight.

"You see?" Michaels said. "Dead to the world."

Michaels had eliminated one of Reese's few options. Reese might have tried to free her at gunpoint, but now that was impossible. He couldn't risk carrying her, unconscious, out of the clinic and aboard the ferry while waving a gun. He would appear deranged, and he would be hopelessly encumbered. Jordan wouldn't hesitate to sic the security guards on him, and quite possibly he would order them to shoot.

"Sleep is what she needs right now," Michaels said. "And I'll control her symptoms with a tranquilizer until I talk to her psychiatrist. Once the dosage has been adjusted, she should be fine."

Reese registered the proviso, and he turned to look at Michaels. "What do mean, 'should be fine'?"

"Well, I'm sure this panic attack is nothing more than a minor relapse, but I'm no psychiatrist. I suppose it's possible that there's a deeper underlying problem that may require more intensive treatment. But don't worry. It's a very remote possibility," Michaels added with a bedside smile. "I shouldn't have even mentioned it."

But he *had* mentioned it, and Reese could guess how Michaels and Jordan intended to proceed. With Jordan's wealth and influence, it wouldn't be hard to find psychiatrists willing to commit Lara to a private mental hospital.

Reese itched to wipe the smile off Michaels's face, but he produced a smile of his own. "I know you'll take good care of her, but I'd like to stay on the island. I want to be here for her when she wakes up."

Michaels shook his head regretfully. "I'm afraid that won't be possible, John—as much as I'd like to have you stay. But I heard Bobby Jordan talking with Billy-Lee, and everyone who isn't absolutely essential must leave. It's something about insurance and liability."

"I see." Reese nodded in feigned resignation. Michaels's excuse was thin, but Reese wasn't going to challenge it. "When she wakes up, please tell her that I'll be coming back as soon as I can."

"Of course. And don't worry. She's going to be fine."

The mood of the people crowded into the dining hall for the late lunch was cheerful excitement. Jordan's staff was enjoying the thrill of an evacuation that was unmarred by risk or even discomfort. Jordan was seated at the head table with Lurleen, Billy-Lee, and Michaels, and he looked buoyant. Apparently he considered the problem of Lara Brooks already solved.

Reese chewed mechanically on his sandwich, forcing himself to eat. There was no telling when his next meal would be, and a long twelve to eighteen hours lay ahead of him. He had ruled out leaving on the ferry and going to the state police. Without proof, his story would sound absurd, and there was too little time to persuade them to investigate. Reese was sure the *yakuza* would be coming on the heels of the storm.

He would have to stay on the island, free Lara, and call in his helicopter pickup at the first opportunity. He hoped he could finesse his departure, but if necessary, he would simply refuse to leave. It might create a scene, but Jordan and Michaels couldn't afford to draw too much attention to Lara's situation.

Reese looked over at the head table as Bobby Jordan rose from his seat. Billy-Lee rapped on his glass with a spoon, and the hubbub in the room immediately subsided.

"Brothers and sisters," Jordan said in his resonant baritone, "I have a few announcements to make. First of all, I want you to know that you'll be seeing the broadcast we taped this morning a week from today. Despite the power failure, I think we have a wonderful service on tape, and I'm sure the special message we delivered to the world this morning will be a blessing to all our viewers."

This was received with enthusiastic and prolonged applause.

"Secondly, I want you to know that we are all going to have a *good* time riding out this storm. Buses will meet you in Lambeth Cove, and I've arranged for accommodations in the best hotel in Portland, where you'll be treated to a specially catered dinner."

Jordan paused as the crowd began to cheer, and he had to raise his voice to continue. "And afterwards," he went on with a broad grin, "Lurleen and I will be joining you for a good old-fashioned camp meeting. The devil may have robbed us of our electricity, but he can't take away the power of the Spirit!"

The crowd roared its approval, and Jordan held up his arms for quiet. "I'm told the ferry from the mainland has been delayed, but so has the hurricane. The ferry will get here around two P.M., and there will plenty of time to make a safe passage down to Lambeth Cove. But I'd appreciate it if you'd gather here fifteen minutes ahead of time, so that you can all go down together and get aboard promptly.

"Lurleen and I would like to go with you, but we'll be flying out after you depart. I must bring my helicopter to a safe haven before the storm hits. But Lurleen and I will be with you in spirit, and we'll all meet up again this evening at the hotel.

"Finally, I'd like you to give a nice round of applause to Billy-Lee, Dr. Mike, and four other stalwarts," Jordan said, pointing to Johnson and his fellow security guards. "They're staying behind to batten down the hatches and ride out the storm right here."

Johnson smiled perfunctorily, and the other three ex-Marine types looked distinctly bored. They wouldn't be bored much longer, Reese thought—not once the *yakuza* hit the island.

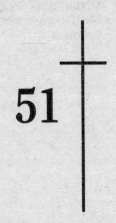

51

As Reese joined the crowd gathered outside the dining hall, Fletch spotted him and came over. "We're not going to have to rough it," Fletch said, laughing, eyeing Reese's clothes. "We're going to a hotel."

"Just getting into the hurricane spirit." Reese had changed into jeans and hiking boots, and he was wearing a lightweight safari jacket. He had brought the extra clothes with no specific purpose in mind, but now he was glad he had. In the jacket's voluminous pockets were Beretta's cellular phone and an extra clip of ammunition. The Browning was tucked in behind his hip.

"Did you get to speak to Lara?" Fletch asked.

"No. She's still sleeping, and Michaels didn't want me waking her."

"It's a shame she's going to be stuck here. Have you heard the rumor?"

"What rumor?"

"About the generators. One of the guys told me that the chief engineer thinks they were sabotaged."

"No way. It wouldn't be the Christian thing to do."

To Reese's surprise, Fletch laughed heartily. "Right. Definitely not."

Billy-Lee had been standing apart from the crowd, apparently trying to count heads, and now he drew himself up to his meager height and called for attention. "I don't see anyone missing," he said loudly, "but if you know someone who isn't here, give a holler." He waited for a few seconds and then nodded. "All right, folks. Looks like everyone's here, so go on down to the ferry and get aboard. Bon voyage!"

Billy-Lee shepherded the group to the brow of the hill, but he didn't follow as the crowd flowed onto the road and started down the slope. Reese had intended to try to slip into the storage shed as the crowd moved onto the ferry, but Fletch was sticking to him like glue.

"Why aren't you with your girl?" Reese asked, and Fletch grimaced and brushed his recalcitrant shock of blond hair back from his forehead.

"Women." Fletch sighed. "You can't live with 'em, and you can't live without 'em."

Coming from the freckle-faced youngster, the world-weary sentiment should have struck Reese as comical, but he was in no mood to appreciate the humor.

One of Jordan's gospel singers started a familiar song, and it was immediately picked up by the crowd. Smiling and singing, Bobby Jordan's true believers marched happily down the road. Besides Reese, only the chief maintenance man didn't join in the singing. Reese saw him trudging along with a dour expression, apparently suffering the blame for the power failure.

The group was still singing as the people in the lead marched onto the ferry slip and trooped aboard. Reese and Fletch brought up the rear, and Reese slowed his pace even more and glanced back up the hill. Billy-Lee had been watching the group's progress, but now he turned away and headed back into the compound.

Reese smiled inwardly. It was the first bit of luck he'd had. That, and the fact that Jarvis still hadn't left with the *Mary Jane*. "Shit!" Reese burst out for Fletch's benefit as they approached the ferry's stern gate. "I forgot the damn diskettes."

"What?"

"I left some proprietary software in the control room."

"Nothing's going to happen to it, and you'll be coming back. What's the problem?"

"You don't know my boss," Reese said with an exaggerated frown as he followed Fletch onto the ferry. He set down his overnight bag and looked up the hill again. No one was in sight. The deck began to vibrate as the ferry's engines started.

"I'll have to go back," Reese said quickly to Fletch, then slipped past the deckhand who was closing the stern gate.

"John, what are you doing?" Fletch called after him.

"I'll make the crossing with Jarvis," Reese called back for the benefit of Fletch and several onlookers.

"Don't be silly, John. You can leave the diskettes."

"Are you coming or staying?" the deckhand interjected sourly, glaring at Reese. "We don't have all day."

"Staying," Reese said, and the deckhand closed up the stern gate.

"Hey!" Fletch exclaimed. "What about your bag?"

"Take it over to the hotel, will you please? Just leave it at the desk."

"Sure, but—" Fletch broke off as the ferry started moving, and he smiled and shrugged. "Okay, John. See you later."

"See you," Reese called back, moving casually to his right until the storage shed beside the ferry slip hid him from view from the top of the hill. He looked across the harbor at the *Mary Jane*. Jarvis had been moving about on the boat, but now Reese couldn't see him.

Reese stayed where he was until the ferry cleared the harbor, turned east, and passed out of sight. The sky was heavily overcast and the sea breeze was picking up, but the leaden sea was relatively quiet. The hurricane was clearly still hours away.

Jarvis was still not in sight, but Reese moved around to the far side of the shed in case Jarvis reappeared. Reese didn't like the situation, but luck had given him an edge. He was still on Miracle Isle, and he was the only one on the island who knew it. He took one last look up the hill and sprinted diagonally up the grassy slope to the cover of the bordering pines.

He was breathing hard by the time he reached the tree line, and he had to rest before he was ready to move on up to the plateau. He climbed up the sharp, wooded slope as quickly as he could and circled around to the rear of the compound to where he could observe the helicopter pad. It seemed just possible that Jordan might try to spirit Lara off the island.

If Jordan did try that, Reese resolved, the preacher was in for an unpleasant surprise. He would have Reese as an additional passenger. The Browning would be Reese's boarding pass.

After the Second Book is opened, let him that is wicked, be wicked still. And let him that is righteous, be righteous still. For judgment shall not be stayed, and each shall receive his reward, according to his deeds.

SAMARIA SCROLL 1, COLUMN 3.7.2

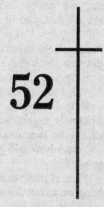

52

Daddy's waiting outside," Billy-Lee said through the open doorway to Lurleen's room.

She was sitting at her dressing table, putting finishing touches to her makeup, and she didn't look around. "I'll be ready in a minute," she said in a clipped tone.

Billy-Lee stepped inside and closed the door behind him. "Daddy's told you what's happened."

"Yes," Lurleen said, leaning closer to the mirror for a final inspection. "He's finally told me everything."

Apparently satisfied, she turned around on her seat and looked at Billy-Lee. "Imagine my surprise when I discovered that Revelation had it all wrong. I can't recall anythin' in there about makin' copies of little ol' pieces of dried-up DNA and stickin' them into a test-tube embryo."

"But it's going to be *all right*." Billy-Lee had half convinced himself, and now he desperately wanted to convince Lurleen. "No one's going to find out. Michaels knows how to deal with the Brooks woman, and if anyone else tries to mess with us, I'll handle it."

Lurleen arched an eyebrow. "By that, I assume you mean

your security guards will handle it. What did you tell them?''

"That the Aaronites sent the Brooks woman. I told them that we caught her wrecking Michaels's equipment after she'd sabotaged the generators.''

"My, my," Lurleen responded unsmilingly. "What an imagination. Breakin' in and wreckin' a laboratory. However did you think that one up?''

Billy-Lee flushed.

"*Did* she sabotage the generators?''

Billy-Lee shook his head. "Why should she? That's how Michaels caught her. The chief engineer just made that one up on the spur of the moment to cover himself.''

"And how did you explain not handin' her over to the police?''

"I said that we don't want scandal. I told them that we'll hang on to her for a day or so to see if she'll tell us anything, and then ship her off the island.''

"Isn't Johnson worried about a kidnappin' charge?''

"It would be her word against ours, and besides, I threw in a bonus for him and his men. I made it a big one. Whatever they have to do from here on out, they'll do. The price may go up, but we can afford it.''

"And what do you think they may have to do?'' Lurleen asked, staring at Billy-Lee.

"I don't know. But we have to protect the ministry, don't we? *Don't we?* Why are you looking at me like that?''

"It doesn't matter." Lurleen rose and picked up her handbag. "We mustn't keep your daddy waiting.''

"What's the matter?'' Billy-Lee demanded as Lurleen walked past him and he followed her into the hall. "What are you worried about?''

Lurleen just kept walking.

"Sweet Jesus,'' Billy-Lee burst out. "We have things under control.''

"The Lord's will shall be done,'' Lurleen said without looking back as she continued down the hall, "whether we know what it is or not. But that's never been enough for your daddy. All his life he's *had* to know. You'd better understand something, Billy-Lee. If that revelation of his goes sour and there's real trouble, you'll be on your own. Your daddy'll crack like an eggshell.''

Reese watched from the edge of the forest as Billy-Lee accompanied Bobby Jordan and Lurleen to their helicopter. Billy-Lee waited until they took off, then headed back toward the dormitory.

Reese moved to his left through the trees bordering the rear of the compound until the dormitory and the entrance to the clinic's dispensary were in view. Billy-Lee had stopped at the entrance to the dining hall to speak to one of the security guards coming from the maintenance building. The man carried storm lanterns and a collection of raingear, and he followed Billy-Lee into the dining hall, where they apparently intended to ride out the hurricane.

A few minutes later, Johnson appeared, walking from the maintenance building to the dining hall with a burden of his own. Johnson was carrying an armload of shotguns. Reese could only guess the reason for the guns, but he recalled the security chief's reference to threats from a fringe religious group. Apparently someone had not dismissed the maintenance engineer's claim of sabotage.

The hurricane was approaching far more slowly than Reese had anticipated, but having seen the shotguns, he gave no more thought to calling in his helicopter before the storm hit. He wanted the cover of the hurricane. If he was caught trying to free Lara from the clinic, Billy-Lee's men would pin them down. Reese wouldn't go for her until the storm was at its height.

53

Reese heard the warning crack of a tree limb breaking above him, and he rolled aside as the limb crashed to the ground. Throughout the forest, pines were being uprooted by the shrieking wind ripping across the plateau, and twigs and branches whirled through the air across the rain-lashed compound. The hurricane had brought dusk early, and the glow of storm lanterns showed in the windows of the dining hall. All the other buildings were dark.

Billy-Lee, Michaels, and the security guards had been gathered in the dining hall for the past half hour, and Reese decided to wait no longer. He got stiffly to his feet and broke from the cover of the woods. Slitting his eyes against the wind-whipped rain, he ran past the helicopter pad and the end of the maintenance building toward the entrance to the clinic's dispensary.

He was wringing wet and chilled, and he ran awkwardly. His rain-soaked jacket weighed on his shoulders and arms, and his jeans clung wetly to his thighs. He was panting hard by the time he reached the entrance.

As he opened the door, the wind caught it and nearly tore

it from his hand. He stepped inside, forced the door closed behind him, and paused for a few seconds to catch his breath. The hallway was dark, and the building was silent. All Reese could hear was the shriek of the wind outside.

He made his way down the hallway and up the stairs to the room where he'd last seen Lara, praying she hadn't been moved. The door was closed, but unlocked, and to Reese's relief, he found her inside. She didn't stir as he approached her bed, but his hopes rose as he saw restraining straps about her arms and legs. Apparently Michaels expected the sedation to wear off before he returned.

"Lara!" Reese said sharply, shaking her shoulder. "Lara, wake up!" She moaned softly, and her eyes flickered, but she didn't awake.

Reese unfastened the restraints and tried again to wake her, but without success. She muttered something and slipped back under. Yet the sedation was wearing off, and Reese decided to wait. Unless Michaels forced his hand by returning too soon, he wouldn't bring Lara out of the clinic until she could leave under her own power.

Water was dripping from his clothes onto the floor, and it reminded him of the wet tracks he must have left behind. He stripped off his soaked jacket, dropped it onto the back of the chair beside the bed, and went into the adjoining bathroom to look for towels. Finding none, he went downstairs.

He found towels in the dispensary and methodically wiped up the tracks he'd left in the hallway and on the stairs. The corridor was so dark that he had to light his cigarette lighter periodically to check his work. Lara was still fast asleep when he returned to her room.

Reese left the door ajar, moved the chair from beside the bed over to the doorway, and settled down to wait. He would have to rely on his ears to warn him if Michaels returned, for the room's window gave him no view of the dining hall.

It was seven-thirty before Lara began to stir, and Reese immediately went to the bed to prod her awake. Outside, the wind seemed to be diminishing, as if the eye of the hurricane was approaching, and he thought Michaels might take advantage of the lull to come and check on Lara.

She sighed in response to his touch and dreamily opened her eyes. The light in the room was so dim that she didn't immediately recognize him as she came awake, and her eyes went wide. She gasped and shrank away from him.

"Easy, Lara. It's me—Reese."

"John!" she cried in relief, and seized his arms. "God, I was praying you'd come."

Reese lifted her into a sitting position, and she clung to him.

"I didn't know what was going to happen," she said, starting to cry as her words spilled out. "What they might do to me. It was horrible. John, they're both crazy."

"It's all right now," Reese said, tightening his arms around her. "It's okay."

It felt to Lara as if the bed were spinning beneath her. Her head throbbed and her dizziness was nauseating, yet she didn't care in those first few moments. Reese had come for her, and that was all that mattered.

But as her mind continued to clear, fear broke in on her again with renewed force. "Where are Michaels and Jordan?" she asked anxiously, pulling back so she could see his face. "Please, John, get me out of here."

"I will. And I promise they won't get their hands on you again. How do you feel?"

"Dizzy," Lara said, pressing closer to him. "Why is it so dark?"

"It's evening, Lara, and we're in the middle of a hurricane. You've been sedated all day."

"All day?"

"Yes. Did Michaels give you more than one shot?"

"I think so," Lara replied, unsure how much of what she remembered was real. "John, we've got to get out of here and tell the staff what's going on. Some are bound to help us. They can't all be crazy."

"There's no one to tell, Lara. There was a power failure this morning, and almost everyone has gone to the mainland. Only Billy-Lee, Michaels, and the security guards stayed behind."

"We're *alone* with them?"

"Yes, but we have an edge, Lara," Reese said quickly. "They don't know I'm here. They think I left with the others."

The reassurance in his voice calmed Lara more than the words themselves, but it couldn't dispel her anxiety. "What about Jarvis? Is he gone, too?"

"Yes. He had to take his boat down to Lambeth Cove."

"Then how will we get away?"

"Don't *worry*," Reese urged, gripping her shoulders and easing her back onto the bed. "Beretta made arrangements for a helicopter pickup in case I ran into trouble. We'll get away, all right, and I'll take you out of here as soon as you're able. Don't try to get out of bed just yet."

"But what if someone comes?"

"I'll take care of him," Reese said with a flat finality that under other circumstances might have been chilling. Now it made her feel safer.

"What happened this morning?" he asked. "Did you break into Michaels's lab?"

There was no recrimination in his voice, and Lara almost wished there were. God, she'd thought she was being so clever . . . "I'm sorry, John. I thought I had plenty of time, but Michaels came back early."

"I know. It was the power failure. Michaels left the chapel to check his equipment."

Lara shuddered. "I tried to talk my way out, but it was no use. He guessed at once that I'd found him out."

"You *found* the finger?"

"I didn't see it, but I know where it is. He keeps it locked in a safe. And John, I know what they're doing! I read Michaels's lab notes. He and Jordan are certifiable—stark, raving mad. They think they can clone Christ!"

"*What?*"

"Well, not really—not the whole man—but Michaels found two aberrant genes in the finger's DNA that he says carry the 'essence of Christ.' He wants to insert them into a test-tube embryo. God, *that's* why they brought that young couple to the island for in vitro fertilization. They want to implant it in Mary Joplin's womb!''

"Is it possible to do that?"

"In principle, yes, but God only knows what effect those genes would have on the fetus if it survives. It's a horrible experiment, John. We've got to stop them!"

"We will."

"Please let's get out of here." Lara pushed herself up into a sitting position. At once a fresh wave of dizziness swept over her, and she grimaced.

"But can you walk?"

"I think so."

"Okay, let's see." Reese picked up her shoes and handed them to her. But he made no move to help her.

As Lara tried to put on the shoes and tie the laces, she felt that she might fall off the bed at any moment. Reese just watched her, waiting to see if she could manage.

"What about this helicopter?" she asked to distract him from her fumbling.

"Beretta arranged to have one for me on twenty-four-hour standby, and he gave me a cell phone to call for the pickup. There's just one problem. The chopper can't fly in before the storm passes, and that's when the *yakuza* will be coming."

"How can you know that?" Lara asked, hardly caring. Her desperate desire to get out of the clinic was all-consuming. Both shoes were on, and one was tied. Only one to go, but the effort almost seemed too much.

"Because that power failure was no accident. Your trusty technician sabotaged the generators last night. You were half-right about the *yakuza*. They wanted people off the island, all right, but they weren't willing to wait."

"Then what are we going to do?" Lara asked, tying the last knot and sliding her legs over the edge of the bed.

"Keep out of everyone's way and wait for our chance to call in the helicopter. Or get off the island on the *Mary Jane*. Jarvis promised me he'd come back as soon as possible after the storm, and maybe he will."

Lara looked at the floor, which seemed a long way down,

and eased herself off the bed. Again Reese made no move to help her, and she willed herself to succeed. The threat of the *yakuza* remained an abstraction. It was Michaels who terrified her, and she was desperate to get out of the clinic.

To Lara's relief, her legs didn't fold up under her.

"How do you feel?" Reese asked as she stood beside the bed, swaying with dizziness and hanging on to the mattress for support.

"Still woozy, but I can—"

Reese stiffened and Lara's throat constricted as they heard the heavy thud of an outer door slamming shut downstairs. "Someone's coming!" she whispered, feeling panic rise in her again.

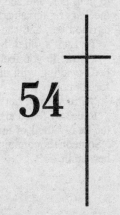

54

I'll bet it's Michaels," Reese said, striding to the door and closing it. "I've been half expecting him to check on you."

He came back, picked Lara up, and placed her on the bed again. "Don't worry," he said as he saw her start to shiver. "I'll take care of him. All you have to do is play possum."

Quickly Reese covered her with the blanket and loosely refastened the restraining straps. "If he comes in here, just lie still with your eyes closed."

"That may not be so easy. I'm shaking all over."

"You'll do fine," Reese said, running his hand lightly over her hair. "I said they wouldn't get their hands on you again, and I meant it."

"Maybe it isn't Michaels," Lara said, and Reese heard the hope in her voice. Michaels had obviously terrified her.

"I hope it is," Reese said, feeling his rage build.

"Why?"

"So we can get the finger," he said, not wanting her to know what he had in mind for Michaels. "If we run into trouble, it could be a useful bargaining chip."

Lara forced herself to stop shivering and kept her eyes on Reese, drawing reassurance from his calm preparations. He returned the chair he'd used to its original position, picked up his jacket, and slipped it back on. Then he drew his gun, checked it, and took up a position where he would be hidden by the door when it opened. The readiness she saw in his expression betrayed no anxiety.

Then he winked at her, and Lara found herself actually able to smile. The look in Reese's eyes and the gun in his hand made it more difficult than ever to picture Reese as a teacher, and again Lara wondered fleetingly what he'd been earlier in life. Whatever it was, she was grateful.

Reese raised a finger to his lips, and Lara heard footsteps coming down the hall. As the steps approached the door, Reese gestured urgently and Lara realized that she was staring fixedly at him. She turned her head and closed her eyes just before the door opened. As she heard the intruder coming toward her, she held her breath, not trusting herself to breathe normally.

Lara heard the door slam shut, and her eyes flew open. Three feet from her bed a startled Michaels whirled to face Reese, who had been hidden by the door as it opened.

"Surprise," Reese said softly.

"Reed!" Michaels burst out, but then he saw the gun and froze.

Lara sat up and hastily freed herself from the straps. She still felt weak and dizzy, but now she was sure she could walk. As she slid off the bed, Michaels, who held a syringe in his hand, recovered from his surprise.

He looked from Reese to Lara, and if Reese had not been there, she would have shrunk from Michaels. "So," he said coldly, returning his eyes to Reese, "you're in this together. How did you get back on the island, Reed?"

"Drop the syringe," Reese snapped.

Michaels let the syringe fall to the floor, but if he was worried, he didn't show it. "Give it up, Reed. You can't stand in the way of God's will."

"Watch me." Reese gestured with his automatic. "Move away from the bed. That's it. Good. And if you don't want me to pull the trigger accidentally, you'll stay put. Lara, can you walk?'' Reese asked without taking his eyes off Michaels.

''I think so.''

''Come on over and stand behind me,'' Reese said, still watching Michaels.

Lara walked to him unsteadily, but her dizziness was fading away, leaving her feeling merely weak. Reese waited until she was behind him, then he said softly to Michaels, ''I want the finger.''

Michaels smiled thinly, without a trace of fear. ''No doubt, but you won't get it from me. That gun in your hand won't do you any good. If you use it, the others will hear. Then you'll be in for it.''

''I don't think so,'' Reese said, his voice dropping even lower.

Lara didn't think Michaels heard the warning in that soft voice, but she did.

''Lara,'' Reese said, ''please wait for me out in the hall.''

''But can't we just—''

''Please wait outside,'' he interrupted without looking around. ''And shut the door behind you.''

Reese waited until he heard the door close behind him, then he advanced on Michaels. ''I've been looking forward to this,'' he said with a smile, and it was genuine.

Reese didn't know if he could beat Michaels into submission, but he was going to try. The man he faced shared responsibility for Allison's living death, and it was payback time. Reese took one last step toward Michaels, counting on the man's reacting, and Michaels didn't disappoint him.

The renegade scientist was strong and quick, but not quick enough. As Reese came within arm's reach, Michaels lunged, trying to sweep aside the gun, and simultaneously threw a right hook. Reese pulled back his gun hand and ducked under Michaels's swing, and before Michaels could recover, Reese backhanded him across the mouth with the gun barrel.

Reese struck viciously, and the blow split Michaels's lips wide open and splintered several front teeth. Michaels staggered back against the wall with an agonized cry. Blood gushed from his mouth, and his eyes went wide with shock, but Reese wasn't finished. He kicked Michaels in the crotch, and Michaels crumpled to his hands and knees, gasping and gagging. Reese shifted his gun to his left hand, balled his fist, and hammered Michaels to the floor with a kidney punch.

"John!" Lara called anxiously through the door. "What's happening?"

"Stay out there," Reese yelled, and his voice sounded unnatural to him.

Michaels was still conscious, but he could hardly move. His limbs twitched feebly as he lay, facedown, gurgling in agony. Reese picked up the syringe Michaels had dropped, slipped it into his jacket pocket, and waited for Michaels to recover.

As soon as he was sure that Michaels would register his words, he prodded him in the ribs with his boot and told him to roll over. Groaning, coughing, and spitting blood, Michaels rolled onto his back and stared up at Reese with eyes glazed with pain and shock.

"Do you want to hand over the finger? Or would you like more of the same before I get around to shooting you?"

"Woarrgh," was Michaels's gurgling response.

Reese dropped to a crouch beside him. "You've got to understand," he said softly. "My daughter was in the laboratory you creeps raided, and now she's a vegetable. I *want* to kill you, Michaels. I'll enjoy it. So, please—tell me you're not going to give me that finger."

Reese wasn't sure he didn't mean it, and Michaels's terrified eyes showed no doubt whatsoever. As Reese rose, Michaels nodded desperately and made an unintelligible noise that Reese interpreted as assent.

"Smart choice." Reese went over to the bed. He stripped off the pillowcase and threw it at Michaels. "Keep that over your mouth. I don't want to make Lara sick. Now, get up."

Michaels clasped the pillowcase over his gory mouth and struggled to his feet.

"Okay. Take us down to your lab."

Michaels nodded and tottered to the door and out into the hall. As he passed Lara, she stared at the blood already soaking through the pillowcase.

"Dr. Mike changed his mind," Reese said.

55

Michaels removed a small, brown glass bottle from its atmosphere-controlled cabinet and handed it to Reese. This was what Reese had so desired, but he felt nothing as his fingers closed on it. The bottle's plastic cap was tightly sealed with a wrapping of tape. It was too dark in the laboratory to see anything clearly, and Reese flicked his lighter and held the flame behind the bottle to illuminate the interior.

"What do you think?" he asked Lara, showing it to her. "Should I open it to be sure?"

Lara shook her head. "It looks right, and we shouldn't expose it to moisture." She looked down at Michaels. He had been kneeling beside the storage cabinet, and now he sagged against his desk. "I don't think he'd try to fool us."

"Okay, Dr. Mike," Reese said. "Lock up the cabinet."

Michaels closed and locked the storage cabinet, and Reese pulled the swivel chair back from Michaels's desk. "Get in under the desk. Slide in backward and draw in your legs."

Michaels stared at Reese uncomprehendingly.

"Move!" Reese snapped.

As Michaels squeezed himself in under the desk, Reese

took the hypodermic syringe from his jacket. "It's time for a dose of your own medicine, Doctor."

"No!" Michaels protested, his inarticulate voice muffled by his hand over his mouth.

"I know it's no longer sterile," Reese said, crouching before him, "but that's life. Take it, and give yourself the shot."

Reese handed him the syringe and flicked his lighter again to be sure Michaels actually inserted the needle and gave himself the full dose. As Michaels dropped his hand from his ruined mouth to push up his sleeve and inject himself, Reese heard Lara gasp.

"It looks worse than it is," he told her, stretching the truth.

As soon as Michaels was finished, Reese took the syringe and stood up. "How long before it takes effect?" he asked Lara, who was staring at Michaels's gory, gaping mouth.

"I—I don't know exactly," she said in a shocked voice. "Not long . . . no more than a minute or two."

"You need something to wear outside," he said to her to distract her from Michaels. "He must have had a raincoat or jacket when he came over. Why don't you see if you can find it—maybe in the dispensary."

"Okay," Lara said weakly, still looking at Michaels.

"Take this. It's getting pretty dark." Reese pressed his cigarette lighter into her hand. Her hand was ice-cold. "Will you be all right?"

"Yes. I'll be okay."

Reese watched her as she made her way out of the laboratory, then he turned back to Michaels. Dr. Mike stared back at him with hate-filled eyes as Reese waited impatiently for the drug to take hold. Michaels's eyes didn't close until just before Lara returned.

She was wearing Michaels's trench coat, and it swallowed her up. She looked small and vulnerable. "I found it," she said, obviously trying to sound stronger than she felt. She was leaning against the desk for support.

"How are you doing?" Reese asked worriedly.

"Not so great. Maybe I'm allergic to whatever Michaels used on me. What about him? Is he out?"

Reese thought so, but he wanted to be sure. "It doesn't matter." He crouched down and pressed the muzzle of the Browning against Michaels's forehead. "I'll just shoot the son of a bitch."

Michaels didn't react, but Lara did. "No!" she cried, seizing Reese's arm.

"I was just testing," Reese said quickly. "I had to be sure he was out."

"Don't do that to me!" Lara exclaimed, and as Reese stood up, she recoiled from him.

Reese's own nerves were stretched taut, and he couldn't suppress the flash of anger her reaction ignited.

"Goddamnit," he burst out. "I warned you, but you wouldn't listen! I'm sorry if it isn't pretty, but you're stuck with me—and whatever I have to do to get us off this goddamned island."

Lara winced. "John, I didn't mean—"

Reese cut her off. "Let's get out of here." He shoved the desk chair into place to hide Michaels. Without a careful search, no one was going to find him. "Is there a rear exit to this building?"

"Yes," Lara said in a small voice that made him regret his outburst. "Between this lab and the dispensary."

"Okay, let's go," he said, taking her arm. "Sorry I snapped at you."

"That's all right."

"No, it isn't. You've been through enough already."

The clinic's rear exit opened onto a wide strip of grass between the back of the clinic and the maintenance building, and it was out of sight of the dining hall. Nevertheless, Reese opened the door slowly and cautiously peered into the gathering darkness. "All clear." He took Lara's arm. "Let's go."

There was little chance of being spotted, but as Reese led her between the two buildings, heading for the woods beyond the DNA lab, he had to suppress the urge to run. Lara was keeping up with him, but she was none too steady on her feet.

The eye of the hurricane had apparently missed the island, for although the wind had moderated for a while, it hadn't died. And now it was back to full force. Violent gusts buffeted them as they came out between the clinic and maintenance building and hurried past the DNA laboratory to the forest. They reached the edge of the pines, and Reese stopped to let Lara rest.

"How are you doing?" he asked, raising his voice to be heard.

"Okay," Lara shouted back, wiping the rain from her face, but he didn't believe her.

Twice she had nearly fallen, and already she was dripping wet. Despite the trench coat, the wind would soon chill her, adding to the misery of the sedative's lingering aftereffects.

"Do you know if Jarvis locks up his cottage when he leaves the island?" he asked.

"Yes—but only so the door stays shut. He leaves the key in the lock. Are we going down there?"

"Yes, but we'll take the long way around to be sure we're not seen."

Screened by the trees on the edge of the forest, they circled around the rear of the compound and made their way downhill through the pines bordering the eastern side of the grassy slope. Reese halted two-thirds of the way down the slope, at a point where the tree line angled away from Jarvis's cottage. The cottage was below them and to their right.

Reese looked back up the slope at the compound. No lights were showing, and he saw no one. "Okay," he said, taking a firm grip on Lara's arm, "let's get on down there."

Despite the growing darkness and driving rain that cut down visibility, Reese didn't like crossing the forty yards of open ground to the cottage. He was too anxious to avoid being spotted, and instead of letting Lara set the pace as they moved down the slope, he relied on his hold on her to keep her from falling. The wind beat against them, stinging their faces with rain, and they repeatedly slipped in the wet grass and stumbled on rock outcroppings.

Just above Jarvis's cottage, an embankment dropped abruptly to the level of the shore road, and Reese misjudged it. He slipped and pulled Lara off-balance, and he heard her sharp cry of pain as she stumbled and tumbled forward. He couldn't catch her, and they both fell and slid in a tangle to the bottom of the embankment.

Reese scrambled to his feet, but Lara didn't rise. "My ankle!" she cried, her voice whipped away by the wind and barely audible above the thunderous pounding of the surf. "Damn! I think I've sprained it."

Cursing his stupidity, Reese seized Lara under her arms and lifted her up. "Can you put any weight on it at all?" he shouted, holding her tightly about the waist.

Lara tried and immediately cried out again. "It's no use. I can't walk."

"I'll carry you."

Reese scooped her up and carried her in his arms to the kitchen door of Jarvis's cottage. To his relief, the key was in the lock, and the moment he unlocked the door, the wind blew it open. He carried Lara inside, lowered her carefully to the floor, and returned to the door. He removed the key, slammed the door shut, and locked it from the inside.

The windows were shuttered, and the moment the door closed, they were plunged into total darkness. The old house creaked and rattled as the wind gusts buffeted it, but the sounds were hardly noticeable against the background thunder of the waves crashing ashore outside.

Reese flicked his lighter. "Christ, it's a rat's nest in here."

"And it smells," Lara added, finding herself smiling, "but any port in a storm."

When Reese had slammed the door on the storm outside, it had been as if he'd shut out everything else as well. Sometime during their flight through the woods, Lara's headache had vanished, along with her dizziness, and for the moment, at least, they were safe. The relief Lara felt was second only to her relief upon waking in the clinic and finding Reese.

"How's your ankle?" he asked, going to one knee beside her.

Lara tried to flex it and winced. "I'm afraid it's sprained."

Gently Reese pulled down her sock and examined her ankle. "You're right," he said worriedly. "It's swelling already."

He extinguished the lighter, but before they were plunged into darkness again, Lara caught the worry in his eyes. He must have been counting on being able to move about at will, she realized with a pang, and now . . .

"I'm sorry," she said into the darkness.

"It's my fault. I was coming down the hill too fast."

"No," Lara said, feeling for his arm. "I mean I'm sorry I got you into this fix."

"Don't be. I got myself into it."

"But if I hadn't gone into Michaels's lab on my own—"

"We wouldn't have the finger. I'm not complaining."

But Lara hadn't forgotten his angry outburst, and it was the flare-up, rather than the words themselves, that made her feel guilty now. Until then, he'd seemed so coldly deliberate—which had made what he'd done to Michaels so shocking to her—but when his control had slipped, she'd heard the strain beneath his anger.

He was afraid for her, she realized, and the worst thing was that she was glad.

Reese rose and used his lighter again to scan the contents of the kitchen, and Lara slipped off her soaked raincoat. He spotted an old flashlight on a shelf on the far wall and went to try it. The batteries were weak, but the beam was still adequate.

"Do you want a chair?" he asked.

"I'm better off on the floor with my leg stretched out." Lara's ankle was throbbing dully, but again she tried to flex it. The pain was excruciating, and inwardly she writhed in frustration. Unable even to walk, she'd become a millstone around Reese's neck.

"What about ice for the ankle?" she asked, grasping at straws. Bringing down the swelling might not help much, but it was worth a try. "Is there any in Jarvis's refrigerator?"

Reese checked and shook his head. "No luck. The trays are empty. But there's Coke and beer. Want something to drink?"

"Yes, please." Lara was belatedly aware of her parched throat. "A Coke."

"What about something to eat?"

"No, thanks. My stomach's still queasy."

Lara sounded exhausted to Reese, but she seemed to have recovered her spirit. Good, he thought grimly; they were both going to need it. He took a six-pack of Coke from the refrigerator and brought it over to her. Then he moved to the window facing the slope and peered through a narrow gap between the planks of the storm shutter. He found he could see all they way up the hill, where the dark outlines of the compound's buildings were rapidly merging with the premature night.

He pulled over a chair from the kitchen table, switched off the flashlight, and sat down. "I'll keep an eye on the compound from here," he said, trying to sound confident.

Lara slid across the floor and settled beside him with her back against the wall. "Want one?" she asked, popping open a can.

"Yes." Lara felt for his hand and gave him a Coke. Though he was thirsty, the pleasure he took in slaking it was only fleeting. He hadn't reckoned with being pinned down, and he had to think, and think quickly.

Even with Lara crippled, no one would find them in the darkness, but if daybreak came before they were able to get off the island, they would be tracked down. To passively await events was now too risky, but the alternative might be even more dangerous.

Lara had opened another can for herself, and he heard her drink thirstily. "Ah, that's better," she said with a sigh of relief. "We're doing all right, aren't we?"

"So far, so good," Reese replied, wondering how long it would be before Billy-Lee missed Michaels.

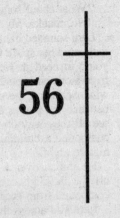

56

"What's keeping Michaels?" Billy-Lee worried aloud, rising restlessly from his chair.

"Relax, boss," said Johnson, who was lounging with his men. They had their chairs tilted back and their feet propped up on one of the dining room tables. "Maybe he's humping the broad."

The other three laughed coarsely, and Billy-Lee felt his cheeks begin to redden. *Damn it, they're laughing at me.* Billy-Lee turned away and went to the window, unwilling for them to see his embarrassment. He'd never felt comfortable with them—and particularly not with Johnson.

Billy-Lee was unused to the swagger and barracks crudity of the men he'd hired, and they seemed to relish his discomfiture. He'd overheard them referring to him and his father as Bible thumpers, which had quickly become Big Thumper and Little Thumper. Billy-Lee had done nothing about it, for he needed them, and he could have tolerated the ridicule of Johnson's underlings.

They were stupid men with unimaginative faces who were clearly beneath him; but Johnson himself was harder to dismiss. He was a hawk-nosed, swarthy man, as big as his comrades and built like a football player, but there was nothing dumb about him. Outwardly he was respectful, but Billy-Lee sometimes detected subtle derision in his watchful eyes that was hard to take.

It was almost pitch-black outside. With the white glare of the fluorescent storm lanterns reflecting off the glass, Billy-Lee could see nothing, but he kept his face to the window until his flush subsided. He couldn't have said why he was nervous. Michaels should have returned long before now, but there was bound to be a simple explanation.

Yet Billy-Lee couldn't escape the feeling that something was wrong. Maybe it was the incessant, angry whine of the wind and the furious, gusting beat of the rain against the windows that had gotten on his nerves—or being cooped up for hours in the dining hall with the four crew-cuts.

No, Billy-Lee decided angrily. It was Lurleen's fault. She'd spooked him, and he couldn't shake her parting words. *If something goes wrong, Billy-Lee, you'll be on your own.* Oddly, the shotguns lying on a nearby table added to his nervousness—as if preparing for the worst was tempting the devil. And what was the worst? Billy-Lee had no idea, and that worried him all the more.

"Relax, boss," Johnson said again as Billy-Lee turned around. "Those crazies you're worried about would have to be *really* crazy to come out in a storm like this."

"That's not what I'm worried about," Billy-Lee lied. "Michaels is a lot older than he acts, and he was only going to check on the Brooks woman."

"You think he may have had a heart attack?" Johnson asked uncaringly.

"I don't know. I just think someone should check on him, that's all."

Johnson nodded. "Good idea," he said, but he didn't stir.

Billy-Lee swallowed his annoyance and reached for his hooded rain jacket. "I'll have a look. I'll be back in a few minutes."

"We'll be here," Johnson said with a lazy smile, and yawned.

57

If Reese had been alone, he wouldn't have hesitated. But he wasn't alone, and if he miscalculated . . . *Damn it, Reese, time's wasting. Make up your mind!* Lost in the turmoil of his indecision, he didn't realize how long it had been since he had spoken until Lara finally broke their silence.

"How long have you been a teacher?" she asked, seemingly apropos of nothing.

"Ever since I got my master's back in '75."

He couldn't blame her for wanting to talk, but the last thing he wanted was conversation. He had to make a decision, or it would be made for him, and he could feel time slipping away.

"What are you going to do after we get out of here?" he asked, just to say something. "Will you be able to cancel your leave and go back to Dartmouth?"

"I hope so. Even if I could find a temporary research position somewhere, I'd want to go back. I felt like I was in a rut and going stale, but right now, that rut looks just fine to me."

"A rut? Michaels told me you're a first-class scientist."

Decide, damn it!

"Some reference," Lara said sarcastically. "The man's a lunatic."

"Don't you think you're good at what you do?"

"Good enough, I suppose, but I'll never win a Nobel Prize."

"How do you know?"

Lara laughed softly. "Trust me."

Reese shifted position to relieve the growing stiffness in his back and leaned forward again to peer up at the compound. The top of the hill was completely shrouded in darkness now, and he could no longer see the buildings. He knew what he had to do. Why didn't he tell her and get on with it?

"John . . ."

"What?"

"How is it you know about guns?" she asked diffidently. "I saw the way you handle your pistol—almost as if it were second nature."

"I enlisted in the army out of high school," Reese said, hoping she would drop it, for he thought he knew what was on her mind. What he'd done to Michaels. She'd had a glimpse of the kind of man he was. Lara said nothing for a moment, and he guessed that she was working out the time frame.

"Were you in Vietnam?"

"Bingo." Reese remembered bitterly her shock when she'd seen Michaels's ruined mouth, and the way she'd recoiled from him. "I suppose that explains it."

"Explains what?" Lara asked, sounding puzzled. "I was just asking, because . . . well, because I want to know you."

Reese grimaced in the darkness. "You mean, to know how I could do that to Michaels?"

"No!" Lara exclaimed. "That's not it at all. Forget how I reacted back in Michaels's lab! Believe me, John, I understand how you must feel about your daughter. I know why you had to get the finger. I know it's more important to you than anything else."

"Is that what you think?" Reese asked in disbelief. "Lara,

I didn't stay behind for the finger. I stayed behind for you."

Lara said nothing for a moment, and when she did start to speak, she broke off as she heard his intake of breath. He'd caught a flicker of light atop the hill. The light showed briefly again and disappeared, but it was warning enough. He could only hope that he hadn't delayed too long.

"Did you see something?" Lara asked, trying not to sound scared.

"A flashlight. They've probably started to look for Michaels."

The warm glow that had suffused Lara when Reese had told her why he'd stayed was instantly quenched as if in ice water.

"Should we get into the woods, John? They're bound to come down here sooner or later, and I can't move quickly."

"That's just it. We can hide as long as it's dark, but once it's light, they can track us down. And if the *yakuza* show up, we'll have more than Billy-Lee's men to worry about."

"But aren't you going to call for Beretta's helicopter as soon as the storm's over?"

"Yes, but what if there's a screwup and it doesn't come? And even if the chopper arrives while it's still dark, everyone on the island will hear it coming. I was counting on drawing them away—or pinning them down while you got aboard—but now . . ."

Abruptly Reese stood up. "Here's the flashlight." He pressed it into her hand. "I won't be needing it."

"Where are you going?" Lara asked in alarm.

"Back up the hill. I'm going to try to hit them before they hit us."

Lara felt the clutch of fear. He would be one man against four or five. "But they may have guns!"

"So have I."

Just the way he said it confirmed her fear. "They *do* have guns, don't they?" she gasped, seizing Reese's hand. "That's why you didn't go after them before. John, please stay here!"

"I hate to leave you here, Lara, but I—"

"I'm not worried about that! I'm worried about *you!*"

"Don't be." Reese reached down and lifted her to her feet. "If I can't take them, I won't try. You've got to trust me, Lara."

"I do," Lara said, caught between her anxiety and her determination not to tie his hands, "but . . ."

"No buts," he said, encircling her waist and half carrying her to the door. "It's the lesser of two risks."

"Are you sure?"

"Yes," Reese said firmly, "but if something does go wrong, don't forget that Jarvis promised to come back here for us after the storm. Try to get on the boat, Lara—with me, or without me."

Lara felt tears start in her eyes, but she had no choice but to let him go. If she tied his hands, they might have no chance at all.

"Lock up behind me," he said, reaching for the door, and Lara threw her arms around him and held him tight.

"I've got to go, Lara."

"I know." She raised her face to his. There was too much to say and no time to say it. His lips were cold as she kissed him fiercely. "Come back safe, John."

Reese could hardly see his hand in front of his face as he scrambled up the embankment above the cottage. Save for the phosphorescence of the churning sea, it was almost as dark outside as it had been in Jarvis's kitchen. The storm was abating, but the wind still swept the hillside in gusts.

Reese was virtually invisible, and the scrape of his boots on the occasional rock outcropping was lost in the thunder from the waves crashing ashore below. There was no need for stealth, and he drove himself up the hill as fast as he could go.

As he climbed, he saw more than one flashlight beam moving erratically among the compound's buildings, and it was clear that a search was on for Michaels. If he didn't hit them before they realized they had real trouble, he wouldn't have a chance.

Reese's lack of conditioning cost him on the climb, and his heart and lungs were pumping by the time he reached the brow of the hill. Just as he came up onto level ground, a light flashed from the Crystal Chapel ahead of him and to his left, and he dropped into the grass. A man emerged from the chapel, crossed in front of Reese, thirty yards away, and turned toward the dining hall.

The stray light from the man's flashlight glinted on the barrel of the shotgun he carried, killing Reese's hope of catching them unarmed. Reese's only consolation was that they weren't sticking together, but he had to let this one go by. He was too winded to close swiftly and silently and take the man from behind.

As the man headed for the dining hall, Reese got to his feet and moved across the road to the side of the Crystal Chapel. Still breathing hard, he edged along the side of the chapel until he had a full view of the quadrangle. As the man opened the door to the dining hall and went in, Reese glimpsed Billy-Lee's short figure just inside the doorway.

Two men accounted for. Where were the others? Reese was sure he had seen more than one man's flashlight beam moving about.

Lights suddenly appeared on the far side of the quadrangle, and two men came out the door to the clinic's dispensary. They were dragging a third man between them. "Boss, we've found him!" one of the men yelled, and Reese recognized the voice of Johnson, the security chief.

Reese gritted his teeth in frustration as he watched Michaels being carried to the dining hall. Johnson had found him much sooner than Reese had expected, and now the security chief was fully alerted. He didn't know what he was up against, but he couldn't believe that Lara Brooks had overpowered Michaels.

Billy-Lee opened the door and they hauled Michaels inside. The moment the door closed again, Reese slipped back the way he'd come. He didn't expect Johnson and his men to remain inside long, and they would be coming out to hunt.

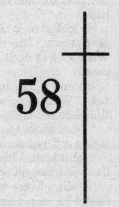

58

Johnson dragged Michael's inert body into the dining hall and let it slide unceremoniously to the floor. Billy-Lee saw Michaels's mouth clearly for the first time, and he almost gagged. "Is he . . . is he dead?"

Johnson shook his head. "He's just out cold. Someone beat the shit out of him, but I don't think he's concussed. Look how he's breathing—like he's asleep. I think he's been drugged."

Johnson looked grimly at Billy-Lee. "My apologies. You were right. That girl sure didn't do this to him. We have company."

"Who?" Billy-Lee asked, oblivious to the uselessness of the question.

"How would I know? Some of those crazies you're worried about. But we'll find out as soon as we round 'em up. In this weather, they're as stuck as we are."

Johnson nodded wordlessly to his men, and they began stuffing extra cartridges into jacket pockets beneath their raingear. Billy-Lee glanced fearfully at the windows, wondering what lurked in the black, howling night. His immediate urge was to call his father, but what could his father do? Until the storm passed, they were cut off from the mainland.

He looked back at Johnson and his men, and he felt a rush of gratitude. They no longer looked stupid to Billy-Lee. Whoever had freed the bitch was in for it, he thought viciously.

Johnson picked up a spare shotgun and looked at Billy-Lee. "Want to come with us?" The other three looked at Billy-Lee and smiled expectantly.

"What about Michaels?" Billy-Lee responded, and their smiles widened derisively.

"He'll keep," Johnson said, "but this is what you pay us for. I just thought you might want to come along."

"I will." There was nothing impulsive in Billy-Lee's decision. He didn't like the idea of going, but staying behind alone was even less appealing.

"Okay." Johnson tossed Billy-Lee the shotgun. "Know how to use it?"

"Yes."

"Good, but be careful where you point it. Okay, guys, let's do it."

As they filed out of the dining hall and the darkness enveloped them, Billy-Lee felt his nerves steady. With Johnson and his men, he was the hunter. No one was going to rob him of his inheritance, he vowed. *No one.*

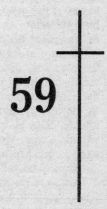

59

Reese had retreated back across the road and dropped into the grass on the edge the slope. He didn't have to wait long. The door to the dining hall opened again, and the tall, hawk-faced security chief was briefly silhouetted in the doorway as he emerged. The three other security guards came out behind him, followed by Billy-Lee, and all five men carried shotguns.

As Billy-Lee closed the door behind him, darkness swallowed up the group. No one switched on a flashlight, and Reese nodded grimly to himself. No lights, and they were moving out in force. Johnson was taking no chances. Only Billy-Lee's presence surprised Reese; he had thought the preacher's son would stay behind.

Reese's brief hope that the men might separate to search the compound again died as he heard the faint sounds of their approach. Seconds later, boots scuffed the roadway ahead of him and to his left, and directed by the sound, he glimpsed their shadowy forms moving away along the road. They were going down to check the harbor area.

By sticking to the road, which snaked back and forth

across the slope as it descended, they were giving Reese time to reach Jarvis's cottage ahead of them, but he had a decision to make: flee with Lara or try to sucker them into a fight on his own terms. As Reese got to his feet and started down the hill, he made his choice.

The roof of Jarvis's cottage was clearly silhouetted against the churning, phosphorescent waters of the harbor, and he raced straight for it, slipping and sliding down the slope. At the bottom of the hill, Reese skidded down the embankment to the level ground beside the cottage and ran to Jarvis's kitchen door. He rapped on it hard, confident that the sound wouldn't carry over the pounding of the surf, cupped his hands around his mouth, and pressed them against the door.

"Lara!" he yelled. "Open up!"

Lara was on the floor when she opened the door, and Reese nearly tripped over her as he rushed inside. "I got up there too late," he said, gasping for breath. "They've found Michaels, and they're armed and coming this way. We've got time to get away, but I'd like to try something else."

"What?" It was a question, not a protest. Lara was keeping her nerve.

"I'll wait for them on the slope just above you," Reese said quickly, "and when they come, I'll make them think they flushed me. If I can draw them up the slope and into the woods, I think I can take them on."

"But how many are coming?"

"Five." Reese heard Lara's sharp intake of breath. "I know what I'm doing," he added quickly, hoping it was true. "Lara, I want to cut down the odds against us. I hate leaving you alone again, but—"

"Stop worrying about me. If you're sure—do it."

"Okay," Reese said gratefully. "I'll need the flashlight."

Lara slid off to one side and fumbled for it on the floor. "Got it." She reached up and handed it to him.

Reese took it and squeezed her hand. "I'll come back here as soon as I can, but if I'm not here when Jarvis comes back, promise me you'll get on his boat and go."

"But, John—"

"Promise me you'll go!"

"All right, I promise."

Despite the reluctance in her voice, he believed her. "That's what I needed to hear."

Reese lay in the grass beside a rock outcropping thirty yards up the slope above the cottage. The rain had all but stopped, but he was soaked to the skin, and the storm's last, fitful gusts seemed to cut right through him. Tension knotted his stomach as he waited for Johnson and his men. Like an aging prizefighter, Reese knew the moves, but his slower reflexes and diminished strength worried him.

Johnson had begun his search at the far end of the harbor, where the road came down to the shore. One of Johnson's men was careless with his flashlight, and Reese had seen a flicker of light from inside the shed beside the ferry slip. Now he had his eyes fixed on the roadway near the dock, where he thought he could detect their silhouettes against the phosphorescent surf beyond.

Reese caught a hint of movement, and then their shadows appeared, moving up the shore road. Reese slipped out his automatic. The shadows came abreast of the dock and halted, as if the men thought someone might be hiding in the darkness at the end of the dock. But the storm surge had all but submerged the dock, and none of the men ventured out to check.

The shadows moved on to the boathouse, and as it was searched, Reese once again saw the brief gleam of an unguarded flashlight. He rose to a crouch and began to breathe deeply, preparing himself for the scramble up the slope. The cottage would be next.

With nothing but the cottage left to search, the need for stealth was gone and the men turned on their flashlights. As they crossed the road toward the cottage, their flashlight beams probed the ground around it and played over its shuttered windows. Johnson, recognizable by his size, was in the lead.

He went straight for the kitchen door, and just before he reached it, Reese scraped the barrel of his gun over the rock on the ground beside him. Had it not been for the surf, the

men couldn't have missed the noise, but none of them reacted. Johnson tugged and rattled the doorknob, and Reese
hastily reversed his grip on the automatic.

Johnson stepped back and kicked hard at the door with
the flat of his boot, but the door held. Before he could kick
again, Reese hammered the gun butt twice against the stone,
and this time he was heard. One of the men behind Johnson
yelled an alarm, and he and another man swung their flashlights in Reese's general direction.

Their beams splashed the hillside just above the embankment and to Reese's right, and he launched himself up the
slope. He scrambled diagonally up the hill toward the tree
line, glancing back to see what was happening. One man had
come up over the embankment, and all five flashlights were
playing over the slope below him; but they didn't have a
direction to follow yet.

Reese waited until he'd almost reached the edge of the
pine forest bordering the slope before switching on his flashlight. Instantly he heard a chorus of shouts from below. He
looked behind him, saw that the men were coming up after
him, and plunged into the woods with his flashlight still on.
The shouts behind him turned to the excited cries of men
caught up in a chase, and he knew he had them on the hook.

Behold those things which shall surely come to pass, the voice said to Simon. And the earth opened, and smoke poured out and darkened the sky. Then arose from the bottomless pit the beast that is Satan.

—SAMARIA SCROLL 1, COLUMN 2.4.1

60

Lara had seen light penetrate the kitchen windows' shutters and knew that Billy-Lee's men were coming. Their flashlights continued to play over the shutters as they approached, and then she saw a sliver of light appear beneath the door. The doorknob rattled, and she held her breath, waiting tensely for Reese to draw them away.

Without warning, the man outside kicked the kitchen door with a terrifying bang that shook the cottage, and Lara jumped. The door was still intact, but she was afraid it couldn't withstand a second kick. Reflexively she drew back against the wall. *Where was Reese?*

Then she heard a man shout, and she sagged against the wall in relief. She heard a second shout, and she slid over to the window at which Reese had kept watch and pulled herself up onto the chair. Immediately her sprained ankle began to throb, but she barely registered the pain as she leaned forward and peered through the crack in the shutter.

Flashlight beams were probing the hillside, and one man had climbed the embankment, but the others were still out of sight. Wherever Reese had gone, apparently they didn't have a fix on him yet. One of the beams swept across the man at the top of the embankment, and Lara glimpsed the evil gleam of a long gun barrel.

Abruptly a faint light appeared on the slope above, and it was greeted by a chorus of shouts. Flashlight beams danced crazily as men scrambled up the embankment. They were all wearing dark ponchos and carrying shotguns, and they yelled like animals as they started up the slope in pursuit.

Billy-Lee panted his way up the slope almost to the tree line before it suddenly hit him. Whoever was running from them was moving fast—too fast. Billy-Lee didn't know how many they were chasing, but it looked like only one. And the bitch couldn't possibly run that fast. Not with her peg leg. She had to be in hiding, but where? They'd looked every—

Billy-Lee stumbled to a halt and shouted breathlessly to the nearest of the men ahead of him, "I'm going back—to check the cottage!"

Only one of Johnson's men heard him, and Billy-Lee felt a tingle of anticipation as the man waved and ran on. Billy-Lee could have yelled the explanation—that their quarry was decoying them away from the cottage—but he wanted no help. He would take care of the bitch himself.

He paused for a moment to catch his breath, but his eagerness wouldn't let him wait, and he started back down the slope as righteous lust welled up in him. Had his legs not already been rubbery, he would have run.

Billy-Lee couldn't wait to get his hands on her. Neither his father nor Michaels had been able to get the truth out of her, but he would find out what was going on. And then he would take his pleasure. She had tempted him mercilessly, and now she would get what she deserved.

Lara saw Reese's faint light flicker and begin to wink fitfully, and she realized that he must have reached the tree line. But he wasn't moving fast enough. The lights behind him were closing on him. Lara felt her teeth cutting into her lip, and she had to consciously stop biting it.

She lost sight of Reese's light as the first of his pursuers reached the tree line. Three of them were lagging behind, and the light of the man farthest behind slowed and then stopped. One of the two lights ahead of him briefly slowed, then continued on up the hill. A chill rippled up Lara's spine.

The light of the man who had halted was moving back down the slope and coming straight toward her. He kept coming, and Lara's heart began to pound. Why was he coming back if not to search the cottage? For several seconds Lara didn't move, paralyzed by helplessness.

Abruptly the spell broke, and she slid off the chair onto the floor. Her first urge was to find a place to hide, but as she scrabbled across the floor toward the door at the back of the kitchen, she realized it would be no use. Even if there was a hiding place, she'd never find it in time.

Reese drove himself up the slope, moving deeper into the woods as he climbed toward the plateau. The pine-covered hillside became ever steeper, and Reese's pace inexorably slowed. His thighs ached, his breath came in whistling, burning gasps, and his already drenched body ran with sweat. His pursuers had stopped wasting their own breath in yelling, and although they were encumbered by raingear and shotguns, they were younger and stronger and gaining on him.

Reese heard them crashing through the undergrowth below him, and he desperately clawed his way up the last of the slope and staggered forward onto the plateau. His heart was pounding and his chest was heaving as he hastily scuffed up the pine needles carpeting the ground and snapped several twigs on the nearest branches. Then he plunged on.

Reese ran forward in as straight a line as possible, marking his trail as he went. He kept going as long as his lead time and flagging strength allowed, then reversed course and came running back the way he'd come. Ahead of him, he saw a flashlight beam glancing off trees on the edge of the plateau, and he switched off his own light and slipped off to the right of the trail he had left. Gasping for breath, he wiped away the sweat running into his eyes and waited impatiently for them to readjust to the darkness.

Johnson was the first up the slope, and Reese recognized

his voice as he urged on the men coming up behind him. Reese crept toward Johnson's light as quickly as he dared. He could hear Johnson's men grunting and cursing as they struggled up the hill.

Backtracking was an old trick, and Johnson might not fall for it, but either way, Reese thought, he now had the bastards on his own terms. He was invisible, and as long as they kept their lights on, they were easy targets. At the very least, he should be able to cut down one or two of them and get himself a shotgun.

Johnson had come up onto the plateau a little too far to the left, and he didn't pick up Reese's trail before the first man behind him reached the plateau. Reese continued to creep toward them.

"Jesus," Reese heard the man pant at Johnson, "where's their light? Which way do we go now?"

"Shut up!" Johnson snapped, sweeping his flashlight over the ground around him. "There!" he exulted as he spotted Reese's trail. "Come on! This way."

The others were only seconds behind, but Johnson didn't wait. He found the second of Reese's markers and quickened his pace. He and the other man passed within five yards of where Reese crouched, and Reese let them go by. He had them strung out, and he'd slip in behind and take the last man first. Undoubtedly that would be fat Billy-Lee.

The next two men reached the plateau together.

"Who the fuck are we chasing?" Reese heard one man pant.

"The girl and whoever sprung her. Who do you think?" the other responded as they hurried after Johnson.

"Then why did fuckin' Billy-Lee turn back to search the old salt's place?" the complainer asked, and Reese's breath caught in his throat.

The answer trailed after Reese as he slipped away, fighting down the urge to break into a heedless run. "That was bullshit, butt-head. The Little Thumper just didn't want to work up a sweat. That's what he pays us for."

61

Lara was trapped, but she didn't want to be taken without a fight. Desperate for something with which to defend herself, she moved toward the kitchen sink, found the cabinets beside it, and felt for a drawer. She found one, yanked it open, and heard the rattle of utensils just as the man outside delivered his first kick to the kitchen door.

Lara reached up into the drawer and winced as her fingers closed on a knife blade. It was a fish knife, or something similar, with a thin, sharp blade, and she pulled it from the drawer. A second kick to the door drew a gasp from her, for she heard the splintering of wood. She seized the edge of the counter and struggled upright, keeping her weight on her prosthetic foot.

Her heart hammered against her ribs, and she could hear the hiss of each breath she drew. The man kicked again, and this time the door flew open with a splintering crack. For a moment, as the intruder swept his flashlight around the kitchen, his dark figure was dimly visible in the doorway. Then the beam found her, and the man directed it into her eyes, blinding her with its glare.

"Who are you?" she challenged hoarsely, clinging to the counter and tightening her grip on the knife.

She was answered by a high-pitched laugh.

"I knew it," Billy-Lee cackled, advancing into the room, but he was winded and paused for breath. "I knew you couldn't move that fast."

Billy-Lee kept the light in Lara's eyes and slowly came toward her. Behind him the door creaked as it swung back and forth in response to fitful gusts of wind. "Say—that's a mean knife you have there," he sneered. "I'd put it down if I were you."

"Stay back!"

Billy-Lee laughed unnaturally. "I've got a shotgun, girl. I could shoot you right now."

"And swing for it!"

"I wouldn't count on that, sweet stuff." Billy-Lee took another step toward her. "My daddy is a powerful man."

Lara thrust the knife out in front of her, but she couldn't see a thing past the blinding light in her eyes. Billy-Lee was still breathing heavily, and she no longer thought it was entirely from exertion.

"Put it down. I could splatter your pretty little body all over this room."

Lara caught the sadistic undertone, and she tried not to show her fear. "Stay back!" she cried as fiercely as she could, but he took yet another step closer.

"I could have told the others," he said from behind the blinding light, "but I thought it would be more interesting to come back for you myself."

Without warning, Billy-Lee lunged forward and drove the shotgun's barrel into the pit of Lara's stomach. The blow doubled her over, but somehow she managed to keep her hold on the counter. Gasping for breath, she tried to straighten up, and Billy-Lee backhanded her across the face.

She spun off-balance, and she cried out as agonizing pain knifed up through her ankle. She crashed to the floor and landed on her back. Still holding the knife, she tried to rise, but Billy-Lee brought his boot down on her right arm, pinning it to the floor.

As Lara fought to pull free, Billy-Lee increased the pressure until her fingers opened, releasing the knife. He kicked it aside with his other foot, and between her own gasps, she could hear him panting. It was an ugly, terrifying sound.

"Who are my boys chasing out there?" Billy-Lee rasped, looming over her. "Who set you free and doped up Dr. Mike?"

Lara gritted her teeth and said nothing, and Billy-Lee increased the pressure of his boot on her arm and jammed the shotgun barrel against her left breast, pushing her down until she was flat on her back.

"Talk!"

Lara stared defiantly up into the blinding light and said nothing.

"It's not a good idea to rile me, girl," Billy-Lee snarled. "You're not the first bitch to interfere with my daddy's holy mission, and I fixed her good. One blow from me, and she never saw light again. From what I hear, she never will. 'He shall smite His enemies and cast them into darkness!' "

"The girl at Harvard?" Lara gasped, and Billy-Lee laughed.

"And I'll fix you, too, if you don't talk. *Who's on the island with you?*"

Lara shut her eyes against the light and said nothing.

"You're a Jezebel," Billy-Lee hissed, and Lara's skin crawled as she felt the gun muzzle slip off her breast, down over her stomach, and probe her crotch. "I've got you now, you Catholic bitch. Oh, you thought you were so clever, pretending to ignore me, but I knew you wanted to ensnare me in lust."

Suddenly Lara's fear was swept away in a flood of loathing and fury. "Don't flatter yourself, you pathetic creep!" she spat. "Even the devil wouldn't waste time on you."

"Bitch!" Billy-Lee rasped, and suddenly the blinding light vanished. Lara heard his gun and flashlight clatter to the floor, and then he was on top of her, crushing her with his weight. His hot, sour breath invaded her nostrils, and he tried to close his mouth over hers. Lara twisted her face away, bared her teeth, and sank them into his cheek.

Billy-Lee howled and reared back. "Bitch!" he panted, tearing open her shirt. "Cunt!"

Lara struck him in the face with her fists as he ripped away her bra, but he didn't seem to feel her blows. She clawed at his eyes, and he struck her hard on the side of her head. The floor seemed to spin and tilt beneath her, and for a moment she lost awareness. Then she felt Billy-Lee wrenching at the belt of her jeans and she started to scream, but she gagged as a wave of nausea swept over her.

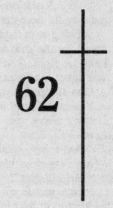

62

Billy-Lee's flashlight illuminated the struggling bodies entangled on the kitchen floor, and the sight loosed a killing rage in Reese as he hurtled through the doorway. Billy-Lee was fevered with lust, and he never heard Reese coming. Reese swung his gun butt at the back of Billy-Lee's head with all his strength and felt the shock of the blow all the way up his forearm.

Billy-Lee collapsed on top of Lara like a poleaxed steer, and she continued to struggle beneath him. Her eyes were squeezed shut and her face was twisted in an agonized grimace.

"Lara!" Reese cried, seizing the back of Billy-Lee's poncho and starting to lift his heavy body.

"Oh, God, John! Get him off me. *Get him off!*"

Billy-Lee's trousers were down around his knees, and as Reese hurled the body aside, his stomach roiled at the sight of the erect penis jutting from beneath Billy-Lee's poncho.

Lara's heaving chest was bared and her jeans had been pulled down, and Reese dropped to one knee to help her cover herself. With a feral snarl, she tried to seize his gun.

"Give it to me!" she screamed. "I'll kill the bastard! I'll *kill* him!"

"No!" Reese cried, pulling the pistol from her grip. "His men would hear the shot."

Sobbing with rage, Lara thrust herself up off the floor, still trying for the gun, and Reese threw his arms around her and held her tight. "Not now. If he isn't dead already, I'll let you shoot him later."

Lara stopped struggling and began to cry.

"Easy," Reese said, stroking her hair. "It's over, and I won't leave you again. This was my fault. I shouldn't have—"

"Don't say that!" Lara protested through her tears. "Don't take the blame for that piece of shit. God, I hope you *did* kill him."

"Lara, we've got to get out of here before his men come back to look for him. Are you okay?"

"Yes," she said hoarsely, looking over at Billy-Lee's body, and as Reese released her, she slid away from it.

She started to cover herself, and Reese went to shut the door. The lock had been torn away, and he pulled over the chair by the window and jammed it beneath the knob to hold the door shut. Then he picked up Michaels's trench coat and brought it to Lara. She had pulled up her jeans, but the buttons had been torn off her shirt and she was holding it closed. Tears still streamed down her cheeks and she was breathing hard.

Reese slipped his pistol back in behind his hip and helped her on with the coat. "I think he's breathing," she said with loathing, staring at Billy-Lee's inert body.

"Forget him," Reese said, picking up the shotgun. "Have you ever shot one of these?"

Lara shook her head, still staring tensely at Billy-Lee.

"Lara!" Reese said sharply. "We have to get out of here, but first I want to show you how to use this. With a shotgun in your hands, no one's going to mess with you."

For a moment Lara barely reacted, but then with visible effort she pulled herself together. She looked at Reese and nodded. "Show me," she said hoarsely.

"After each shot, you have to pump the slide to eject the spent shell and load in a new one—like this." Reese checked the safety and worked the action once, ejecting a live shell. "Now you try it," he said, pressing it into her hands. "The safety's on, so the gun won't go off."

Lara awkwardly worked the slide, ejecting another shell.

"Again. . . . Good, that's it."

Reese took back the gun and reloaded the ejected shells. "You pull the trigger to shoot and then pump the slide for the next shot. That's all you have to know. I'm taking the gun off safety now. It's ready to fire, so keep your finger off the trigger. Okay?"

"Okay," Lara said, taking the weapon in her hands. She still looked badly shaken, but Reese could see her determination to overcome her shock, and it heartened him.

He discarded Jarvis's weak flashlight and picked up Billy-Lee's. As he did, he spotted the fish knife on the floor and on impulse slipped it into his boot.

Billy-Lee's body twitched suddenly, and he emitted a soft groan.

"John! He's waking up."

Reese paid no attention. "We've got to get out of here." He switched off his flashlight and plunged them into darkness. He'd picked up a chilling sound from outside—faint, but rising steadily above the thunder of the surf.

"Hang on to the shotgun," he said, and scooped her up in his arms. He carried her through the pitch-black darkness to the door and kicked away the chair. Behind them, Billy-Lee groaned.

"But he's coming to!" Lara protested in alarm as the door swung open and Reese carried her outside.

"Forget him," Reese snapped, feeling his way down the steps. "We've got to get up to high ground. We're sitting ducks down here."

Lara dug her fingers into Reese's shoulder. "But, John, I didn't tell you! Billy-Lee is the—"

"Listen!" Reese hissed between clenched teeth, and for the first time Lara registered the engine drone above the surf's thunder, rising steadily and accompanied by the beat of helicopter blades.

"You listen!" Lara cried as Reese carried her onto the shore road. "It was Billy-Lee who attacked your daughter! He *told* me!"

Reese stiffened and his stride broke, but at that moment a searchlight stabbed down from the black sky, illuminating the churning harbor waters. Reese broke into an awkward run.

"No time," he growled through clenched teeth as the helicopter swept in from the sea.

"Is that Jordan coming back?" Lara cried.

"*No,*" Reese panted. "*Yakuza!*"

Reese stumbled and almost fell. The bright column of light was racing straight toward them, but there was no way Reese could outrun it. He was exhausting himself. "I'm too heavy for you," Lara shouted in his ear. "Put me down!"

Reese ignored her and labored on, his gasping breath hissing through his gritted teeth. For an instant the searchlight beam caught the end of the wooden dock, and the helicopter abruptly swung right and slowed.

"They've veered off, John. Please put me down!"

Reese heard the helicopter pilot change pitch and glanced back. The chopper hovered for a moment, then its searchlight beam slid shoreward along the dock. It could swing back in their direction at any moment, but Reese knew Lara was right.

He was only halfway to the cover of the storage shed beside the ferry slip, and he knew he'd never make it. Chest heaving, he lurched to the side of the road and collapsed with her against the embankment, praying for luck. The searchlight had reached the shore, and the beam played briefly over the boathouse before sweeping toward Jarvis's cottage.

As the beam splashed it with light, Reese saw Billy-Lee come stumbling out the door. The pilot hovered and kept the searchlight trained on Billy-Lee, who tottered down the steps, swaying drunkenly.

"Daddy!" Billy-Lee cried, staring up into the light and

waving his arms, and Reese felt rage rise in his throat. *I should have killed him.* "Daddy!" Billy-Lee cried again.

Lara leaned close to Reese to be heard above the noise. "It *is* Bobby Jordan!"

Reese heard the hope in her voice and wished she were right. "No," he replied, panting for breath. "That's not his chopper."

As the helicopter continued to hover, four flashlights appeared at the top of the hill in front of the compound—Johnson and his men. They could see Billy-Lee in the searchlight beam, and they started down the hill toward him. The pilot had seen their lights, and the helicopter rose. As the searchlight beam started moving up the slope toward them, Billy-Lee scrambled madly up the embankment after it, yelling incoherently.

Reese got to his feet. "We have to get up to the plateau, Lara! Once Michaels talks, those guys in the chopper will come after us. We'd be sitting ducks down here."

"But don't carry me, John. Let me try to walk."

"Okay," Reese agreed, lifting her to her feet, and he slipped his arm about her waist. Lara held on to his shoulder and they started up the shore road toward the bend beyond the ferry slip, where the road hooked around to run uphill.

High on the slope, the searchlight came to rest on Johnson and his men, and they waved at the helicopter. They continued down the hill toward Billy-Lee, and the helicopter followed them. As Reese and Lara passed the ferry slip and started up the road to the compound, Johnson and his men reached Billy-Lee.

Reese could see Billy-Lee staring up at the light, and he heard him shout "Daddy" again. Then he toppled backward, and one of Johnson's men had to catch him before he fell. Reese saw Johnson look up at the helicopter and give the thumbs-up sign.

"Jesus," Reese said to Lara. "They still think it's Jordan."

"Are you sure it's not?" she asked, and then she gasped in pain as once again she put too much weight on her sprained ankle.

"This is too slow, Lara! I'll have to carry you."

"You can't—not all the way up."

"Yes, I can, but not in my arms." Without giving her a chance to argue, Reese crouched and folded her over his shoulder. He straightened up and trudged forward. Above them, on the other side of the slope, Johnson and his men had turned and were climbing back up to the compound.

They were slowed down by Billy-Lee, and Reese was relieved to see the helicopter staying with them. He needed all the time he could get. Panting and sweating with the increasing strain, he doggedly continued up the road.

As Johnson and his men neared the top of the slope, the helicopter rose sharply and began to explore the compound with its searchlight. Reese drove himself faster, ignoring the warnings of his body, desperate to reach the plateau. The helicopter completed its circle of the compound and dropped toward the pad behind the maintenance building.

63

Kenji had seen Tanaka tap the pilot and point, and the helicopter had veered and dropped like an express elevator. From Kenji's seat in the rear, he could see nothing in the black void beyond the windscreen, but he'd known Tanaka must have spotted the island. The four *yakuza* toughs squeezed into the back of the cabin with Kenji had stirred restlessly, like hounds before the hunt.

Buffeted by the dying storm winds, the helicopter had lurched sickeningly as it lost altitude and then hovered. Kenji gritted his teeth to stop himself from vomiting. His hands were ice-cold and clammy, and he expected to throw up at any moment. How much of his nausea was due to airsickness, and how much to nervousness, Kenji neither knew nor cared. He only knew that he wanted it to be over—the flight, the unbearable tension—everything.

In response to Tanaka's commands, the pilot flew on for a moment and hovered again—and again and again. *Why aren't we landing?* Finally the helicopter rose and flew in a wide, slow circle, and to Kenji's relief, he realized that they were landing at last.

Tanaka twisted around and shouted over the mind-numbing roar in the cabin to his men, but to Kenji, his voice was lost in the engine's thunder. Kenji wasn't really listening. His mind was turned inward as he struggled to prepare himself.

Kenji's left leg gave way as he jumped from the helicopter, and he fell to his knees. Tanaka seized his arm and pulled him upright as the other *yakuza* scrambled out after him.

"Are you hurt?" Tanaka asked over the whine of the helicopter's engine winding down.

"No. My leg fell asleep." Kenji peered tensely into the darkness around him. Tanaka had briefed them on the complex's layout, and he thought he could detect the black mass of the nearest building. To his amazement, he suddenly found himself more excited than afraid.

"Remember, stick close to me," Tanaka said into his ear, careful not to be overheard. In front of his men, Tanaka scrupulously pretended that Kenji was in charge. "Put on your mask," he added, pulling his own black hood over his head.

Kenji was dressed as Tanaka and his men were, in a black jumpsuit, and even at close range they were visible only as shadows. Kenji heard the snick of gun bolts as the *yakuza* readied their weapons. He, too, carried an American military rifle, but although its magazine was loaded, Tanaka didn't expect him to use it. Tanaka had instructed Kenji how to operate the weapon, but he'd only given it to him for show.

"The men I saw were armed with shotguns," Tanaka said quickly to his raiders, "but it's not because of us. They acted as if they think we're friends, so let's wait and see if they come to us. Remember," he added sharply, "this isn't a killing raid. No one gets hurt unless it's absolutely necessary."

The *yakuza* pilot emerged from the helicopter and readied his own rifle. Kenji had been present when Tanaka had briefed the raiding party, and he knew that the pilot would remain with the helicopter to safeguard their escape. Two of Tanaka's men carried explosives in their backpacks. One would plant a bomb in the communications center to delay discovery of the raid, and the other would take care of the computer system to ensure that no data from the sample survived.

"Here they come," Tanaka said softly as several flashlight beams appeared, and he issued terse instructions. His men split into pairs and disappeared into the darkness to either side of the advancing flashlights, preparing to close in from the flanks. Tanaka stayed put, and the pilot crawled into firing position beneath the helicopter.

"Get down, Hamada-san," Tanaka whispered, and Kenji lowered himself to the ground.

As he bellied into the wet grass, he could feel his heart beating, but still with excitement rather than fear. There was no turning back now. Was that what had liberated him? Or had he been changing bit by bit and simply not realized—

One of the approaching light beams swung up from the ground in their direction, and Tanaka switched on the powerful, narrow-beamed flashlight slung beneath the barrel of his rifle. Quickly he played it into the eyes of the advancing group, blinding them.

There were five of them—four big men in hooded ponchos, carrying shotguns, who were shepherding a much smaller man, who looked ill. He was walking under his own power, but the men beside him kept a steadying hold on his arms.

"Hey!" cried the tall, hawk-nosed man in the lead, squinting against the glare. "What's with that light? Reverend Jordan! Your son's been hurt!"

They were less than thirty yards away, and Tanaka raised his rifle to his shoulder. "Drop your weapons immediately, or we'll shoot!" he barked in English, and his men switched on their own lights, transfixing all but the hawk-nosed man in the lead.

He reacted too quickly even for Tanaka. The man brought up his shotgun in a blur of speed, and Kenji winced as the shotgun boomed. Tanaka's body jerked, but then he fired back. The short burst from his automatic rifle sent the man spinning to the ground.

"Drop your guns or die!" Tanaka thundered.

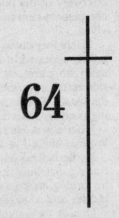

64

Lara bit off a cry of pain as Reese collapsed on the side of the road with her beneath him as they hit the ground hard. He rolled aside, gasping for air, too winded to ask if she was badly hurt. Every muscle in his body seemed to be quivering, and his thighs ached unbearably. They were still twenty yards from the last roadbend at the top of the slope.

Lara reached out and touched his burning face, which was running with sweat. "My God," she said anxiously, "you'll have a heart attack."

I'm not that old, Reese wanted to say, but he hadn't the breath to speak. He lay there with his chest heaving, tensely aware of time slipping away. The helicopter had landed, and the pilot had cut the engines. Reese rolled onto his stomach and struggled to his knees.

"No!" Lara exclaimed. "You've got to rest."

Reese didn't argue, for he was too exhausted to rise. He stayed on his knees, sucking in air, with his heart pounding from overexertion. "Can you crawl up the rest of the way?" he gasped.

"Yes, but where are we going? Into the woods?"

"No, not yet. I want to see what they—"

A booming report from behind the compound cut Reese off, and it was immediately followed by a sharp, staccato rattle.

Lara seized Reese's arm. "What was *that?*" she gasped.

"Shotgun," Reese croaked, still out of breath, "and an M-sixteen on autofire. Go on, Lara—straight up, if you can. I'll catch up."

Lara started crawling up the last of the grassy slope, and as she disappeared into the darkness above him, Reese gathered what strength he had left and started up after her. He caught up with her, lifted her to her feet, and together they moved across the road and onto the compound's lawn.

They had come up to the left of the Crystal Chapel, with the seaward end of the research building directly ahead of them. Reese led Lara forward until they could see diagonally across the quadrangle to the far end of the clinic and the dining hall.

The night was still pitch-dark, and the muted thunder of the surf below masked small sounds. Reese could afford to wait to see what happened before getting Lara into cover in the woods. Seconds after they went to earth, flashlight beams darted past the far end of the clinic into the quadrangle. Men were coming from the helicopter pad at the rear of the compound.

Lara saw two dark figures advance into the quadrangle, sweeping the area with their flashlights, and Reese whispered to her to lie flat. She didn't need to be told to hide from the sinister shadow men, and the sight of them chilled her as they flitted across the compound toward the dining hall.

"Scouts," Reese whispered, and incredibly she heard relief in his exhausted voice. Was it because they'd reached the plateau? High ground, low ground—what difference did it make? What was he waiting for? Why not get into the woods and as far away from them as possible?

The two men reached the dining hall, and as they burst through the doorway, they were briefly silhouetted against the light inside. Both were clad in black jumpsuits and black, hooded masks, and Lara saw that their flashlights were slung beneath the barrels of rifles. They remained inside no more than thirty seconds, and as they came back out, three more raiders advanced into the quadrangle, herding Billy-Lee and his disarmed men before them.

She could see that one of the security guards was wounded—Johnson. Two of his men were supporting him between them, and he was dragging one leg. Billy-Lee was walking without assistance, but he moved like an automaton, his arms unnaturally slack at his sides. Once again the smell of him filled her nostrils and she could feel his crushing weight. Revolted, she looked away.

One of the men emerging from the dining hall called out in Japanese, and there was a brief exchange with one of the *yakuza* herding the captives toward the dining hall. The man who'd called out ran toward the entrance to the clinic's dispensary, and his partner took up a position beside the doorway to the dining hall. He remained there as the raiders hustled Billy-Lee, Johnson, and his men inside.

"Kuroda must have told them who's on the island," Reese whispered. "I think that guy went to look for you, but they don't know I stayed behind," he added with grim satisfaction.

Reese was still breathing hard, but now he sounded as coolly controlled as he'd been in the clinic. Lara couldn't understand it.

"Look at that man they posted outside the dining hall," he whispered to her. "He hasn't even bothered to get out of the light from the windows. These guys act like everything's sewed up, Lara. They must think they've bagged everyone but you."

"But what happens when they don't find me? And what will they think about Michaels?"

"I don't know," Reese whispered, "but maybe Johnson and his men will keep their mouths shut until they figure out what's going on."

65

"Tie up those security guards and bandage that one man's wound," Tanaka said to his *yakuza* as he propelled the dazed, fat young man to a chair at one of the dining tables and forced him to sit. Kenji thought the man resembled the one he had glimpsed in the stairwell the night of the break-in, but he couldn't be sure. The man stared up at Tanaka with wild, glazed eyes and shook his head, as if trying to clear it.

"Keep an eye on this one," Tanaka said to Kenji, and went to examine the man they'd found lying unconscious on the floor. Tanaka shone his flashlight on the man.

"That's the lab director!" Kenji exclaimed. "But what happened to his face?"

Michaels's gaping mouth was a gory mess, yet Kenji's usual reaction to the sight of blood was strangely absent. He didn't understand the change that had come over him, but he relished it. His queasiness had vanished with his fear, and the sudden lifting of his lifelong burden was exhilarating.

Tanaka kicked Michaels sharply in the ribs. The lab director didn't even twitch. "He's not going to tell us anything,'' Tanaka growled, and as he turned, Kenji spotted blood oozing from a half dozen tiny wounds.

"You're wounded, Tanaka-san!"

"The shot was nearly spent," Tanaka said dismissively, going back to the man in the chair. "Four guards, the lab director, and the preacher's son," he said, ticking off the personnel they'd expected to find. "This one must be the son."

"Are you Billy-Lee Jordan?" Tanaka asked sharply in English.

"Who are you?" Billy-Lee gurgled, staring up at Tanaka. Kenji saw fright in Billy-Lee's eyes, but no understanding.

"Yes, that's Jordan," snapped the hawk-nosed security guard. "Leave the poor bastard alone. Can't you see he's out of it?"

"What's your name?" Tanaka said, turning and advancing on the hawk-nosed man, who lay on the floor with the other guards. Tanaka's men had bound them hand and foot and tied them together around a support pillar. All wore sullen, angry expressions, but the hard eyes of the hawk-nosed man were genuinely fierce.

"Johnson. What's yours, asshole?"

"What's wrong with your boss?" Tanaka demanded.

"Beats the shit out of me. Maybe he slipped and hit his head. All I know is, he went down to the harbor and didn't come back. We had to go looking for him."

"With shotguns?"

"Billy-Lee was expecting trouble, but he didn't tell us you'd be gooks."

"What?"

"Gooks," Johnson spat. "Chinks—Japs—whatever the hell you are."

"What happened to the lab director?" Tanaka snapped. "Did he slip and fall, too?"

Johnson didn't answer, and Tanaka dug his boot into Johnson's wounded thigh. Johnson jerked and ground his teeth, but he refused to cry out. "You're lucky," Tanaka said. "The bullet missed the bone and the artery. What happened to the lab director?"

"He has fits," Johnson gasped as he saw Tanaka's boot move toward his thigh again, "and he had one tonight. He was hurting himself, so we gave him a shot of something he had on hand in case of an attack."

"I have only one more question for you. Where's the archaeological sample?"

Johnson responded with a blank look, but Tanaka saw Billy-Lee Jordan react. Turning to Kenji, Tanaka smiled grimly. "The preacher's son understood *that*," he said in Japanese.

At that moment, the *yakuza* Tanaka had sent to search the clinic returned. "No sign of the girl. The clinic's deserted."

Kenji saw Tanaka hesitate, but only for a fraction of a second. "Maybe we were misinformed, but it doesn't matter. The men are accounted for."

He turned on Billy-Lee. "You know what we want. Where is it?"

Billy-Lee desperately tried to feign incomprehension, and his clumsiness made it clear that he hadn't been faking until now. His face was deathly pale beneath his tan, and his staring, terrified eyes were unnaturally wide. He looked like a man who'd awakened from a dream into a nightmare.

"Where is it?" Tanaka demanded, and when Billy-Lee said nothing, Tanaka took a quick step toward him.

"No, don't hurt me!" Billy-Lee squealed, almost toppling backward as he came out of the chair. His voice was high-pitched and distorted, but it was the voice Kenji had heard the night of the break-in. Billy-Lee Jordan had been the man who'd struck Allison.

Tanaka shifted the rifle he cradled so that Billy-Lee was staring straight into the muzzle. "I won't hurt you," he said coldly. "You won't feel a thing when I splatter your brains. I'll only say this once, Mr. Jordan. Give us the sample, or die—right here, right now."

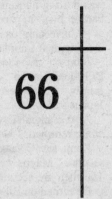

66

"Look at that," Reese whispered tensely as two of the raiders drove Billy-Lee out of the dining hall and prodded him toward Michaels's laboratory with their rifle butts. "They're not worried about finding you missing. They're going straight for the finger."

The anticipation Lara heard in Reese's voice scared her. "What are you thinking?"

"That it's time for you to get undercover," Reese whispered back. "I want you to crawl over into the woods."

"*Why?* John, what are you going to do?"

"Maybe nothing, but if they make a mistake, I'll take advantage of it."

Lara's throat constricted, and she didn't trust herself to speak. She recoiled from being left alone again, but it was fear for Reese that tightened like a band around her throat. He was going to try something. She *knew* it.

Reese waited tensely for Lara's response, hoping she wouldn't balk. How could he refuse if she asked him to stay with her? He couldn't—not after what had happened the last time he'd left her alone.

Billy-Lee and his captors had reached the entrance to Michaels's lab, and Billy-Lee was unlocking the door. Incredibly, he appeared to be recovering. By rights, Reese thought fleetingly, the blow to the head he'd received should have cracked his skull.

"All right," Lara whispered. "I'll go."

"Good," Reese responded with relief, and he reached out and squeezed her arm. "Get into the trees directly across from us, and stay put so I'll know where to find you. And hang on to that shotgun."

"Won't you need it?"

"No. Keep it, and go."

Seconds after the darkness swallowed Lara up, one of the two *yakuza* who'd remained in the dining hall came outside, said something to the lookout, and came running across the quadrangle in Reese's direction. Reese started to slither backward, but as the man passed the Prayer Tower, it became clear that he was heading for the computer room. Reese drew his pistol and stayed where he was.

Hardly believing his luck, Reese watched the *yakuza* run to the door to the computer room and slip inside. Reese's pulse quickened in anticipation. They had made a mistake.

As the door closed behind the raider, Reese rose and ran toward the research building, confident that the careless lookout outside the dining hall would neither see nor hear him. In seconds, Reese reached the end of the research building, where he was safely out of sight of the dining hall.

He intended to ambush the *yakuza* inside the computer room as the man came back out, and Reese moved along the building wall to the side of the door. His breathing steadied as a cold determination settled over him, and he slipped the knife from his boot. He had never killed with a knife, and he wasn't looking forward to it, but he had to kill silently.

Reese heard a faint noise from behind the door, and he dropped to a crouch and tightened his grip on the knife. The door swung open, and the raider's flashlight beam splashed the ground in front of Reese. As the man stepped through the doorway, Reese lunged sideways, slipped beneath the man's rifle barrel, and drove his blade up under the man's ribs with all his strength.

As he thrust in the knife to the hilt, the handle shivered violently, and Reese felt the hot gush of blood pouring over his hand. He stifled his revulsion as the raider jerked and stiffened with a gurgling gasp, and as the man toppled back through the doorway, Reese caught the rifle before it fell.

He switched off the gun's flashlight, pointed the weapon in Lara's general direction, and winked the light three times to signal that he was all right. She must have seen something of what had happened, but he hoped she'd not seen too much.

Reese stepped over the corpse in the doorway and dragged it inside. As the door swung closed, shutting out the noise of the surf washing up from the shore, Reese heard the static hiss of a transceiver the dead man carried. He switched on his own flashlight, set it on the floor, and hastily wiped his blood-covered hand on the dead man's jumpsuit. Then he checked the M16.

A round was in the chamber and the safety was on. Reese shifted the select lever to autofire and laid the weapon down. The rifle already carried a thirty-round magazine, with a second magazine taped alongside it, but Reese wanted as much ammunition as he could get. He found no spare magazines in the *yakuza*'s pockets, but the dead man had a pack strapped to his back.

Reese pulled the knife out of the corpse, wiped the blade and handle, and slipped it back into his boot. Then he rolled the body over to search the pack. Instead of ammunition, he found an unfamiliar electronic unit with a short antenna. He pulled it out and studied it a moment before he realized what it had to be. He couldn't be sure it was a radio detonator, but he could think of no other use for the device. He rose and went looking for the bomb.

67

As Kenji watched Billy-Lee fumbling with the safe's combination lock, the night of the break-in came rushing back to him in vivid detail. Again—as he had so many times in his nightmares—he heard Allison's piercing cry of fear. The guilt he felt afresh only intensified Kenji's loathing for the man on his knees before him.

Billy-Lee had already bungled the combination once, and as he reached for the door's handle, he looked up anxiously. "Open it," Kenji said, and the voice he heard was that of a stranger. He had never wanted to hurt a man before, but he wanted to now.

Billy-Lee depressed the handle, and the safe's door swung open. Surprise stayed Kenji's reaction, but Billy-Lee recoiled from the empty safe as if he'd found a viper inside. "It *was* in there!" he cried defensively. "I swear it!"

Kenji no longer knew himself as frustration and loathing swelled to rage, and Billy-Lee saw it.

"No!" Billy-Lee cried, throwing up his arms and scrabbling back against the wall. "Michaels must have moved it! Ask him! Ask Michaels!"

Kenji felt Tanaka grip his arm. "He's too frightened to lie," Tanaka said sharply in Japanese, taking his transceiver from the holster on his belt. "We'll have to get it out of the lab director," he said, and spoke into the transceiver. "Obe, see if you can wake up the drugged scientist."

Tanaka received an immediate response and nodded in satisfaction. "He started coming around a few minutes ago," he said to Kenji, and then into the transceiver, "Slap him awake, Obe. The sample isn't here, and the scientist knows where it is. See if you can get it out of him while he's still confused."

Billy-Lee flinched as Kenji angrily seized him and hauled him to his feet. "You'd better not be lying," Kenji snarled at the man who'd derailed his life, and as Tanaka called to his other men to check in and report, Kenji propelled Billy-Lee toward the lab exit.

"Wait, Hamada-san," Tanaka said sharply as Kenji hustled Billy-Lee toward the corridor leading to the outside entrance. "Sakai's not responding."

"Maybe his set isn't working," Kenji said, paying no attention. He still thought Billy-Lee might be lying, and he wasn't willing to wait to find out.

"I don't like it. He should have come out by now. *Sakai!*"

Kenji heard the concern in Tanaka's voice, but he discounted it as the overprotective caution of a nursemaid. Heedless, he pushed Billy-Lee ahead of him into the corridor. Tanaka had shown him how to operate the rifle he carried, and as they approached the outer door, he snapped back the bolt. Kenji wasn't sure what he wanted more—the sample, or for Billy-Lee to try to run.

68

Reese found the bomb in the room housing the computer mainframes, a thick, plastic-wrapped package and an electronic unit with a glowing red indicator light. The bomb's explosive looked to Reese like C-4, or some other variant of plastique, and there was plenty of it. The *yakuza* obviously wanted to destroy Michaels's computer records.

Reese's first instinct was to switch off the receiver unit, but he remembered Lara's horror at the experiment Michaels had planned, and he immediately changed his mind. He slipped the radio detonator into his jacket pocket. When the time came, he would wipe out Michaels's data himself.

As Reese came back through the computer room, he heard a voice emanating from the dead man's transceiver. The language was Japanese, but there was no mistaking the curt tone. Whoever was speaking was in command.

Reese detached the transceiver from its belt holster, discarded his flashlight, and picked up the M16. Impatiently he waited for his eyes to readjust to the darkness. The *yakuza* commander spoke again, and another Japanese voice responded. Reese understood only the first word: *"Hai!"* A brief exchange followed, and Reese turned down the transceiver's volume and slipped outside.

As he crept to the corner of the building, he heard the *yakuza* commander's voice again. "Sakai!" the man snapped, and waited for a response. The response was silence. Reese eased into a prone firing position and lined up his sights on the raider still standing outside the dining hall.

"Sakai!" the *yakuza* commander repeated more sharply, and Reese guessed that Sakai was the name of the man he'd killed.

Any second now, the raiders' commander might realize that something was wrong. Reese steadied his aim on the lookout in front of the dining hall and started to squeeze the trigger.

Abruptly a light appeared at the door to Michaels's laboratory, and out of the corner of Reese's eye, he saw Billy-Lee come stumbling out. Behind him came one of the raiders. Reese held his sights on the man outside the dining hall, but he eased up on the trigger. If the *yakuza* behind Billy-Lee came out far enough, Reese thought, he might get two of the bastards at once.

"Sakai!" cried the commander again, and this time the tinny voice from the transceiver was echoed by the same voice, coming through the open doorway to Michaels's lab. The commander had moved to the outer door, but he wasn't showing a light. He was suspicious, all right, and Reese waited no longer.

He made sure of his aim and loosed a three-shot burst at the lookout. The M16 bucked against his shoulder, and he heard a shriek. The man in front of the dining hall spun and fell, but the scream had come from a terrified Billy-Lee. As Reese swung his sights toward the raider behind Billy-Lee, the preacher's son bolted.

Reese expected the gunman to drop to the ground and switch off his light, but inexplicably the man wasted precious seconds on Billy-Lee. The *yakuza* fired wildly, and Billy-Lee collapsed like a sack of meal. Belatedly, the raider threw himself to the ground, but Reese already had him in his sights.

The man's flashlight winked out just as Reese fired, but he was sure his burst had struck home. Instantly, muzzle flashes flared from the dark entrance to Michaels's lab, and bullets chipped the corner of the research building and stitched the ground as Reese rolled to cover.

Reese almost didn't make it, for the *yakuza* still inside the dining hall had been alerted by Reese's first burst, and he fired from the entrance at a better angle. A ricochet zinged past Reese's ear, and a bullet plucked at his jacket. Two more short bursts dug up the ground and chipped the corner of the building before the *yakuza* guns fell silent.

Reese peered around the corner. The flashlight on the ground beside the body of the man in front of the dining hall still burned, but it was pointed away from the clinic. Reese could see neither Billy-Lee's body nor that of the gunman who'd shot him.

Reese's pulse pounded at his temples and he was breathing quickly in response to the adrenaline flooding his system, but he felt a surge of elation. Thanks to a stroke of luck, he had eliminated three of the bastards, and only two were left. The odds had shifted dramatically in his favor. He turned and pointed his rifle in Lara's direction and winked the flashlight three times to let her know he was still all right.

Abruptly a burst of Japanese sounded from the transceiver on the ground beside him, and he picked it up. The moment the exchange was over, he cleared his throat and pressed the transmit button. "Are you guys ready to say *sayonara?*" he asked as coolly as he could manage.

Two long seconds passed, and then the *yakuza* commander replied in accented but fluent English. "To whom am I speaking?" he asked with studied calm.

"It doesn't matter. Three of your men are down, mister, and I'm willing to leave it at that. Do you want to call off the fight?"

"Are you proposing a truce?"

"I'm proposing to let you get out of here while you still have the chance."

"I'll have to consider it."

"Then show me some lights while you're thinking,"

Reese snapped. "I want to know where you are."

"If you do the same."

Reese turned on the flashlight beneath his gun barrel, briefly played the beam on the ground beyond the building's corner, and switched it off again. Over the transceiver, he heard an exchange in Japanese, and lights winked from the clinic and the dining hall.

The *yakuza* leader said something more in Japanese and then switched to English. "We'll reply with our lights every time we see yours."

"Don't think too long. If I decide to put a few rounds into your chopper's engine, you're stuck here."

The *yakuza* leader spoke rapidly in Japanese, and Reese heard a reply. Then there was silence, and the seconds stretched out.

"*Well?*" Reese demanded. "I'm running out of patience."

"Tell me something. Have our paths crossed once before? In an office building in Massachusetts perhaps?"

The man was stalling. *Why?*

"Show me your lights!" Reese snapped, flashing his own, and again lights winked from the clinic and the dining hall. But Reese didn't trust the silence. He was about to shift his position when the *yakuza* commander spoke again.

"I can see we have no choice but to withdraw," he said, but something told Reese he was lying.

At that moment, Reese sensed movement behind him, and he whirled to face the unexpected danger. Even as he turned, he knew he'd be too late.

Time stood still for Reese as he tried to bring his M16 to bear on the indistinct, shadowy figure of the man sent to take him from behind. In the midst of his desperate attempt to survive, a part of his mind registered his mistake. He had counted five *yakuza*, but there was a sixth. Reese's gun was still swinging toward the raider when he saw the flaring muzzle flash as the man fired from the hip.

A sustained burst would have cut Reese down, but the raider didn't get the chance. Coincident with the muzzle flash, a booming shotgun blast catapulted the *yakuza* toward

Reese, as if swept from behind by a giant broom. The man staggered forward, and Reese squeezed the trigger and cut him down at point-blank range.

"John!" Reese heard Lara cry from the woods, and only then did he realize what had happened. Lara had moved up closer to him, and she had saved his life.

"I'm okay!" he yelled, deliberately confirming his position to the surviving raiders before he shifted. Afraid they might be rushing him, he scooped up the dead man's weapon and sprinted toward Lara. She called to him again as he neared the trees, and he veered to his left.

"John," Lara gasped in relief as he dropped into the undergrowth beside her.

"Quiet," he whispered, readying his rifle. "They may be coming."

He could feel Lara shivering beside him as he peered into the darkness, straining to detect a hint of movement or catch a telltale sound. Seconds later, Reese caught a faint, indistinct voice coming from the transceiver he'd left beside the research building, and he expelled his breath in release.

"They're not coming at us," he whispered, putting his arm around Lara. "At least not yet. Are you all right?"

"*Yes*," Lara whispered back. "Now that you're here."

But her teeth chattered, and she was still shivering. "Hang in there," he said, pulling her close. "They've lost four men. If they have any sense, they'll quit."

"I'm okay. It's just that I was so scared," she whispered, the words coming out in a rush. "I know you told me to stay where I was, but all that shooting—and I couldn't see what was happening. And when I saw that man slipping up behind you, I . . ."

Reese felt her shudder. "You saved my life," he whispered, "but you didn't kill him. I did."

But Lara's thoughts had raced on. "Even if they leave, John, Billy-Lee and his—"

"Billy-Lee's dead. They shot him when he tried to run."

"Good!" Lara responded fiercely. "Damn him to hell."

Reese's initial relief that the *yakuza* hadn't rushed him was slipping away as the silence in the compound stretched out. *Where are they? What are they up to?*

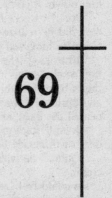

69

Kenji lay facedown, paralyzed with pain he could never have imagined. It stabbed him in the chest with each shallow breath, and his leg felt as if it were being seared by a hot iron. But this was nothing compared to the agony in his hip.

"He's alive," came a faraway voice, and through the pain he felt hands probing his body. "There's blood all along his side, but I can't tell . . ."

"Give him a morphine shot, and then we'll roll him over and risk some light."

Kenji tried to scream as hands twisted him onto his back, but the searing pain in his chest cut it off. He opened his eyes and through a blur of tears saw shadows above him and a tiny sliver of light.

"Thigh's torn open, but it's still only a flesh wound. Hip bone's smashed, and his chest . . . I see bone splinters, but no penetration. Bullet must have glanced off the rib cage. I think he'll make it, Tanaka-san."

"I'm not afraid," Kenji sighed, but there was no response from the shadows above him.

"None of us will make it if we don't get going. You take his legs."

A shadow appeared over his face and came closer, closer. "We're taking you home, Hamada-san."

"Did you get the sample?" Kenji asked, but for some reason he couldn't hear his own voice, and the shadow didn't respond. It didn't matter. He wasn't afraid, and he knew that he would never be afraid again. That was all that really mattered.

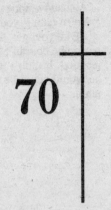

70

John!'' Lara exclaimed as she heard a whine rising from the rear of the compound. ''They're going!''

''Yes,'' he responded, getting to his feet, and the release she heard in his voice seemed nothing compared to the relief flooding through her. As the helicopter lifted off and the *whap-whap-whap* of its whirling blades filled the air, Reese lifted Lara to her feet and hugged her.

Lara clung to him, laughing and weeping with joy at the same time. She raised her eyes, trying to see his face in the darkness, but he was looking up at the helicopter as it swept low overhead.

Without warning, a deafening blast shattered the night, and they both winced. ''My God, what was *that*?'' Lara cried over the helicopter's roar.

''I don't know,'' Reese shouted, ''but I think they just blew up Jordan's communications center.''

Lara still couldn't put weight on her sprained ankle, and she almost lost her balance as Reese bent down to pick up his rifle. ''Come on,'' he said, switching on the flashlight beneath the barrel. ''We'd better check on Michaels and the others. My guess is they're tied up, but we don't want them getting loose.''

"I'm too beat to carry you," he added, handing her the rifle. "Hang on to this for me, and put your arm over my shoulders."

He reached up and grasped her wrist with his left hand and encircled her waist with his right arm, and they left the woods with Lara limping awkwardly beside him. In the darkness she could barely see the body of the man she'd shot, but she was glad Reese shifted direction and blocked it from her view.

"Maybe we can pick up some crutches in the clinic's dispensary," Reese said.

"God"—Lara laughed, feeling giddy—"I can't believe it's really over."

"If that was the communications center blowing up, I hope my cell phone works."

"Billy-Lee had one in his Jeep," Lara said, and she had to stifle a reflexive stab of fear as she said his name. *Thank God he's dead.* "What do you think it was?" she asked tearing her thoughts away from Billy-Lee. "A time bomb?"

"It was probably detonated by radio. The extra man I missed was probably busy planting it. The radio signal must have been on a different frequency, or the one in the computer room would have blown, too."

"There's a *bomb* in there?"

"But it won't go off," Reese said quickly. "I took the detonator off the *yakuza* who planted it. It's in my pocket."

"Then blow it up, John! I know Michaels will be going to jail, but let's not take chances. What he wanted to do was horrible. Blow it up!"

"Okay, but first things first."

The flashlight on the M16 the lookout had dropped was still burning on the ground in front of the dining hall, and Reese was relieved to see that it didn't illuminate the body of the man he had killed. Lara would have nightmares enough as it was, he thought, without the memory of all the corpses scattered about. The door to the dining hall was open, and

Reese could hear scrabbling sounds and muttered curses from inside.

Reese and Lara were just five feet from the doorway when they heard a gurgling snarl to their left and behind them. Lara gasped, and as Reese twisted them around, she swung the flashlight beam in the direction of the sound.

Fifty feet away, Billy-Lee was tottering toward them like a zombie with a rifle in his hands. The left side of his head and half his face were red with blood from the grazing bullet that had knocked him cold but failed to kill him. Squinting against the flashlight's glare, he raised the M16 he'd obviously taken from the body of the man Reese had shot in front of the clinic.

Reese hadn't time to reach the pistol in his waistband or seize the rifle in Lara's hand, so he lunged toward the open doorway, carrying Lara with him. Behind them he heard the staccato blasts of the M16 on autofire as Billy-Lee loosed a wild burst. Bullets stitched the ground and chewed up the half-open door as Reese dove with Lara diagonally through the entrance.

They hit the floor and skidded across it, and Reese gasped as his head banged against a table leg. Lara was clinging to him, and he fought free of her arms and roughly pulled her farther out of the line of fire.

"I dropped the gun!" Lara cried as the firing abruptly stopped. "It's *outside*!"

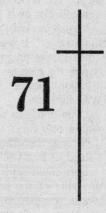

71

Billy-Lee half fell to his knees and dropped forward into the grass. The earth rocked beneath him and the pounding in his head was agonizing, but he didn't care. *Satan's black angels have fled before thy wrath, O Lord, and I have the strength of ten men. Now shall I smite the last of Thine enemies!*

Billy-Lee's lips drew back and he shook with silent laughter as he pointed his rifle at the doorway, which was fully illuminated by the flashlight on the rifle the Jezebel had dropped. *Come out, come out, whoever you are.*

Billy-Lee's eyes slipped in and out of focus, and as he stared at the doorway it became two doors, sliding apart and coalescing again. One, then two. One, then . . . A figure's head and shoulders appeared in the doorway—the figure of a man on his belly, *like a serpent.* The world spun, and as Billy-Lee pressed the trigger, he spewed vomit.

Lara gasped as bullets splintered the doorjamb inches above Reese's head, and he barely pulled back in time. She knew the rifle she'd dropped was only feet from the door, but it might as well have been a mile.

"What do we do now?" she asked, feeling strangely numb. The shock of seeing Billy-Lee had dissipated almost immediately, as if her nerves had burnt out.

"Yeah, asshole," someone sneered. "What are you going to do now?" It was Johnson's voice.

"I'll have to go out after him," Reese said to Lara, ignoring the men tied up behind them.

"Don't, John!" Lara urged. "Billy-Lee looked half-dead. Wait him out."

"I'm going to take the son of a bitch," Reese responded with a cold fury.

"Reed!" another voice cried before Lara could protest. "Reed, is that you?"

Lara could hardly see the man lying bound on the floor to one side of the security guards, but it was Michaels, his words mangled by his ruined mouth. "Reed!" Michaels cried again as Reese stood up and turned toward him. "What's happening? Who were those men?"

"Who gives a shit!" Johnson snapped at Michaels. "The Japs are gone. That's Billy-Lee out there."

"Japs?" Michaels responded dazedly. "Why were they after God's precious . . . *Reed—what have you done with the finger?*"

"Shut *up,* for Christ's sake," Johnson growled as Reese slowly advanced on Michaels. "Hey, Reed—I know you. The computer guy, right? Are you the one we were chasing? Look, man, I don't know what's going on, but Billy-Lee is out there with an M-sixteen and you've only got a pistol. Let's you and me cut a deal."

"Billy-Lee?" Michaels cried with renewed energy. "Oh, praise God! Thy will be done!"

Reese knelt beside Michaels, and there was just enough light for Lara to see the gleam of the blade as he drew a knife from his boot. "What are you going to do?" Michaels asked anxiously.

"Cut you loose," Reese said, feeling for the cords around Michaels's ankles.

"That's right, cut me loose!" Michaels exclaimed triumphantly as Reese sliced through the cords. "No one can stand in the way of the Lord. But the Lord is merciful, Reed, and so are we. Just give us back the finger.''

Reese hauled Michaels to his feet and pushed him toward the doorway. ''John,'' Lara asked in alarm, ''what are you going to do?''

''Dr. Mike is going to fetch my rifle for me—assuming Billy-Lee doesn't shoot him.''

''No!'' Michaels burst out.

''Move!'' Reese snapped, jamming his gun into Michaels's back and pushing him forward. ''Or I'll shoot you myself.''

''You can't scare me,'' Michaels responded with an unnatural laugh. ''The Lord is with us. Give it up, Reed,'' he shouted as Reese continued to shove him toward the door, ''or you'll never get off Miracle Isle alive.''

Lara heard the manic assurance in Michaels's voice, but Reese didn't seem to care as he continued to push Michaels ahead of him. And when the ploy failed, Reese would go out after Billy-Lee anyway. *He hates Billy-Lee too much. He isn't thinking.*

Reese had muscled Michaels almost to the doorway when a wild thought struck Lara, and she seized on it.

''Don't be stupid, John!'' she said as sharply and coldly as she could manage. ''Michaels doesn't know it's over. Why don't you tell him?''

To Lara's relief, her tone arrested both men, and Michaels twisted around to face her. ''Tell me what?'' he demanded. Lara couldn't see Reese's face as he stared at her, and she prayed he would give her the time she needed to improvise her trap.

''Why do you think we came here?'' Lara sneered at Michaels.

''You're *Catholics,*'' Michaels hissed. ''You do what the pope tells you.''

''Exactly,'' Lara snapped back. ''And do you actually think we wanted that rotting scrap of flesh and bone? Do you think for one second that the Church—the *true* Church—would tolerate the blasphemous lies of that ridiculous scroll?

We didn't come to steal that decaying finger, you idiot. We came to *destroy* it!''

"What have you done with it?" Michaels raged, trying to pull himself free of Reese's grip.

"What time is it, John?" Lara asked.

"What difference—"

"What *time* is it?" she snapped, fearful of the impatience she heard in his voice.

"Ten o'clock," Reese said without looking at his watch.

"So," Lara said quickly, anxious that Michaels not register the mystification she heard in Reese's voice. "Only six minutes to go."

"What are you talking about?" Michaels demanded, his voice rising sharply.

"You heard that one time bomb go off, didn't you?" Lara said with calculated venom. "Your computers are next, and that cursed finger of yours is sitting right on top of the bomb."

"No!" Michaels bellowed as if in agony, and he lunged for the door. "Billy-Lee, get the finger!" he yelled at the top of his voice. "It's in the computer room! The computer room!"

Billy-Lee blinked and tried again to focus his eyes as he heard Michaels shout. Dr. Mike's distorted voice seemed to come from far away, as if he were shouting from the far end of a long tunnel. But Billy-Lee understood, and he struggled to his feet.

Get the finger! Computer room. It's in the computer room! The computer room!

Billy-Lee reeled and almost fell as he turned toward the research building and stumbled into a run. The earth pitched and rolled as he ran, and he gasped at the pounding agony in his head, but he kept running. *He had to get the finger!*

Without warning a black mass rose up in front of him, and he nearly ran headlong into the side of the Prayer Tower. Gasping for breath, he fumbled for the gun's flashlight and switched it on. Behind him he heard Michaels still shouting at him: "Get the finger, Billy-Lee!"

But not for you, Michaels, and not for Daddy! For me and my ministry!

Reese looked at Lara, but he couldn't see her face.

"Do it," she said hoarsely, and he stepped through the doorway.

He could see Billy-Lee's flashlight beam dancing crazily as it neared the door to the computer room, and he took the radio detonator from his pocket. Michaels was halfway to the Prayer Tower, but he was trying to run too fast with his hands tied behind his back. He stumbled and crashed to the ground face first.

Reese extended the detonator's antenna, and when he flipped the toggle switch, a red indicator lamp came on. Billy-Lee had reached the outside entrance to the computer control room, and Reese saw his light disappear. Michaels was struggling to get to his feet, but in his haste he toppled forward again. Reese waited another two seconds and pushed the firing button.

A brilliant white light flashed behind the windows at the seaward end of the research building, and Reese winced as the explosion blew them out with a deafening blast. Michaels, who had started to get up again, fell back in shock. Reese slipped the detonator back in his pocket, picked up the M16, and walked across the lawn to Michaels.

The scientist was no longer trying to get up. He lay in the grass, twitching and writhing as if in pain. "Forgive me, Lord," he moaned over and over, and as Reese came up to him, he saw that Michaels was weeping.

72

Reese straightened up behind the wheel of Billy-Lee's Jeep, which he'd parked in front of the dormitory, and looked at his watch. Exhaustion weighed on him, and for a moment the watch face remained a blur. Almost 11 P.M. What was keeping Lara?

He sounded the Jeep's horn, and less than a minute later, Lara emerged from the main entrance, carrying a flashlight Reese had found in the dining hall.

"I was coming," she called, swinging toward him on crutches he'd liberated from the clinic. "You didn't have to honk."

"What took so long?" he asked, and the voice he heard was gratingly hoarse. *Christ, I've had it,* he thought as he reached across to help her into the passenger seat, *and we're not done yet.*

"As long as I was changing into dry clothes," Lara said cheerfully, "I thought I might as well try taking a shower. The water was only lukewarm, but it was worth it. My hair's going to be a mess, though. No dryer."

The response astonished him. Having just come through

hell, it seemed impossible that Lara could worry about her hair. In contrast, Reese felt completely drained. Relief was not enough to buoy him, and he felt no satisfaction, much less a sense of triumph. He'd done what he'd come to do—what he'd had to do—but the vengeance he'd so desired left him feeling empty.

"Is that our ride?" Lara asked as she picked up the sound of an approaching helicopter.

"Let's hope so," Reese said, starting the engine.

Lara reached over and gripped Reese's arm. "Why so glum? We're home free!"

"Looks that way," Reese said, letting out the clutch, "but we still have loose ends to tie up."

"Let Beretta and his people worry about that."

Reese shook his head. "I'm going to see Jordan," he said as he drove around the end of the dormitory onto the road circling the compound and headed for the helicopter pad. "There's an easy way for us to finish this, and a hard way. I've had a talk with Michaels, and I think we can take the easy way."

"What do you mean?" Lara asked, raising her voice above the swelling roar of the incoming helicopter.

"I'll explain once we're on our way."

As they neared the landing site, the helicopter's searchlight swept over them and flooded the pad in light. The helicopter began its descent, and Reese stopped the Jeep and helped Lara out.

"*When* are you going to see Jordan?" she yelled over the deafening noise.

"Now. I'll have the pilot drop me off at Lambeth Cove, and I'll pick up my car."

"I'll go with you," Lara shouted.

"No! You go on to Beretta. I want him to know what's happened. Tell him that I'll call him as soon as I've finished with Jordan."

As the helicopter touched down, Reese saw that the chopper's identification number had been covered by a canvas shroud. The pilot throttled back, and Reese and Lara made their way to the helicopter, their heads bowed against the downwash from the whirling blades. The pilot opened the cabin door, and Reese lifted Lara into a rear seat.

"I was told there would only be you," the pilot shouted at Reese. He was a hard-looking man about Reese's age, and he wasn't amused.

"You were told wrong," Reese shouted back, climbing in beside the pilot and closing the door. "Let's get out of here."

"Okay, Mac," the pilot snapped, and pulled pitch. The helicopter shot straight up, and Reese felt as if his stomach had been left behind.

As the helicopter leveled off and flew out to sea, Reese leaned toward the pilot to be heard over the roar in the cabin. "I want you to drop me off at Lambeth Cove, a short hop down the Maine coast from here."

The pilot scowled and shook his head. "Those aren't my instructions."

Reese was in no mood to argue. He pulled out his Browning and jammed it into the pilot's ribs. "I'm giving you new instructions."

Thus spoke Simon: From the face of him who overcomes false prophets shall God wipe away all tears.

—SAMARIA SCROLL 1, FRAGMENT 24

73

The young night clerk in the hotel where Jordan was staying eyed Reese dubiously as he entered the lobby and crossed to the desk. "Can I help you?" the clerk asked coolly, obviously put off by Reese's matted hair, unshaven face, and wet, dirt-smeared clothing.

"You can. You have a group from Bobby Jordan Ministries staying here. I'm part of the group, but I got left behind. One of the party should have checked my luggage with you. The name is Reed. John Reed."

"Yes, sir, I can check on—"

"I'm sure you can check on it, but while you're fetching my luggage, I want to see the Reverend Bobby Jordan. What's his room number?"

The clerk cleared his throat and pointedly looked at his watch. "It's really quite late, sir," he said officiously. "Is he expecting you?"

"No, but if you're worried about it, buzz his room and tell him that John Reed is here to see him." If Jordan didn't remember the name, Reese thought, Lurleen certainly would. "And tell him that I've just escorted Lara Brooks off the island."

"What island, sir?"

"Just tell him, kid. I guarantee he'll want to see me."

Reese rapped on the door to Jordan's suite, and the preacher opened it immediately. Jordan's face was puffy from sleep and showing his age, and he had dressed hurriedly. His shirt-tail was only half tucked in and his hair was mussed. Now that he was face-to-face with him, Reese almost changed his mind.

"What's the meaning of this?" Jordan demanded, trying to mask his anxiety with angry indignation. "Do you know what time it is?"

Reese just stared at him.

"What's this about Lara Brooks?" Jordan huffed ineffectually. "The poor girl is ill."

"She's feeling better now. Escaping Miracle Isle did wonders for her. Do you want to talk about it out here," Reese added loudly, "or inside?"

Jordan retreated hastily, and Reese walked into the suite's sitting room and shut the door behind him. Lurleen was not in sight, but the door to the bedroom was partially open.

"What do you mean, she escaped?" Jordan demanded, still trying to sound angry, but his restless, anxious eyes gave him away. He was scared. "I don't know what you're talking about."

"Maybe your wife does," Reese said, looking toward the bedroom.

Immediately the door opened wide, and Lurleen appeared. In contrast to her husband, she looked coolly self-possessed. She had dressed with care; she was freshly made up and not a hair on her bottle-blond head was out of place. "Good evenin', Mr. Reed," she said icily, and her steely eyes scanned his unkempt appearance from head to foot.

Reese walked to a chair opposite the sitting room's sofa and sat down. "Have a seat," he said to the Jordans.

"I demand to know what you're doing here!" Jordan burst out.

"Shut up, Bobby," Lurleen snapped, and Jordan wilted.

Lurleen went to the sofa and sat down, and Jordan came

over and perched beside her, staring at Reese as if he were a bad dream. His initial bluster had been paper-thin, and now there was not a trace of the commanding presence he projected from the pulpit.

"I take it you've managed somehow to bring the girl off the island," Lurleen said to Reese. "Are you a Catholic, too, Mr. Reed?"

"My name is Reese, not Reed."

The name didn't register with Lurleen, but Bobby Jordan stiffened. Lurleen glanced at her husband and looked back to Reese. "Does that have some significance?"

"I have a daughter. Allison Reese. She was in the Harvard laboratory the night your son broke in."

Lurleen's expression froze, and for an instant he saw a hint of fear in her eyes—but only for an instant. Jordan was blinking rapidly and no longer looking at Reese.

"I see," Lurleen said, maintaining her icy calm. "Have you come here to tell us that you're going to the police?"

"No."

"Ah." Lurleen's eyes flickered. "Then let's get down to business, shall we?"

If nothing else, Reese thought grimly, Lurleen was a survivor. She had no idea of what had happened, but at the moment, at least, she was focused on the one question that was vital to her: Could she make a deal?

"What do you want?" she asked. "Money? That can be arranged, but there are limits. You can make trouble for us, but that's all it would be—trouble. Bobby Jordan has an impeccable reputation, and whatever charges you and the girl might level at us, it would be your word against ours. You have no proof."

"Wrong," Reese said, and he drew the bottle containing the finger from his jacket pocket.

Without warning, Jordan abruptly came to life. "No!" he cried, his wide eyes fixed on the bottle, and he jumped up. "That's God's precious gift!"

Reese rose to meet him, and as Jordan lunged for the bottle, Reese batted his arm away and threw him back on the sofa. Jordan tried to get up again, but as his eyes met the muzzle of Reese's gun, he flinched and fell back, breathing hard. Lurleen hadn't moved.

Reese looked down at her. "You know what's in the bottle, don't you? It's all the proof I need to put your Bobby in a striped suit."

"What happened?" Jordan asked dazedly, staring up at Reese with vacant eyes, and his lower lip started to quiver. "What have you done?"

"Quiet, Bobby!" Lurleen snapped, not taking her eyes off Reese. "You still haven't told us what you want, Mr. Reese."

"Lara and I already have what we came to Miracle Isle to get. What happens next is up to you. We left a mess behind tonight—a mess that will have to be explained to the police. If you're clever enough to explain it without involving us, you'll never hear from us again. But if we're dragged into it, we'll tell our story. Bobby will go to jail, and you'll lose your money machine."

"What mess?" Lurleen asked icily.

"Apparently there's someone else who wanted this bottle. I don't know who, and I don't know why. But tonight, six thugs raided your island. They flew in by helicopter on the heels of the hurricane."

"That's absurd!" Lurleen responded, glancing at her husband, but Jordan was no help to her. He continued to stare up at Reese with vacant eyes.

"You'll believe it when you find the bodies lying around." Lurleen's eyes widened. "And the wrecked buildings the raiders blew up before they were driven off. As I said, it's a real mess."

"But what *happened?*"

"Explaining that is your problem, and you'd better make it good."

"Please," Jordan pleaded dazedly. "Don't take God's precious gift."

Lurleen looked at her husband in disgust.

"When you get to the island," Reese said to her, "you'll find Michaels and the others tied up in the dining hall. If you stick as closely as possible to what actually happened, you should get away with it. Just leave me and Lara out of the story. We weren't there. You took us both off the island when you left yesterday afternoon in your helicopter.

"I've had a talk with Michaels, and he's ready to play along. If your security guards won't keep their mouths shut for money, you can remind them that if we talk, they'll undoubtedly go to jail with your husband. If you screw up, Lurleen—Bobby, here, will be facing charges of conspiracy, kidnapping, theft, and attempted murder. That's a promise."

Reese's last words penetrated Jordan's daze, and tears spilled from his eyes. "Don't forsake us, Lord," he sobbed. "O God Almighty, deliver us from Thine enemies—"

"Shut *up!*" Lurleen snarled, and for a moment Reese thought she was going to hit Jordan. But she quickly recovered her icy composure and turned back to Reese. "All right. If we do cover up, what then?"

"I've already told you. If you keep us out of it, we're quits."

"Why?" she asked suspiciously. "I don't understand."

"You don't have to understand. Do we have a deal?"

"Yes." Although her voice remained cold, she was not quite able to hide her relief.

Reese took one last look at Jordan, who was muttering incoherently to himself, and walked to the door. If he stayed even a second longer, he thought, he might change his mind.

"Why?" Lurleen asked again as Reese opened the door. "Why are you letting us cover up?"

Reese turned back to her. "Because I'm willing to settle for biblical justice. You know the passage, Lurleen—'Eye for eye, tooth for tooth . . .' " Lurleen was staring at him uncomprehendingly.

"I lost a daughter," Reese said, going out the door, "and last night, your husband lost his son."

He didn't wait for a response. He closed the door behind him and walked away.

74

Reese arrived early the following afternoon at the posh and very private clinic where Beretta was convalescing. Overwhelming exhaustion had forced him to stop at a motel, where he'd immediately phoned the number Beretta had given him. To Reese's surprise, Beretta had answered, and although his voice had been weak and sometimes barely audible, Reese was sure that he'd understood all Reese told him.

Eight hours' sleep, a shower, and a change of clothes had improved Reese's appearance, and the young woman at the reception desk greeted him with a friendly smile. "Yes, Mr. Reese, we've been expecting you. Please sign our register, and I'll show you up to Mr. Beretta's room."

"Do you know if Dr. Lara Brooks is here?"

"Yes, she is, Mr. Reese. She just returned from lunch."

Lara's pulse quickened as she heard a man and a woman coming down the hall, and she recognized Reese's step. He'd left her barely twelve hours ago, yet she couldn't wait to see him. They'd parted in such haste—with so much left unsaid.

Beretta's bed had been cranked up so that he was in a semireclining position, and he managed a grin as Reese entered. "Well done!" he exclaimed with as much enthusiasm as his weakness allowed.

"I'm glad you're satisfied, Al," Reese said, but his eyes had found Lara, seated in a chair in the corner, and his smile seemed reserved for her.

"Satisfied is an understatement," Beretta said to Reese. "You vastly exceeded my expectations—and those were high from the outset."

"We were lucky," Reese said, coming toward Lara.

She started to reach for her crutches, wanting to rise, but then he was there, smiling down at her. "Hi," she said, grasping his hands, and she saw at once that Reese felt as constrained as she did by Beretta's presence. She desperately wished they were alone.

Beretta coughed spasmodically, a thin, painful sound that betrayed his condition. Reese gently squeezed Lara's hands and turned back to Beretta. The man from Opus Dei coughed again, and he grimaced, but his dark eyes were as alert as ever.

"Lara told me all about your ordeal," he said hoarsely, looking past Reese to smile at Lara. "She's a remarkable young woman, but of course I don't need to tell you that."

"We're not out of the woods yet," Reese said.

"But I think you *are,* Reese. I've already told Lara the good news. Jordan is playing along, and he seems to have concocted a plausible story."

"How do you know?" Reese asked quickly.

"We've been monitoring wire services, and two hours ago, the AP reported the raid on Miracle Isle. According to the story, the bodies of three unidentified Asians were found dead, and the police think that the dead men were Aaronites—some obscure religious cult led by a man named Martin Leeks.

"They're suspected of violence in the past, and Jordan claims that Leeks had made death threats against him. The news account states," Beretta added dryly, "that the attackers were heroically driven off by Billy-Lee Jordan—who, unfortunately, was killed while trying to remove a bomb they'd planted.''

"Let's just hope Jordan can make the story stick," Reese said. "I know they won't find any prints on the guns we left behind, but . . .''

"Don't worry," Beretta said confidently. "It's just bizarre enough to be believed. Reese, we're boundlessly grateful that you chose to end this discreetly.''

Reese heard Lara stir in her chair behind him.

"John . . .'' she said tentatively, and he turned. "Are *you* satisfied?" she asked, looking at him intently. "Are you sure you want to let Jordan go?''

For an instant Reese felt a stab of guilt as an image of Allison curled on her bed flashed into his mind; yet he knew he'd made the right choice.

"Yes. It's better this way. Finished.''

Beretta cleared his throat with uncharacteristic diffidence. "Do you have the finger with you?" he asked, and Reese turned back to him, impatient to close things out. Now that he knew Jordan was covering up, it seemed they'd cleared the last hurdle, and he itched to leave with Lara. He couldn't wait to be alone with her.

Reese withdrew the brown bottle from his jacket pocket, and he saw Beretta's eyes fix on it with no less intensity than he'd seen in Jordan's eyes. To Reese's surprise, Beretta's hands trembled slightly as he accepted it.

"God's precious gift," Reese said.

"What?" Beretta asked distractedly, tearing his gaze from the bottle.

"God's precious gift," Reese repeated. "That's what Jordan called it. Is that what you believe, too, Al? Do you really think that finger came from the body of Christ?''

"I don't know," Beretta said in a strange voice, staring at the bottle, and Reese realized that he was seeing another side of the man entirely. All trace of the coolly pragmatic operator had vanished.

He looked up at Reese and shook his head. "What I may or may not believe is irrelevant. It's for the Church to decide, after long and prayerful consideration. Only God knows the answer, Reese. We can only hope that He will reveal it."

"Good luck," Reese said, and he extended his hand.

"You're not intending to leave now, are you?" Beretta responded in surprise. "Cardinal McDonough is already on his way here. He's taken a personal interest from the beginning, and as I told Lara, he's anxious to meet you both and extend the Church's heartfelt thanks."

"No thanks are necessary." Reese took Beretta's hand and shook it to make his refusal final. "What I did, I did for myself."

"Perhaps, but we're in your debt nonetheless." Beretta looked past Reese at Lara. "Have you thought any more about Foster's offer?" he asked her.

Reese didn't understand, and as he looked at Lara, he saw her eyes flicker in apparent confusion.

"I didn't want her sabbatical leave ruined," Beretta explained to Reese, "so I put some wheels in motion. Professor Foster at Berkeley is one of the top men in Lara's field, and he has a real interest in her recent work. He's more than willing to have her come to Berkeley for the year, and it would be a terrific opportunity for her."

"That's great," Reese heard himself say, trying not to betray his dismay. With a sinking feeling in the pit of his stomach, he realized that until now he hadn't thought beyond the moment. But they were back in the real world now, and Lara had her career . . . What if she wanted to go?

Lara was looking at him questioningly, and as their eyes locked, Reese didn't know what to say. *Christ, if only Beretta weren't—*

And then Lara smiled—a slow, wonderful smile. "It was very thoughtful of you, Al, but I think I may have another offer."

"Yes," Reese replied, heedless of the catch in his voice. "You do."

75

Dusk was darkening into night as Reese turned off the main highway onto a country road, and Lara guessed that they were nearing the nursing home.

"You're awfully quiet," she prompted.

"Sorry," Reese said, tightening his arm around her shoulders. "It's just that—"

"You're thinking about Allison. Of course, you are. I just don't want you to think you have to hold it in, that's all."

"I don't know how many times I've come to see her, and I never got used to it. Maybe I never will. But I was wrong when I thought that nothing could make it any easier. Having you with me makes it easier."

"I'm glad." Lara closed her eyes and rested her head against his chest.

"Lara, I love you more than I can say."

"I know," she murmured, and the contentment she felt was beyond measure.

Reese opened the glass door at the entrance to the nursing home, and Lara preceded him into the dimly lit common room. The pungent odor of disinfectant still hung in the air, the nighttime stillness in the old house was the same, and the same four elderly women sat at the card table in the far corner. Everything was the same except Reese, and he felt as if he'd been away far longer than ten days.

"Good evening, ladies," he called.

"Good evening," the foursome chorused.

"You haven't come around for a while, Mr. Reese," chirped one of the women. "We missed you. It's a shame you're too late to see the cardinal. So *impressive* he was in that beautiful scarlet robe."

"What cardinal?" Reese asked, startled, and he glanced at Lara.

At that moment, Mrs. Filbert came into the common room from the Alzheimer's wing and came hurrying across to Reese. "Mr. Reese," she said a little breathlessly, "I tried to reach you at home, but you'd already left."

"Is anything wrong?"

"No," she said, looking distractedly at Lara.

"Mrs. Filbert, this is my fiancée, Lara Brooks."

"Oh," Mrs. Filbert said with a surprised smile. "I'm pleased to meet you, Miss Brooks. Congratulations to you both!"

"Thank you," Lara said.

"Mrs. Filbert," Reese interjected. "You said you were trying to reach me?"

"Yes, and I'm sorry you missed them, Mr. Reese. I told them that you'd called and would be coming, but they said they couldn't wait."

"*Who* couldn't wait?"

"Why, the cardinal and the priest who accompanied him," Mrs. Filbert responded in surprise. "Didn't you know they'd be here?"

Mystified, Reese looked at Lara.

"Was it a Cardinal McDonough?" she asked Mrs. Filbert.

"I'm not sure," she replied, clearly flustered. "I'm afraid I didn't catch the name. I didn't know you were Catholic, Mr. Reese."

"I'm not."

"Oh," Mrs. Filbert said in confusion. "They said they'd come to see Allison, and I just assumed . . . Oh, I hope I didn't do wrong."

"No, I'm sure you didn't," Reese said. "You say they came to see Allison. Do you know why?"

"To pray for her. I just assumed you must be Catholic, Mr. Reese. I hope you don't mind."

"He doesn't, Mrs. Filbert," Lara said quickly. "John did Cardinal McDonough a service, and I'm sure his prayers for Allison were a way of saying thank-you."

"That's right," Reese said.

"Oh, I'm glad," Mrs. Filbert said in relief. "You know, some people are very sensitive about that sort of thing." She smiled diffidently and shook her head. "I'm a Presbyterian myself, and I must say it was a bit strange. They had this little ivory box that they carried the bottle in, and—"

"What bottle?" Reese interrupted, more sharply than he intended.

"A little brown glass bottle that they touched to Allison's forehead. Holy water, I guess. Is something wrong, Mr. Reese?"

"No," Reese replied, forcing a smile, "not at all. We'd like to see Allison now."

"Of course, but I'll show you the way. We had to make some changes while you were away, and Allison has a new room. I'm sure you'll find it satisfactory."

As Reese and Lara followed Mrs. Filbert into the Alzheimer's wing, Lara caught Reese's eye. "Don't be angry," she whispered. "It's just their way of trying to repay you."

"Was that it?" Reese whispered back, finding it difficult to keep his voice low. "Or were they using her as a guinea pig? A 'true relic' might work miracles, right?"

"Don't think that way," Lara whispered. "They're grateful to you, John. That's all."

Allison's new room was at the very end of the corridor, and as Mrs. Filbert reached the threshold, she stopped short and looked back at Reese with an astonished expression. "Mr. Reese, I think I should call the doctor."

Alarmed, Reese reached the door in two quick strides, and

he saw at once what had startled Mrs. Filbert. Allison was no longer curled on her side in a fetal position. She lay on her back, breathing deeply and evenly, just as if she were asleep.

"Did they move her?" Reese asked sharply.

"Certainly not, and when I looked in on her just a few minutes ago, she was the same as always."

Reese started forward, and Mrs. Filbert grasped his arm. "Please don't get your hopes up. The change is surprising, but it may mean nothing."

"I know," Reese said, walking toward Allison's bed, and he did know. If one ignored the wasting of her body that had occurred over time, Allison looked merely asleep. But it was bound to be nothing more than another cruel trick of nature, he thought, and he refused to be taken in. He didn't believe in miracles—in brown bottles or otherwise.

Reese looked down at his daughter and reached out to stroke her shorn auburn hair. "Hi, Alie," he said as he'd said so many times before. "It's Dad."

"John," he heard Lara gasp behind him as Allison appeared to stir in response to his touch, and he turned to tell her that it was just a random movement of no significance.

"John!" Lara said more urgently, staring at Allison, and as he followed her gaze, he saw Allison's eyelids flutter. In disbelief he watched her eyes open and turn toward him, and then her lips moved. Through the sudden rushing in his ears he heard his daughter's voice, barely above a whisper.

"Hi, Daddy."

Epilogue

Midnight. The witching hour. Not the best time to be reading passages from the inner Samaria scroll, Beretta thought. Father Wilson was still translating the coded scroll, and Beretta had been given photocopies of the passages deciphered in the past two weeks. He would have liked to think that it was the hour and the silence in the clinic that made the ancient conjuring rituals' dark visions so unsettling, but deep down he knew that Cardinal McDonough's parting remarks were responsible.

He put aside the translation and tried to distract himself from his thoughts. He reached for a letter he had drafted that he intended to append to his report to Rome. Beretta had written the letter with some hesitation, and he wanted to read the final paragraphs one last time:

"The possibility that the finger's DNA contains a gene which halts cellular senescence is a question that can be resolved scientifically. It would appear that the results of such an investigation would be pertinent to the consideration of the finger's authenticity, and in addition, we have it on Professor Singer's authority that they might be of medical benefit to mankind.

"Should it be decided that surrendering the finger to further scientific investigation is worth some degree of risk, I venture to recommend Lara Brooks as the scientist to be given the task. She is fully competent to do so, and she is trustworthy beyond doubt. Furthermore, there is no one more deserving of the scholarly rewards to be received, should the results of her experiments prove to be of scientific significance.

"Along with this recommendation, however, I am compelled to emphasize that there are potential risks associated with such a course. There remain those, outside the Church, who know about the scrolls, and such knowledge has a way of spreading."

Satisfied that there was nothing he wanted to delete or add, Beretta put down the letter and pressed the nurse's call button. He was becoming increasingly uncomfortable, and he needed another shot of painkiller. Beretta detested needles, but he suspected he would have enough trouble sleeping, even without pain. He couldn't get Cardinal McDonough's last words out of his mind.

"It's very odd," Cardinal McDonough had remarked to Beretta as he was about to leave. "In the midst of my joy in hearing of the girl's recovery, and even as I thanked God for it, a passage from Saint Luke suddenly came to mind.

"You know, Al, if God has given us a true relic of Our Savior, then despite the trappings of magic, we might have to view the scrolls as having been divinely inspired."

"Apocalyptic prophecies included?" Beretta had responded with a smile.

"Would that really be a stranger thought than the possibility that we have both held in our hands the finger of Jesus Christ?"

"I suppose not," Beretta had replied, unsure if the cardinal was speaking seriously or not. "But if that's the case," he'd added lightly, "we'll know soon enough. According to the scrolls, our time is about up."

"Yes," Cardinal McDonough had said, "and perhaps that's why the passage from Saint Luke popped into my head when I was told of the girl's recovery. For if it truly was a miracle, worked by the finger of Our Savior . . .''

"What passage from Luke?" Beretta had asked, and he knew he would not soon forget the words the cardinal had recited:

> But if I with the finger of God cast out devils, no doubt the kingdom of God is come upon you.
> Luke 11:20